NIA'S RESOLVE

ALSO BY SIBERIA JOHNSON

Lovesick (New Adult Romance)

Nia's Resolve

Ivory's Ruin

Serena's Grace

Riley's Inferno

Paranormal Erotica

Sin, Secrets, and Summoning

& more TBA

NIA'S RESOLVE

THE PLAYBOY SYNDROME

SIBERIA JOHNSON

A LOVESICK NOVEL

This book contains topics that may be sensitive to some readers, including explicit sexual content, profanity, and mentions of assault.

To find out more about Siberia's books, visit her website (https://beacons.ai/siberia) and join her exclusive reader group (www.facebook.com/groups/sweetsinners).

Editing by Shawsome Reads Editing Services
Proofreading by Lindsey Clarke

ISBN: 978-1-963206-01-2

She's fallin' in love now
Losin' control now
Fightin' the truth
Tryin' to hide
But I think it's alright, girl
Yeah, I think it's alright, girl, ooh

Despite her past she can't help the attraction
He tells her that he's nothing like the last one
He redefines in every way what love is
She fell for him and hasn't gotten' up since

RUSS, "LOSIN' CONTROL"

Dedicated to those who won't give up on love,
and to my husband, who has never once given up on me.

CONTENTS

ONE

Caspian

When men are hungry, they hunt.

The craving for love and lust is as old as time, a tale of the heart that loops on constant repla y. Once the intro begins to hum its hypnotic tune, all are powerless but to dance along. Some hold on to the golden thread of happily-ever-after while others become inebriated, stumbling in search of answers they don't yet have the questions for.

Blind to his part in this eternal composition, Caspian set down his textbook and leaned back from the small study table. Flipping through monotonous pages was pointless now. Not when he could be scouting out his newest target.

The campus clock tower rang in the distance, a forlorn bell signaling the end of another hour, and the hall bustled with a surge of students. A sea of uncharted opportunity. They all hurried to and from class, tapping on tinted glass screens or chatting in newly formed cliques. Studious ones carried large bags suitable for books and binders, and the more lax paraded on with little to nothing more than a pair of headphones.

Most didn't note his presence, but the few that did either squared their shoulders in a masculine rivalry or blushed

1

under his unapologetic gaze. Their attention was nothing new. Normally he welcomed a well-executed advance, but today he would pick the prize, not the other way around.

He let his eyes drift from one potential muse to the next, measuring their worthiness and appraising their unique styles. University came stocked with an endless supply of attractive women—blondes and brunettes, miniskirts and sundresses, small waists and thick thighs—yet none stood out.

A handful of women he'd already fucked mingled with the rest, but their appeal had gone. He needed something new. Someone exciting.

Unfamiliar.

A girl who would give him a challenge and make up for the sour taste left from last semester. This time, he'd learn his lesson. Some girls took extra effort to crack, and he'd be prepared to take the long route. After he played the game well enough, she would be on her knees singing his praises—and that would make his predestined victory all the better.

Wait.

Head on a swivel, he locked onto tantalizing hourglass curves. *Her.*

Hips swaying with purposeful stride, a plump peach ass filled out the pair of faded blue jeans as she passed by. Although hidden in the crowd, her aura spoke volumes. The poise of her posture held a certain regality, feminine yet determined. She didn't need an entourage to look like a queen.

A stack of typical freshman textbooks was pressed to her supple chest, but one in particular piqued his interest. She clutched the thin notebook with extra care, its pages encased in intricate, perhaps even handmade, leather. It looked more like a personal journal than a composition notebook, certainly not meant for the scrawl of lackluster class notes. No, that book would contain something more important. More valuable.

If it was anything similar to his own sketchbooks, then she

might be exactly what he'd been looking for. But like a breeze that vanishes as soon as it's noticed, the back of her cherry-red hair disappeared through a pair of lecture room doors.

His lips curled into a half smile, pulse quickening. Sophomore year had brought him a fresh batch of home-cooked girls ripe for the taking, and she was the cream of the crop. A wave of intrigue pricked over his skin and settled between his legs. This would either be very good or very bad, but either way it would be exciting.

Outside of personal leisure, attending university had been a monotonous chore. A requirement imposed by the two people in his life who couldn't agree on anything else. After their recent divorce, his parents forced a formal education down his throat with a silver spoon—as if they thought ensuring his success would make up for their failures at home. In any case, early on he decided to use the space how he wanted.

He tapped his foot on the scuffed tile floor as gears in his head sprung to life. He could either make a move now or find her after forming a proper plan. But planning wasn't his forte, and letting another second pass without seeing her would be a waste. The first option it was.

He snapped the neglected textbook shut and swung his backpack over his shoulder, eying the double doors she'd gone behind. No one else had filed into the room, meaning there wasn't a lecture being held right now. Was she lost? Or was she resigned to be alone?

If the redhead was new to campus, then surely she'd appreciate someone showing her the ropes. Effortlessly, he could transform himself into a personal tour guide, and there were a few VIP spots he'd grant her access to if she was nice. It was no secret he was well equipped *and* well endowed, his sculpted muscles just as useful in the bedroom as they were in the gym.

Stepping forward, his thoughts raced ahead. That journal

stole so much of his curiosity that he hadn't gotten a decent look at her face. What shade would her eyes be, framed by that bright red hair? Would they burn into him when she looked his way? What about her lips? Would she be a tease or lure him in with a bashful smile?

How would her eyelashes darken her eyes, or her cheekbones highlight her face? What expression would she wear when he caught a real glimpse of her and she of him? Would she let slip the secrets she kept in that special journal?

The thought of her was like seeing a big, colorful lollipop in a candy shop window and dropping everything to go buy it. He appreciated the tiny taste he got, and for a moment he became even more enticed by the sample than seeing the whole thing. Humming to himself, he hoped this wasn't the end of good surprises. The sweet taste of her soft skin was almost palpable on his lips. The satisfaction of hearing her moan his name faintly echoed in his ears.

Sturdy strides carried him to the closed oak doors and a hammering heart chiseled away at his chest. Hitting on girls had been his second nature, but this time a certain thrill saturated his veins. This was a great start to the new school year, hopefully a sign of many more breathtaking girls to come.

His smile widened at the thought, prying the door open.

Yes, the first of many.

TWO

Nia

Not even the calm atmosphere of an empty lecture hall could hone her focus. The first assignment of college stared up from the worn desk, but she struggled to scrape up enough motivation to start. Nia raked restless fingers through her ruby hair and shivered as the ends tickled her shoulder.

Her vision glazed over as she leaned back, the hard plastic chair echoing her groan of protest. Arched windows along the wall let in columns of light that illuminated a vaulted ceiling and intricate oak trim. Leaving for college had been her chance to excel, to carve out a life all her own, but hollow essays did nothing to soothe the whiplash of the past week.

Saying good-bye to her mom felt like a distant sting, overridden by the chaotic first week of moving into the dorms, orientation, and trying to find where the next class would be and when. On top of it all, the other freshmen girls were too wound-up scouting hot parties and hotter boys to bother with studying. Finding friends would be harder than she thought.

As exciting as their parties sounded, she couldn't view hooking up through rose-tinted glasses. No man on this planet could guarantee her happiness, so in the end, what did they have to offer? A long, winding roller coaster that only led to more trust issues and broken hearts? She'd take a rain check on that one. After witnessing her mother's toxic routine, she'd vowed never to follow in those same footsteps. Her future didn't have tolerance for regrets.

That's why all of her romantic pursuits belonged to formatted, black-and-white pages. There was one universal truth she didn't need to question—fictional men were a gazillion times better than real ones.

She looked down at her journal and ran a finger along its spine. The world of words served as her sanctuary, a safe place. A single sentence could transport her to a world where the sun always set in a symphony of soft shades, and her feet didn't have to stay rooted to the ground. As long as those fantasies were kept sealed away, she could allow herself to dream.

In fact, that's exactly what she needed. A writing sprint was the change of pace her brain had been missing. She unfolded the leather cover and opened to a blank page, inhaling the scent of fresh paper. Faint scratches of her pencil chased away empty silence, and whatever came to mind poured out between the lines.

A name. A mere murmur in the distance. Awoken prophecies once cast away and forgotten. Knowing before seeing, hearing before speaking, fate proved its worth. Hand in hand, their hearts beat as one. Rising, feeling, needing. Two bodies entwining—

The main doors opened with a whoosh, and she nearly toppled out of the seat. Her pencil clattered to the ground as steady footsteps echoed through the room. There wasn't supposed to be another lecture for the rest of the day. Did someone else use this spot to study? She should have watched and waited before assuming she'd be alone.

Her head snapped up as the intruder approached, pace lazy and confident. Purposeful.

Jet black joggers hung at his hips, and a school jacket

wrapped around muscular, broad shoulders. If the university used him to advertise, there'd be too many applications to count.

"My bad, I didn't mean to startle you." He bent to pick something off the floor, but she couldn't tear her gaze away from his form.

Tension snapped across her skin. He must've walked straight out of a magazine—so what was he doing *here*? As he stood, she had to tip her head back to see his face. Tousled black hair cascaded down in loose curls that framed his sculpted features, and his eyes glinted with an intensity that seemed out of place. Like a dark storm cloud looming on a calm day.

A smooth-as-butter smile spread across his seductive lips. Then, their eyes connected.

He demanded all her attention. Froze her automatic flight response. A ripple of nerves coursed through her body, and the way his eyes honed in on her sucked the breath right out of her lungs. If he were in a novel, he'd definitely be the main character. Or the antagonist, that would suit him better. He didn't look like a nice guy, and he certainly wasn't a hero.

Hadn't he said something?

"You dropped this." He offered her the pencil. She quickly grabbed it back. "Hey, are you all right?"

His friendly words came from a voice that rumbled against her heartstrings, settling deeper than she wanted to admit.

"I was just leaving." Grateful that her voice wavered considerably less than her hands, she shut the journal and shoved her assignments back into a folder.

"You don't have to." He splayed his palms in a display of innocence. "I thought you might be lost. You look new."

She bristled—so he came in because he saw her and not for his own reasons? As much as that should flatter her, she didn't like the sound of it. Besides, she knew his type, and the charm wouldn't fool her. Her skin already burned too hot under his false pretenses.

"I'm fine." She yanked her backpack over her shoulder, grabbing the pile of scattered books and folders on the desk. This was not the time to be disorganized.

"Come on, you'll make me feel bad. Don't leave on my behalf." He took the liberty of sitting at an empty desk beside her and stretched out his legs. "If you're studying, I promise to not disturb you. I have some work to do myself, so if you don't mind, I'll join."

She did mind.

A refreshing—annoying—mint aroma came from his direction and aroused her senses. No way would she be able to study with him so close, especially when she could feel his intrusive gaze roaming over her. The large room began to feel smaller and smaller as nausea crept into her gut.

"I do mind, so I'll be going." She stood without daring to give him another look and stepped over his impertinent legs.

He made her heart stutter, and she didn't want to think about what that meant.

"Can I ask one question?" Already halfway to the door, she didn't bother responding. "Hey, all right, all right—take it easy. I'll leave you alone. Just wanted to know what was in that fancy book of yours, 'kay?"

She stopped before she reached the exit. Fighting off the reaction he wanted from her, she turned with a level head and shot him a cool glare. "My *fancy book* is none of your business."

"So it seems." His eyes glittered. "Tell me, do you always get this defensive, or is it just me?"

She set her jaw, refusing him the gratification of an answer. He got up from the chair and walked over, extending his right hand. "Name's Caspian, by the way. Nice to meet you."

THREE

Caspian

ALL HE NEEDED WAS HER NAME. AND AN HOUR OR TWO TO ROCK her entire world.

The second their eyes clashed, he knew this was what he'd been looking for. Not only was she drop-dead gorgeous, the room glowed with her presence.

About time he found someone on his level.

Never before had someone made his pulse race with such exhilaration, who affected him without even trying. His well-practiced charm was hard to maintain when she stared right through him like this. As if he didn't matter in the least. All the effort to make her smile and blush batted to the side without a second thought.

Bringing up the journal *had* gotten him a response, but an icy one at that. Her frosted blue eyes stared at his outstretched hand and her dainty fingers stayed firmly wrapped around a stack of books. So tense...somehow he had to get her to drop that sky-high guard.

The tip of his tongue tingled with anticipation at tasting her smooth skin. Every part of it, from those pouty lips down to the swell of her breasts and the delicacy between her thighs. Time to play a little cat and mouse.

"Just so you know, I came here to get away from other people. I'd rather not be bothered by..." She motioned to him as a whole. "...this."

He chuckled, the jovial timber bouncing off the walls. His reaction earned a scowl that he appreciated as much as her attitude. That adorable frown made it hard to focus. What other expressions could he paint on—

"I'm serious."

And that voice of hers, swirling around his ears like a silken scarf—how could he not be smitten? If only he were the center of her admiration instead of irritation. Regardless, he could work with it. His smirk turned into a genuine smile. This one wasn't looking for a tour guide, that was for sure.

A playful, throaty groan escaped his lips. The kind he knew women liked to hear. "I can't know your name?"

She didn't even take in a breath to respond, her lips sealed shut.

Well then, he wasn't worth half a sigh. Usually girls couldn't help themselves when he gave them his full attention. She'd be one of those scenic route types, the ones who wanted him to play along as the doting boyfriend before opening up. That wouldn't be a problem; he welcomed the chance to challenge his skills. *This* was the kind of test he would enjoy.

"My loss, then." He dropped his hand. "Ladies first, as they say. The room is yours. But do warn me if you put my name in that burn book."

She adjusted her arms, pressing the stack of books closer to her chest and inadvertently pushing up her tits. "It's not a burn book."

Oh, but he'd already been burned. The heat from her gaze licked up his skin as he raised an eyebrow. "So, I'm safe?"

"From what?" she mumbled, taking a step away from the exit, yet not toward him either.

"From falling for you. I'm very susceptible to love spells, you know." She snorted, and he decided to take a leap of faith. "You know what I think that book is?"

She tipped up her chin, the only form of acknowledgment he was going to get. The motion exposed the elegant curve of her neck, and he bit his lip. "I think it's a place for all the things you don't want anyone else to see. Things that keep you up at night. Maybe some things that get you hot and wet when you're alone."

He raised his eyebrows. She continued to glower.

That wasn't a no.

He stepped back to give her more space and lowered his voice. "Like all the ways a kiss can make other parts of your body tingle. How fast a man can make you come, or how long he can keep you on edge. If he'll enjoy eating your ass as much as he wants to lick your pussy—the answer is yes, by the way."

He paused and looked down in amusement, absorbing everything from the clench in her jaw to the rosy flush blossoming over her cheeks. She shouldn't have bothered with makeup. Her natural hues captivated him quite thoroughly. "Things I can make your reality."

She stood her ground, yet her voice came out huskier than before. "As I said, it's none of your business. And even if it did contain those things, it sure as hell won't mention you."

This girl would be the death of him.

Very well, he could give her some distance. As difficult as that would be, he wasn't so desperate that he couldn't take a hint.

"I'll see you around, stranger." He tipped his head and walked past, not sparing a look back. The click of the door sealed the fact he wouldn't get any action tonight, and the growl inside tapered to a pathetic whine. But he'd already been hooked and was determined to reel her in. Now he had something to focus on besides sleep-invoking courses and tedious workouts.

His first attempt hadn't been a complete failure. She would be thinking about him.

In the meantime, thoughts of her invaded his mind—the wide arch of her eyebrows framing cat-like eyes, the slight bronze hue of her skin that darkened when she got embarrassed. And that mouth. Her first words carried a sting but came from such soft and full lips.

She embodied everything he'd been craving. Those gentle curves were much better than he envisioned, and they fit her steely personality perfectly. The idea of discovering her secrets kept locked away in that journal was just as thrilling as the thought of stripping her down. He couldn't help but imagine how she would moan his name as he pleased her—again and again.

He wanted to pin her against one of those old Roman columns, clad in a white dress and looking like some sexy goddess. The campus had a few of those columns somewhere... Or maybe she wasn't a human or a goddess but a mythical siren. That would explain why she had seduced him with only a few dirty looks and reprimanding words. Would she be just as dirty in bed? Or did her kisses taste of sugar as well as spice?

A few paces down the now-empty hallway, he leaned against the wall and tried to imagine a fight for dominance in a passionate kiss. He actually questioned who would win. Maybe he'd let her take the lead at first. After all, the breathy moans women made as he took over were such a turn-on. And hers would be especially delicious.

A giggle echoed in the halls as a group of students walked past. Lingering stares landed on him, but when he returned the favor, they were quick to glance away.

Their attention meant little when his mind was already

occupied. Even now, he wished to see his icy redhead again, recalling how *she* hadn't looked away. To his introduction, she'd offered a strategic counter, although she probably hadn't seen it as such.

She didn't want to be bothered.

Oh yes, he knew of many possibilities besides bothering her, but what would she want most? If he got his way, he'd test out some theories the next chance they met.

Hopefully, he didn't have to wait too long. She could quite possibly turn out to be his most rewarding conquest yet.

FOUR

Nia

August sun beat down on the picnic table as she ate lunch with a small group from the dorms. They'd stumbled upon a cute café at the edge of campus and had agreed to rest before walking downtown. This weekend was the perfect opportunity to explore her new city, homework and presumptuous playboys tucked away as mere unwanted memories.

Nia nibbled on her plain bagel and soaked up the balm of sunshine, running her toes through the grass. This excursion hadn't been too bad, and from bits and pieces of their conversation, she got to learn more about her neighbors.

For the most part, she let herself fade into the background. Various chit-chat about the Greek organizations and the guys that belonged to each held no interest for her. Some topics were so predictable that she wondered if they were in a television show.

Except, she didn't have the script.

It was hard to gauge whether the other girls were pretending to be shallow or if they enjoyed their life filled with gossip. Fictional characters were so much less complicated. They came with less risk, and she could read into their thoughts without putting herself on the line. Even the villains could earn her sympathy in some way or another. And none of them would call her out when she wanted to be alone, unlike *someone* who took advantage of quiet girls in empty lecture halls.

Caspian's implication about her journal had hit a little too close to home.

Her gaze wandered to a freshly mowed hill, eager to think of something pleasant rather than to dwell on him. This time, she veered away from the explicit and conjured a simple scene that would be part of any sweet summer romance.

A young woman smiled in the midday sun, basking in the company of her doting boyfriend. Their picnic came complete with a red checkered blanket and a basket full of fruits. The girl giggled again at the man murmuring in her ear, then he leaned over and—

"What have we here? Such an enchanting sight," a familiar voice chimed from the sidewalk. "Do you ladies happen to be new to campus?"

Dammit. Closing her eyes, she prayed not to see the one person she'd hoped to avoid. But her daydream had already vanished, and when she turned, a devilishly handsome face smiled back at her. She scowled.

Her dorm neighbor, Serena, took the lead in dazzling Caspian, bracelets jingling as she brushed a strand of blonde hair behind her ear. "Yeah, we're all freshmen. How did you guess? Are you a student?"

Caspian flashed a smile and slid onto the bench across from Nia, laying on the charm thicker than she thought possible. "I am, but I've been around. I could gladly teach you a few things if you want."

Nia groaned. Somehow, this was much worse than their previous conversation. Why did he have to show up twice in one week? Once had been more than enough for him to get stuck in the creases of her brain like gum on a shoe.

Crossing her legs, she drifted off again to the green hill. She held no reservations about ignoring Caspian in favor of her own fictitious couple. The story ramped up with a more intense scenario, and with a small sigh, she retreated into the ecstasy of wandering hands and curious tongues.

The man leaned in for a kiss, lips trailing down the girl's neck as both fell backward onto the soft grass. Dancing on the line of too much public affection, he pinned her hands above her head and whispered sweet nothings into her breasts, filling her whole being with butterflies.

Wait.

Oh, hell no, that's what Caspian said, wasn't it—all the ways a kiss can make other parts of your body tingle? How dare he invade her thoughts as well as her space...

"Nia, earth to Nia...you've been out of it again." Serena's glossed lips poked into a pout as she stabbed Nia's shoulder with a slender, manicured fingernail.

"Hm?" Nia glanced over, careful to keep her focus on Serena and not give Caspian the satisfaction of her attention. Why was he still here?

"Did you notice our new friend?" Serena motioned to their extra-friendly campus pest. "He's a sophomore and offered to give us a lift if we need to get groceries or just want to get out of town—right?" Caspian responded with a brief nod. Serena smiled back, then turned to Nia and whispered, "He's really nice. You shouldn't ignore him like that."

Ugh. Now interaction would be inevitable. But so far, he hadn't mentioned they already met once, and she was grateful he didn't put her on the spot. If being polite was necessary, then she'd just have to bite the bullet.

"Hello," she said dryly, focusing on his sooty eyelashes to avoid direct eye contact. The last time their eyes met, something weird happened, and it had been bad enough without spectators.

"Nice to meet you, stranger—or it was Nia, right?" Caspian's teasing smile widened.

Instantly, she regretted playing along. Her name. That's what he'd been after.

He redirected his attention to the others and let her be. At least he wouldn't force her to talk if she didn't want to.

A breath of relief escaped her lips. But her mind still churned with leftover tension from the daydream, and since he wasn't looking in her direction, she chanced another glance across the table.

The sunlight angled in just the right way to highlight the color of his dark eyes—blue. The kind that was deep and dangerous. Cast against a cloudless sky, his eyes shone like refined sapphires, flecked with sprinkles of silver as elusive as rays of moonlight. A traitorous blush crept over her cheeks as she cursed his sharp jawline and those oh-so kissable lips.

Lips that wove illusions and lies...no matter how good they sounded. She'd had more than enough experience with people who held up a façade only to reveal their true nature when others weren't watching.

"It's not polite to stare, you know." Caspian met her head-on with those entrancing eyes. "Not that I mind, but if you keep it up, I'll be mesmerized into going home with you." His foot nudged hers under the table.

Serena and the others gaped at her, their faces colored with shock and jealousy. Nia quickly transformed her expression into a scowl. She didn't intend to get noticed by them, or by Caspian for that matter. He winked, and the heat in her cheeks turned up a notch. What the hell was he playing at?

Amid scrambling about for a reply, he released her from his gaze and turned back to the others. "So, where were we?"

The moment ended as swiftly as it had come. The tension in her chest eased, and she pulled out her phone to occupy herself for the remainder of the conversation. This time, none of the others seemed to care.

"Hey, Nia." Serena tapped her on the shoulder, lighter than earlier. "Do you want his number before we head off downtown? He said we could all have it."

"No, I'm good," she dismissed, not looking away from the phone screen.

"Okay, that's fine. In any case, I have it." A hint of relief etched into Serena's voice.

As good-looking and charismatic as Caspian was, it didn't surprise her that Serena wanted him to herself, and she had no qualms with that. Her concept of inconsequential intimacy had been ruined for a long time now.

Pushing the dark thoughts to the back of her mind, Nia closed out the game on her phone as Caspian parted ways. Good riddance.

As soon as he got out of sight, one of the girls turned to her. "Okay. I *know* you think he's hot. I mean, I was low-key staring, too...so why didn't you get his number?"

Jade green eyes inquired as much as the girl's soft-spoken words. A name from earlier surfaced—Ivory. Over the course of the afternoon, Nia had found herself migrating toward her more than the others. They were similar in some ways, though Ivory did better at holding her own in conversation.

"Oh, it's uh, it's not like that," she replied, trying to brush it off. "I thought about basing a character off him for a story. It looks weird, I know, but I'm really not interested in him at all."

"Ah, I understand." Ivory smiled. "You're a writer, then?"

"Umm..." She'd rather not talk about her personal life, but looked like that was the only way to get out of this mess. "It's a side hobby, nothing serious."

Graciously, Ivory let the subject of Caspian drop. "Oh, okay then... Can I put my contact in your phone? I think yours is the only one I don't have."

Nia relented. "Sure, but you should know I'm bad at replying."

She handed her phone to the cute brunette, who then hunched over the table and typed in her info.

While waiting, she took in a breath of fresh air. Maybe on her way back, she'd stop on that hill and write down the scenes she thought of, taking extra care *not* to picture *him*.

FIVE

Nia

CASPIAN WAS A DAMN CURSE.

Cerulean eyes that told of hidden treasure. Words lurking in the depths of her mind, and a voice that echoed in places she had long forgotten. It was as if he could reach in and dismantle her without even trying.

As the group explored downtown, she made notes of unique places that would be great settings for a story—an abandoned gift shop, boarded up yet still marked with a sign painted in bright colors, a cute corner park, and a wall of graffiti covered in cryptic messages—but in each location *he* would appear in her mind as a character in the background.

Determined to not let him derail her day, she decided to stop into a salon and told the others to meet her back at the dorms. It was about time to touch up her roots anyway, the red had already started to fade.

In her first turn of good fortune, an appointment fell through, so a stylist was able to see her as a walk-in. The name on his badge read Adrian, and he was young and friendly, but not overbearing. Nothing like a particularly annoying *someone*.

Nia watched through the mirror as Adrian separated her

hair with the end of a paintbrush. Stubble along his jaw balanced a long cut of auburn hair with the ends colored pale pink. Whether it made sense or not, she trusted stylists more when they had their dyed, too.

"This is a busy time of year," he said, making small talk. "As you can see, we're constantly booked. I suggest taking a card so you can make an appointment next time."

"I'll grab one on my way out," she agreed. "A rush would make sense with all the new students."

"Yup," he hummed. "Mind me asking if you're one?"

She began to nod, but stopped when it shifted her head too much. "I am."

"Ah, then I hope you're enjoying the experience." He dabbed crimson at her roots, a cold sensation spreading from where he worked. "But remember to not get wrapped up in the excitement. I've seen too many people fail their first semester."

"I appreciate the advice," she replied. It wasn't like she planned to go out and party anyway. The less excitement in her life, the better.

Adrian nodded. "Okay, now we'll let this sit for about 25 minutes, and then I'll wash it out."

Nia pulled out her journal and distracted herself while the color set in. Leaving out character info for now, she jotted down the places she'd seen and some plot points.

After time ran out, Adrian came back to give her hair a rinse. This was always the best part, and the reason she went to a salon instead of doing it herself. The feeling of water on her scalp left her calm and refreshed, and her mind drifted to a steamy shower scene.

Palms slid over hot, wet skin. Bodies pressed against cold tiles. Secret places and forbidden touches were too enticing, too sensitive to every touch and kiss after hours of aching need. Black hair plastered to the side of his pristine face, droplets of water intensified the lust in his eyes, and...

No! Not him again.

Drawn out of her thoughts, she stared at the ceiling and frowned until Adrian finished, then blow-dried her hair. She reached up to examine a lock, marveling at the soft and smooth texture.

"Do you like it? I think the color matched up perfectly," Adrian said, standing behind her.

"Yes, it looks great. Thank you." If nothing else, this would cheer her up. Not that she wanted to impress anyone. "I'll be sure to ask for you again the next time I come."

Adrian chuckled as he walked her over to the check-out counter. "I'm flattered, but any of our stylists would do just as good of a job."

She quickly paid and headed home, wanting to take another look over a few spots on her way back. If she couldn't find a project to distract her from writing about Caspian, she might be stuck with writer's block forever.

ო

"Yeah, I'm sure," Nia spoke into her cellphone, trying not to find the stereotypical conversation too amusing. "Mom, I checked the washing machines and dryers. I'm okay, really." She leaned the chair on two legs, happily sequestered in her dorm.

"Oh, good...and I know you'll be fine, honey. I'm so glad you're growing up to be an independent woman, but I'll always worry. It's my job."

Her lips gave in and turned up in a smile. Being away from home, and consequently her stepfather, had been one of her biggest blessings, but her mother's voice and caring words always warmed her heart. "Thanks."

"And..." A sigh came from the other end of the line. "I know you're a good student but do try to make some friends. I'm not just talking about boys—find someone who you can have fun with every now and then."

"I know," she said. "If I find someone whose version of 'fun' matches mine, then I'll be sure to lend them some of my books." An inner voice silently mocked her words. The girls she had gone out with today had walked past the library without a second glance, though she'd stopped by on her way from the salon.

"I think—" her mother began but got interrupted by a booming voice in the background. Nia dropped the chair back onto all fours as an involuntary shudder ran down her spine.

"Ah, that's Rob. He just woke up, and he was up late so well...you know how it goes."

"Yeah, it's all right." No more needed to be said on the matter. Some things were better off left between the lines. "I'll talk to you later, Mom. Love you."

"Love you bunches!" her mom replied, then ended the call.

Nia took a moment to close her eyes, banning negative thoughts and pushing out the sour memories associated with that house. She'd moved miles away. This was her space, and she was safe.

The cookie-cutter dorm room looked rather unremarkable —plain and blank, but it was hers alone. With one additional loan, she'd secured a spot in a single-occupant room, and it'd been worth every penny, plus interest. Much like her preference for empty lecture halls, she opted to be alone at night rather than sleep next to a complete stranger.

Most of the people she knew looked forward to roommates, but the last thing she wanted was to walk in and find someone entertaining guests—or otherwise engaged—when she needed to sleep or study. Granted, the walls were so thin she had already noticed her neighbor participating in some extracurricular activities, but with any luck, she'd learn to tune it out.

Nia set the phone down and pressed a finger to the mouse pad of her beloved laptop. The screen awoke from the gentle prod and revealed the document she had been typing when her mom called. Getting resituated in her desk, she went through the notes she'd jotted in her journal from earlier. Most characters didn't have names yet, so she scrolled through the contacts in her phone for inspiration.

Then she froze, eyes landing on the one name she had been avoiding. How the hell did *his* contact end up here?

Heart racing, she tried to remember when he could have gotten his hands on her phone. Or...when Ivory had taken her phone, had *she* put in Caspian's contact info?

She clicked on the edit option, thumb hovering over the delete button, but couldn't bring herself to press it. If Ivory had given her the contact information, then Caspian didn't know she had his number...and he didn't have hers. This could be the perfect opportunity to prove he really was a bad guy, then write him as a character to break the curse. No doubt he had too many women's numbers saved to remember them all, so she could easily pretend to be someone else.

Before making any hasty moves, she sent a quick text to Ivory.

> You put Caspian's contact into my phone?!?

IVORY

> Lol. Maybe; I plead the fifth.

> He doesn't have my number, right? If he does, I swear I'll murder you.

> He doesn't know. Don't worry.

> Okay. He better not know anything, and don't tell him anything about me either.

OK ok! Relax, my lips are sealed. What happens now is up to you two.

Whatever.

One more thing...give me a random name?

Caspian ;)

Nia tossed her phone down in exasperation. That wasn't a random name at all!

But it happened to be the one she needed. Picking the phone up, she started a message to "Caspian<3", the way Ivory saved his contact. Of course, she had no idea how fast he'd reply to some unknown number or a chick he didn't care about. All she could do now was wait for a response.

SIX

Caspian

More of a curve here. Yes, that's it. So graceful. Perfect. No—

Bits of used eraser cluttered the sketch paper as he removed the last line. Not quite right. His forehead creased as he examined the piece. After fifteen years of drawing, he still couldn't do hands right. Looking down at his own, he tried to transform it into a woman's. Smaller knuckles, more refined fingers, a gentler constitution...

The human figure had always entranced him. In younger years, a growing collection of wooden mannequins populated his desk, and rough sketches decorated the margins of his sparse class notes. He graduated from stick figures long ago, moving on to detailed nude figures and the occasional portrait. His favorite subject by far had become drawing different sex positions and of course, practicing them when he got the chance.

Drawing let him focus, a state of relaxation not unlike meditation. Analyzing the human form was more complex than people believed and provided a great filler for times like this—he hadn't gotten laid in almost two weeks. Others turned

27

to porn, but he found it crude and tasteless compared to real art. The fine lines of sensuality proved much more enjoyable than merely watching the act of sex.

His current project featured a woman poised on a stool, elbows bound behind her back with a rope wrapped around her stomach to frame delicate breasts, then dipping lower and knotting between her labia. He'd color her in later, giving special attention to the two taut peaks on her chest and the pink pearl peeking out behind the intricate knot at the apex of her legs, meant to be the center of the piece.

His degree in business served as a front, meant to hold down a decent job that would support him enough to continue his hobby. The pursuit of art was his true passion. He would have gone to an art school if given the choice, but the first time he brought that up to his parents had also been the last. Tuition and housing proved to be more than he could afford on his own, even if he managed to juggle a full-time job along with classes.

No one knew he drew these days. The spark of creativity had flickered when he went off to college but never went out. His parents had all but forgotten. However, it wasn't something he could simply stop.

A piece of art caught a single moment that would fade in real time. It could capture those rare occurrences of pleasure that never lasted very long. Drawings were lifeless; they came without desire or protest. On canvas, he didn't have to deal with the sorrow behind someone's false happiness or the withered state of their soul hidden within. If he wanted his subject to smile, all he had to do was draw one.

Art became the only way he saw true beauty in human existence. The subjects he drew were his creations, and they came with no backstories and no aspirations. Their only purpose was to bend to his whim and depict a reality he wished he could create. A much harder task had been to fix the broken pieces of real people. He saw his parents try with each other—and fail.

When he noticed someone's suffering, he also knew he couldn't take away their problems. So, he opted to turn a blind eye. He couldn't be a savior. Couldn't change reality. Nowadays, he drew to pass the time and ignored the rest.

A knock came at the apartment door. He paused to look up. Adjusting his eyes to the dim glow of the desk lamp, the only light on in his apartment, he realized how much time had passed since he sat down. The sun had already disappeared.

Straightening at his desk, he placed some pages of homework over the unfinished sketch.

Another knock, more fervent this time.

"Leave me alone. What the hell do you want?" he called.

Silence. He huffed and went over to crack open the door.

"Sup, dog breath." His former roommate, Adrian, greeted him with the traditional—and irritating—nickname. No matter how many times he insisted he didn't carry mints because of an insecurity, Adrian wouldn't drop the moniker.

Propped in the doorway, his friend stood in a leather jacket over a black shirt and jeans, hair tossed up in a bun. Must've just come back from a shift at the salon.

"Why are you here, puke hair?" Caspian grumbled, returning the friendly insult with his own, referring to the light pink tips of Adrian's hair. Besides living across the hall, Adrian was the only person he bothered to talk to on a regular basis. Anyone else would've had the door slammed in their face.

"You've been out of it all week, man. Still haven't gotten any pussy, have you?" Adrian joked, smiling despite Caspian's glare.

"Don't remind me. What the hell are you here for?"

"Still want to go out tonight? Word is half the student population will be at that party. Maybe even some hot professors." Adrian raised his eyebrows, a hopeful look in his golden eyes.

"Shit, I forgot." Caspian leaned against the door and pushed back some hair that had fallen over his forehead. "Half the student population?"

Adrian gave a knowing scoff. "Chances are your freshman girl will be there. If she's not, I will personally drag her there so you can get out of this slump. You'll never score if all you do is mope around in your room."

"I'm not moping."

Caspian's phone vibrated in his pocket. Groaning, he hoped it wasn't some chick he slept with last year and ditched the next morning. They kept crawling out of the woodwork. But seeing Nia would be the one reason worth risking getting mauled by wet panties tonight, if Adrian hadn't exaggerated the amount of students attending.

"I don't know. Nia didn't come off as the party type." He opened the message and read as he spoke.

"Oh, you're on a first-name basis now?" Adrian chided. "How did this one not end up with a dim-witted nickname?"

Caspian wasn't listening well enough to reply. He frowned. The text was from an unsaved number. At the very least, he made sure to save the contact for every girl he hooked up with. An unknown sender hadn't surprised him before, so who could this be?

UNKNOWN

Hey, it's Kate. What are you up to rn?

Showing the screen to Adrian, he asked, "Do you recognize this number?"

Adrian glanced down. "What, not one of your old flings?"

"No. Even the blocked ones still have contact names. I don't remember a Kate, either." His frown deepened, seeing no previous messages from the sender.

"A scam, then," Adrian concluded. "They're getting more clever these days."

"Hate those damn people or bots, or whatever they are," Caspian muttered as he typed in a brief reply to "Kate."

> Who is this?

> Kate, don't you remember me? We hooked up a few months ago.

"Shit, man, if it's a scam, they're good. This is too realistic." He tilted the phone to show Adrian again.

"Looks like you forgot about one." Adrian shrugged off the topic. "Doesn't matter anyway. Not until you can get your mind off that freshman. Did she even give you her number yet?"

"Mn..." he began to respond but got distracted while typing another response.

> No, I don't remember. What do you want?

> I'm missing a contact photo for you. Could you send one? :) pls

> Send me a photo first, and we'll see.

While he waited for her reply, Caspian lifted his head to acknowledge his friend again. "What was that?"

Adrian shook his head. "You really need to snap out of it. So much for my wingman, not that I needed one. I asked if you had that girl's number. I could ask around for it tonight if you're not going."

"No. I got all her friends' contacts, but she's holding out on me."

Adrian narrowed his eyes and gave him a sideways glance. "And suddenly, an unsaved number texts you?"

"What are you getting at?"

"You told me she was obviously interested but wary,

31

probably afraid she'd catch cooties—or worse—feelings. Personally, I'd be more concerned about Chlamydia..."

"Shut up and get to the point. You know I'm clean."

"Could be your girl." Adrian turned, casting an uninterested glance down the hallway. "She's too timid to talk to you directly, so she asked her friends for your number."

Caspian weighed Adrian's words. Maybe he was right, and the mysterious sender had been Nia. Adrian had a habit of picking out things about people without talking to them. He knew which girls would be easy, their sense of humor, and who would give trouble later. Caspian learned to not question Adrian's intuition, and after all, the skill could be useful as hell.

An image of a girl with long black hair popped onto the phone screen, a picture from the unknown sender. Caspian recoiled at the sight and shook his head. "This ain't her."

Adrian sighed without looking at the photo. "Reverse image search for it. I bet you a thousand condoms she got that off Google."

He did a quick fact-check, and as much as he hated it, Adrian was right. The photo had been posted a couple years ago on some recruitment page connected to the university.

"So, you think it's Nia?" he asked.

Adrian waved his hand. "I'm guessing the party is a no-go tonight. Keep texting her, and I'm sure you'll figure it out soon enough." He walked over to his room, leaving Caspian alone with the phone.

In the little over a year since they met, that guy had never read a girl wrong. Adrian had pulled Caspian out of more than enough sticky situations to earn his trust. So, turning back into his apartment, he sent off a string of messages to verify their hunch.

He was in.

SEVEN

Nia

CASPIAN<3

If you are who I think you are, then this should be fun.

SHE CURLED HER KNEES UP TO HER CHEST AND GLANCED AT THE photo Caspian sent, excited the conversation was going well. Then deflated upon a closer look.

It showed him in front of a mirror, casually revealing a thirst trap worthy of an eye roll. His face had been cropped out, leaving a portrait of his jaw down to his waist. Shirtless. Toned skin and a set of immaculate pecks blended into a seamless, well-defined six-pack.

Oh, and by the way, this is a real photo of me, unlike yours XD

Her face flushed. How had he already called her bluff?

Bastard must've used reverse image search...but if he knew she sent a borrowed picture, then who did he think he was really talking to? And why text back?

She closed out the messages and again considered deleting the whole thing. This was a waste of time.

...Was it? After all, he had taken the time to respond.

She rubbed the indent between her eyes, trying to wake up her frontal lobe and invigorate the flow of logic. But curiosity pricked at her subconscious. Did he know she sent the messages? That was impossible. He didn't have her number, and they had only spoken a few times.

No harm would come from continuing the conversation. She could delete the messages anytime, and he couldn't force her to reveal her real identity.

Reopening the conversation, she glazed over his impressive physique. These muscles weren't the bulging bricks often described in erotic fiction—no, he looked more polished, attractive even...

No! Shaking her head, she reprimanded herself for thinking of Caspian like that.

Then she sat upright. If he could search up her image, she could do the same. Chances were nothing would turn up, but it might be worth a shot. All she needed was something to develop a character. After she got what she wanted, she'd move on and forget the conversation ever happened.

Pulling up three different search engines, she uploaded the photo to each. The first two came up blank. The third had a single result. Not an exact match, but the background fit, and this photo even included his head. Seemed Caspian liked to reuse selfies.

She clicked the link and discovered a personal blog written by a girl at their university. A series of posts stretched over the course of six months and documented the blogger's freshman year. Nia scrolled down to the earliest date and began to read, the rest of the room fading as she became immersed in the screen.

The tone of the posts started happy and carefree. The blogger embraced her college experience, got by with average grades, and went to the occasional party. At one of these parties, she met an irresistible flirt—obviously Caspian—and he managed to steal a kiss along with her phone number.

Nia clicked her tongue. His smug attitude made more sense now. He was used to getting what he wanted. Ignoring her imagination as it drifted to what a kiss from him might be like, she skimmed the next few posts.

The blogger wrote about having the time of her life, even mentioned thoughts of dating Caspian long-term. He thrilled her and became an adventure, someone she wanted to make memories with. But she hadn't been ready to go all the way, and after only a week of knowing each other, he stopped responding to her messages.

The following week's post was a slew of capital letters. They broke up. The picture Nia searched was posted next to one of Caspian in bed with another woman.

Through a muddle of words and curses, she pieced together what happened. From the girl's perspective Caspian had acted like a boyfriend, but on his end, she was only some girl he met at a party. The blogger didn't know he'd also been texting her friend and that the two ended up sleeping together. When the two girls finally talked about the situation, they were both devastated. Their college romantic comedy turned into a tragedy.

Nia wasn't surprised. She didn't expect Caspian to be any different. Still, something deep in her heart sagged with an invisible weight. She passed off the feeling as simple disappointment in reality. He had no power to break her heart, and no man ever would. It didn't matter what he did in his sex life because she would never be a part of it.

She scrolled back and studied the photos of Caspian's smile

and handsome smirk. Were they real or posed? How did people ever find true love? Was such a thing even real? She hoped so but wasn't going to cross any fingers.

Bookmarking the page, she glanced at the clock. Late enough to turn in for bed, which was good because she didn't feel like writing or returning to her conversation with Caspian.

One thought kept circling her mind. She wanted to write this character based on Caspian's personality as much as possible, but couldn't bring herself to imagine him as a heartless villain. Sure, he called her out, but as soon as he noticed her discomfort, he'd stopped.

A part of her wanted to believe in him like she believed in fairy tales, sparkles and all. There had to be some redeeming factor about him, even if he didn't show it to the world. After all, she came off wrong to a lot of people around her, but there were reasons for that. She didn't think she was a bad person, and she didn't want to believe Caspian was, either.

The assured aura that rolled off him reminded her of Prince Charming—captivating, determined, and steadfast. Yet the blog pointed toward him being the obstacle of happily-ever-after.

Maybe if she found out more about him by pretending to be Kate, her mind would be at ease. If she could just put him into words, then he'd stop haunting her.

She sighed and returned to her room, crawling under crisp, cool sheets. A fortress of blankets sheltered her from worry, and sleep came like a welcome vacation.

Through the blur of slumber, two sets of voices called out. An old box TV produced the first set. Characters from her favorite childhood show. Anticipation bubbled up, and like a young child, she ran toward the sound and settled herself in front of the big block screen in her living room.

Bright and happy cartoons overshadowed the other set of voices: her mother and the man she adamantly refused to call stepfather. The adults kept their voices hushed in the beginning, but their argument rose as the back door opened and then slammed closed.

Soon, bangs echoed through the stale air—a fist being slammed into rickety walls. Normally this was as bad as it got, but today an eerie heaviness lingered in the room and clung to her like humidity.

Eventually her mom came out and set dinner down on a paper plate, telling her to eat and they'd join her later. She didn't speak to avoid being a nuisance, eating the macaroni and cheese as quietly as she could. The afterimage of her mom's pursed lips and deepening worry lines imposed over the carefree actors on the TV.

A loud crash came from the kitchen. She flinched as her mom shouted, "I'm sick and tired of dealing with your shit, Rob! I'm done living in this fucked up hellhole..."

The back door burst open, and heavy steps approached. "You bitch!" Her stepfather's baritone resonated through the walls. "I pay the bills. I support you and your brat! Don't you think I deserve some thanks?"

"How dare you think you deserve anything! I told you this was your last chance, and I am *done*. Done being your slave, done laying down whenever you—"

The crack of a hard slap silenced the room. Nia froze, eyes downcast as pinpricks danced across her skin.

"You..." her mom's voice wavered, no longer strong or determined. Broken. "Please, just stay away from her..."

Nia turned from her plate and watched the burly man enter the room. Eyes wide, her body refused to move as a plea caught in her throat.

That's when she woke up. A cold sweat glued her legs to the thin bed sheets, and half of her arm had gone numb. She sucked in a deep breath and wiggled her fingers. Dampness wet her pillow—the tears she'd been unable to shed then were finally sliding down her cheeks.

The dream had been more a memory than a nightmare. A few details were off, but the emotion rang true. That's another reason she couldn't have a roommate. She wouldn't want to explain her night terrors. They didn't come as often as they used to, but they never fully went away. Maybe they never would.

She searched in the dark for her phone to take her mind off the fading scene. A bright blue light illuminated the room and chased away her monsters as Caspian's messages appeared on the screen.

Did Caspian have someone he loved? Would he ever turn into someone so terrible?

Without thinking about the potential repercussions, she sent him a text. It was too early in the morning to expect an answer, so she put her phone down and snuggled back into a comfortable position.

Picturing her own prince made her heart beat a little steadier. A man who would hold her as she slept, who would make her laugh instead of cry. And most importantly, one who she could love instead of hate.

She woke the next morning to a notification on her phone —a text from Caspian. Vaguely, she remembered sending something during the night but couldn't remember what. At least it was Sunday, and there was no rush to get out of bed. But after opening the message, she froze, struggling to process what she'd sent.

> Do you have a girlfriend?

To make matters worse, he'd responded.

CASPIAN<3

I was reserving that position for you ;)

Her mind raced. Who did he want to be his girlfriend? The imaginary Kate? Or her? Did he mean it, or was he just joking? And why was that stupid heart still by his name?

Tossing her phone aside, she buried her head in pillows and decided to deal with the issue after breakfast.

EIGHT

Nia

WINDING THROUGH A MAZE OF INSIPID HALLWAYS, NIA ENTERED the cafeteria clad in pajamas. Light from the overhead fluorescents faded into sunlight streaming through wide windows, and the dull roar that normally filled the tiled chamber had toned down to muffled mutterings of Sunday morning apathy. A welcome smell of eggs and sausage filled the air.

She spotted a familiar group picking at their breakfast and chatting, then Ivory caught her looking in their direction and waved. She waved back and quickly moved through the serving line to get a plate, swiping a cinnamon sugar muffin off the sidebar.

After sitting down next to Ivory and greeting the rest of the group, Nia expertly blended into the background as the others continued in conversation, content to eat her breakfast and listen. She pinched off a bite of cinnamon deliciousness and popped it in her mouth.

"I guess he's just not the party type."

"Which is weird because I totally pegged him as one."

"Yeah, Serena did, too. Now she has to come up with a new way to get his attention."

The other girls laughed at the last statement. Now that she thought about it, seeing them without their ringleader was unusual. And it sucked that they talked about Serena behind her back. None of them were any better.

Keeping her thoughts to herself, Nia pursed her lips and glanced at Ivory to catch her reaction. Ivory leaned in and caught her up to speed. "We went out to a party last night. It was supposed to be a big thing, but the guy Serena hoped would be there didn't show up. He even told her he'd be going beforehand."

Ivory hummed and raised an eyebrow, setting down her fork. "That's her side of the story anyway. The dude completely ignored her texts last night. Anyway, Serena got pretty wasted, so she's probably asleep right now. That, or too hungover to get out of bed. I'm gonna go check on her after this and bring a get-well snack." Ivory held up a napkin filled with mini muffins and fruit.

"Oh, okay." Nia didn't have much to say about Serena's love life. If anything, her perspective would only make matters worse. "Thanks for filling me in. You went to the party too, I'm guessing?"

Ivory nodded and then looked down, much too interested in the design of maple syrup on her plate. "I didn't stay long. But it was fun, and there was one guy...well, it doesn't matter because I didn't have the courage to talk to him."

"I understand," Nia offered, taking another bite of her muffin. "There's always next time."

Ivory sighed. "It's fine. I shouldn't put weight into people I meet at parties anyway." She pushed back her plate, looking more invested than she implied, or should've been, for not having talked to the guy. Still, Nia hoped it worked out for her.

"So…" Ivory gave her a sly sideways glance, jade eyes alight with curiosity. "Have you texted him yet?"

Nia looked over, caught off-guard. "Who?"

"You know…the number I gave you."

Who…? Oh.

She retorted with an exasperated sigh. Of all topics she absolutely *didn't* want to discuss but desperately needed advice on, it was Caspian. She stared at her plate, feeling about as put-together as her crumbling muffin. "I might have sent him a text, but there's no way I would let him know who it came from."

The words from his last message flashed in her memory. *I was reserving that position for you.* She sighed again—the most accurate way to express how she felt about the whole ordeal. "I don't know. I can't trust a stranger who randomly walks up to a table of girls and starts hitting on them, but I can't seem to get him out of my head, either." She ran her fingers through her hair and pulled at a knot. "*Oww,*" she groaned, more from mental stress than the pulled strands of hair.

"There's no need to beat yourself up." Ivory cracked a smile, then her face softened. "Maybe he's supposed to be in your head. Did you ever think about that?"

Nia glared at her. "If he's supposed to be there, why am I so annoyed? All I want is peace and quiet… I didn't come to college to find love."

"And that's exactly why love has found you!" Ivory declared with a sweet smile. "Okay, okay," she relented when Nia attempted to send a hundred daggers at her through a single look.

"That may be a bit much, but I'm just saying." Ivory twirled the straw around in her smoothie. "He didn't pay attention when any of us looked at him, but when you did, he pointed it out. There's no harm in talking to him if you're attracted."

"There's a lot of other fish in the sea for him to fry," Nia replied. "I'm sure last night he got it on with some hot chick without a second thought. I'm the only one wasting energy on this." She also knew that, at least six months ago, he had definitely played the field. If one girl posted his picture along with a rant, there were bound to be others to replace her, and she wouldn't let herself fall for the same trap.

Ivory gave her a weird look. "Yeah, I guess so..."

To prove her point, she asked, "He was at the party last night, right?"

"No...he wasn't."

He wasn't? So, instead of going out last night, he texted her. Maybe there this story had more to it after all. "Does he actually mean it?" she muttered, then clapped a hand over her mouth.

"Mean what?" Ivory's eyes widened and she set down her smoothie.

"Uh..." Damn it, she couldn't backtrack now. Not when Ivory was so tuned in. "He said he was," her throat constricted, "interested in whoever he thinks is texting him. But I'm sure he doesn't know it's me."

Ivory's face lit up with a sly grin. "I can ask what he thinks, if you want."

Nia stared at her in surprise. "Wait! No, you can't tell him anything!"

"I know, I know," Ivory said as she stood up, taking her tray back to the bins.

Given a moment to think, she contemplated the offer. Having Ivory ask would be easier than beating around the bush herself. She trusted Ivory to keep her word more than any of the others, but would finding out really be worth the effort?

If she didn't do something, could she ever get him out of her head?

Ivory came back and picked up her napkin of goodies for

Serena. It was now or never. "Actually, would you mind?" Nia kept her voice hushed.

"Sure, I'll be super discrete." Ivory gave her a wink.

"Thanks." A smile tugged at her lips. "Let me know what kind of response you get."

"Of course, silly. And do yourself a favor and relax a little." Ivory grinned and walked out of the cafeteria with a farewell wave.

Left with a mix of anticipation and dread at Caspian's response to the big question, she tried to not imagine every horrible outcome of this ploy. Did she want what Ivory said to be true—for him to be interested in her? Or would she just be another check on his list? Should she even care?

ᘂ

Another brain-numbing assignment waited back at her dorm. At least now the space wasn't so bare. Over the past week, she'd added little embellishments to the room, a few throw pillows here and airy curtains there that swayed when she left the window open. Yet they weren't enough to settle her mind.

She could only take so much actual work before turning to her newest piece of writing, the one where Caspian debuted as a main character. Now, although not the best in quality, at least she had a photo of him to work with, but his unreadable expression did nothing to help develop his character.

As his face stared outward from the digital screen, she couldn't conjure up a single suitable idea. The more she thought about him, the more she questioned what she knew. The conversation with Ivory hadn't helped, either.

Resting her head on her palm, she shut the laptop screen. This wasn't about some fictional character or a frivolous story on digital pages. Caspian was a real person, and she had started to develop a real curiosity about him. Not attraction—definitely not that. Attraction was too much of a fickle thing.

She thought she'd been attracted to her first and only boyfriend and assumed he'd been attracted to her. After all, he did make the first move by kissing her in the courtyard after school. It had caught her off guard, and he walked away right after, but when rumors started that they were going out, neither denied it.

The relationship turned into a stupid role-play after that, consisting of the occasional night out and half-hearted make-out sessions. She hung out with her friends, he talked with his, and their worlds stayed separate. The only time he ever responded to her texts or greetings at school was when he wanted to show his friends he had an actual girlfriend.

They didn't make each other laugh, couldn't have a deep conversation, and never even discussed what he liked about her. Romance wasn't a part of their interaction. But, with intimacy came attachment, and she didn't want to regret losing whatever they had. Then a friend told her he'd been kissing another girl, and it ended. Just like that. They never spoke again, as if they never knew each other. She'd suffered in silence, not wanting to admit something that hadn't been real could physically hurt so much.

A week after the breakup, she found out the truth. He'd only kissed her because of a stupid dare; he never really cared in the first place. As much as finding out poured salt in the wound, what his friends did after had been worse. She still couldn't bring herself to dwell on it. Even so, those events solidified her belief that men were shallow—their interest in women limited to sex appeal and ego.

Her desire to get to know guys after that became nonexistent. Until now. More than anything, she wanted to use this chance to find out if Caspian would prove her right about men, because surely he would.

She forced herself to open her planner and attempt to return to schoolwork. There was no use pining over a guy who might not be interested in her.

Not two seconds later, her phone dinged.

A message from Caspian.

NINE

Caspian

So, you interested?

Even though he was confident she'd reach out, waiting had become boring. He twisted in the pile of sheets and clothes on his mattress and clicked through mundane notifications on social media.

The time for breakfast had already passed, and lunch hour was steadily passing by as well, but he didn't feel hungry. Not in that way, at least. Nor had he been motivated to head over to the gym.

Last night ended in a breakthrough he couldn't ignore. It didn't matter why Nia asked if he had a girlfriend. The question meant she thought about it—and she wanted it to be her.

On top of his newest form of entertainment, messages from last year's flings had begun to trickle back into his inbox. Stale memories accompanied a myriad of meaningless names, and he blocked each of them in turn. He'd witnessed first-hand how girls who pretended their time together was special, who thought that meant they were *entitled* to more, only led to bigger problems.

Nothing was a bigger turn-off.

Half of the guys he knew had run through them anyway—the same girls who gave *him* shit for sleeping around.

Women will swindle you out of your hard-earned money, your time, and most of all, your respect as a man. Trust yourself over anyone else.

That had been the fatherly advice he received, and as far as experience proved, he had no reason to doubt it. If lasting love did exist, he hadn't seen it. The first seventeen years of his life felt like a scam, a lie from parents who only pretended to love each other. All he wanted from women was a good time, not the selfish demands and drama that grew with proximity.

While waiting for his next text from Nia, he unfollowed several similar girls to clear up the useless images on his feed. Finally, a notification banner dropped down on his screen.

ICE GODDESS NIA
Interested in what?

Odd she didn't remember. Had she not taken him seriously?

My offer. It's exclusive, mind you.

What offer are you talking about?

Being my girlfriend.

His patience almost ran out before the next reply came in.

...I'd like to know more about you first.

Ah, now that sounded like her—curiosity beneath a layer of reservation. Heat spread in his chest, just enough anticipation to get his blood pumping. She hadn't taken the jump into conversational territory before, and it added a thrill to the chase. Every step forward impressed him.

Nia didn't flounder the same way others did. When she said she wanted to know more about him, he believed it. She was the kind of girl to want to be invested in a relationship before committing. He responded without hesitation.

> You want more? If the photo wasn't enough, we can arrange a closer look in person ;)

That's not what I meant.

> Then you're not opposed?

I certainly will be if you keep messing around.

He chuckled. If only she knew how serious he was.

> What do you want to know?

Um, well, who are you? I mean, we really don't know much about each other.

> All right. My name's Caspian, nice to meet you. I think we went over this already, lol.

Ugh. I guess I have to ask more specific questions. What motivates you?

That question stunned him into an upright position. Most girls went for the typical 'what are you studying' or 'do you play sports.' Some even shamelessly asked for his dick size—he hoped, for their sakes, *those* had been drunk messages.

Regardless, he'd never been caught unprepared to answer a question.

> You motivate me.

It was no lie. Here he lay undressed in bed, acting like a teenage girl texting her crush. All because of Nia—because he needed to see how far she'd take him.

> *eye roll* Really? How can a girl you met at a random party motivate you?

Oh, so she still wanted to pretend to be "Kate"? He could work with that.

> You were too cute and such a tease, leaving without a kiss. Can't stop thinking about all your secret fantasies…and believe me, I appreciated your bluntness more than anything else.

> Did you think I'd forget how you asked me to suck on your clit? That you wanted to feel me moan as you come?

He smirked, imagining the blush that must be on her face. How he wished he could see it. What he didn't have to imagine was the tent setting itself up in his boxers. Stretching one arm above his head, he focused back on the conversation at hand. That pick-up line might have been too direct, so he switched back to a more passive style.

> That's okay. I know your answer.

> What motivates you?

This time her reply came easier.

> I'm generally not a motivated person.

Interesting. He wondered why Nia hadn't talked herself up. From what he observed, she had plenty of motivation. Enough to study the first week of classes and enough to reach out to him, although she didn't come across as very social.

> Okay. Then what motivated you to reach out to me?

Oh, I uh, needed a contact picture?

> Needed to see me again that bad, huh? Did you like the one I sent ;)

Your face wasn't even in it.

A grin irresistibly spread across his lips. Nice to know his face meant more than a group of generic muscles.

> Is that a yes or a no?

Can you please just tell me something real about you? Something meaningful?

Meaningful.

He meant everything he told her, but of course Nia would want more. Humming to himself, he tried to think of a reply that wouldn't leave him too vulnerable. With any other girl he'd be worried opening up would make him less desirable. When women felt on the same level as a man, then suddenly he wasn't worth their time. Why else would they fall in love with supernatural beings and fictional fairy tales? He couldn't be either of those, despite trying to come across as such.

Nia would want a real answer, though. So he did something he wasn't used to. He was honest.

I don't think of many people around me as friends. To me, most people are fake. They won't tell you what they really think about you until you get on their bad side. If you want the realest thing about me, it's that I don't trust people.

That's the first thing you've said to me I believe :)

He relaxed. A colon next to a parenthesis had never put him at ease before, but hers did. A knot within him uncoiled—she believed him.

Your turn.

What do you want to know?

Tell me something real about you. Something meaningful.

Sure, he could've asked about the color of her underwear or if she called his name when she made herself come, but for some reason it felt better to leave the playing field even. And he was almost—*almost* more interested in the answer than picturing her naked while she typed it.

I don't believe in men. I haven't met a single one that wasn't selfish and unreasonable.

Selfish and unreasonable? Not the worst thing he'd been called.

Fair enough.

Wait. He reread her last message. She hadn't been referring to just him. Thinking back, he noticed she had been more on edge than most girls when he introduced himself. What kind of guy had been bad enough to give her that impression of *all* men? His chest tightened.

Then his stomach rumbled with a loud protest, and he decided to digest that piece of information after whatever meal it was currently time for.

The phone lit up as soon as he put it down. Without thinking, he glanced at the screen. A message from Adrian— not who he'd hoped for. Standing at last, he threw on a pair of sweatpants and headed to the kitchenette.

The contents of his fridge were meager at best. The last bit of milk had gone sour and the only thing that moldy loaf of bread was good for was feeding the birds. Luckily, the container from last night's takeout stood apart on a lone shelf, and Caspian decided it was about to face its ultimate demise.

A few minutes later the microwave dinged, and he sat down with a half-full tray of steaming lo-mein noodles. His phone went off again. If that was Adrian, it better be for a good reason. Grabbing his phone, Caspian stuffed another forkful of greasy food into his mouth and opened the message.

IVORY (NIA'S FRIEND)

Hey. I have a question for you.

Go ahead.

Some people were talking about you at the party last night, so I wanted to get an answer from you directly. Are you seeing anyone? Or have anyone in mind?

I have someone in mind.

Ah... I knew it. Who is it?

Why do you want to know?

Just curious ;)

The usual reply. Why were women always so predictable? He rolled his eyes. Clearly, Ivory or someone else in their friend group, had an interest in him, and they were poking around for information.

You'll find out soon enough.

Are you serious about this girl? If it's one of my friends, you should know I don't deal with broken hearts very well. I'll come after you.

Lol. Serious as I've ever been.

Somehow, that's not very reassuring.

How about I just show you? That is my specialty, after all...

TEN

Nia

A KNOCK SOUNDED OUTSIDE HER DORM, AND SHE GOT UP FROM the desk to open the door. An exuberant Ivory waited with a suspicious smile plastered across her face. Nia rolled her eyes and stepped aside, hoping that meant the mission with Caspian had gone well. Except Ivory's definition of "well" was yet to be determined.

"I couldn't get a straight answer, but he *did* say he would tell me," Ivory burst out before Nia could get in a greeting. "Under certain conditions."

"That...doesn't sound good." Nia closed the door and motioned for Ivory to take a seat beside her on the bed.

Settling into the comforter, Ivory crossed one leg over the other. "It's nothing crazy, I swear." Her face softened into a sympathetic plea, and Nia tried to erase the doubt etched in her own. "Caspian asked if our group had any plans for this weekend, and I said 'no' cause we don't, and then he invited us all to the club on Saturday." Ivory clapped her hands together, her face lighting up again while Nia's darkened. "He said he'd ask the special girl out then and there if we all came."

"*All* of us?" She squirmed. "What does that mean exactly?

Aren't there only two of you who are old enough to enter the club?"

"Oh, I guess he has connections." Ivory wiggled her eyebrows. "And I think by 'all of you' he meant those of us he met at lunch last weekend. There's a couple more he didn't get to meet, but I'm sure he can get them into the club, too."

Nia sighed. "So...I have to go this time."

Going into a club didn't thrill her. The thought of being surrounded by people who only came to get drunk and dance sounded like a panic attack. Especially with all the attention Serena was sure to attract with her sweet-as-honey persona. One day, she'd get stung by one of those adoring honey bees.

The location almost outweighed her desire to figure out Caspian. But...if he really was rejecting hordes of girls for a special interest, then this was a prime opportunity. She strongly doubted he had her in mind, and it wouldn't be all too bad if she could hide in a corner and watch the show.

Ivory leaned back, supporting herself with an arm as strands of brown hair fell over her shoulder. "Yeah, pretty sure you have to go if you want to see who he asks out." She giggled, then sobered. "If you're uncomfortable with it, then do what feels right for you. But if you're worried about going someplace new, we'll all be there with you. I don't plan on drinking, so I can help if anything gets too weird."

"Thanks," Nia replied, relieved to have her support. "I'm still not sure, but I have a week to think about it, right?"

"That's right. If you don't want to go, it's no sweat. I'll probably ask if he can still get a few of us into the club." Ivory looked up with questioning eyes. "That is, if you don't mind."

Nia shrugged. "Why would I care? You don't need to ask for my permission."

"It's just I know you want that special girl to be you, and I don't want you thinking I'm trying to steal him away, that's all," Ivory said.

"I do not," she protested, cheeks flushed as her hands fidgeted.

Ivory sat up and patted her leg, then stood and walked toward the door. "You keep saying that, girl. I'll give you some space to think it over. If you need anything, you know where to find me."

"Thanks, Ivory." Nia smiled, grateful she had found someone to talk to who didn't press her.

"My pleasure." Ivory flashed a cute smile, then waved and left the room.

Unsettled by the new absence and left with her looming decision, Nia sat back down at her desk. Homework was so not happening—good thing she had finished all her assignments for tomorrow. Then again, would she feel any better until she got Saturday night over with? Tapping a restless pattern onto the desk, she wrestled with herself.

What was she even worried about? This would merely be to investigate Caspian's character. Any normal girl would go after him—he personified tall, dark, and handsome. No one would question if she went along. Even without seeing that intense look in his eyes from their first encounter, the more she communicated with him, the more she realized how captivating he could be. Like how he could alter himself to fit different situations, like water being poured into an assortment of containers. Why miss out on a chance to see him again?

Her mind slipped to the message he sent last night when he admitted to not trusting people. Bitterly, she thought maybe that was because he used every girl he talked to, and all guys had a bad habit of being trash.

What if...she hesitated at the thought but didn't shut it down like usual. What if she could just be his friend? And he could be hers? The thought of building any sort of bond made her apprehensive, but thinking of him as a friend, an ally, felt better than being a potential partner or love interest. That way, he wouldn't threaten the reinforced cage protecting her heart. He could peer in without getting too personal.

A part of her wanted to know what he would see if he looked close enough; if he had an unhindered glimpse at who she was, would he turn and walk away? Would he want to leave behind the girl with a dysfunctional past and a lonely future? Or would he relate to one of her fragmented pieces?

As she picked up her phone and reread their messages, a new one came in.

HE WHO SHALL NOT BE NAMED
Meet me at the club. at 10 p.m. Saturday.

Why?

I have a surprise for you.

Shaking her head, she clicked her tongue at his arrogance. Foolish of him to think she'd go simply because he told her to —good thing she already knew what this was about.

I won't go without a good reason. I want to know if you plan on killing me or not.

Should I take that as a compliment? I am quite skilled, but more in the art of pleasure.

She puffed her cheeks and blew out a long breath. Just when she thought they might have a normal conversation, he had to pull this crap. Were all men motivated solely by sex?

Must you be so predictable? Try again.

All right then, what would make you happy?

How about a normal conversation?

That's what we were just having.

You're crazy.

Crazy for you.

This was ridiculous. A guy who only knew pick-up lines couldn't make her happy, even in the areas he boasted. She learned how to take care of herself years ago, and no egotistical flirt could make her think otherwise. Sure, she read about all the kinky stuff that sounded good on paper, but the only person who could satisfy her was herself.

I bet you don't even know what love is.

Who said anything about love? …but tell me then, what is it to you?

She couldn't answer.

Unsure of where this conversation was going, she put her phone down and leaned back in the stiff chair.

An incoming message dinged. Debating on whether or not to open it, she huffed as another persistent ding came in. Was he going to distract her all day? Irritated, she unlocked her phone and read his messages as they kept coming.

If you were mine, and I was yours…I'd take you to a nice restaurant, then bring you home to be my dessert.

I'd hold your hand as we walk down the street and hold your pussy when we're alone.

I'd kiss your lips when you come in the room, and nibble on your nipples when you come in bed.

> I'd count how many times I can make you smile and how many ways I can make you moan.

> & I'll illustrate every word, if you give me the chance.

Her head spun.

She really needed to learn to give up on talking to him. That was all a bluff, and she wasn't so dumb or horny to fall for it. Words like those weren't hard to type—she had firsthand experience.

> That...wouldn't make me happy.

As if he would understand.

The first few blog posts resurfaced in her mind when the girl had been in a blissful daze. Maybe he wasn't lying. That girl fell head over heels for a reason. But one thing was certain: Caspian had no concept of commitment. Girls were no more than entertainment to him, dating his version of playing a game.

She left him unread and turned her phone off. There, now she could study in peace.

Overcome with a newfound motivation to plow through any scrap of homework, she pulled out her notes and saw the last thing jotted down.

Give Caspian someone to believe in.

That had been in reference to the character she'd made to represent him, yet something about it rang true for the real one.

Even though she didn't want to think about him at the moment, she knew avoiding the problem wouldn't make it go away. Instead of admitting she'd already made her decision about Saturday night, she began writing a short scene to let off steam.

Music blasted through the club, carrying their heartbeats and drowning out every thought that passed through their minds. All flashing lights and cheap perfume. Their sweat only added to the exhilaration, bodies bumping into each other, hands wandering through thin clothes, lips murmuring dirty secrets into eager ears that would soon come to fruition...

Closing her eyes, she abandoned the real world for one of her own and let any worries melt away. If only love in real life could be as easy as it was in her head.

ELEVEN

Caspian

"Hey, puke hair, you coming tonight or not?" He shifted the phone and ran a hand through damp hair from a post-workout shower.

"What's happening again?" Adrian asked.

"The club, with that group from the dorm."

"Right, your girl's gonna be there."

The smirk on Adrian's face was audible, but Caspian chose to ignore it. "Yeah," he replied. "You're sure she'll show up?"

"Don't be so anxious, dog breath, it'll throw off your game," Adrian chided.

Caspian shook his head and snorted. "You really know how to piss me off."

Half a dozen girls had been sufficiently smitten since last he went to Adrian for advice, but Nia was proving to be a different story. Memories of his last failure resurfaced in full force, including how much of a drag it was to involve his friend in these things. But the teasing would be the worst of it. It hadn't been easy for Adrian to earn the title of friend, but he had, and Caspian knew what he said wouldn't get passed around outside the two of them.

This time, he'd make sure not to get caught off guard.

"From what you've told me, you can bet on her being there," Adrian confirmed. "What makes her so special? I've never seen you this fixated before."

"Dunno, it's...different with her." He didn't care to dig deeper than that. "So, you coming or not?"

Adrian ignored the question. "Cause she's different, or you're different?" he mused.

"Come on," Caspian muttered, glancing at the clock as he sat down to stop himself from treading circles in the carpet. "I don't have the energy to waste on your philosophical debates right now."

"Sure you don't," Adrian replied. "In any case, she seems decent. But sorry man, I already made plans for tonight."

"So much for being my wingman," Caspian grumbled.

"Just returning a favor." Adrian's tone shifted back to a tease. "Go break a leg."

Caspian scoffed. "Thanks, but I'm not an actor."

He hung up in order to silence whatever clever remark would get thrown out next. Sometimes talking to Adrian felt like a massive headache, but at least he got the confirmation he was after. She would be there.

Tonight he would see his ice goddess again face-to-face, and that meant it must be the right time to make the next move. For once, he wanted to get to know a girl—not as a girlfriend, but as a bare minimum friend. A glimpse into her world, even her choice of outfit or subtle body language, was all he needed from tonight.

He'd hoped Adrian would come along to keep the rest of the girls company, but the club could provide enough willing volunteers. Either way, he planned to focus his time and attention on Nia. She deserved it, since he hadn't felt this inspired in a while. Almost long enough to wash away his bitter memories.

Another glance at the clock revealed that at last, it was almost time to head to the dorms—he'd offered to pick up Ivory and Serena knowing Nia would tag along too.

He sprung off the couch and rummaged through various piles of clothes, but that only made more of a mess, and none of them were suitable anyway. Foregoing his usual lack of effort, he pried open the dresser with a rattle and fished out an untouched button-up shirt. That would do, maybe with a pair of crisp jeans. He combed a few fingers through his hair and as a final touch, used a spray of his favorite cologne.

All set.

Thoughts settled and hopes high, he snatched his wallet and car keys, locked the door, then strode out of the apartment complex. A black sky greeted him as he popped his collar, the air pleasant and warm with the promise of changing tides.

The dorm building wasn't difficult to find. A few paces inside, he spotted the cluster of girls he'd met before. One stood taller than the rest, her blonde hair falling down an exposed back and clothed in tight black fabric that accentuated slim hips. Immediately, he pictured Nia in a similar outfit and tried to search her out. But she wasn't with the others.

"Oh, hey! Caspian!" A petite girl with light brown hair waved from a few doors down. "We're, uh, almost ready..."

Ah, that must be Ivory.

"Excuse me," he said, parting the sea of lip gloss and winged eyeliner. A chorus of coy compliments fell short of his ears as he made his way toward the dorm Ivory had popped out of. Worry crept into his heart. What if Nia had decided not to come after all?

A hushed conversation crept through the cracked door.

"Nia, you can't be serious!"

"I'm just not sure! Do you really think—"

He interrupted with a rap on the door frame. Both girls turned, Ivory in a simple dress with a star pattern, while Nia donned pajamas. His eyes lingered on the scrawled poem stretched over Nia's chest then tracked up to her flushed cheeks.

Ivory's exasperated look transformed into a smile, while Nia's turned to annoyance. He noted the uncertainty in Nia's eyes and renewed his vow to make sure she had a good time. "Am I interrupting?"

"No, not at all," Ivory responded before Nia could object. "I was just helping pick out what to wear." She spared a glance at the bed, where several sets of clothes had been laid out, along with matching shoes.

Nia shot Ivory a menacing glare.

He chuckled and nodded politely at them. "Mind if I see the options?"

Any outfit would be stunning. Hell, she could skip clothes altogether, and he'd be more than happy.

"No need, I figured it out," Nia answered and stepped in front of his view of her bed.

Ivory sighed. "Can you give us five minutes?"

He shifted away from the door and turned his back to the wall. "No problem, take all the time you need, ladies."

Nia huffed before he retreated completely. "It's fine. Give me a minute so I can change."

"Need any help?" He threw a smirk in her direction, then turned before a projectile gave his face a makeover. He'd take that as a no.

Ivory stepped into the hall across from him as Nia closed the door. A few moments of silence passed before she spoke. "Thanks for taking us out."

"Yeah, no problem," he replied. "How many of you are coming?"

"Half a dozen, I think. Some are meeting us at the club." She shuffled her feet, tapping her toe on the floor. "Just...don't pressure her too much. She's not taking this lightly, you know."

He looked up and searched Ivory's downcast eyes. Was Nia that worried about tonight? He opened his mouth to respond, but got cut off as the door opened.

Eager to see what Nia had chosen, he turned at the same time she stepped forward, and she stumbled right into the solid wall of his chest. His automatic response would have been to catch her—if he wasn't already trying to catch his breath.

She gasped as her hand shot out to brace herself on his arm. "Don't stand right there! Geez," Nia huffed.

His skin heated as she removed her touch and hurried over to Ivory, who offered a bright compliment. He couldn't help but pull his lip between his teeth, eyes traveling over her flattering burgundy jeans. A simple black top hugged her chest and fell off one shoulder in an obvious tease. His pulse already raced twice its normal speed—how was he supposed to last the night without slipping that thin fabric over the other shoulder?

"You picked the perfect outfit," he said, the corner of his lip curing into a smile. He took a mental note of her style. It would make a great addition to one of his drawings.

A blush took over her expression. "Well, I didn't put it on for you."

"Mn." He knew better—she went out of her way to pick out something nice, and he'd be sure to give her all the appreciation she deserved. "If that's the case, would you take it off for me?"

Shock flared across her face, covered quickly with indignation. "I changed my mind. I'm staying here."

"Wait." He stepped in front of her door to cut off her escape route. "Come. For me."

She glared back, then flicked her gaze between his torso and the doorknob. "Fine. And Ivory, make sure you keep that pepper spray ready. I think we're going to need it."

Serena approached them from down the hall. "Everyone who had a ride already left for the club. Are we ready now?"

"Yeah, I think so." Ivory glanced at Nia to verify. "Right?"

"Sure," Nia responded, clearly avoiding his gaze as she gave her friend a tense smile.

"Then let's get going," he said and pushed off the wall.

TWELVE

Nia

STREETLIGHTS AND BLURRED BUILDINGS WISPED PAST THE CAR window as she tried to keep her eyes averted. The backseat seemed safe enough, with Ivory settled in beside her and Serena taking the lead next to Caspian.

But the night view wasn't nearly as interesting as the spearmint-scented man in the driver's seat. Every few minutes, she'd chance a peek out her peripheral vision. And every time she glanced up, deep blue eyes would flick to meet hers from the rearview mirror. Quickly she retracted her gaze, as if Caspian's attention had inflicted a burn.

Even though she should interact with him—for research purposes—she couldn't bring herself to hold eye contact. Pushing down the bundle of nerves in her stomach, she tried to at least appear normal on the outside and pay more attention to the conversation.

"—you guys are crazy!" Ivory scrunched her face in mock horror. "I'd never ride a motorcycle, too risky for me. Just the thought of what could happen when you get in an accident..."

"You're pretty much okay if you wear a helmet and don't

drive like a maniac," Caspian replied, grinning like a Cheshire cat.

"I'd give anything to feel the wind in my hair," Serena chimed in. "Wearing a helmet defeats the whole point."

"What about you, Nia?" Caspian asked, a twinkle in his eye. "Would you ride?"

The air conditioner must have stopped working because the temperature just went up a few degrees. The image of Caspian in a black leather jacket careening around a corner on a motorcycle was too perfect to admit.

"I'd...I don't think I could handle one. They're pretty heavy," she responded, struggling to retain her composure. The skin on her fingernails became much more interesting than it should've been.

"If I rode with you, would it be better?"

No.

"Wouldn't that just make the bike heavier?" she retorted, impressed her reply came out coherent.

Caspian laughed. "Trust me. I can handle some extra weight."

The deep rumble of his voice reminded her heart of its rhythm, and she smiled, proud she had made him laugh. His laid-back energy diffused through the car and eased the knot of tension inside her.

"What kind of music do you all like?" he asked, glancing through the mirror.

Careful to keep a straight face, she tentatively met his gaze before he looked back at the road. The moment ended before it became too awkward or heated, and her small smile tugged higher at the corner of her lips.

Guarding the spark of happiness like a secret, she returned to staring out at the city lights and expected everyone to respond to his question in her place. Instead, a sharp stab dung into her side as Ivory elbowed her.

Serena took the liberty to answer first. "Pop, all the way."

Nia took a deep breath to steady her nerves, then offered a reply to avoid any further *encouragement,* "Anything, really." Hopefully that was dull enough to not draw any attention and satisfy her accomplice, but Ivory gave her a sideways glance with raised eyebrows.

Then Ivory offered her own response. "Rock or alternative."

Hands clenched, Nia bore a hole into the side of Ivory's head with her stare. That wasn't true...rock and alternative were *her* favorite genres, not Ivory's. Why...?

Ivory pursed her lips and tilted her head as if to say *try harder, Nia.*

Caspian fiddled with the radio until he found a rock station and looked at them. "Like this?"

Instinctively, Nia nodded in response. Heat flared in her cheeks, and she swiveled back toward the window. She needed this car ride to be over.

"Do you go to this club often?" Serena asked, directing the question at Caspian.

Of course he did, or else he wouldn't be so confident about it. Unable to help herself, Nia watched him from the corner of her eye.

He hummed. "Not as much, recently. I've been" —his eyes flashed to meet hers— "distracted." The last word came out hushed, almost a whisper.

Her blush intensified, and she forced her attention to the passing storefronts. Was he being genuine, or was it all an act? It'd be too easy for him to play the part for a few hours, to live the life that novels so often glorified without caring what was written on the next page.

Her mind drifted away from the conversation and down a more risqué path. If they were characters in a story, she'd be wearing a skimpy dress like Serena's, while a sexy R&B song played in the background. Caspian would look just as charming as he did now, with his ruffled hair and unbuttoned collar.

A one-night stand wouldn't matter because the narrative would simply end. No need to construct a happily-ever-after. Why fret over real feelings when she could write perfect ones instead, even if they were only a collection of moments?

In her fantasy, she would've purposely worn lacy lingerie under the skimpy dress. Maybe even none at all, while he would steal small glances and fleeting touches the whole ride. Everything would "click." It would feel right, and magically, she wouldn't be anxious anymore. They would both be relaxed and excited and utterly, inescapably, aroused.

With one hand on the wheel, he rested the other over her thigh as they engaged in pleasant conversation. His fingers were warm and heavy yet left such gentle caresses as he inched up further and further. The minutes ticked by, stretching on and on as desire pooled between her legs. The car rolled to a stop. In a single heartbeat, they clashed in a primal kiss. Hot and demanding, his mouth dominated hers with tender passion, making every right move. His hand finished its course along her thigh and—

"Nia, are you okay?" The real Caspian's voice broke the spell. "You seem a little dazed."

"Oh, uh, it's a little hot in here," she said, cursing herself for not having a better response. How could he not see right through that? If his imagination went as wild as hers...she shrunk into the seat.

"You should have said so," he replied and turned on the air full blast. Serena curled up as the cold current hit her legs. Nia cringed, unnerved about causing everyone else discomfort. She shouldn't have come after all. Was it too late to turn around?

"Just a few more minutes until we arrive," Caspian announced.

Guess not.

They found a parking spot and pulled over across from a

large building. Its bright neon sign lit up the sidewalk—a symbol of the club suit of cards.

Clambering out of the car, Nia hung back to stay out of sight and trailed behind Caspian, while Ivory bridged the gap between the two. Serena's heels clicked on the sidewalk as she raced ahead.

They entered by the check-in counter, where the other girls greeted them with an assortment of stilettos and sequins, full of bubbling laughter and fluttering lashes on elegant faces primed with makeup. Music blasted through the establishment, vibrating under her feet. Bouncing lights and bodies came into view through a set of glass doors in the foyer.

Everyone else prepared for a fun and easy night out, but Nia paled in comparison. Going into a busy club with people she hardly knew didn't seem fun or easy. She watched as Caspian chatted with the bouncer and the rest of the girls got their hands stamped. This was her last chance to back out.

No, she couldn't leave. Not yet.

Turning, she admired how Caspian looked so sure of himself. This was more his scene than an empty lecture hall or outdoor café. Shoulders set and relaxed, sleeves rolled up to reveal smooth forearms, he had the presence of a leopard prowling in the night.

Maybe if she focused on him, everything would be all right. If he were standing next to her, maybe being in a mass of unknown people wouldn't seem so suffocating.

He caught her gaze and came to her side. "Still feeling unwell?"

His closeness didn't aid her already flushed cheeks. Minted breath mingled with his cologne and spiked the air. She tried to fight off the urge to lean in closer, but this place formed a massive, tumultuous sea, and she needed a buoy. A nervous tic started up as her finger tapped against her thigh.

"Are you sure it's okay to be here? I'm underage." She

looked away from his face. A face that probably saw how pathetic she was, how much of a wreck she felt inside. A surge of nausea threatened to choke her. What was she doing here with a guy she just met?

"Is it too much? I can take you home if you want," he whispered, bending down. A large, soothing hand slid into hers, and a steady current of energy flowed up her arm.

"Can I ask a question?" he said, passing off his previous one.

"I guess."

"When I first saw you, confidence exuded from your every step. You looked like a queen." He tipped up her chin.

Leveling her eyes, she put on a brave face. This wasn't the time or place to be showing weakness. "What do you mean, when you first saw me?"

Could that be why he'd been so intense that day? Had he purposely walked into that lecture hall? For her?

Caspian bit his bottom lip. "Never mind that. Why are you unsure of yourself now? What can I do to bring the real Nia out of her shell?"

He didn't understand? He'd admitted he didn't trust anyone, so surely he concealed some things the same way she did. The chameleon couldn't understand the tortoise, yet both wanted to hide.

Cobalt eyes locked onto hers, and he continued with a slight grin, "Or do I need to tease you more? I kinda hoped to see your smile again without getting the pepper spray involved, but you could always make it up to me with a kiss."

"Not gonna happen," she retorted in a fiery tone that betrayed her frosty demeanor.

"Are you sure? My lips would still work if I'm blind."

This guy.

She rolled her eyes. "Nice try."

He gave her hand a squeeze. "I want to show you something."

Eyes wandering from his dark, wavy locks down to his broad chest, she squeezed back and followed as he led her to the dance floor. Caspian held his fair share of mysteries, and it made her want to learn them all. Even if it meant getting out of her comfort zone.

THIRTEEN

Caspian

"LET'S GO," NIA DECLARED, TAKING HER FIRST STEP ONTO THE bustling main floor.

Excitement burst through his chest. When they first arrived she had looked like a lost mouse, ready to bolt at any indication of danger. But now her confidence returned, and it complimented her as well as the colored lights dancing across her skin. He hoped it stuck around, if only a while longer.

His hand dwarfed her thin fingers and tiny palms. The small gesture came as a new kind of intimacy, almost insignificant compared to the constant grinding all around them, but he could only feel Nia. Pulling her closer, he didn't plan to let go until he was sure she'd stay.

He wondered what had drawn out her bold side. Was it his proximity? His words? The only effect he seemed to have on other women before was an increased sex drive, but this seemed deeper. Each up and down with Nia provided far more stimulation than the predictable triumph he'd grown accustomed to. A steady thrum in his chest hinted at more, that maybe these circumstances with another woman wouldn't be the same, but he didn't dare to examine that closer.

The club's high ceilings lit up with neon lights, displaying brief flashes of the crowd that decorated the second-story railing and a large open bar on the main floor. Everything here was already familiar to him, but he walked slower to let Nia adjust.

Taking a quick sweep of the room, he noted how everyone else was getting along. Some of the girls stood on the sidelines, sipping drinks as they talked among themselves. Ivory sat among them, enjoying the view from a table near the large windows and sneaking glances at him and Nia.

Serena and the rest of her squad had made their way to the middle of the dance floor, already engaged with a few new acquaintances. She caught his eye from across the room and curled her lips in a sultry smile. Her gaze meandered down his body, hips swaying, and dropped her eyes to his waist. Then her face darkened and her smile faded. Nia's hand slipped away from his. Serena turned back at her friends as if nothing happened.

He glanced back to catch Nia, but it was too late—she'd already wandered halfway to a stool in the far corner of the bar. This wasn't his plan. Setting his jaw, he watched through the crowd as she sat down with her back to him.

At least she'd found a place to get comfortable instead of walking out. The corner would be quieter and less crowded, better for conversation. He needed to fix whatever thoughts she'd gotten in her head and keep her improved mindset from earlier.

He silently watched her sip a glass of ice water. As fun as it would be to break her out of her trance, which seemed to be a habit of hers, he wanted to see what she was up to. Up to this point, he had no clue what she actually thought. Especially about him.

Facing forward, she looked down and pulled something out of her purse. He cocked his head. What had she brought?

A pencil. And that journal. In past years, he'd pulled out similar items many times, but these days, he'd been too busy collecting girls on his arm to pull out a sketch pad.

Intrigued and fed up with merely watching the action, he slipped onto the stool next to hers. "Can I get you something more exciting than water?"

Her eyes remained focused on the notebook. "I don't like the taste of alcohol."

The corner seat at least seemed to keep her calm. Legs crossed at the ankles, shoulders set back, she resembled the Nia he remembered.

He set an elbow against the counter. "Then you haven't been drinking the right stuff. Let me treat you. I can ask for a virgin one if you prefer."

She snorted. "Is that what *you* prefer—virgins?"

He smirked. "I prefer you. No other requirements."

She rolled her eyes as if she doubted him down to the very core of his being. "Wouldn't taking out the alcohol defeat the purpose of proving your point that I've not been 'drinking the right stuff'?"

A grin lit up his face. "Say no more, baby girl." He raised a finger to catch the bartender's attention. "Sex on the Beach, no vodka, and keep everything else."

The bartender nodded and pulled out some bottles from behind the counter. Nia's attention shifted back to the paper, where her scribbles went on for a quarter of the page. A crease formed on his forehead, and he leaned onto the counter to get a better angle.

The way her hand glided across the paper made it seem like whatever she wrote was significant. But instead, his gaze traveled up her slender arm to her shoulder. He sucked in a shallow breath as he noticed her exposed bra strap. Would she let him trail butterfly kisses down that shoulder to her chest? Would she moan low and long if he sucked on her nipple?

The things this woman did to him.

"Sound like something you'd like?" he teased, jealous the notebook got more of her attention than him.

"What?" The pencil stopped moving, and she looked up with sparkling eyes.

"Sex on the beach."

The tip of the pencil snapped. "What did you say?"

Her expression made it hard not to laugh, but he held it in.

Then the bartender set down a frosted, bright orange drink in front of them. Nia spared a glance at him, and he nodded to the glass, pressing his lips together to prevent himself from ruining the moment.

"Oh, the name of the drink," she whispered to herself.

"Yeah." He grinned. "Unless you want it to mean more?"

A dark look flashed across her face. Repressing whatever comment surfaced in her head, she lifted the drink and tasted a tiny sip. Then sipped some more.

She appeared as elegant as ever, red lips delicately perched on the rim of the glass. Ironically, as she quenched her own thirst, his multiplied tenfold. He rolled on his lip between his teeth and fought the urge to steal those lips for himself. The mental images he had wrestled to keep at bay came flooding in, his mind not the only part of him reacting to the scene in front of him.

"Not bad..." she remarked, setting the glass down.

"I knew you'd like it." He felt a little too pleased with himself. "Take out the strong liquor and you get a delicious cocktail even non-drinkers can appreciate."

She paused, and her eyes flicked up to his. "Are you waiting on a drink?"

"Mn, no, I don't drink when I'm out to have a good time with a good girl."

She frowned. "Then why are you here, wasting time with me when you could be out there dancing with someone?"

He chuckled at her oblivion and dragged a hand over his face. Was he really going to do this? Tonight, he planned to bring Nia into his spotlight—fading into the background didn't suit her. This wouldn't be the only time he proclaimed infatuation with a girl, however, it would be the first time he wasn't sure how it would be received.

"I wanted to put a smile on that pretty face of yours," he said. "You look like you're feeling a little better, anyway."

She blushed and glanced down. "Yeah, I guess so. Thanks for the drink."

The tip of his finger lifted, wanting to reach out and brush a loose strand of hair behind her ear. But he didn't, afraid she'd recoil again at his touch, or worse, that it would spark something he knew couldn't be taken care of tonight.

"So...what's the journal for?" he asked.

FOURTEEN

Nia

NOT AGAIN.

Here he went, catching her off-guard. And when she was already out of her element, no less. She couldn't figure out why he cared. A player should be out on the dance floor with some girl who wanted his attention, not with a wallflower like her.

The last thing she wanted was to start telling Caspian all her secrets, unraveling her hobbies, daydreams, the reason she came tonight at all...and the journal held the heart of it all.

She met his dark eyes with a glare. Even through the moving lights, she could see the intensity in his gaze. What did he want? Those sapphire eyes trapped her in the same way they had before. Something about him intoxicated her, his attentiveness headier than any liquor.

Then she realized—this scene, this feeling of energy in her veins that came from the beat and Caspian's gaze—it was perfection. She *had* to write it down. A part of her searched for this, whatever it was, for a long time, and she might never experience it again.

Digging a pen out of her bag, since her pencil had snapped,

she scribbled a few notes. Only after a few seconds did she remember Caspian had asked a question and was waiting for her answer.

Her hand stopped, fingers frozen. He'd probably read everything. The words about him.

Her skin crawled with heat. She reached for the cocktail and sucked down half the sweet, tangy liquid.

"I like to write," she finally choked out.

Why try to avoid him? Why fight it? After all, what could really come of her exposing a bit of herself? He didn't know she had been texting him—he didn't know anything.

Then why did this make her so nervous?

Humor and curiosity danced in his eyes. "About physics?"

She cocked her head sideways and re-read the words.

A pull of uncertainty, evenly matched with the chaotic force of fate. A personal gravity that keeps you together despite the cracks threatening to tear down everything inside. Then, at the same time, a pitfall in your stomach as you finally take the dive.

"...something like that," she responded, closing the journal and putting it back in her bag.

"Do you write a lot?" he asked, persisting with the questions.

"Yeah." She took another sip of her drink to cool down and turned to look at him once again. In front of her sat the one person she wanted to examine, to observe and figure out his true nature. Right now, she should make sure to take in all the details.

He sat comfortably, almost careless. One arm rested on the sleek countertop as he propped a foot on the lowest rung of the stool, knees spread wide. His shirt pulled taut across a chest chiseled beyond what should be legal for their proximity, and the width of his shoulders was twice her size. His jaw cast a faint shadow on his neck as neon lights buzzed in the background. Defined cheekbones highlighted smooth skin—

"What do you write, then?"

She gave a weak shrug. "Different sorts of things."

Her eyes continued to critique him. A solid button-up shirt with jeans...business casual? Compared a hoodie and sweatpants, it seemed like he'd tried—

"What are you currently working on?"

She huffed. If he kept this up, she'd get nowhere.

"Can we just...stop," she blurted. Conversing had become too overwhelming, and he needed to be quiet, to let her take everything in without interruption.

The corners of his lips sank down. "Stop what?"

She closed her eyes before responding. "Stop acting like we want to know each other. I'm not here to entertain you or make small talk. All I came to do was observe."

Faintly she recognized the impact of the bold words, but tuned out all the noise. The lively music in the background, his smooth voice beside her, the frenzied consciousness of her thoughts...things that only muddled the situation.

According to her wishes, he remained silent. She sighed in relief at not having to answer any more questions. Then, as she opened her eyes again, they widened in shock.

He'd pulled off his jacket and was slowly unbuttoning his shirt, exposing the smooth, refined muscles underneath.

She snapped her eyes up to his. "What are you doing?"

Smirking, he kept eye contact as he took his time to finish undoing each button. She watched with wide eyes as his hands moved lower, one button at a time, down to his six-pack and then showing off the elastic of his underwear. A defined 'V' pointed below a thick black band, to which she dared not allow her eyes to wander.

"Letting you observe me." His voice was low, barely audible over the club's music.

That...was not what she expected. Not at all.

Should she be complaining? She didn't know yet. The

booming bass drum drowned out the pounding of her heart, but she could feel it beating hard in her chest.

Every carnal thought she had entertained came to the forefront of her mind. A tiny part of her wished his fingers were hers, gliding gracefully over his chest and abdomen. Of course, she'd seen all of this before on a digital screen, but putting a face on top of his body, so close she could reach out and touch him, was really too much.

On top of it all, and much to her torture, he stayed absolutely silent. Colored lights danced across his bare skin.

"Why?" she breathed at last.

Instead of taking the bait he so shamelessly laid out for her, she forced her eyes to stay connected with his.

"You wanted to observe me, didn't you? I thought this would be more fun."

He wasn't wrong. In fact, she hated that he was right.

"But I didn't mean," she hesitated, "all...of that."

He smiled, baring pearly teeth in a devious grin. "Well, this is more the kind of thing I observe when I draw people."

"You draw?" she choked out.

He shifted to lean on the counter again, the ripple of movement in his chest hard to miss. "Yeah, but it's kind of a secret. You're the first person I've told in a while."

"Oh, okay." She swallowed, struggling to regain her composure. "So, what do you draw?"

"If I tell you, will you tell me what you write?" Though swathed in the shadow, his eyes gleamed a deep blue as he held her gaze. Something akin to a spark of static energy jolted her heart.

She nodded.

"I draw erotic scenes," he continued. "Mostly sex positions, but sometimes I just sketch whatever comes to mind."

A flush of heat spread over her body, delicious and

alarming at the same time. "I guess you could say I write whatever comes to mind, too."

Caspian's eyes sparkled. "What's on your mind tonight?"

You.

"Someone—" She coughed, choking on her honesty. "Um, *something* that keeps bothering me."

His smile only widened. "In that case, I'd like to read what you write about that...thing."

"No. Not happening."

"Oh..." He exaggerated his amusement with a raspy chuckle. "I'm a big boy, I can handle it. I'm sure it's nothing worse than what I draw."

She rubbed her hands over her thighs in an effort to calm her nerves. "Still, you wouldn't want me to see any of your pictures, right? Yeah, it's the same type of thing...artists get subconscious about their work."

"Then we'll make a trade, my art for your writing."

Well, it hadn't been hard for him to sidestep that one.

Was he really offering to show her his explicit drawings? Her thoughts raced with possibilities, and she couldn't decide if this was a ruse to get her attention or a chance to find common ground.

He pulled a phone out of his pocket, tapping it a few times before leaning even closer to her. Their shoulders brushed, skin to skin, and the smell of his cologne wrapped around her. In the back of her mind, she wondered if her other senses would enjoy him as much as her nose seemed to.

"Here, you can scroll through them," he said as he handed her the phone.

She took it and looked down at the drawings. Some in color, others in black and white, a few basic sketches. All of them very good.

All of them very lewd.

Couples bent over each other in sex positions she hadn't even imagined, while some were erotic portraits of people making out. The details stood out to her on a few of them, as if he had already read her writing and made it come to life. Scanning over every photo, but careful to not linger on any one in particular, she admired his work.

The content didn't embarrass her, but rather the fact that the very attractive artist sat mere inches away. Now she knew for a fact the kind of things he was capable of imagining. And he was watching her, practically shirtless. If Caspian could draw these in such beauty, she didn't want to think of what he could do in the three-dimensional world.

"So, which do you like best?" he asked softly, voice dropping an octave.

She quickly looked for a less shocking image, pointing to a black and white pencil drawing of two hands lazily clasped together, naked bodies entwined in the background.

"This one, I guess," she whispered.

"Mn, that's easy, it starts like this..." He reached over and entwined their fingers. "But for the rest, I'd have to demonstrate back at my place."

Her face must have been about to combust in flames.

"Then we could try this, for example..." He scrolled to a picture of a couple—naked, obviously. A woman sat on her lover's wide lap, back to his chest as his hand conveniently covered the spot between her legs. His other hand squeezed her perked breast, a hard dark nipple standing out between his thick fingers.

She knew exactly how she'd write this scene, carried away with every word she'd use to recreate his drawing.

Without permission, she imagined herself and Caspian in the same position. An undeniable tingle crept between her legs. The first thing that came to mind fell out of her mouth. "I could write a scene like this."

"Now then, I really need to read your writing," he whispered in her ear.

FIFTEEN

Caspian

"Don't get any ideas," Nia hissed a little harsher than necessary.

Reclining to give her space, he tried to relax his coiling nerves and feverish heartbeat.

So, she had a rebellious side. He'd been right about the thoughts she kept in that journal. Were they all sexual fantasies? Or was there more to it?

He wondered if she had written a scene with a similar setting, surrounded by intoxicating music and the thrill of dancing with a handsome stranger. Being in such a place with her certainly did wonders for him.

The faint smell of vanilla drifting from her hair wasn't helping, either. She lacked the sickeningly sweet perfume most girls bathed in, and her subtle allure only made him want to get closer. But it was too soon for that.

"Just because I read and write about that stuff doesn't mean I do it," she clarified.

"It doesn't mean you don't." Everyone did *something*.

Nia took up her drink and finished it off. "Well, I don't need *you* to please me, so don't get too full of yourself."

He smirked. "Is that so?"

"Yes, exactly so. I don't need a boyfriend, a playboy, or any man, for that matter." She turned to him with white-hot fire in her eyes.

How badly he wanted to get burnt. This was the Nia who had eaten away at him for weeks. Finally, she had come out of her shell. And he hadn't been the only one to notice. Quite a few hopefuls had cast wandering glances their way, but to his delight Nia focused on him alone. "Well, if you say so. Though I could add to the experience."

She frowned. "I'm fine going through my whole life without sharing that experience with anyone."

He paused, searching her shifting expression, and again getting a sinking feeling in his chest. "Your whole life? That's a big commitment."

"You know that saying, if walls could talk?" She pinned him with a somber look that defied the carelessness of those dancing behind her. "Well in my house they did, and that was enough of an experience for me. I'm good on my own. Sex, love, relationships—I don't need them. I've never seen it lead to anything I'd want."

He opened his mouth. Then closed it. For the first time in his life, he found himself truly speechless. Despite the constant flashing of bright lights, Nia looked as if she were in a dark, lonely place.

"Sorry...if I said too much," she mumbled, withering. What had this girl been through?

Stacking her elbows on the counter, she let her forehead rest in her palms. After all the awkward gazes and flirtatious exchange of words, this was the trigger that made her hide. His heart stirred with a desire to protect her from whatever demons she had been running from.

"No, come back," he whispered. He understood what it was like to hate your home life. What she shared was significant, and he didn't want her to deal with it alone. "I don't think you said too much at all. In fact, I'd like to hear more."

"Why?" She shifted to watch him through the corner of glossy, ice-blue eyes.

"I'm not here to hurt you, Nia." His arm screamed to reach out to her. But he didn't want her to crumple further. "I only want to listen to your story. What did the walls say, when you were growing up?"

Her back and shoulders rose with a deep breath, then she closed her eyes and began to explain. "I heard everything. The shouting, blaming...the name-calling. No amount of sex could help my mom keep a man or find one worth keeping. They all turned against her, shamed her for giving up her body and couldn't care less about what damage it caused." She opened her eyes, boring a hole into the counter. "I don't want that."

He cringed...what a nightmare. The arguments from his parents' divorce were enough, but he'd been able to find an outlet through boxing and art. If she had learned to associate sex with unhealthy relationships, her hostility toward intimacy made perfect sense.

"That must have sucked." He paused. "So, you've given up on men?"

"Yeah," she mumbled. "They're all the same, in the end."

"Then let me prove you wrong." The words came almost too naturally.

Nia lifted her head. "You don't mean that." She eyed him warily, thin eyebrows arched in suspicion.

"Oh, I think I do." Despite his mixed feelings about it all, he maintained a confident façade.

Anything to convince her to spend more time with him. And whether he wanted to be in this position or not, he couldn't pull out now.

He knew he wasn't the exemplar of all men, far from it. At the very least, he was better than whoever had been around Nia at home—and he had a sneaking suspicion there was someone else she hadn't told him about—but he also wasn't exactly the guy 'worth keeping.'

His habit of chasing whatever he wanted finally backfired. Although he didn't worry so much about his ability to be a decent guy as much as he worried about actually trying. The warning from his father echoed in his heart, and for a moment he feared somehow this would be a trick. The same way his parents believed their love had been fake all along.

However, Nia had been genuine from the beginning, and her fear of men suddenly made all the other comments make sense. At least for her sake, Caspian wanted to prove himself. Men weren't all monsters. If nothing else, he could show her that he meant no harm.

"And you think you're proof men can be decent?" She laughed, right in his face.

Despite the insult, he couldn't help but chuckle along. It was the first time he heard her laugh, and he instantly wanted to hear it again. Step number one of his new goal became just that—to make her laugh more often.

"I can be decent when I want to be," he teased. "And you're not about to pretend you don't want me right now."

Shaking her head, she blushed and looked down, a smile finally dancing on her lips. The soulful music seemed to dissipate as he watched, an ache growing in his chest. "But really though, let me show you that you don't have to steer clear of men forever. I promise I won't do anything unless you want me to."

She met his eyes. "I'm sorry, Caspian. I'm not looking for a relationship."

He leaned forward, wishing these stools had been placed a little closer together. He wasn't going to let her run away. "Then make it one date."

No one could say he didn't make a good salesman, and he had the most practice pitching himself.

She steeled her eyes and crossed her arms, meeting his energy head-on. "You know I won't even kiss you, right? Why would you go out with me?"

"Because I want to." An easygoing grin spread across his face, wrinkling the corners of his eyes. Her challenges never ceased to spark his enthusiasm. "Haven't you enjoyed yourself tonight?"

By the sheepish look on her face, he could tell she had. It hadn't been so hard to get her relaxed, and the feeling was definitely mutual.

"It's...not what I expected. Kinda nice, actually," she admitted.

"Then it's a date?"

"*One* date."

He swallowed his grin, elated at their progress. Now he was certain this wouldn't be the last time he saw her. A decent conversation had brought them so far. Even if he only got one date for now, it was all he needed. Having fun once in a while didn't have to leave her hurt.

"Then," she spoke, hesitating, "you came here tonight to ask me out, didn't you?"

"Yeah, I did."

"Did you know it was me texting you all along?" Her words hung in the air as she played with her now empty glass, twirling it around in her hands.

"Does that matter?"

"It's just embarrassing, is all..." The bottom of the glass clunked against the wood counter. She covered her face with her hands, cutting her sentence short.

She was too cute getting all flustered—but he didn't want to leave her feeling uncomfortable. He stood up and closed the distance between them. Gently taking her hands between his own, he looked at her as she struggled to hold eye contact. "Don't you think I enjoy talking to you?"

"Well..." She smiled meekly and rolled her eyes. "A little too much, I guess, since now you've got to go on a whole date with me."

Rubbing the back of her hands with his thumbs, he faked an annoyed sigh. "It's that terrible, huh?"

A playful gleam sparked in her eye. "Actually, I think I'm more embarrassed by what *you* said. Why on earth would you say all those things to a girl you hardly know? And that picture..." She shuddered.

"...didn't even have my face in it, right?" he finished. They both laughed.

"Speaking of, mind putting your shirt back on?" She took her hands from his and pulled the fabric closed over his chest. Her touch melted into his skin.

"Ah, but surely you like this look," he teased.

"No," she said tersely, her blush giving her away.

"You know, I normally let the girls do the *un*buttoning, but I'll settle for doing things the other way around this time." He winked and let her fit the shirt buttons back into their appropriate holes.

She rolled her eyes and pursed her lips, working her way down from his collar. "Why do you insist on joking around like that even after everything I told you?" Her tone became more serious than before. "Clearly, there won't be a time for things like *that*."

"Nia," he sighed. "Let me set this straight. You don't have to do anything with me, you don't even have to be here right now, just say the word and I'll walk away. Or I'll try to. The point is, that won't stop me from wanting you. I'll always say what's on my mind, even if you disagree."

Having finished with the buttons, she placed her hands in her lap and stared up at him. After a moment, she responded.

"Don't expect me to reciprocate. And I swear if you try anything, and I mean anything—"

"—I won't," he said. "Forcing you is not my objective. But I won't be hiding my thoughts, either."

"What's so fun over 'n the corner?" a disheveled Serena cut in, coming over to stand behind Caspian. "You two seem t'be gettin' along."

SIXTEEN

Caspian

SERENA'S PREENED HAIR FELL INTO FLUFFY DISARRAY. THE HOURS of dancing and drinking and laughing had ruffled her up, cheeks now flushed and makeup smudged. The tell-tale sign of inebriation glossed her eyes—a look he recognized all too well.

"Do you need something?" he asked, turning to face her with Nia at his back. He knew right away she wasn't in a good state. Serena had passed her limit quite a few drinks ago.

She took a step toward him and stumbled in the process. Before he could react, Nia rushed forward to assist.

But instead of accepting the helping hand, Serena pushed her friend to the side. Nia teetered and he placed a steadying arm around her waist, gently directing her behind him.

"I can stand on my own," she slurred defiantly. Her words were partially lost to the thrum of the music, now at odds with the scene in front of them. "Saw you two havin' such a good time, figured I wanted t'join." Serena smiled like a little girl who had just flagged down the ice cream truck. The smell of liquor seeped from her breath, too strong for perfume to hide.

Caspian took a step away and pulled Nia with him.

Normally he'd offer a ride home, but that probably wasn't the best idea.

Not bothering to pay Serena attention, he looked over her head and scanned for one of the girls from the dorm who had brought a car. Spotting one who wasn't holding a glass or bottle, he turned to Nia and pointed out the girl.

"Why aren't you looking at me?" Serena grabbed at his face, but he dodged, catching her wrist and lowering it.

"Hey now, we're gonna get someone who can take you home." Nodding at Nia, he asked, "The girl in the yellow dress, she came with you guys, right?"

"Umm." Nia scrunched her face and searched the crowd. "Oh, that's Avril, I think." She seemed distracted as her attention pulled back to Serena. "Is she going to be okay? She's in bad shape for only a couple hours of clubbing."

"I'm right here!" Serena whined, her voice rising.

Maybe inviting all of the girls hadn't been such a good idea after all. At least he hadn't had anything to drink and could think clearly.

"Do we have a problem here?" the bartender asked, taking stock of the situation.

"No, just getting this lady a ride home," Caspian replied. "We got it covered."

"Mm. Get it covered then." The bartender gave him a pointed look.

He returned the sentiment with a curt nod and offered his credit card. "Here, for my tab."

Beside him, Nia quivered, arms crossed and face pale, like she was the one about to get sick.

"What's wrong?" he asked.

Serena jerked her arm out of his grasp and plopped down on a stool next to them. Those nearby moved away to make a buffer of a few feet. Smoothing a strand of unwieldy golden hair, Serena gazed at him and wiped at her eyes, smearing her eyeliner more than it already was.

He returned his attention to Nia, worried about her reaction, or lack thereof.

"It's—I'm fine," she responded, voice barely above a whisper. "Let me grab Avril." His eyes followed her red hair as she jostled through the maze of bodies.

"You're not going to text me back, are you?" Serena's words cut through his thoughts like a dull knife. Her voice now weak and defeated, she pretended to sober up, sitting as straight as she could and pulling on the hem of her dress.

Eying her, Caspian set his jaw. The answer should be obvious. "No."

Silence shrouded a tense friction between them, neither giving in, both watching the other. Eventually, Serena stood up but remained firmly planted in front of him. He wondered if she wanted to stand there or just couldn't figure out which way to move her feet.

"Hey Serena, been looking for you, girl!" Their friend in the yellow dress, Avril, hooked her arm around Serena's. "We should head out soon. I've had my fill of this place."

The words went unnoticed as Serena remained focused on him with pleading eyes. He cleared his throat and addressed Avril, "We were just heading out, too. Is there anyone else that needs a ride?"

"Don't worry, I think all the others went home except for me and Ivory," she said.

At hearing the familiar name, he looked over Avril's shoulder and found Nia talking with Ivory. Nia seemed to have calmed down and didn't look as pale as before, but he wanted to be there with her—and as cheesy as it sounded, to hold her again.

He thought the club would be a great place to show her off

and maybe bring out a different side of her, but that wasn't what had happened at all.

"Don't worry about me. I actually have another ride home." Serena brushed nonexistent dust off her dress and smiled, covering her previous disappointment with a cheery demeanor. Multicolored lights danced overhead, yet she paled to a stoic melancholy.

"It's really no problem," Avril insisted, but Serena had already staggered away.

"Serena!" Nia called, causing her to look over. "You're not okay, come back with us."

A sneer flashed across Serena's face as she continued her wobbly catwalk to the dance floor. He watched their exchange, not wanting to mess things up more than he already had. Ivory went to catch up with Serena, and Nia shot a worried glance in his direction, to which he offered a shrug.

"Well, we tried," Avril sighed. "I'll keep an eye on her for the time being."

"You sure?" he asked.

"Oh, we'll be all right," Avril replied. The way she maneuvered around the club told him it wasn't a new scene to her. Good, she'd be able to step in if needed. Serena should have someone on her side.

"I planned to stay longer, but I think it's best if we head out." He ran a hand through his hair and let out a breath, nodding to Avril before going to Nia.

Head down, but as stunning as ever, she stood a few feet away. The larger groups of people dwarfed her small body in a way that made Nia stand out like a single soul on a merry-go-round. The world twirled around her, ever spinning onward in the direction it was programmed to go, while she stood alone, lost in its complexity.

"Don't take what she said or did too personally," he told her, bending over to speak in her ear.

She snapped out of the trance and looked up at him. Gone were the small crinkles around her eyes and the shine of suspicion in her pupils, replaced by something he was afraid to uncover. She didn't seem taken off guard by Serena, but it was clear it dampened her spirits.

Offering a smile, he reached out his hand to her. "Do you want me to take you back now?"

"Yes," she said in a hollow voice as if trying to hold herself together. He knit his eyebrows in concern.

"Do you know if Ivory wants a ride, too?" he asked, not wanting to dig up any skeletons lurking in her closet in the middle of a busy club.

"I told her she should stay with Serena." Nia looked around, and he followed her gaze to where Ivory watched over a drunk Serena dancing without a care in the world. "She needs her more than I do right now."

Ass in the air, dress barely covering her thong, Serena let hair drape over her face as she bounced and swayed with the beat of the music. She leaned further into her partner with a smile plastered over her lips. The entire dance floor fed off her unabashed energy, but her bubbly nature had vanished.

"Just you and me, then?"

Nodding, she turned to walk toward the exit without any further confirmation.

"Hey," he called, grabbing her elbow. She pulled away and glared at him with daggers in her eyes. What was with this sudden mood change?

"Hey! Hold on, what's the matter with you?" He had to pick up the pace to walk beside her.

"I don't want to talk right now," she replied and pushed open the exit door.

"Nia," he groaned, standing in the doorway.

"I *can't* talk right now," she whispered more delicately, a crack lingering in her voice.

The music subsided to a faded rumble as the door latched closed behind them. Pale streetlamps replaced the club's lighting. Hiding her face in her hands, Nia stood on the curb, a statue of solitude.

"Nia..." he repeated.

Maybe he had gotten into this deeper than originally planned.

SEVENTEEN

Nia

HER CHEST ACHED. EMOTION THREATENED TO SPILL OUT ALONG with the tears, and it was all she could do to stand still. If she moved even an inch, she might shatter. The slightest breeze might crack her calculated composure and let Caspian breach her defenses. She prayed the darkness around them would swallow her up.

It had been fun, at first.

Talking to him at the bar had even felt a little normal. Like a blanket on a chilly day or a warm candle flickering at night. He made her feel good. Safe. For the smallest fragment of time, she allowed herself to believe he harbored some semblance of real feelings for her.

Then Serena came crashing in and reminded her—flooded her heart with the chilling memories of her mother, drunk and heartbroken. Time after time, night after night, year after year. Her destiny couldn't be the same. She'd do anything to not follow that same path. The only way out was to avoid falling in love in the first place. It only blinded those caught in its snare.

How could she have stumbled into Caspian's trap? Why had she let him talk to her at all? Everyone else could see him for the playboy he was. They wanted to get in his pants just as much as he wanted to get in theirs, but they'd never trust him with their secrets or life story.

This had all been a dream, a figment of her overactive imagination. Caspian wanted her for his own pleasure and was playing her the same way he had countless girls before.

Every small touch that lit up like a million firecrackers under her skin meant nothing to him. He would never understand what she saw when she looked into his mystifying ocean eyes, the yearning for love she constantly had to banish from thought. And when she made him smile, it shone a ray of light that only illuminated the damning wounds on her weathered heart. Some scars never heal, and hers were being opened back up. This had to stop.

"Talk to me." Caspian's voice reverberated from behind and breached her gloom, bringing her back to the dark street and empty curbside. His hands wrapped around her arms.

She flinched, skin prickling on impulse. His movements halted. They both stood frozen.

"Nia, were you...?" he whispered.

Too ashamed of her past to reply—unwilling to reveal the depth of her wounds—her lips sealed. She'd already opened up too much.

"Let me help you." Those words, now so soft and tender, echoed more loudly than if he had shouted.

A tremble rolled through her like the clap of thunder after a bolt of lightning. Pressure built behind her eyes, followed by the yearning to cave in, to crash headfirst into whatever he offered. Caspian always had a way of making her want things she shouldn't.

"I can't trust you. I can't do this. Not with you," she said, trying to remain calm.

"I'm only taking you home." The incomprehension in his voice was palpable.

That's right. She sucked in a breath. Get home, then she could break. "Right, sorry." She wiped a few tears away from her eyelids and focused on the pavement. "Where did you park again?"

"First, tell me what's wrong," he insisted, turning her around to look at him.

She closed her eyes and tried not to notice the scent of mint that filled her nose. "It's nothing."

"Look at me."

Not that.

Anything but that.

Cupping both sides of her head, she sensed him bend down to her eye-level. Warmth spread from his rough fingers to her cheeks, the night air in stark contrast to his comforting touch.

"Caspian...don't..." she whispered, at war with herself over falling into his arms or breaking free of them.

He chuckled, warm breath tickling her nose. "Afraid I might kiss you? That's against your rules, remember?" He spoke the words above her lips, their implication undermining his light tone.

Shoving him back, her eyes flew open in a flare of anger. Before he waltzed into her life, she had been happy enough, content to never want a man, and never felt a need for one. That was her normal—he didn't have the right to change that, to *fix* her. Not when this was another walk in the park for him.

"I'm done with your jokes, Caspian. Take me home," she demanded.

Smile fading, he stared at her, the streetlights casting shadows that concealed half his face. "Okay."

They walked in silence back to his car, the clinking of keys the only sound to break through the tension that wound itself around them.

The radio turned on as the car came to life, playing the music he had put on for her on the way there. Now in the passenger seat, Nia turned away and leaned into the window. After this, she would delete his number. Delete him from her life completely.

A pang in the heart nudged another tear from her eye. Was it too late? Did the affection he gave her tonight so easily eclipse her safety net of fiction? All the stories she wrote were fantasies, not meant for real life, but somehow, Caspian made her feel maybe they could come true.

"Why me?" she whispered under her breath. Part of her wanted to know why she had been dealt this particular set of cards, why fate, or God, had put her in this situation. Another part wanted to know why Caspian picked her out from all the girls available to him, but she didn't expect an answer.

"I relate," came the reply, catching her attention. "Not to everything, but for a time, I wanted to run away from my life, too. Did run away, in a sense. My parents got divorced a little over two years ago, during my senior year in high school. It got pretty bad, and well...it's still pretty bad." He paused to take a deep breath. "So, I know... I know how much parents can screw up your life. From what you've told me, you never got the chance to be happy."

That only made the fissure in her heart deeper. Being reminded of her past didn't cheer her up. Still, she would've never imagined he had anything less than a simple, happy childhood. Her old curiosity about him reared its head, and she turned to look at him.

"I'm sorry to hear that," she responded quietly.

To her surprise, he smiled. "I have my own life now; college gave me that much. And as soon as I get a lame desk job, I can work on art in my spare time and build the life I want. Believe me, I get not wanting to trust other people with your problems."

He was being open with her about himself and his real emotions, which made him all the more human.

Glancing over, he took the wheel in one hand and reached out the other, offering it palm up. "But, for some reason, I want you to."

"You want me to what?"

"Trust me." He shook his head, laughing at himself. "I'm such a hypocrite, Nia. But trust me. For our one date, at least."

That charming smile came back, and she cursed herself for the way her heart fluttered. Hesitantly, she placed her hand in his. Was this a peace offering? Or a silent agreement of some sort?

Caspian gave up a piece of himself. He knew something about her, and now she knew something about him. Yet his words were only a part of the puzzle, the side he wanted her to see.

"Okay." She found herself agreeing before having weighed her options. After all, one date couldn't end in heartbreak.

"Thank you," he breathed, braiding his fingers with hers. A rush of air filled her lungs, and something rooted deep within her expanded. The feeling of opening up, just a little.

"Do you feel any better?" he asked.

"Mhm, yeah. It helps to know your story a bit. I mean, that's what I've wanted to know all along."

He chuckled. "Why would you want to know my story?"

"I...don't know. It's what I like—stories. I guess it's also because you come off as a jerk, and I wanted to know if that was true." She traced the outline of his fingers with her own.

Such a trivial thing, to hold hands, but she'd never done it with a man before. Her ex had never reached for her hand. Not having a father left certain holes she didn't even know existed. A man's hand. It felt so much bigger than her own. Sturdy, in a way. His skin wasn't rough from work but wasn't smooth like hers, either. She wondered what other new things she'd experience with Caspian.

"You *really* think I look like a jerk?"

Nia scoffed and rolled her eyes. "Sure you do. You look like a jerk who thinks he can sleep with anyone he bats his eyes at."

"Ah, so I'm a sexy jerk," he teased.

"What? No—"

"Thanks for the clarification." He gave a mischievous wink.

She couldn't help but laugh. He was trying to get on her nerves on purpose. If only she could steal some of his confidence for herself.

Looking at her through thick eyelashes, he put on a serious face. "When are we going for that date, baby girl?"

His flirting wore down her composure, but she'd never let him know it. Eyes locked straight ahead as he pulled up to the dorms, she mentally checked her schedule. "Wednesday afternoon. My classes end at noon that day."

"Then I'll pick you up at noon on Wednesday."

"Sure. See you then." She opened the door and hopped out before he could get away with anything else.

EIGHTEEN

Caspian

HE LEANED BACK IN THE DRIVER'S SEAT, WATCHING FOR ANY SIGN of Nia as his car idled in the parking lot behind the dorms. Would she stand him up? He'd go in and get her if it came down to it. For now, he sent a quick text.

> It's noon, baby girl.

Their night at the club had shown him so much about her and left him wanting so much more. But to his disappointment, the self-assurance he first saw had yet to make a second appearance. Getting close to others really did seem like a burden to her, but beneath the armor of indifference he also saw how genuine and kindhearted she was. The ghost of her presence still lingered in the passenger seat. Holding her hand had made the world slow down, made him feel like he had a bigger purpose.

He couldn't remember the last time he felt like that.

The chime of his phone interrupted his thoughtful silence.

SEX ON THE BEACH

> I literally just stepped out of the classroom.

The sass in her words brought a smile to his lips as much as her new contact name. Taking her to bed was still his goal, but he wanted her to enjoy it as much as he would. Moreover, he didn't want to leave her broken. If it took a million steps along a figurative shore before they got there, then he'd gladly count each one.

> Doesn't change the fact I'm here waiting for you.

> Well, you're going to be waiting a bit longer because I need to drop by my room first.

Sighing, he turned off the engine. It would be easier to go to her room and wait there. Plus, that way he'd see her sooner.

He caught the door as another student came out and made his way to Nia's room by memory. The halls were quieter today, and memories from his year in the dorms flooded back. Those were the beginning of his glory days. When he learned the power a fit body had for women who liked sex as much as he did. Any and every girl had been appealing back then.

Now, his tastes were more refined and more recently, stuck on a single woman in particular. Already, he had told her about his art and opened up about his less-than-glorious family situation. Nia took everything in stride, not judging or disappointed that he wasn't more impressive. Still, the thought of causing her any kind of disappointment irritated him.

She had a certain vulnerability about her, and he wondered if she did fall for him, how far it would go. When women were only invested for one night, it was easy to forget about them the next day, but he had a feeling she was an all-or-nothing kind of girl. Seeing her freeze up at the club still pulled at his heart.

This ploy to prove himself as a stand-up guy was riddled with pitfalls, but here he was, doing it anyway. Chasing after a girl with real expectations could very well lead to the fate his father spoke against, but he couldn't let go. It didn't feel wrong.

He reached her dorm and knocked. No reply. He leaned against the door, deep in thought. All he wanted was to prove intimacy was nothing to fear. For him, it had been everything he hoped for and more. He wanted nothing less than to hear her laugh, to listen to her sigh his name as they let go of everything else.

"You're really standing there waiting?"

Sweet yet crisp with scrutiny, her voice stopped his train of thought completely. He turned to see a smile pulling at the corners of her lips.

He smirked—she *was* happy to see him. "Yes, and it's about time I got something in return for my efforts, don't you think?"

"Yeah, one date, and that's it." She shouldered her way between him and the doorknob. "Move it, Caspian." Gaze wandering down to her ass, he bit his lips to avoid saying something that would get him slapped.

"Aw, I think I deserve more than that," he teased, loving every inch where her body touched his. Icy eyes glared up at him, and he noticed she'd put on more makeup than usual. "Okay, okay, hear me out. You'll let me take you wherever I want today, no questions asked."

"That sounds awfully suspicious," she said as she opened the door. "I retain the right to call 911 at any time."

Following her into the room, he acquiesced, "As long as there are no questions."

While she put down her bag and carefully unpacked her laptop, he observed how she kept her room. The bed frame, desk, and dresser were the generic stuff provided by the college, but she had covered up the bland shades with sheer sky-blue curtains, while deep indigo and sapphire pillows created a mountain of fluff on the small twin bed.

"So where are they?" he casually asked, scanning the room.

Nia shuffled around her desk, distracted by sorting papers. "Uh, the what?"

"Your vibrators."

Whipping her head around, mouth agape, she scrunched her face in a look that said more than words. "Why the hell would you ask? It's none of your business."

"Not yet." He cocked his head and studied her reaction.

"I'd say *fuck you*, but you'll take it as an invitation," she muttered.

"Guilty as charged."

She huffed, but before turning around spared a glance to the bottom drawer of her dresser.

Noted.

He didn't mind the cold shoulder as he continued to peruse her natural habitat. Paperback books from the library were stacked on top of her dresser, and a small silver frame caught his eye. The photo inside displayed a younger Nia, hugging a woman who had almost an identical face, mid-length blonde hair and blue eyes. She must be Nia's mother. They both looked happy, but their smiles were obviously put on for the camera.

His attention shifted to a mini fridge in the corner, and he went to open it, hoping to find something to grab for himself. To his disappointment, there were only bottles of water and some berry yogurt.

"No soda?"

"Who told you to go through my stuff?" she shot back, arms crossed over her chest as she leaned against the desk.

Enjoying her eyes on him more than he should, he went to inspect the necklaces dangling from a jewelry stand in front of a small set of drawers and a mirror. The pendants were all simple but elegant. One in particular stood out—a golden heart on a thin chain.

"Can you be done invading my privacy?" she hissed.

"Mn, no questions, remember?" he hummed, testing the limit of her temper. She hadn't called off the date yet, and besides, he liked seeing her fire.

"Well, I'm finished, so you need to be done too."

"Did I tell you how beautiful you look today?" Locking eyes with her, a genuine smile lit up his face at her conflicted response. She started to smile but then narrowed her eyes, settling on irritation. Necklace in hand, he walked closer. "With this, the look would really be complete."

A blush colored her cheeks, and she rolled her eyes, reaching out to take the necklace.

"Ah—" he said, pulling out of her reach, "I'd like to put it on, if you don't mind."

Something flashed behind her eyes, and after a moment of hesitation, she drew her hair up in one hand to expose the elegant slope of her neck. "If it means we get to leave, then fine."

He had to suck in a breath in admiration at seeing her skin —and the fact she let him touch it. Placing the necklace around her neck, it was hard to not lean down and plant kisses along her shoulder. Her sweet, addicting scent clouded his thoughts. Every curve of her body was indescribable. The urge to run his hands over every place his eyes landed fought with his self-restraint. His fingers lingered a second longer after closing the clasp, and he traced around the thin chain to the heart charm that rested flawlessly in the center of her collar bone.

"Perfect," he whispered under his breath.

The faint sound of her exhale preceded her reply. "Now, let's go."

Barely making it out in time before she shut the door and

locked it, he turned to look at her again, but she had already taken off down the hallway. With long strides, he easily caught up to walk beside her. "Can't wait to start the date, I see."

"More like I can't wait to get it over with."

NINETEEN

Caspian

THE SMELL OF HOT, FRESH FRIES AND THE CRACKLE OF carbonated soda filled the car. Music settled into the background as they drove up a winding road lined with trees. His secret getaway.

They were about ten minutes outside of town, and Nia had given up on trying to figure out their destination—at the cost of many failed attempts. Patches of leaves had started to turn orange and red, even pink, but most still clung to the verdant green of summer.

Reaching over, he snuck a fry from Nia's lap and popped it in his mouth. It would be a waste to not enjoy any before they turned lukewarm.

"Hey!" she said, swatting at his hand a second too late.

Crunching down on the fry, he flashed his teeth in a victorious grin. "I'll let you have one of mine, fair?"

"Then I'll take it right now." She reached into the brown bag and pulled out a single fry. "Fair's fair."

He shook his head and chuckled. "Not even gonna wait until we pull over? Never seen someone so protective of their french fries before."

He'd smiled more in the last twenty minutes than all the past three days combined. Most of the time that was because Nia did something unexpected, like her possessiveness over fries, but it didn't bother him in the slightest. Seeing someone really be themselves, even if it was awkward or uncomfortable at first, revitalized him.

Her gaze went back out the window, to his disappointment. "It's because when my mom took me out to get fries, I would always steal hers and say the same thing. But I never remembered to give her any of mine." A mischievous smile crept across her lips.

"Oh, so because *you're* a shameless fry thief, then it's assumed *I* must be too," he said, making a left turn. "We're almost there."

"Mhm," she hummed, not sparing a glance in his direction as she continued to peer outside.

Being with her made him feel lighter. Since the night at the club, they'd exchanged a few texts, but nothing too personal. He liked to imagine either her sweet smile or a scowl whenever he 'interrupted her day'—as she liked to put it.

Today, he wanted to discover another moment like the one they had at the club, one where they connected on a level he hadn't shared with anyone else.

"I've never seen anyone do that," he said, watching in amazement as Nia stuck a fry into her vanilla shake and took a bite.

"What? Fries and ice cream?" She nibbled at another fry coated in the sugary cream.

"Doesn't the ice cream make the fry cold and soggy?" He wrinkled his nose.

"Not at all. It's the mixture of the salt and the sweet, the cold and the hot, that makes it such a great pair." She bit down on a fry emphatically, closing her eyes and humming with contentment.

"You should try it," she said, holding out a new fry with a small dab of the vanilla shake.

He opened his mouth wide, leaning closer.

"Ew, no way. I'm not going to feed you. Just take the fry with your hand," she insisted, pushing the fry toward his hand.

"Worth a try." He took the fry and squinted at it before biting down. The sweetness of vanilla and heat hit his tongue first, then salt kicked in to compliment and bring out more subtle flavors.

"Mm, you're right." This unusual snack was delicious.

"Exactly. And now that you've had your taste, you don't get anymore," she said, biting back a smirk.

"You know one taste won't be enough," he shot back. "Not when it comes to you."

Licking the rest of the salt off his fingers, he wondered how she'd react if he pulled over and wrestled that shake away, maybe making a strategic spill or two so he could sneak in a taste of her as well.

But it had been a pain to convince her to let him pay for the food in the first place, and they didn't need any unnecessary squabbles so early on.

"Here we are," he said, making a turn into an empty parking lot. Picking a spot in the middle of the open space and away from the road, he shut off the engine and took in the sight in front of them.

"Ohh...this is nice." She sat up to get a better view.

The entire college campus and most of the town spread out beneath them. From this vantage point, they could watch as the inhabitants ran about the maze of buildings like miniature figurines. The best part was most people didn't come up here since it was off a lesser-known service road. It was the perfect place to come and chill for a few hours, especially when being around people started to get on his nerves.

"I knew you'd like it, but it's in a secluded area, so I figured your overactive brain would assume I was taking you here for some ridiculous, sinister intent."

"Well, I wouldn't have come here with you at night, that's for sure," she said. "Are you going to eat your burger now? I feel bad for finishing most of my food while you had to drive."

"Yeah, definitely starving over here...especially since you banned me from enjoying my new favorite treat." He stuck out his bottom lip in a pathetic pout.

Sighing, Nia held out her shake. "Here, you big baby."

"I'm kidding. Enjoy your food." He reached for the bag instead of her shake.

"What? I decided to be *nice* for a change, and you're *joking around*?" Pretending to be offended, she crossed her arms over her chest.

"Come on, I take it back, okay?" he prodded.

She glared at him, but her eyes were filled with heat instead of her usual criticizing cool and made him all too aware of their proximity. He laughed off the increased pounding of his heart. "Your eyes are amazing. They remind me of those macro snowflake pictures, where the ice is all crystallized into beautiful patterns like they floated here from another world."

Staring back, her face faded from annoyance to astonishment, then colored a delicate pink. "Flattery will get you nowhere," she mumbled, crunching on another fry.

Taking in the view himself, he bit down on his burger—the biggest one on the menu. "My dad would take me to get burgers since before I can remember. We wouldn't talk much, maybe about sports or something he needed to complain about from work. Made me hate the idea of becoming an adult." He paused. "But it was his only space to be sane. Even more so after the divorce. Now I've turned into him," he scoffed. "This is my place to be sane. That's why I knew you'd like it."

Nia put her shake in the cup holder. "I do like it. Reminds me of when my mom and I would go out on particularly depressing days. Just to leave the house, leave it all behind, and try to forget. We'd..." She stifled a quiet laugh. "We'd take a coin and flip it, heads for right and tails for left."

"Sounds fun," he replied. Aside from the part about wanting to forget. Examining her face, he noticed this was a sore subject. She stayed quiet. Sad. He saw the calm after the storm—a heart-wrenching emotion that slipped in and out of her like the tide.

"It was. Some of the few times we didn't spend arguing over something that didn't really matter or things that really did matter, but I guess I shouldn't have had an opinion on it. One day, we ran into an old antique shop neither of us knew existed, and other days, we'd get fries or ice cream, or both." She smiled, looking down as she entwined her fingers.

Caspian's brows knit as he crunched the paper wrapper and tossed it back in the bag. "Do you have anyone to talk to about that kind of stuff?"

"Ha, no," she replied. "I had a friend in high school, but she moved away junior year, and we lost contact. I was too busy trying to get spotless grades and writing essays for college scholarships since then. I don't have much of a social life, but I prefer it like that." She sighed, voice quieting. "Better than making friends just to lose them. I prefer to write, share my thoughts with a pen and paper and no one else."

Pain hung in the air, and he didn't know if it came from Nia, his empathy, or remnants of sorrow from his own hard times. All three were very real.

"Can't fault you for that," he said. "Human nature does lean more toward evil than good."

She didn't reply, and he reached for her hand. Luckily, she let him take it, and gave him a turn to play with her fingers. Sliding his thumb up and down her palm, he rubbed her small knuckles between the pads of his fingers. "You know, my dad told me to stay away from women because they were selfish."

Turning, Nia eyed him with disbelief. "Aren't men the selfish ones? They've repressed women for centuries."

He shrugged. "I've seen it happen on both sides. My mom acted selfishly, tore our family apart in exchange for a pay raise and extravagant vacations. It came out my senior year of high school that she had been cheating for years, and that's what finally unraveled everything."

"Caspian," Nia whispered, placing her other hand on top of his. Both went silent.

The sun cast long shadows across the town, buildings outmatched in height by the length of their darkened counterparts. Light sparkled in rows of windows that angled just right, and the greenery glowed as if enjoying its last few hours before nightfall.

TWENTY

Nia

THE WARMTH OF HIS HAND—A LACK OF EMOTION IN HIS DEEP voice.

A casual smile on his lips that hid a story of untold consequence.

Caspian had been dealt the other side of her deck of cards, one where his mother chose to leave, and his father stayed. Reaching up with the hand not entwined in his, she rubbed the warm metal of the tiny heart charm around her neck.

"She really did that?" she asked, searching his face for the emotion he hid so meticulously.

"Yeah," he sighed. "Said my dad worked too many hours to have her living a middle-class life." His eyes focused on their connected hands, as if in them he could see memories from his past.

"So why..." She cut herself off. Even with this experience, he ended up cheating. Or maybe he didn't see it that way in his head. The image of Caspian tangled in the sheets with another woman flashed in her mind and she let go of the necklace. "I guess you didn't get the best dating advice?"

He chuckled. "My mom wasn't around much, and my father

125

didn't offer anything valuable. After their divorce, he only gave me warnings."

"About women?"

"Mn, yeah. Not against sex in general, though. A guy wouldn't give that up, but I've never had a serious relationship. Can't say the divorce didn't affect that."

"I figured as much." If he'd ever taken a girl seriously, she was sure they'd still be together. The fatal flaw in his technique was only putting in enough effort to get sex.

"It's that obvious to you?"

She would have rolled her eyes if his ignorance didn't feel so personal. After all, wasn't she just another conquest to him? "How many women have you actually cared about, Caspian? Don't you ever wonder if they want more from you?"

Frustration and resentment from remembering her mother's painful experiences boiled to the surface. Did he have no clue?

"Why pretend to be something I'm not?" he said, using one hand to comb through his hair. "I don't offer these women a long-term relationship. They don't offer me one, either. You just go with the flow and get what you get."

Retracting her hand from his, she put it back in her lap and clenched her fist. "You...you *did,* though." She stared out the window. Anywhere except at him. "When I asked if you had a girlfriend, you said you were reserving that spot for me."

"And," he emphasized. "I meant that. Maybe I want to try something different for a change."

Somehow, that was difficult to believe.

"Don't lie to me," she hissed, eyes averted. "All you talk about is sex. So, tell me now if that's what you want. Why are we here, anyway? Is this what you do, bring girls here on dates to win them over?"

"First, I've never brought a girl here, Nia. It's only been you.

Do you want to know why?" he asked, voice barely above a whisper.

"Why," she demanded. It wasn't a question.

"This is *my* place, and it's not like I can just relocate because you can't find this view anywhere else. Every time I come here from now on, I'm going to think of you. I'm going to remember this evening." He turned his head away, letting out a breath. "Remember you, and you're the first I want to remember. The first I want to sit here and talk with. You're real with me despite shying away from everyone else. As much as I enjoy the thought of stripping you down and coaxing every moan of pleasure out of your lips, I want this, too."

What was she supposed to make of that? One minute, he talked about being real, and the next, he spouted some steamy fantasy. Hollowness gnawed inside her, begging to be filled by him, by his arms around her and his promises of affection.

"Also, I haven't mentioned anything sexual since we've been in the car until you brought it up. That should tell you something."

His words dove into her mind like dangerous sharks. Words were words; they could all very well be lies, but she couldn't ignore the truth in them. Yet a wave of concern twisted her gut —her judgment was fatally flawed, heart poisoned, and she believed whoever she trusted would eventually turn.

If it could happen to her own mother, she wasn't immune. There was no magic manual about dating or falling in love, no manuscript that listed every possibility and how to react when her head and her heart were at odds.

"How do I know you won't get tired of me one day? Turn around and take back everything you said? You can't be serious about a relationship on a whim."

A moment passed before Caspian spoke quietly as if not to scare her. "You gave me one date, Nia, and I want to make the most of it. Maybe even get a second. There's a part of me that responds to you in a way I can't describe, a part I want to explore, and I've never been more serious about that."

The sky turned red as the setting sun dipped between long stretches of clouds on the horizon. On the other end of the city, darkness crept into the pale blue of dusk and revealed stars that kept their light veiled until the world sank into sleep.

She had a million questions that needed answers, but most importantly, if she fell, would he stick around to catch her? "Are you willing to actually commit?" she asked. "To a relationship?"

"Yes." He reached over and gingerly tugged at her chin with his hand. "If that's what you want this to be."

Letting him turn her head, she searched his eyes. The confidence and intensity he usually wore wasn't there. Instead, his pupils had dilated, the expanse of his soul staring straight back at her. Memories of the personal things he shared floated to the surface of her mind. How he admitted to not trusting anyone, how he had wanted to run away from his life, and how the pain of his past still affected him.

"Nia, at least let me try," he whispered.

A barricade within her crumbled, one brick at a time, until it turned to a pile of dust, reminiscent of the stars billions of lightyears away.

"Okay." She nodded, and the beginning of a smile formed on her lips. "I guess you can have a second date."

Releasing a breath, he relaxed his eyebrows and smiled. "You really are something else."

"Well, it's not like the bar has been set very high," she joked.

"Nothing I've experienced compares to this." Their whole evening had been filled with peace, and it made her feel whole. Alive.

"What do you mean?" he asked, voice tinted with concern.

"It's just, I..." She turned to look out the window as his fingers nudged hers. At this point, her heart had grown accustomed to the feel of his hand, and the methodic movements of his fingers against hers played a soothing melody that eased her agitation. "My first and only other boyfriend didn't take me on dates, and I never had a dad to eat burgers with."

"You didn't have a father? What happened to him?"

She feigned a lighthearted laugh. "He wanted nothing to do with me, so I wanted nothing to do with him. As soon as he heard the news of my mother's pregnancy, he left. No note, no contact info, no regrets."

"How could he not want you?" Caspian said. The sharp edge of anger cut through his words, and his emotion caught her off guard.

"Hell if I know or care," she muttered, staring into the dimming landscape. Of course she cared, but long ago she'd shoved those feelings in a box and buried them deep.

"Why would he go and screw up your life before it even began? He had no right..." Caspian cut himself off, pausing to take a breath. "I guess it's not my place."

"You're not wrong, but it is what it is." She turned to look at her hands. "And he wasn't the last to screw up my life."

TWENTY-ONE

Nia

CASPIAN TOOK IN A MEASURED BREATH. "WHO ELSE?"

A pool of shadow had gathered at her feet, and a streetlight clicked on, intensifying the highlights, and deepening the growing darkness. She needed to do this, to at least to recount the events. He didn't need to know exactly how it tore her apart, only that it happened.

She took a moment to strip the pain from the next words that left her mouth. "My ex and I got together because he kissed me in seventh grade. Not that we did anything else, but I went along with it. One day, some of his friends told me he was waiting for me in the bathroom. So I went, but he wasn't there. Only them, the three of them." The lump in her throat grew larger. "They told me I was 'too pretty to be with one guy,' then they grabbed me."

Caspian clenched his jaw at her words, grinding his teeth, but he remained silent and gave her space to speak.

She took in a lungful of air to remain in the present. "They pushed me in the corner. Before I knew what was happening, they had covered my mouth, and—" The crack of Caspian's knuckles pierced her wavering voice. "—I fought back, but they were bigger and stronger."

She stopped, shutting off the images in her brain and forcing a monotone voice. "My clothes ripped, but I managed to run away. They were his friends, and my ex never said anything about it. Nothing changed. Like it didn't even happen."

She looked up after a deep breath to see Caspian staring straight ahead—jaw firm, a slight crease in his forehead. All he'd done was listen, but that was enough to calm her agitation.

"So, that's part of why I can't be intimate. When I get close to people, the memory creeps up, and it's not something I can ignore." Her muscles tightened, nails digging into the back of her hands. A part of her felt good to release the long-kept secret but remembering came with a heavy burden.

More than wanting Caspian to know, she wanted him to respect her experience. As difficult as it was to share, she needed him to acknowledge why she balanced on the edge so often. This was his chance to walk away and go back to a life where he could get an undamaged girl.

"That should have never happened," he muttered. "Men can't *force* themselves on women they want. There's no pleasure in making someone terrified of you, of putting them through that kind of stress." He reached up and touched his temple, then blinked and shook his head. "I'm sorry. You're the one who should be mad, not me."

She finally managed to swallow the lump in her throat and nodded, relieved that he didn't judge her. "That's the thing, I'm not mad. I'm just...scarred. I can't let it happen again."

"I'd hate men too if one pounced on me with a kiss and his friends tried to rape me," Caspian said, clenching his jaw.

"It was just a dare—the kiss, I mean. Maybe the other part, too." She shook her head. "My ex wasn't all that into me, and looking back, I could tell. I never felt anything when he touched me. The whole relationship was entirely worthless."

Now, it seemed like a cruel joke. In retrospect, she could see every wrong turn she made, but it was too late to change anything. All she could do now was try to protect herself.

Rolling his shoulders, Caspian looked deep in thought. Then he glanced up and held her gaze. "You deserve better."

"Don't you think I know that?" she scoffed. For years, she had written and dreamed about a love she yearned for but no longer believed could exist.

"Yes, but you deserve to at least know what a good kiss is. A do-over. You deserve another first kiss."

Her breath caught at the sight of him, eyes glinting in the faint light. The warm glow of a streetlight outlined his sharp features, and every detail in his face made hers up. The face of someone who listened, who didn't push if she wasn't willing to give. Someone who she had just handed a piece of her soul and, most of all, whose soul she craved a part of more than anything else.

"Are you offering?" she asked, already knowing the answer.

"Mn, are you asking?" he countered.

In a moment of apprehension, she flicked her eyes down and away from his. The concept was tempting, almost too much so, but it was still their first date. And nothing good came from hasty kisses in a dark car. "This isn't exactly what I imagined my first kiss would be like, either. Although I enjoy being here with you, if I really do get a do-over, I'd want a better location and time."

"I'll agree to that."

"Also..." She hesitated before finishing, rolling her bottom lip between her teeth. "How do I know you can give me a good kiss?" Risking another glance up, she peered at him just long enough to see his own lips, parted and plush, as they curled into an unmistakable smirk.

"Give me your hand," he said, extending his own.

The first time he offered his hand, she'd snapped to leave

her alone. Now, however, she reached out and accepted his familiar one. Ripples of shimmering energy defused from her chest and sparked at her fingertips.

His firm yet delicate grip held no insecurity. He held her as one would hold the stem of a flower, tight enough to not let it fall but not too much as to crush it unintentionally. As her heart pounded against her ribs, he grounded her, steady and reassuring. Angling his wrist so her knuckles rested over his fingers—like a prince holding a princess's hand—he locked their eyes, gradually bringing their hands to his lips. The wing beat of a thousand butterflies swept over them, and she felt the pillow of his lips, the faintest breath of contact between his soft skin and her first knuckle.

She shivered. Heat radiated from his touch and seeped into her bones. Now she wished he was holding more than just her hand. Keeping every muscle in her body still to hold out for one more, she let herself plummet into the whirlpool of his deep blue eyes. And he gladly kept her there.

Hand claimed, he brushed his lips over to her second knuckle, pressing more firmly. All she could focus on was the delicate caress of lips, how her heart jumped at the simple contact, and her thighs squeezed tighter.

Then he transitioned to the third, parting his lips enough to let the tip of his tongue sear her with its heat. Jerking her hand, she recoiled and held it to her chest. Her lungs expanded with the memory of how to breathe, but her tongue couldn't recall how to speak.

"How was that?" he asked in a low voice, edged with a huskiness that sent her heart into overdrive.

"I, um, I think you passed," she said, finding her voice amidst the loud thuds of a racing pulse.

"Mn," he hummed as if envisioning something. "Good." Then a pause fell, one that only lasted seconds but seemed to stretch on for the whole of the night. "I should take you back.

You have classes tomorrow and said you wouldn't come here with me at night."

"Yeah," she agreed. "I did say that."

They drove with the subdued murmurings of the radio in the background, her hands carefully guarded by her side. Today had been eventful, and she almost wanted it to last longer, to hold on to her newly discovered connection with Caspian, but she didn't push her luck.

Her eyelids slid closed with every slight bump in the road. Absently, she wondered if she was drifting asleep or waking from a dream. Either way, it had been better than even she could've imagined.

TWENTY-TWO

Caspian

A REEL OF HER EVERY WORD AND EXPRESSION PLAYED THROUGH his head. Even now, as cold water washed the heat from his body, Nia's voice rang in his ears.

The accusations hurt most of all, but he couldn't help but examine the truth in them. Outside of sex, he and his past partners had only shared a cocktail of flirtatious words and glances. It was an easy win-win for both sides: a night of pleasure paired with convenient amnesia in the morning. But there were consequences—there always were. He just chose to look the other way.

Granted, every woman he slept with had been more than eager to take him to bed. He didn't act like the scum that took advantage of Nia. Balling his fists against the shower tiles, a flare of anger burned through his veins. There were so many things wrong with what had happened to her, so much sorrow he wished he could kiss away. But he was smart enough to know that's not how it worked.

No matter how many gifts, how much tuition, or how many words of praise his parents offered, nothing could change the misdeeds of the past. Forgiveness only came with due acknowledgment, and there had been little to none of that.

He hung his head, shutting off the shower valve and shaking droplets from his shaggy hair. Nia had no examples of good men in her life; no wonder she adopted an attitude of disgust. He felt like he applied to a job with his dream salary, but for which he was severely underqualified, and yet somehow managed to get hired.

He had to make good on his promise—to try and do right by her for as long as she stuck around. That started today, the official do-over.

After mostly drying himself off, he went to the bedroom and pulled on a pair of boxers and sweatpants. Then the doorbell rang. He stopped mid-reach for a t-shirt. Was she *exactly* on time?

Checking his phone, he saw it was a few minutes early.

They agreed to meet at his apartment since the park Nia wanted to visit was a couple blocks away. He offered to pick her up, but she refused, insisting she didn't need to depend on him for rides all the time. At least it only took twenty minutes to walk from his building to the dorms.

Sauntering over to the door, he opened it wide with his most charming smile. "I've been waiting for you."

A plain white t-shirt and bell-bottom jeans never looked as sexy as it did on her. If he had known such simple clothes could be so stunning, he would've never bothered to put lingerie in his drawings. She also wore the same heart pendant as last time. But what really stabbed him in the heart was her cute face, shifting from boredom to nervousness and settling on shock in a split second.

"Come on in." He stepped aside, smug that she couldn't seem to look away from him.

"Put on a shirt," she grumbled and walked past, cautious to not let their bodies touch.

"You've already seen it all, so what's the issue?" A lazy smirk stretched over his face.

After closing the door, he turned to see her leaning against the kitchen counter. Half of him expected a reprimand for the dirty dishes in the sink and clutter scattered over the couch and desk, but it never came. Nia gazed out the window at the other end of the open living room, arms folded over her chest.

"How was your calculus class?" he asked, knowing it was her last lecture of the day.

"It went by fast enough. I finished this week's homework, so I really only need to show up for the quiz." She caught his eyes again.

A droplet of water from his hair landed on his bare chest, and he flinched at the sudden cold. Nia bit her lip and looked down. "Just got back from boxing at the gym," he said, bringing her attention back to him. "What do you say? Am I working out hard enough? Or hardly working?"

She let out a frustrated sigh and dodged his question. "You need to pull your pants up. Sagging isn't sexy."

He chuckled and walked closer. That blush of hers always had a mind of its own, and he made a point to always notice it. "Remind me again, which way is up?"

She shot him a glare, putting on her attempt at a poker face. At this rate, it wouldn't surprise him if he showed a blush as well, especially with the embarrassing line about to come out of his mouth.

"Cause when I'm with you, my world turns upside-down."

He added a wink for good measure.

"For goodness sake," she hissed, reaching out and yanking his pants up over his hips.

"That's definitely *not* the right way," he teased, then adjusted the seam so it rested at the same line as the elastic of his boxers.

She rolled her eyes. "Are you going to drop lame pick-up lines all day, or are we walking to the park?"

"I'll be right with you, ma'am," he said as he disappeared into his bedroom.

One shirt and two sprays of cologne later, he returned to find her typing something on her phone. A message? To whom? He peered over her shoulder. That wasn't the messaging app. It was a notepad.

Countless stars and endless dreams could never measure—

She jumped and leaned away. "Don't sneak up and spy on me!"

"I never got to see your writing...remember our agreement at the club?" He arched his eyebrows.

She stuffed her phone in her pocket. "I remember, but with *that* behavior, you get a demerit."

"You know, you really should have explained the rules from the beginning. Or else I don't know when I'm breaking them."

"The rules are you ask before you look." She met his stare with her own and pursed her lips, reminding him exactly why he needed to get to the park.

If only he could kiss her right now. He lowered his voice. "What if I want to touch?"

Her eyes widened. "Y-you," she stammered, tripping over the words, "—you ask. You ask then, too." Clearing her throat, she turned and headed for the door.

Hm. That certainly was an improvement over the flat rejections he'd gotten earlier. Did she want him to ask?

One thing was certain, if she thought turning around and showing him her ass would deter him, it didn't. Yet something told him if he asked for what he really wanted, he wouldn't be getting it.

Sighing, he followed her and grabbed a jacket on the way. She unlocked the door for herself and stepped out, giving him the same look he got when they left from her dorm, like she was the one in charge.

He couldn't help but laugh. Who was he kidding—she was obviously the one in charge from the moment he set eyes on her.

"What are you laughing at?" She narrowed her eyes, waiting as he locked the deadbolt from the outside.

Running a hand through his damp hair, he looked at her and forgot whatever it was he should say next. The keys jingled as he threw them in his hoodie and stepped toward the exit. "I have a question for you, baby girl."

"Hm?" She drifted to his side, fiddling with her pockets.

He reached for her hand and let it slide into that particular spot where it fit perfectly in his. "Since every time we try to have normal conversations, they turn into confessions from our messed-up pasts, I came up with a hypothetical situation to start our evening."

"That sounds nice." She smiled in a way that turned his heart inside out.

"All right. If there's an emergency and you have to leave your house or dorm, and you can only save three things, what would they be?" They stepped outside, where the cool evening air washed over them. Only an hour or so until sunset.

"Ummm, okay," Nia hummed.

He kept a meandering pace as she thought over her answer, enjoying the sight of summer as it matured into autumn. A few leaves tumbled across the sidewalk, and late-blooming flowers spread their petals in a triumphant last stand. Though none of it compared to the cute redhead at his side.

"I would bring my laptop, that's number one...and my laptop charger, of course. Does that count as a separate item?"

"Let's just say the laptop and the charger are one, so you get two more," he answered.

"Okay. Then there's my journal..." Her eyebrows furrowed in concentration. "And my phone. Your turn."

"My first item would be..." he let his voice trail off as if in thought, but he already knew his answer.

TWENTY-THREE

Caspian

"My first item would be...you," he finished.

"Caspian, that's..." Looking down at the crosswalk under their feet, Nia sighed, appearing at a loss for words.

"What? Isn't that a good answer?" He quirked an eyebrow. She was the first girl he'd even *think* to say that about, much less speak it out loud.

"*I* can't count. Why would I be in your house?"

For starters, so he could hold more than just her hand. "I can think of quite a few reasons..."

She squeezed his hand, too flustered to appreciate his sideways smirk. "That's not the point. Can you please think about what you say before it leaves your mouth? Winning me over with flattery won't work."

"Why not?" Didn't all girls like to be the center of affection? Doting over them had always put him at an advantage, and with Nia it came so easy.

"Because it isn't real," she huffed. "I don't want to feel close to you because you're constantly feeding my ego. I want to feel close because we *are* close. I want to *mean* what we say." She raised her free hand and tugged at the heart charm resting on her chest.

He studied her disposition as they walked under large oak trees lining the sidewalk, how her honey skin reflected the last rays of sunlight filtering through the leaves, and the cool cast of evening outlining her graceful features. A layer of loneliness hid behind determined eyes—she wanted real connection. Most likely because her life had been devoid of it, much like his had lately.

If anyone deserved to be complimented, to be loved, she did. He could shower her with the most extravagant praise and mean every word. "I do mean what I say. What if I'm flattering you *because* I feel close to you?"

"Do you? Isn't it your usual trick to flatter women so they open up to you?" she countered.

Exhaling, he considered. His track record wasn't the cleanest on that front. "You're right. Most of the time flattery is a tool to attract women, but you're the exception. I want you to know that you're special to me."

Nia released the necklace at her chest. "I can't assume I'm an exception. Too many women do that and end up getting hurt."

He gave her hand a squeeze and relented, "Okay. I'll just have to up my game then. No more generic flattering."

She half laughed, half sighed in response. "I guess that works."

They stopped at the edge of the small park. Families had long since gone home for dinner, and only one group of rag-tag teenagers could be seen hanging out under the pavilion. Looked like they wouldn't have any interruptions.

As tempting as it was to claim her lips right here and now, he forced himself to keep a hold on his self-control. Nia had a vision for this evening, and he wanted to make it better, not ruin it.

Although he was sure his lips could make anything better.

"Um, so..." She looked up at him, not quite making eye contact. For having chosen their location, she looked completely lost.

He gave her a reassuring smile and reached up to tuck a strand of ruby-red hair behind her ear. "Do you want to play on the merry-go-round or the swings first? The slides were always my favorite, but I think I'm a little too big for them now."

A delicate laugh rang from her lips. Every muscle in his body ached to pull her into him, to turn her lips just as red as her hair.

"The swings were always my favorite," she said, chewing on her lip and looking past him to where a set of swings hung unused, still and silent in the faint breeze.

"After you," he murmured.

As she walked ahead, she tilted back her head and stretched her arms wide, basking in the fresh air. At that moment, the setting sun took on a lavender hue and cast a mystic glow on everything it touched.

Inhaling, she smiled from ear to ear and closed her eyes. Then turned to face him. "Ready?"

Before he could untie his tongue, she bounced off in a spur of energy and sat on one of the swings. The chains had been wrapped around the top pole several times, so the seat hung higher than the others and left ample room for her feet, not that she needed much to begin with. He laughed as she pumped her legs, gaining some momentum, but not much.

"Need a push?"

"Um, sure." She held her legs out straight and peeked at him through the corner of her eyes.

He walked behind the swing and gave her hips a healthy shove, enjoying his view. Her hair flew back as she swung forward, and a chorus of giggles floated to his ears.

"I love how it feels like you're flying," she said as she came back toward him.

He pushed her out again, and she went high enough to make the chains lag, suspending her in the air. "Makes you feel like you can conquer the world, right?"

"It does!" Her voice brightened with a lightheartedness he rarely got to hear. Hair wisped around her neck, and she beamed as her head hung upside-down to watch him.

When she swung toward him again, he whispered, "Because you *can* conquer the world, Nia."

Her eyes widened.

The swing's momentum slowed as she swung up and descended again, and she pulled her head up to look forward. At the moment when he would usually push her back out, he wrapped his arms around her waist and captured her in a strong grip.

"Caspian!" she squealed, body tilted in mid-air.

"Looks like I've caught you." His voice came out deeper and huskier, and hints of vanilla enveloped him as he dipped in closer and nuzzled her. "I couldn't help myself, you're too beautiful when you forget to worry."

Too slow for his racing heart, but fast enough to feel every inch of her in his arms, he walked forward until the swing was level with the ground and circled to face her. His hands returned to perch on her hips, drawing lazy circles in the strip of satin skin at her waist. Eyes big and round, Nia watched as he bent down, almost brushing noses.

So close.

"Do you trust me?" he whispered, searching her face.

"I want to," she responded breathlessly, sending shivers down his spine.

Hips flush, he fit himself into the space between her thighs and took in a deep breath of her blissful scent. "Put your arms around my neck."

She released the metal chains and slid her hands up and over his shoulders, hooking them behind his head. Not once did either look away, a gravitational tug binding them together. He signaled her with a squeeze, and she wrapped her legs around his waist, bringing them even closer.

A cold breeze blew her hair back and revealed the entirety of her face—the graceful arch of eyebrows, the subtle highlights of cheekbones, and petite, full lips.

Fire consumed him. It licked up his skin and burned through his clothes, but he held himself at bay. Adjusting his grip to support her weight, he lifted her off the swing. She tensed, arms taut.

"I won't drop you. You're easy to hold," he murmured, breath fanning against her parted lips. The plump of her ass filled his hands. He clutched her tighter, closer.

Almost there.

Assured, she let one hand wander up his neck, fingers dancing up the back of his head and teasing through his hair. Her eyes were softer now, dilated and pinning him in place.

His breath hitched.

With a slight pull, she guided his head to hers and kissed him.

TWENTY-FOUR

Nia

THE MOMENT THEIR LIPS TOUCHED, SHE LOST HERSELF TO THE sensation of *him*.

Broad chest pressed to hers, their body heat spread like wildfire. At first his lips were cautious, cradling hers with utmost care. He smelled and tasted faintly of mint, but something else crept up, a masculine scent that drew her in. All of her senses lit up to absorb as much as they could.

The soft curls of hair weaved between her fingers like strands of fine silk, and she melted into his all-encompassing touch. His arms were big and firm and strong—*he* was strong.

More, she urged, pressing into him and pulling tighter at his locks.

Noting her pleasure he prodded deeper, nibbling and sucking on her lip until she let him in. His tongue swept over hers, claiming its place as he tilted his head to deepen their contact.

Returning the favor, she pulled his lip between her teeth and savored the growl that rose from his throat. Her body molded around his, Caspian responding in kind to each and every movement. The totality of their kiss and a growing tension in her core told her making out wasn't all he was an expert at. Not by a long shot.

She broke away for air, lips stinging with satisfaction. It was almost hard to open her eyes, fluttering as she saw his piercing sapphire gaze framed by thick charcoal lashes.

"Now tell me if I didn't live up to your every expectation," he muttered, breath caressing her parted lips in a seductive, ghostly kiss.

Her body buzzed, craving a second taste. Maybe even a third. She glowered at her thoughts.

"Half of that is *my* credit, thank you very much," she joked, much more breathless than intended.

"You're right, baby girl," he replied, grinding her hips into his own. "In fact, it's about time I find out what else you can do."

Her pulse skyrocketed, and she swallowed a moan, gripping his arms tighter. This couldn't be real.

Caspian awakened something stronger than any fantasy she dared to write, but she wasn't ready to confront it. Especially not when they had become so inexplicably tangled. When did their bodies mold so completely? And how could it feel so addictive?

"Uh, nope. Put me down." She squirmed, jumping out from his arms before he could try anything else. As it was, she wouldn't be getting much sleep tonight, and he'd take all the wiggle room he could get. Or rather, the least amount of wiggle room.

The wind became more chilling without his body nestled with hers, so she wrapped a hand around his arm and pulled him close. Casual contact was much easier to process than a full embrace. She pressed her head into his shoulder and looked away from his face. Cologne wafted into her nose as she nuzzled into him, the soft fabric of his jacket providing both a hiding place and warmth from the night air. She hadn't even noticed the sun setting.

"I'm serious, you are amazing," he said, catching her chin with his hand.

Letting him draw her gaze up, she smiled. The joy in Caspian's expression infused into her chest. "I had a really good evening too, thank you."

"Are you hungry?" he asked, his thumb tracing over her bottom lip. "We could grab something real quick, or order take-out to eat at my place."

His offer was tempting, but she already felt her common sense slipping away. It would be wise to not take things too fast and let the night end on a good note.

"I better head back to the dorms."

"Let me walk you there." He dropped his hand from her face.

She nodded, grateful to stay with him a bit longer. Before they left the park, she looked up and searched the sky for any stars bright enough to be seen. Sure enough, a handful twinkled in the twilight. Their glow burned into her memory. This experience was a night she'd treasure just like a glimmering star. One spot of light—that's what Caspian had become in her world of shadow.

"I just remembered," she said, shivering as goosebumps rose on her arms. "We never finished listing our three things."

"I suppose I am quite the distraction," he teased, pulling off his jacket and handing it to her.

Rolling her eyes, she shrugged on the jacket, warm from his body heat. "You're not cold?"

"No, besides, it looks better on you." The jacket sagged around her small frame, the sleeves bunching over her tiny wrists.

"It's nice and warm, and very big. Just how I like it." She smiled over at him. Finally he acted like a gentleman.

"Mn, good to know you like warm and very *big* things."

Even through the dim light, she could see his cheeky smile and characteristic wink. "Oh, please. *Cocky* much?" She bit back a grin at her own innuendo. His belly laugh warmed her more than the jacket did. "*Anyway*, what are your three things? Not including me." She'd been more than eager to hear what Caspian would choose, if maybe he had some secret stash of importance.

"Since *you* are off-limits..." he hummed and reached over to hold her hand. At this point, she'd become accustomed to the feel of his fingers and the way hers curled around his large palm. "I'll take my phone, so I can call you, my car keys, so I can pick you up, and my wallet, so I can take you out somewhere nice."

"That's your answer? For real?" She arched her eyebrows. "Nothing else worth saving? You don't keep anything sentimental?" Ironically, they were walking past his apartment building, so she gestured to it. "You're okay if this whole thing went up in flames?"

He quirked his head and took in a long, deep breath. "Sentimental, that's what you want? Well, I'll keep my answer —my art is all backed up. I only have one photo that isn't digital, and it's in my wallet, so it was already on the list. I make sure to keep everything important to me safe."

She gripped his hand a little tighter. What if, one day, he considered her one of those important things? What if he would keep her safe?

"Is it an older print?" she asked. Most of the photos she had now were taken on a phone and saved automatically, but a few from her younger days had been scanned into the computer.

"Yeah. I was four years old," he replied, not going into much detail.

"Why not back it up like your drawings?" After she asked, she wondered if she'd overstepped. Caspian rarely talked about personal things. Although he had been opening up more.

"Not sure if I want to keep it." He shrugged. "Then again, I do carry it around with me. I suppose I'd rather it be out-of-sight and out-of-mind than gone forever. I have the feeling I'll want it one day, even if I don't want it now." He reached into his pocket and handed her a plain leather wallet.

Once it had probably smelled like a new car, shone under the light, and folded with a crisp exactness; but time had taken its toll, and now wrinkles creased the surface, one corner worn from being repeatedly shoved into a pocket. Cautiously she peeked inside. Something about searching through his various I.D. cards, money, and personal keepsakes felt more intimate than holding hands. A condom tucked in the corner flap caught her eye, but she ignored it. Instead, she took out his driver's license, and stopped under a streetlight to get a better view.

"How did you manage to take a good photo at the DMV?" she blurted, shocked at how his hair fell just so and the blue of his eyes stood out, even in the typical mug shot.

He shrugged. "It's a natural talent."

She rolled her eyes. Next came his school I.D. card and buried behind that, she found an old photo. The edges were ripped, and a long scratch ran down the center like a scar. It must have been taken a while ago, since Caspian looked like a toddler.

His mom held him snuggled on her lap while his father stood behind them. The photo could pass as a hallmark poster, their smiles bright and cheerful, fitting together like a perfect family. A pang of sorrow resounded in her heart because she knew it hadn't lasted.

As much as she wished she had at least one photo like this, she didn't. But even if she did have memories of a happy family, it wouldn't help. What good was a happy past if it led to a painful future?

Wordlessly, she returned the photo and passed his wallet back. She understood his sentiments. The photo was just as hard to keep as it would be to lose.

When he'd stuffed the wallet in his pocket, she placed her hand back in his. He gave her a squeeze as they continued to stroll down the sidewalk.

"I'm not even supposed to have that photo," he said. "My mom would go on these vacations to get away—from my dad and me. One day after she got home, I found her purse out on the counter." He paused, looking up and swallowing, his Adam's apple bobbing down. "The next time she left, I wanted to have something of hers, so I went through it. Ended up keeping that and a pack of mints."

They went silent for a long time as she watched their feet step on cracks in the concrete. "Do you still see your mom? Or talk?"

"No. She'll probably come to my graduation, but other than that..." He ran a hand through his hair. "I get the feeling she resents I decided to live with my dad, I dunno. After the divorce, he became more of a walking dead than a man, so I figured he needed the company. She stopped reaching out to me a year ago, and when she stopped, so did I."

"Do you think two people can fall in love and stay in love?" she whispered, voicing her thoughts out loud. Immediately she held her breath, realizing the awkward implication. "In general, I mean."

Another squeeze came from his hand, and she looked up to see him watching her. "I don't have the answer to that," he murmured.

She nodded, wishing she'd never brought up the topic. Of course he wouldn't know. He spent most of his time chasing a steamy night, not long-term relationships. Only hopeless romantics and delusional people cared about true love.

He surprised her by speaking up again, "One thing I do know...is you make me want to believe in a love that can last."

TWENTY-FIVE

Nia

IF SHE THOUGHT HIS FLIRTING HAD MADE HER HEART SKIP, THE sincerity of his confession made it stop altogether.

By the time they stood in front of the dorms, she concluded it was best to spend some time alone and let her heart get straightened out by her head.

"Thanks for walking me back," she offered as they came to a stop next to the entrance. Looking up at Caspian, she expected to see a teasing smile or hear a witty remark, but he just stared back.

That intense look stopped her every thought, every word that formed before it reached her lips. He looked at her like she was a puzzle, and he wanted nothing more than to sit down and put it together.

Or take her apart, piece by piece.

The longing behind his eyes reflected distinctly in her own heart—a yearning to be lost with him. To let go. Let him take over.

After a second that froze time, he broke the trance. His voice came out low and raspy as he groaned, "I'm going to be thinking about you all night."

Exactly *what* he'd be thinking about, she didn't have to guess. The chills that triggered went straight to the apex between her legs. "Me too."

As soon as the words left her mouth, his hands were on her. One wrapped around her back, smoothing its way under the barrier of her thin shirt and burning a hot imprint over her skin. The other came up to rest around her neck, his fingers stroking the hollow of her throat.

Not missing a beat, she grabbed his arms and rose up on her toes to catch his lips, even though he would have closed the distance himself. This time neither held back, their kiss insatiable. He devoured her on the spot. Her hands gripped his biceps and shoulders, feeling their way around as her balance faltered. His fingers splayed out on the small of her back to keep her upright. She had never known such intimacy or such an acute craving to fall into the abyss of touch and entanglement. Whatever he had to offer, she wanted it.

They slowed to a languid pace, skin against skin, lips dancing a passionate tango. Caspian's drawings floated up from her subconscious, and her heart raced out of control at the thoughts that followed. The sheer force of desire building up became too much to comprehend, so she shut off her brain and only let herself feel skin-deep. Which, at the moment, was a lot to take in.

If he had asked her to go with him, she would have followed. Anywhere.

And that thought shook her wide awake.

She broke away. This was too much too fast—she couldn't allow herself to give in. She had to hold her own and to pull herself out of the stupor before it went too far.

"I need to go inside," she whispered, hating how her voice was breathless and shaky. Clearing her throat, she stepped away. Caspian caught her hand.

"Nia, let me see you again tomorrow." His eyes pleaded more than his words.

"Okay," she agreed, unable to deny him. "I'll text you, all right?"

He pursed his lips as if it wasn't the answer he wanted, but it was enough to keep him at bay. "Call me. Call me if you can't sleep tonight. Promise."

She sighed. At least over the phone, there would be some distance between them. "All right, I will. But," she emphasized, "I'll probably be up late answering to Ivory and the others since I've been avoiding them. Don't stay awake waiting for a call, okay?"

Instead of giving any confirmation, he squeezed her hand and let go. "Have a good night, Nia. Try not to fantasize too much about your helluva sexy boyfriend." He finished with a trademark wink.

Wait, *boyfriend*?

She spun on her heel and disappeared inside the dorm, not willing to take his words as more than the tease they were. Today she had overdosed on Caspian, and it made her knees much too weak.

No more than two steps down the hallway, a familiar brunette spotted her and waved.

"Hey! How's it going?" Ivory called out, green eyes bright and inquisitive.

Nia knew Ivory wouldn't ask for specifics but had to be dying to know about her and Caspian. And since she'd hesitated to tell her mom about her budding love life, not sure she'd get the best advice anyway, these conflicted feelings had no other outlet. Ivory seemed like the safest option.

"Hey, Ivory," she said. "Actually, if you're not busy, I have some updates..."

"Oh my gosh, yes! Please," Ivory blurted.

A smile pulled at the corners of her mouth, and Nia stepped

into the dimension of purple known as Ivory's dorm. Everything from the fuzzy rug on the floor to the fabric tapestries hung up on the walls was a bold violet, including the glowing purple stars that were sprinkled over the ceiling. A lamp with a warm light bulb cast a welcoming glow over her neat bedspread and the extra-large bean bag in the corner.

"Take a seat! On the bed or a chair, wherever," Ivory encouraged as she clicked the door shut.

Nia took up a neutral location on the rug, leaning into the overstuffed bean bag. "First, I wanted to ask..." she paused. "Is Serena still upset? I haven't seen her hanging out with you and the others lately. Ever since last weekend and the whole club thing I've wondered how she's been." She didn't want to pry but couldn't ignore what happened either.

Ivory plopped on the floor across from her and hummed. "Oh, I think she's okay. She decided to go home with some guy she met at the club—I guess he's an upperclassman and now she always goes to hang out with him at his frat house. Even though she says it's studying, we all know better." Ivory rolled her eyes.

"Oh okay," Nia said. "It might be childish, but I've kinda been avoiding her, well avoiding everyone...I don't know how they'll react to me being with Caspian."

"Hold up, you're actually together?" Ivory squealed, eyebrows arched in anticipation. "Is that his jacket?!"

She looked down, forgetting that she still had on Caspian's oversized jacket. His warmth lingered along with the fragrance of his minty cologne. She nodded sheepishly.

"I am *so* happy for you two," Ivory gushed with a smile. "And honestly, if it's not meant to be between him and Serena, then that's how it is. Let yourself follow your heart."

Ivory was the first person she'd met who came across so effortlessly caring. Maybe making a friend wouldn't be impossible after all. "I just want to make sure there's no bad blood between me and Serena. I don't need drama blowing up in my face."

Ivory nodded. "I understand. I think being turned down hurt more than she'll admit—"

Nia cringed. "I really didn't mean for that to happen."

"You didn't do anything wrong," Ivory assured. "Everyone has to deal with rejection once in a while."

That was true. "Rejection still sucks, though," she added. "That's why I never wanted to get involved with Caspian, but I don't know. It just happened. And actually...I think I really like him."

"Don't worry. I'll always be a friend to Serena and to you, too." A sympathetic expression played across Ivory's gentle features. "I can't pick sides in these kinds of things. I only want everyone to be happy. If Caspian makes you happier, that's a good thing."

Nia returned her heartfelt smile. "You really are a lifesaver. Thanks for always looking out for everyone."

"Aw, shucks. Enough about me." Ivory leaned forward as if to catch the slightest whisper or reaction. "I wanna hear about you and Caspian."

The fibers of the rug became infinitely more intriguing as Nia ran her hands through them, trying to sort out how much she should share. "There's not much to tell. I mean, there's a lot I *feel* about it all, but I'm not sure I can put those things into words."

"Come on, don't leave me hanging," Ivory begged.

Nia laughed, then summarized the events of their two dates and concluded, "It's been a while since I could be so open with someone."

"Gosh, I am such a hopeless romantic," Ivory sighed after listening with rapt attention. "I'm melting."

Nia sat on her hands to keep from fidgeting, fighting down the unsolicited furl of girlish elation in her chest. "Every time we get physical, it's just so, I don't know, heavy. Too much to absorb. It scares the hell out of me because I don't know where his head is at, relationship-wise."

Ivory nodded, strands of dark hair swaying with the movement. "Yeah, sounds like you're falling for him hard, girl."

That was the truth, and it hurt to hear so plainly spoken. Nia hid her face with her hands. "Ugh."

"Aw, don't be so worried," Ivory comforted. "Shouldn't you be happy he's into you?"

She peaked out from between her fingers. "That's the thing. I don't think either of us knows what to do with all these feelings. I don't want to..." She covered her eyes again. "I don't want to end up like my mother."

"What happened?" Ivory's voice softened, laced with concern.

"She falls deeper in love than anyone I know, and men just seem to take advantage of that."

"Oh, I can see why you'd be worried with Caspian." Ivory confirmed her fears. "But I'd still give him a chance. From what you said, all you have to do is take it one step at a time. If he can handle that, which *obviously* isn't his nature, then that's a good sign. A guy should never push you beyond what you set as a boundary."

"That...makes a lot of sense," Nia whispered. "Thanks for letting me talk to you."

"Oh, on the contrary, thanks for talking to me." Despite the energy of her tone, Ivory yawned.

"I should let you get back to what you were doing, and besides—" A yawn of her own interrupted Nia's sentence. "All this romance stuff is tiring me out."

With a giggle, Ivory nodded. "Let me know if you need anything."

"Will do," Nia replied, rising to her feet and heading to the door. "Have you seen that one guy again? The one you never got to talk to?"

A smile graced Ivory's lips, but it didn't reach her eyes. "Oh, no. Not yet."

"Then good luck," she said, opening the door. "I'm rooting for you."

TWENTY-SIX

Caspian

Skin tingling from an ice-cold shower, he stared at the ceiling from on top of his bed. The darkness enveloped everything around him, but despite it being one o'clock in the morning, he was wide awake.

Nia hadn't called yet. Maybe she wasn't going to.

After she responded to his goodnight text, they hadn't talked. If he could only hear her voice, the wait to show her real pleasure wouldn't be so bad. But what he felt was real too, wasn't it? Not just the touching and kissing, but their discussion and the sound of her laughter. The way his chest tightened when she smiled.

He usually refrained from drawing people he knew, but with her, it was hard not to. For once, he wanted to capture the essence of a genuine person. Maybe make a small animation. All of her expressions were nuggets of gold worth panning in a river for hours to uncover.

His brows knit as he thought of how she'd fled into the dorm building. It had all gone so well, he'd half expected an invite inside, but then something must've spooked her. Had he done something wrong? He'd held back the entire evening, giving her space and the freedom to set the tone. Up until the end, she'd been her usual self, the honest and pensive Nia that touched more than the surface of his skin.

Whatever caused her concern, it bothered him. Which only bothered him more.

He was already more invested in this, his first semi-serious relationship, than he thought he could be. Or should be. Maybe more than Nia herself.

When she was around, he constantly forgot about impressing her and instead lost himself in the moment. He'd never brought out that picture of his family. Had his emotions about it thrown her off? Did she feel he had no right to mull over his past?

Beside him, his phone lit up with a call and illuminated the wall. He grabbed it, fumbling for a moment before his thumb pressed the answer. He hadn't even read the screen.

"Hello?" he spoke into the darkness, holding his breath.

"I couldn't sleep." Nia's voice came from the other line.

He closed his eyes. That felt better. But something sounded off, a waver in her voice that normally wasn't there.

"You've been crying." He meant it as a question, but it came out as a statement.

"Is it that obvious?" she whispered.

"What's wrong?" He held his breath as he waited for her answer. This would be so much easier if she were next to him.

"I think I like you, Caspian."

His heart fluttered.

Wait—that was upsetting? "You like me...and that makes you cry?"

"It's confusing," she mumbled. "I want to take things slow with you, but my chest feels like it's going to explode."

He knew the feeling. "Did I upset you?"

What he'd give to be beside her at this moment, to hold her

close and make her feel better. Then again, that wasn't taking things slow.

"No. More like I upset myself." She paused, but he let the line stay silent. Those words had to come with an explanation —he wouldn't drag it out of her, but he would wait until she let him in.

And she did. "We're just beginning to get to know each other...I want to know more before we take things too far." Her voice sounded calmer now, still small, but she spoke freely. "I want to know you before we get physical."

Before. That meant he had a chance at an *after.*

He let out a slow breath, lost in the memory of her soft, luscious lips. For him this was asking a lot, but for her, it must be an innocent request. Innocent, like the rest of her that he wanted to claim so badly. Even when she did agree to more than kissing, he knew he wouldn't get the whole package right away. This gradual getting to know-each-other business really did a number on him.

Then, he understood. "You're afraid of how I make you feel?"

"Um. Maybe," she squeaked, voice timid and wispy.

His body relaxed in relief and a hint—no, a healthy dose— of pride. That was a good thing. Or, he thought it was. "Okay. I understand. I won't do anything else unless you ask."

To be honest, he didn't mind going slow as much as he expected to. As long as she kept him around, he'd get her to open up.

"Thanks, again," she said, sounding more at ease.

"My pleasure. Can I see you again tomorrow?"

"Tomorrow?" she asked, apparently having forgotten his request from when they parted earlier.

"Yes," he breathed.

"I have to study." She paused. "You can join me, though."

"Then I will. What time? Can I meet you after your class gets out?"

"Okay, sure. My last class ends at 3:30, at the Memorial building with all the large lecture halls."

He'd never forget that place. "Where we first met?"

"Mhm," Nia hummed in confirmation.

"Then I'm looking forward to it." His smile must have been audible. Even if he couldn't press her into the wall and show her exactly the kind of things she'd feel when his hands sought out her soft and warm center, seeing her would be enough. For now, at least.

"How are you always available?" she inquired, her tone reprimanding. "Do you ever go to class? Or study?"

"Well, now I study with you."

She laughed. That sound fit her so much better. "I'm amazed you haven't flunked out. How do you have time to mess around and party?"

Again, he felt scolded. Not in a bad way. "That's because I know what I'm doing, baby girl. In all sorts of subjects."

She groaned. "I'm going to sleep now."

He chuckled. "Sweet dreams, my sweet Nia."

"You too," she whispered.

"Not gonna say my name?" he chided. A visual wasn't necessary to sense her exaggerated eye roll.

"Good night, Caspian." The words came out as a sigh, and he'd never liked the sound of his name so much. Then she hung up.

Darkness cloaked the room again, and he swung his arm across the bed to set the phone on his nightstand. Good, now he knew where Nia's head was at. He could work on her body tomorrow.

Groaning, he turned on his side and closed his eyes, consumed by thoughts even he wouldn't dare draw.

3

The next morning, Caspian leaned against the university's old brick wall and eyed a steady stream of passing students. The previously unoccupied hallway now felt congested and stuffy. Most people glanced away, if they dared to make eye contact at all. He wasn't trying to look intimidating, but today he didn't want to catch any fish either—so to speak.

Finally spotting the one he wanted, his lips parted in a grin. Nia made her way out the double doors, red hair swaying along with that confident stride he remembered.

"Hey, how was class?" he called out. At the sound of his voice, she looked up, a shy smile curling the corners of her lips. She managed a small wave and wove a path through the crowd to stand next to him.

"Hey, Caspian. Class was boring, as usual." That blush came back, her pink cheeks contrasting cool, crystalline eyes.

He reached out and caressed her jaw, tilting her chin up to plant a chaste kiss on her lips. Just as sweet as he remembered. "Then maybe I should join you next time, make sure you aren't bored."

Eyes wide, it took her a split second longer than usual to respond. "Let's, uh, see how studying goes first."

He bit his lip to stop himself from mentioning how he'd much rather study her body. Biology was important, after all.

Slow.

Yeah, better stick to Principles of Project Management. Even though he knew there was definitely a part of her that didn't want to take it slow. He just had to draw it out.

"To your favorite empty lecture hall?" he asked, running his hand down her forearm, and interlacing their fingers.

"You know all my secrets," she muttered, face scrunching in an adorable pout.

He chuckled and resisted the urge to pull her into an

embrace. The last thing he needed going into an empty room with her was a hard-on. "Only the ones I happen to stumble into."

A laugh lit up Nia's face as her eyes shimmered. "You don't seem like someone who stumbles very often."

"It's been happening more when you're around," he admitted.

Joyful Nia was truly a sight to behold. He wondered if he could ever be mad at her, with such a cute face and radiant smile.

The initial surge of pedestrians died down, and she led him to the lecture hall that sparked their first meeting. The memory came back crystal clear, but he had to admit that walking beside Nia was much better than viewing her from afar. He'd never hoped for anything more than a fairly enjoyable bachelor's life, but he couldn't see how that would ever compare to what he had experienced these past few days. If only it could last a little longer.

TWENTY-SEVEN

Nia

CASPIAN SAT STILL, PEACEFUL EVEN. IT ASTOUNDED HER. Textbook open on the otherwise clear table, he read in silence as she worked on her own assignments.

After the first ten minutes, she had prepared to bat down his inevitable distractions. After twenty, she started to get worried. Once an hour of successful studying passed, she became deeply concerned for his well-being.

He didn't even use a highlighter; the only sound to break his reverie was the occasional turn of a page. His mint cologne that she thought would be distracting had actually helped her to concentrate, but she'd become restless. Scanning his body, she weighed the options of nudging his foot or poking his side. Would Caspian be ticklish? She giggled at the thought.

His striking blue gaze met hers and silenced the laughter on her lips. Heart stuttering, she cursed herself for breaking his concentration. Now it was even harder to focus on anything except him.

"What?" he asked.

Her eyes widened. "I...I wasn't laughing at you, I promise. And I wasn't staring on purpose." She bit her lip, remembering when he'd caught her doing just that at the outdoor café. "This time," she mumbled.

Soft, rumbling chuckles filled the room. "Oh, Nia, you can stare at me all you want." His eyes darkened. "Just know, there will be consequences."

The lecture hall didn't contain enough air to fill her lungs, not enough oxygen to get her brain to function. Her body, on the other hand, seemed intent to know whatever it was he implied. She opened her mouth to protest, but nothing came out.

His demeanor lightened again. "Are you done studying?"

"Oh—" She relaxed, mirroring his smile. "Almost. I lost my motivation for a few minutes there."

Caspian quirked an eyebrow. Not willing to give him another chance to open his mouth and throw her off, she continued, "Give me another few minutes. I'll be finished by then. Would you be good with that?"

"Mhm." He nodded. The enticing smile of his grew wider. Now that she knew the wonders of his lips, she craved them more than she knew she should. She had to stop thinking about last night and get back to her usual, rational self.

Tearing her eyes away, she considered the pile of papers in front of her. They looked as appealing as a stack of soggy potato chips. "Have you really been reading your textbook this entire time?"

Caspian peered over again, and on cue, her heart skipped a beat. "Yes, I have."

"You don't get...distracted?"

The chair creaked as he leaned back and clasped his arms behind his head. "It goes without saying that you can be very distracting." He paused, making her squirm. "Which is why if I don't focus completely on the task at hand, neither of us will get anything done."

Oh.

"Are you trying to distract me, Nia?"

Immediately, her face burnt to a crisp. She was most definitely not trying anything. Truth be told, maybe she did want him to be the one to distract her... No. No way. Slow was good. Slow was necessary.

"It was just a question. Don't go reading into things," she quipped.

He laughed. At least she knew he didn't take her remarks personally.

Composing herself, she pictured a tranquil, endless ocean. No more making waves. She tucked some hair behind her ear and tried to replicate the persona of a proper businesswoman. "I wouldn't want to distract you from your studies. If you need more time, let me know."

"I can stop whenever you're ready. I'd much rather do other things together when you let me," he said.

Tightening her self-control, she kept her face forward. Whatever look Caspian was giving her, it would probably end their ability to study altogether.

The squeak of plastic against metal signaled he resumed his usual position, and she let out a deep breath to ground herself. She shuffled her papers and placed them back down, the corners perfectly aligned. Her head slumped into her hand, elbow propped up on the table. As much as she wanted a break, if she stopped now, she knew he'd sidetrack her for the rest of the day.

Thumbing through her books, she pulled out her writing journal. Almost a week had passed since she last wrote anything, mostly due to her excursions with Caspian. Their conversation at the club surfaced. *Now I really need to read your writing.*

To his credit, he had been very forthcoming with his drawings. Well, with a lot of things in the sex department. Yet at the same time, he had been patient with her and even now, agreed to sit in silence instead of the "other things." Time with him could be either hot and heavy, or sweet and simple like today. They were like magnets that flipped at random, attracting then repelling each other.

But really, it was only her who flip-flopped. Caspian knew what he wanted from day one. He came up to her without knowing a thing about her, singled her out. Was all this time and effort just to get her in bed with him? None of it seemed logical. Nia pushed the troublesome thoughts to the back of her mind.

In any case, she needed a creative outlet, and he deserved to see a snippet of her writing. Allowing someone else into her world of words wasn't utterly new. Sometimes she posted online, but she kept it anonymous. Not even her mother or high school friends, and certainly no one at college, had read her stories.

Despite the novelty of sharing, giving this part of herself to Caspian sprouted delight. It was like a pact between them, a mutual appreciation for breathing life into their secret thoughts. She wondered if he only drew erotic scenes or, if like her, also kept a few gems of undefiled innocence.

Picking up her pencil, she began to scrawl out a message in the best way she knew how.

For the first time, I swam headfirst into the sea. Raging waves and clashing strokes of lightning weren't unknown, but being close made the storm rage with new life. A daunting task, to struggle against such a force. Yet I trusted the pull of my muscles to keep me afloat as my heart fought endlessly against the chill of the water.

I expected to drown, to sink into the fury of the sea. But if by chance I didn't, I wondered if treasure was hidden in the eye of the storm? Perhaps acceptance of fear is the only way to move forward. Perhaps, embracing the possibility of failure is the only road to success.

Expressing her feelings in a symbolic way felt much safer

than explaining out loud. Before she could doubt herself, she ripped out the page and slid it across the table. In a hurry, she picked up her pencil, wincing at how she fumbled to hold it correctly.

With trembling fingers, she began on the first integral of her Calculus homework. Math was black and white, and it'd be a good enough distraction until she calmed down.

On the last problem her mind began to wander. Was he ignoring her note? This was such a juvenile idea...she cursed herself for acting so elementary.

The faint rustle of a paper sliding over the desk came from beside her. Lifting her gaze, she saw Caspian's hand retreat from a sketch drawn on the bottom half of her torn page. She picked it up and examined the illustration.

A man arose out of the sea, carrying in his arms a beautiful woman in a long dress. Waves and lightning crashed behind the pair, but the man remained fixated on walking ashore, where a beam of sunlight illuminated his path. Both the figures were drenched, the hard lines of the man's muscles in contract with the soft curves of the woman's body.

Warmth burst from her chest and encircled her being. So, Caspian was capable of being romantic.

She began to tuck the paper safely into her notebook, then paused. Silence in the room wove around her as Caspian's presence and his drawing added fuel to her imagination. The rest of the scene crept into her head, and she placed the paper back down, turning it over to write on the back.

A cold torrent wrestled with my limbs until foreign warmth encased me. Steel arms held me close, rescuing my beating heart. He pulled us from the waves and brought us ashore, where the drum of his heart eclipsed a clap of thunder.

I drew my gaze up, his chest firm and smooth under my inquisitive fingertips. His eyes wandered down, and the air grew heavy with static, burdened by a force greater than that of the sea. I

savored the way he drank me in, how he roamed over the swell of my
pebbled breasts aching for his touch.

Body, mind, and soul—would he savor all three?

She carefully slid the paper over and promptly blocked out the surge of adrenaline, rushing to finish the last problem of homework. If she hadn't crossed the line yet, this note definitely did the trick.

When done at last, she forced herself to look over. The paper had been carefully placed beside her, with one line scribbled in Caspian's handwriting.

How could he not?

TWENTY-EIGHT

Caspian

HE COULDN'T DO THIS ANYMORE.

Studying in a lecture room was one thing, with the university's old uncomfortable chairs and the possibility anyone could walk in, but studying in his apartment was another.

When he suggested they go to his place to study, he didn't mean to *actually* do homework. Nia hadn't gotten the memo.

He sighed. That was all right. He wanted her to feel comfortable, but he grew more restless by the second. All she'd done was sit down—on his cheap futon, right in the middle of his life like it was hers, too—and that did something strange to the center of his chest. Of course, other body parts were *very* aware of her presence, but he'd gotten used to that.

For the past half an hour, he watched her switch between scribbling in a notebook and typing on her laptop, noticing all the little details he'd skimmed over before. Like how a strip of ruby hair kept falling in front of her face, and she'd push it behind her ear with those pretty unpainted nails. Every so often, her chest would rise with a sigh. And as she concentrated, like right now, she'd nibble on her bottom lip.

Fuck. He couldn't take his eyes off her, but he had to, or else she wouldn't be studying for much longer. The last thing he wanted was to be exactly the guy she thought he was—the kind who only saw what he wanted without considering what mattered to her.

He swiveled his desk chair to block her from his line of sight and pulled out his phone. A notification from an hour ago crossed the screen. A message from his dad. Clicking on it, he read through the simple text.

DAD

> Hope you're doing well and having fun. Be sure to balance out those parties with schoolwork every now and then. Your mom said she put more funds in your account.

He snorted. The last line sounded more like he was an employee rather than a son. Why couldn't she bother to send him a message herself?

He didn't expect anything different, though. His parents were still working out paperwork from the divorce, so chances were she threw it in as a side comment to an otherwise mandatory conversation. He typed a brief reply.

> All good. Thanks. I've actually been more focused recently. How are things with you?

Glancing over his shoulder, he thought about mentioning Nia. His dad would probably like her—even with his stance on relationships. Since she'd been around, he'd done better in school, and she held just as many reservations about making things official as he did.

He didn't know why, but that had started to bother him.

> Same old, same old. House is quiet.

He remembered what that felt like. They could both sit in silence for hours. However, something felt different about the silence after the divorce. Instead of their quiet being comfortable because there was nothing to say, it felt more like suffocation—like guilt and the invisible weight of regret.

Turning to his computer, he clicked off the school's assignment page and brought up some of his backup files, where he kept scans of all his drawings. During the worst months of the divorce, his art had become more abstract, often structural sketches without color or faces.

"Hey," Nia said, breaking through the melancholy.

He looked up. "Mn?"

"I finally got through the reading. What about you?"

"I uh...couldn't focus," he admitted, combing a hand through his hair. "Got distracted looking through some of my older stuff."

Papers ruffled as she put away her books and then padded over to stand by his chair. "That's the picture you showed me at the club, right?"

Upon a closer look, he found the thumbnail she'd pointed to and enlarged it. Sure enough, that was the one she picked from his portfolio—two clasped hands with a naked couple spooning in the background.

"Yeah," he said. "I drew that in high school."

"Oh," she hummed, bending down to look at the screen.

"Here." He swiveled to make space between himself and the desk and spread his legs. "You can sit on my lap."

She tossed an icy glare from over her shoulder in one of her classic *I-know-what-you're-doing* looks.

"I promise I'll behave," he insisted, wishing she hadn't caught on so soon. But he needed to touch her in some way or another, and this bending over would only make things worse.

"You better not have planned this all along," she admonished, and took a tentative seat.

"Good girl," he hummed low without thinking. A lovely hue crept up her face. He smirked and wrapped an arm around her waist. "It's not something I plan, by the way. It's you."

She rolled her eyes and shifted to look at the computer. "What was your inspiration?"

He groaned under his breath. "But you do have to stay still."

She huffed, wiggling around more. "If you hadn't noticed, your lap isn't the most comfortable at the moment."

Yes, he'd noticed.

He'd very much noticed.

"That's exactly why you have to stay still," he hissed, tightening his arm around her waist. "Unless you'd like to help my lap get more *comfortable*."

She twisted to glare at him, and another groan rumbled from the back of his throat. Whatever response she had planned died, lips falling open as she saw what must have been a very dark and not-so-subtle warning look in his eyes.

She pursed her lips but stopped squirming. That blush from before darkened. "Are you going to answer the question or not?"

He sighed and forced himself to focus back on the photos. "I think I was practicing perspective. See how the hands are bigger than their bodies? They're in the foreground, which makes them the focal point."

She hummed. "Most of your other pictures have the sex as the focal point, but in this one..." She paused to study the photo, its reflection lighting up in her eyes. "This one is more romantic, almost poetic."

"Mn." His thumb slipped under her shirt and found a patch of silky skin. "At that time, I guess I was trying to figure out romance."

"Did you?" she asked quietly, eyes still on the screen.

"I..." He exhaled at the flood of memories and set his forehead on her shoulder, taking a deep breath of her scent.

This was the exact opposite of what he was supposed to say—what she wanted to hear—but he couldn't lie. Not to her. "I came to the conclusion it wasn't real. I decided romance was only something people used to get what they really wanted."

Her hand slid over his, entwining their fingers.

"Knowing you, though," he added, raising his head to brush his lips against the delicate curve of her neck. "...I've been questioning a lot of that."

"Oh," she breathed, and though it was one word—one syllable, it sounded distant. He gave her fingers a light squeeze.

"What do you think I really want?" she asked. "From you?"

The question surprised him, although he didn't have to think long about the answer. "To be someone you don't have to be afraid of."

As the words hung between them, their meaning stretched, bridged some previously unspoken gap and molded into a new thought. Not a complete thought, a glimmer of one. If he succeeded, if fear wasn't there, what else would arise in its place?

Security? Trust?

A deeper emotion, something more potent, maybe even more dangerous? Would she want that? Would he?

He lifted his head to look in her eyes, but whatever she felt about his answer retreated. That strand of hair had fallen out from behind her ear again, and he tucked it back, his fingers clumsier and not as well practiced at the motion as hers. He smiled, trying to lighten the mood. "What were you like in high school?"

A cute smile tipped up her lips, brighter than the diminishing sun rays showing through the window, and she looked down. Dark mascara-painted lashes fanned out against her cheekbones. He took a mental snapshot, even though it was second-rate to the real thing.

"I was hopeless," she murmured. "I'd read romance books all day and wished—" She bit her tongue to cut herself off.

"Wished what?" he prompted, giving her side a playful squeeze.

She laughed. "Well..." Her finger traced little patterns up his arm that tickled his hair. "It's silly, but after reading particular scenes, I wished I had someone to practice with. Like kissing and stuff," she clarified in a whisper. "I thought part of why my ex cheated was because I was bad at it."

He cupped her chin and brought her eyes back to his. "I could kiss you all day, Nia. You're not bad at it."

This idiot had thrown away something he would die for a tiny taste of. What a fool. At least now he was here to set the record straight and savor all her kisses. "You can practice anything with me," he said. "I'll be your personal book boyfriend."

She tried to stifle her smile, but he tickled her, and it broke free in a fit of laughter. "I worked really hard to outgrow that stage, you know."

Leaning in closer, he whispered, "Are you sure about that? Nothing you still want to try, hm?"

Her breath hitched, and she turned away. "Maybe... there's one thing."

"Tell me," he said, holding his breath. Hoping she wouldn't back out.

"It's..." She hesitated, then removed his arm and stood up. "Close your eyes?" She bit her lip, and although his heart hammered with anticipation, he did as he was told.

"Um, can you lean back more?"

Was she trying to give him a heart attack? If that's what she wanted to test out, it might very well happen.

He leaned into the chair, and it reclined a few notches. Every inch of his skin pulled taut, aching for a hint of contact. Then tiny, barely-there tickles ran along the side of his face. He twitched, then realized it was her hair. Not the place he'd been hoping for, but his pulse raced nonetheless.

Like mana descending from heaven, her lips brushed against his, warm and tender and delicate. Something about them felt different...reversed. She'd kissed him upside-down.

For a second, he remained as still as possible—much to his agony—and relaxed his lips. That single place of contact between them became excruciating, so good and so enveloping he could no longer feel anything else. Her shape and feel mesmerized him all over again.

That's what he wanted, to create a catalog of her, of every way she could melt for him. To discover the particular feel and taste of every part of her, to know how many ways she could get him to feel things no other woman had.

Her hands slid down his chest and curled, bracing herself against the muscles she found there. Slowly he started to kiss her back, gently sucking on her lip.

A bad kisser? She was fucking fantastic.

He reached up and tangled his hands in her hair, brushing it up and away from their faces. With added confidence, she grazed his lips with her tongue, and he deepened the kiss with a groan, feeling her teeth and tangling his tongue with hers.

He gasped as she pulled away, and breathing in came with a pang of disappointment. Oxygen should be unnecessary if it meant kissing her just a little longer. Her silhouette was lined with fading gold light as she stared down at him from behind the chair, a special gleam in her eye. A gleam he liked very, very much. A gleam he wanted to bottle up and keep forever.

Then she giggled. "It's hard to tell if the position was good or if it was just you."

He smirked, his ego growing far beyond the allowable limit. "Half of the credit goes to you, doesn't it?"

"That's right." She beamed at hearing her quip repeated. "Although...I'm sure you've had much more practice than me."

"Doesn't mean I don't have my own bucket list." He raised his eyebrows.

"What do you mean?"

He swiveled the chair and tenderly brushed the tip of his finger against the hinge of her jaw. "Have you ever been kissed here?"

Flicking his eyes to hers, he watched her expression shift from curiosity to understanding, then flicker between desire and embarrassment.

She shook her head and then whispered, "No."

Leaning in, he replaced his finger with his lips and gave her a light kiss. One that barely made contact with her golden skin but sent tingles down his spine. He drew a line from her jaw to her collarbone and imagined his hand sketching the curve of her neck, or playing with lights and shadows as they danced around her form. "Here?"

"No," she said, voice growing shaky.

He skimmed his lips down and placed another light kiss above the collar of her shirt. Her breath hitched and he moved his finger lower, over the top of her shirt to the edge of her bra. It was all too easy to envision her laid bare, to see the perfect portrait he would paint of her.

"Here?"

"N-no."

Sliding his hand down to her waist, he pulled her closer and pressed a kiss over the swell of her breast. His thumbs slipped under her shirt, the thin cloth much too thick of a barrier. He needed to taste her skin. Feel her heat. Needed to absorb all the little trembles that ran through her body, feel all the places she'd gone soft and show her all the places on his that were very, very hard.

Dancing his fingers up her stomach, he bent down to follow with his mouth, but her muscles tensed. Her hand closed around his wrist, and he stopped.

"It's um," she whispered, clearing her throat. "It's getting late. I should...I should get back to the dorms."

His head fell against her, and he retracted his hand. "Okay."

Every cell in his body hated the next words to come out of his mouth. But he said them anyway. Said them because if he didn't, he wouldn't be able to pull away.

"I'll take you back."

TWENTY-NINE

Caspian

"Get this—when I was young, I wanted to be a farmer. That or a firefighter." The wind carried Nia's laughter as they walked down the sidewalk.

He chuckled along, enjoying their leisurely stroll. The autumn air was crisp enough to keep his mind clear and body cool, despite the temptation beside him. Thankfully, today he had already endured the cruel and unusual punishment called homework. At first Nia's dedication to school was unbearable, but it became less so as they grew more comfortable with each other.

"I'm not sure what I was thinking," she continued. My little head was so full of wild dreams."

He hummed. "Isn't it still?"

She'd filled that journal with dreams, and even though he tended to focus on the ones about him, surely there were many more.

"Oh. Well..." Her voice lowered. "The difference is I used to believe in them, back then."

He knew what that was like.

"Then, what do you want to be now?" he asked.

"I..." She paused. "I haven't decided. Something simple, I think, like a bookkeeper or a clerk. At the end of the day, I want to be able to go home and not worry about bills, but I don't want to stress over deadlines or have to manage people either."

He considered her answer as they turned down the path that led to the dorms, frail leaves crunching under his feet. "You don't want a job that involves writing?" Words lacked the visual element he loved, but Nia could weave them almost effortlessly.

"Oh *right*," she said with sarcasm. "That's the last thing I'd want the world to know me for. I'd rather enjoy the things I write without others complaining that it's cheap or talentless."

"I would appreciate it."

"I'm sure you would and use it as an excuse to have your way with me."

He bit his lip. "Really now, and what exactly would that entail? Do share the details of my ways and how they involve you."

She rolled her eyes and jostled him with her shoulder. "You know what I mean."

"I really don't." He tried his best to sound innocent when his thoughts were anything but.

She shot him a glare, then flipped the question back on him. "What about yourself? Why not become an artist?"

His jaw clenched. He hated himself for being such a hypocrite. If he had known he'd meet her, then maybe he could've been more prepared to be who she needed. Screw appeasing his parents if it meant he had the credibility to encourage Nia to pursue what made her happy. "I would want that. I...have a minor in art, actually."

Well, now he did. He'd make it official later.

"Oh," she said. "I think that's great."

They continued down the sidewalk, feet shuffling on the cement as the dorm building drew closer.

He couldn't help but notice how she avoided intimacy with

him more often and wondered why she refused to go further. Her body betrayed her desire for physical connection, but she shut herself down every time it came down to the line. He'd never seen someone so intent on punishing themselves.

Clearly, he could offer her what she wanted—what she needed. Her body craved him, and the reverse was equally apparent. The longer they ignored the mounting desire between them, the more intense it became.

"If you could live anywhere, where would it be?" she asked.

"Wherever I can get my hands on you," he answered. Location wasn't important; the people around him were.

She shook her head and laughed, careful to not brush against him as he opened the back entrance and let her pass through. "You have a one-track mind, Caspian."

His heart swelled. "Doesn't matter if I like the destination, does it?"

"Can't argue with that." She paused in the front of her dorm and pulled the key from her pocket. "As far as destinations go, a dorm room isn't the most exciting."

"I think I can fix that."

Right now, he didn't want to be anywhere else.

She swung the door open a little faster than normal and took a rushed step inside. "Or maybe *you* need to be managed. Careful, you never know when a girl keeps handcuffs."

"Kinky, sign me up."

"That's not what I meant." She threw a not-so-playful glare over her shoulder and tossed the keys on her desk. Icy daggers in her eyes highlighted the rosy blush coloring her cheeks.

He smirked and locked the door behind him. A very Nia atmosphere greeted him, the soothing blue décor and simplistic style reminiscent of a tranquil meditation room. The faintest trace of vanilla mingled with her scent and made him want to stay forever.

She turned and eyed him with suspicion, face draining of

color. "Are you saying you've used handcuffs before? Want to use them?"

Letting her squirm, he debated on how he should answer. This was getting fun. "I'm saying I'm not opposed."

"Well, I am," she squealed, voice jumping an octave.

"To being cuffed or doing the cuffing?"

"Caspian...I'm serious." Hands planted on her hips, she glowered up at him. "And it's late, so you can't stay long. I shouldn't even let you come in."

How incredibly cute. He deserved a gold medal for being able to keep a straight face. "Are you going to time me, then?" Given the right circumstances, he only needed five minutes to cure her current condition. The air between them was practically sparking.

"No." She slouched on the edge of her bed with a huff. "All this walking made my feet sore," she admitted.

"Then you should've let me drive you to my place or wherever. I'll take you anywhere." He sat next to her, the bed dipping with his weight and shifting their bodies together.

"No, it's okay," she sighed. "I wanted to be outdoors. Fall is settling in and—"

"Let me," he softly interjected as she started to unlace her shoe. Eyes jolting up to his, she took in a shallow breath and let him loosen the knot, then slid the shoe off her foot and tossed it aside. It landed haphazardly in the middle of the floor with a dull thump.

When she didn't continue speaking, he filled the silence for her. "I could drive you to some places I know. We could see a bunch of trees changing colors if that's your thing." He set her foot against the inside seam of his jeans and motioned for the other one. "I won't even tell anyone if you get a pumpkin spice, mocha-whatever."

"I prefer apple cider." She turned her hips to bring the other foot to his lap and leaned back with one hand on the bed.

Another dull thump and the second shoe landed a few feet away from the first.

"Mn." He slid his thumb under the hem of her sock, caressing her ankle. Every inch of her skin was so smooth and silky.

"Thanks...that feels nice," she half sighed as he worked his fingers down to the arch of her foot.

Lingering on the sight of her reclined body, he swept his gaze up to her face just in time to catch a glimpse of the battle behind them. Dammit, she was trying to block him out. His lips pressed into a line, but this time, he wouldn't stop. Couldn't.

"Nia," he murmured, her sock now discarded on the floor and his fingers rolling small circles into her bare heel. The glassy pale blue of her eyes met his, and he held her attention as he spoke. "You're tense."

A trademark blush colored her cheeks. "I'm fine. I like this."

His fingers resumed their kneading, working up to the pads of her toes and massaging the sensitive space between.

When he looked up, her eyes had drifted shut. A delicate smile graced her lips, and he bent down to place a kiss on the top of her foot. Her leg twitched, but at the same time, she stifled a contented sigh and relaxed. Slowly his thumb traced a line that his lips eagerly followed, trailing to her big toe and around the side of her ankle.

"Relax, lean back," he whispered, picking up her other foot and putting the first against his pants seam. She took in a deep breath, the sheets rustling as she leaned into a pile of pillows. A heavy exhale announced her easing nerves, and he repeated the process on the other foot.

She entranced him, his craving unparalleled. The glow of his affections radiated off her, and she looked absolutely exquisite. Instead of stopping at her heel as he had on the first foot, he continued to press his lips up her leg. His skillful fingers inched up the thin fabric of her sweatpants, and he palmed the warm, supple skin of her calf. The steady thrum of his pulse awoke his body, their uneven breaths and the scent of her growing arousal a heady combination.

Making his way upwards, he savored the satin texture of her skin, and his lips parted in awe—verified, she tasted as good as she felt. His teeth grazed along the inside bend of her knee, and he indulged in a small nibble.

She jerked, gasping at the same time.

"Wait."

THIRTY

Nia

A JUMBLED GROAN RUMBLED AGAINST HER SKIN AS CASPIAN pulled away. Steady breaths were about the last thing left in her control, and even those were getting out of hand.

She cursed her pounding heart. He could not have this much power over her. Any power over her. Yet not only her body but her soul wanted to reach out and return his touch. Sealing her eyes shut, she fought to clear her head.

His hands left her legs, and she bit back a whine. The entire week, she'd been forced to confront these growing impulses. A fire in the depth of her being that burned whenever Caspian was around and crackled for fuel when he wasn't. Any attempt at extinguishing it only fanned the flames more.

Time and time again, she stubbornly emptied her head of perverse thoughts, only to have it filled again with images of him and the allure of his drawings. Any and every place they went became erotic, tainted by imagined sexual positions she wasn't sure even existed.

It was supposed to have been one date.

Then that became two, and other non-date dates after that.

There wasn't a line to cross anymore, just a plain of gray and no sense of direction. She'd lost track of which side she came from, if she wanted to go back to black or white. No one tempted her as much as him—in every way. She'd become vulnerable, and that was why she had to put an end to their night.

His very three-dimensional touch unraveled her. All clarity of mind dissipated under his influence. He confounded her, and now he hovered over her on his hands and knees, undoubtedly staring as she curled into an awkward ball. The mattress shifted as Caspian's weight redistributed to one side, and the heat of his body settled in beside her.

"Come here," he murmured, tugging gently at her wrist. She dared a look up at him. Leaning against the headboard, he sat with legs outstretched and arms beckoning. "Let me hold you."

That seemed safe enough, and she was grateful to be close again. He guided her onto his lap, which formed a surprisingly perfect nest. With one large hand cradling her head, he pulled her into his chest and wrapped the other arm around her shoulder. The steady thrum of his heart echoed resolutely into her ear.

She melted. Soft lips pressed to the side of her head as Caspian wove mindless patterns into her skin with the pad of his thumb. His body felt sturdy yet gentle—a perfect fortress.

This was the first time she'd let a man hold her like this. For just a moment, she let herself be cradled, cared for in the most innocent manner. She slowly accepted his affection as it seeped into the pores of her skin.

"Thank you," she murmured at last.

"You okay?" His lips moved against her forehead, warm and soft like fleece, as his breath played with loose strands of hair.

"Yeah. I had to clear my mind," she answered.

"Of something bad?"

No, of something too good to be true. If only he knew how he affected her, how attractive he was. Oh wait, he did—and that was the problem.

"No." She shook her head and tried to sound as non-lovestruck as possible. But her logic fizzed as the gently rough texture of his hands, warm breath and soft lips brushed over her temple. With every inhale her chest expanded into his, their shoulders rising in sync.

"Why do you refuse to let yourself feel?" His delicately spoken words pierced her defenses.

That wasn't the response she expected. Normally she was the one who asked questions, but she'd been utterly unprepared for this.

Gliding his hand to her chin, he tilted her head to face him. Deep blue eyes gazed into hers. "There's nothing to be afraid of. Even if it's bad, you can tell me."

Surrounded by warmth and security, those words weren't so hard to believe, but would he always be here to offer that same promise? No, there was no assurance of a future together. All she could cling to was the fragile here and now.

Her stomach twisted as she remembered the things she *knew* to be afraid of. Abandonment. Heartbreak. Lies. All that had happened to her in the past, before she'd even been born, and she had little faith her luck would ever change.

Her pessimism was the last thing she wanted to discuss, so she said instead, "I do feel. I just don't let emotions control me."

Although, she wasn't doing a very good job of it at the moment. The problem was he made her feel too much.

If she acknowledged the ache in her heart that Caspian filled, then it'd force her to remember why it was there in the first place. She couldn't want him, or anyone for that matter, because as easily as they walked into her life, they could walk out. Her father had been harsh proof of that.

These past few days had been a dream, and she'd almost let

herself forget about his past and the girl in the blog. That didn't change the truth, though. A player was just in it for the game.

He closed the small gap between their lips with a delicate, open-mouthed kiss.

"How do you feel about that?"

Her heart fluttered, begging to be unlocked from its cage. That was a feeling she could never replicate on her own. Guilt rose at the uninhibited response, but before she could focus again on the negative, a surge of want and need overpowered everything else.

What was the question again? Oh yes, how did she feel... Her hands found their way up his shoulders and around his neck, pulling him down for another sinful taste. The defined muscles of his chest brushed the concealed yet equally hard and defined peaks of her nipples.

Caspian felt good. Very good, in fact.

"You haven't answered," he whispered, lips moving against hers.

"This feels..." She paused to think of the right word. "Natural."

Self-indulgence with him didn't feel like heartbreak or deceit or abandonment—quite the opposite.

She felt his lips smile, and hers followed suit. They kissed again, and she reveled in the experience without giving mind to the consequences. Hands mingling in his hair, she held on tighter until they were pressed together with everything she had. Their lips locked in a feverish attempt at conversation and words she didn't begin to comprehend flowed from her tongue to his.

"*Nia*," he groaned, the single syllable of her name a prayer uttered by a desperate, wayward saint—its beckoning call too enticing to leave unanswered.

Leaning in further, she shifted to straddle him and fully covered his mouth with hers. His hands gripped her hips and melded them together, the fusion chasing away rational thought as hopes and dreams sprouted from his infernal touch.

His hardness grew beneath her, pressing exactly where she needed him most. She ground into him, and he returned the favor, hands guiding their movements as he slipped lower and lower, kneading her soft skin and driving her mad.

A sigh threatened to leave her lips, but she swallowed it, not ready to concede her helpless state out loud. Then, as if he could sense her wavering, Caspian deepened the kiss, mouth hot and tender, teasing and tasting as he rewarded her enthusiasm. Heat bloomed within and intensified with every rock of her body against his.

She moaned helplessly.

Letting herself fall to the whims of physical sensation, the force that channeled through her was more intense than anticipated. Much, much more. The times she pleasured herself paled dramatically in comparison.

"What do you want, Nia? You need to tell me." Caspian's mouth migrated to her jaw, breathing the words into her tingling skin.

Her body did more thinking than her brain, reacting as his lips trailed fairy kisses to her neck, where he nipped at her earlobe and sent a shiver between her thighs. Even the slightest touch put her on sensory overdrive. She clung to him, balling the fabric of his shirt in her hands and savoring the ecstasy.

"Tell me, and I can give it to you," he whispered.

She tried to speak, but it came out as a jumbled sigh.

Lazily emerging from between adept lips, his tongue tickled her already tingling skin and glided from her ear down to the hollow of her shoulder. He sucked gently on a spot that made her toes curl, and another strangled mewl escaped. His hands made putty of her insides as they descended closer and closer to the apex of her legs.

"Caspian..." she breathed.

"Mhm?" he hummed, biting down and nearly sending her over the brink.

"Please..."

What was he doing to her? What *else* could he do to her?

THIRTY-ONE

Nia

His hands, his mouth, his lips...they were an oasis in the middle of the desert. And right now, she was drowning.

The truth she had ignored for so long, hidden far away from herself and the world, finally reared its ugly head. She desperately craved to be touched and worshiped in a way only another could provide—to be wanted.

Caspian's mint cologne washed over her as he brought his lips to meet hers again, granting another satisfying kiss. Anticipation spiked deep in her stomach. The time for questions and waiting was gone. All that mattered was feeling him here and now. Surrendering to what she had only written about for far too long.

"I have an idea, something you'll be familiar with." He placed a simple, lingering kiss on her swollen lips.

She opened her eyes, forgetting when they drifted closed. Caspian looked down at her, a smile carved into vibrant red lips and ruffled dark hair falling over his face.

Was this what it felt like to lose herself? Were her doubts and fears worth holding on to? Not only did he feel and sound wonderful, but he looked wonderful. Drinking in the sight of him was enough to take her breath away—the depth in his hooded eyes and confident set of his shoulders.

"Stay here," he said, picking her up and placing her on the edge of the bed. "Don't move."

She watched, raking her eyes over him as he walked straight to her dresser, bent down, and opened the bottom drawer. Embarrassment flooded through her. How did he know where they were?

"Pink or purple?" he asked, referring to her two vibrators.

"Pink," she mumbled as heat swept over her face.

Caspian closed the drawer and walked back, the small pink device in hand.

"Cute," he muttered, turning the smooth cylinder in his hands, its diameter equal to one of his fingers.

Her gaze dropped to her lap, where she fiddled with her hands. The look of desire in his eyes did wonders to her body, but now that she had a moment to breathe, she realized something she hadn't thought of.

She never cared about impressing others. Now, that was about to backfire in her face, the one time she wanted to be admired. A weight crushed her chest as a feeling of insignificance washed over her.

"Don't you know how beautiful you are?" Caspian hummed, caging her between his arms and bending down to place a kiss on her forehead. His thumb traced lightly over her lips.

"Am I—to you?" She had to know.

He turned her chin to face him, eyes filled with absolute certainty. "You are."

"But compared to..." Her voice faded, and she could only finish the sentence in her head: *all the other girls you've slept with...*

His lips sloped into a frown. "If I wanted to sleep with

someone else, I'd be with them. Plenty of girls are easy enough to undress."

So, if he decided at some point to want someone better, it would be a slice of cake. That wasn't very consoling. Her body tensed with rising doubts. Maybe this wasn't—

"Nia," he sighed. "I'm with *you*. When I say you're beautiful, I mean it. Your brilliant mind..." He traced his fingertips over her forehead, sweeping down to tuck a piece of hair behind her ear. "Your ability to listen and see potential in others..."

He kissed her eyes, one by one. "Your vision to better yourself, to want good in the world..."

His hand traced down her neck and over her collar bone. "The way you speak honestly, value truth."

"And yes, these beautiful breasts..." The tip of his index finger ran over her nipple, hidden by her bra but peaked in arousal.

"Your smooth skin..." He lifted her shirt, thumb skimming her belly button. "And this..." He lightly cupped her sex, the warmth of his touch making her gasp. "I want all of it."

She held his gaze for what seemed like an eternity. Lust filled his sapphire eyes and coiled in her core.

How could she refuse?

She opened her mouth to respond but found no words. Caspian's wanton lips came to her rescue, and his hands held her face while the intense feelings from earlier washed over her a second time. Groaning into his mouth, she moved closer and matched his fervor.

"That's it," he whispered. "Fuck, baby girl, I've needed you."

His hands sought out the waistline of her pants and leisurely slid underneath, but impatience got the better of her and she pulled them off in one decisive motion. Her skin flared with heat. Each and every nerve lit up, aching for more of his attention.

"Shit," he breathed as his fingers brushed over her slick

folds, then dipped in to expose her wet heat. "*Shit*, you're so wet. So soft."

"Then do something about it," she replied.

She had severely underestimated the power of a man's touch. His seeking fingers sent her spiraling so much faster and were so much more intoxicating than in her fantasies. Caspian was fully prepared to take exactly what he wanted, and that might be the very thing she wanted, too.

His zealous reply came out through his lips, his hands, his entire body, and for the first time she didn't want to be the one in control. She wanted to forget all the things that had held her down.

"Back to my chest," he instructed, positioning her between his legs. His fingers withdrew and she whined in frustration, but then sighed as she felt every dip of muscle in his chest. A delicate bite to the shoulder elicited a distorted moan from her lips. Then, the vibrator pressed into her palm.

"Go at your own pace," he whispered, breath tickling the spot he just kissed as his hand pushed hers toward her center. Though her body lit up with sensation, the thought of having an audience was unnerving.

Need rose again as his lips roamed between her neck and shoulder, and instinctively she found her hand reaching to find relief. Caspian hummed encouragements into her skin as the cool touch of the wand slid over her clit. The feeling of familiar arousal flooded her, already so turned on she didn't need vibration. Smooth movements granted her an outlet at last, all her breath leaving in one prolonged sigh.

"Damn, you moan so pretty for me," Caspian whispered. His hand slipped behind her and unclasped her bra, her hardened nipples brushing against the fabric of her shirt. The tip of his fingers grazed over the delicate skin of her ribs, and she shuddered, moaning again as he weighed her breasts one after the other.

Her legs opened wider, body contracting as she pushed the tip of the vibrator inside herself, arching her back. The heat of Caspian's hands hardened her nipples until they hurt, and she whimpered as he pinched and lengthened her breasts with skilled fingers. With his other hand, he reached between her legs and found her clit.

Oh. *Oh.*

The pad of his thumb kept an unyielding tempo, the pace of a man with single-minded determination. His touch wasn't soft like her own fingers, but wasn't rough either, and the double— no, triple stimulation had pleasure ripping through her like a tidal wave.

He certainly knew his way around a woman's body, and right now she was anything but upset about it.

Hand quivering, she tried to work the vibrator with a steady pace but failed miserably. Too much demanded her attention. Reading her mind, or rather her body, Caspian shifted and carefully took over the wand. Tilting it with ease, he hit deeper, firmer, and shattered her from the inside out. All remaining control slipped as passion consumed her.

The last of her emotional barricades snapped in two.

Legs shaking, she became helpless against his skill. Her mewls mingled with gasps for air as she fought the tension building in her core. This was more intense than she'd ever known, and cresting the peak scared her. But there was no stopping. No going back.

"Say my name," he breathed into her ear.

She couldn't even remember her own.

He slowed just enough to draw out her pleasure, waiting for a response. The one brain cell still active recognized his voice, and she whispered his name, the taste lingering on her lips.

The taste of his victory. Which at this moment was sweeter than the forbidden fruit itself.

She strained as she braced for impact, jaw gaping open in

bliss. At the exact moment she began to combust, Caspian switched on the vibration.

And it was game over.

Crying for mercy, she came undone as he held her to his firm chest.

Wave after wave of gratification washed over her, turning her bones to jelly and stealing away her last bit of sanity. The world turned black, and through a pinhole of whatever nerves weren't burnt out, she felt him gradually slow and peck a kiss into the crook of her neck.

"Beautiful."

THIRTY-TWO

Caspian

SO PERFECT. EXQUISITE.

He feathered his fingers over Nia's stomach as she came down from the high, admiring the beauty mark next to her belly button. Gradually, her breaths returned to a natural pace. She'd been as erotic as he'd imagined, and marvelously responsive to his touch.

He'd happily stay like this as long as she let him, but he'd be lying if he said he didn't crave more. To send her back into ecstasy and savor some of his own. With how he felt at the moment, he could go all night...but this was still a first for her, and he was trying to respect that.

Nia stirred, turning to read his expression with soft, relaxed eyes. "Um." Concern etched into her voice. "Should...I?" She peeked at his obvious arousal straining against his pants.

A chuckle rumbled from his throat. He wrapped an arm around her waist and pulled her into him, using his body for comfort instead of pleasure. "Are you up for that?"

Doubt flickered in her expression.

"I'm not expecting anything," he added. If she were apprehensive about returning the favor, he wouldn't guilt her into it. He held no delusions that she'd jump him out of the gate, and he had plenty of ideas to get her ready and willing.

"Oh, okay." Her gaze dropped down. "I'm a mess, aren't I?"

"A beautiful mess." He pressed a kiss to the corner of her mouth, relishing the flare of red that darkened her cheeks. "A mess I've been waiting to see ever since I first set eyes on you."

She went stiff, then leaned away to hook her bra and crawled out of bed. A pang of emptiness resonated in his chest.

"Do you want to leave?" she asked, avoiding eye contact as she dressed. "It's okay if you do."

That was a question he wasn't used to. Normally, he wouldn't have stopped so early on, and out of exhaustion when finished, never really cared what girls did when they were done. It was the first he'd been expected, or cared enough, to bridge the gap.

"No," he answered and got up to embrace her. Tension eased in his chest as he brought his lips to her forehead. "We can do whatever you want."

"Whatever I want," she repeated in a whisper. Her breath hitched, hands balling the fabric of his shirt. If they weren't standing so close, he wouldn't have heard her mumble, "Because you got what you wanted, didn't you?"

"Wh—" Glancing down, he saw a tear sparkle in the corner of her eye. "Hey, what's the matter?"

His hand cupped her cheek and brushed away the offending tear. Small crinkles spread across her face; the pristine, content expression from before evaporated like morning dew. His heart dropped at the loss.

She sniffled and turned away. "This is what you wanted all along...since you saw me in the lecture hall, right?"

"Y—" This felt like a trap.

"You didn't even know me." She looked at him as pain flashed across her face.

"That's not the point." He tried to pull her back to him, but she stepped away. "I waited until I *did* know you. Don't you get it? I *want* you, Nia. I did, and I do." He'd take her any way he could get. Was it a crime to want all of it?

"You wouldn't understand," she said quietly, then motioned to the now cold and rumpled bed. "Getting a girl to take her clothes off is normal for you. You may not feel anything from it, but for me, it's..." She took in a shaky breath and steadied her voice. "I thought it meant more than that."

"I do feel, Nia," he whispered. "I feel a lot from it."

A pause filled the empty space between them. "How many?" she asked under her breath. "How many girls have you gotten to undress without a second thought?"

"Does that matter?" he grit out. Despite his efforts to hide the emotion in his voice, the words came out harsher than expected. "You just came apart for me, and this is how you react?" It hurt to know she still compared herself to all the girls he *clearly* wasn't with. If he wanted, he could leave this room and find a handful of girls willing to do a lot more than strip for him. He thought he'd already settled these doubts.

"It matters. I want to know," she insisted. Fluorescent lights bore down as the atmosphere became less serene with every passing minute.

He sat back on the bed and relented, dragging fingers through his hair. "Fine, I lost count. Does that satisfy you?"

"Two weeks..." she muttered. "We've only been seeing each other for two weeks, and I let my guard down." A cloak of bitterness covered her like a security blanket, yet underneath glinted the snare of shame. "I told you I wanted to take it slow—but turns out I'm no better than the rest, am I?"

"No." This would be so much easier if she would believe him. "You shouldn't question yourself like this. Ever since I saw you, I saw something I wanted. Not in a physical way, in a..." Words stuck to the back of his throat. "In a...almost every way."

He'd gathered a lot of reasons to want her since that day, but he'd had plenty enough from the start.

"Would you have even waited this long if I didn't make you? Would you have made the effort to care?" She looked up, a pool of sorrow gathering around her eyelashes.

He clenched his fist at her question. They both knew the answer: he wouldn't have.

She turned. "How can I know I'm not just another piece in your collection, even if I am harder to chase? Hell, that would make it all the more rewarding, right?" Her accusation hit him like a cold stone. "This is all a façade."

"It's not." A part of him was breaking, not being able to touch her or console her. But in the end, he had no defense. His history spoke for itself—it always had. Words would only make it worse, and he couldn't rip his heart out and shove it in her chest, couldn't transfer all these emotions into a form she'd comprehend.

Unable to watch anymore, he looked away. Her mountain of doubt crushed down on him. He hated all of it and was in no position to deal with both of their wounds. "So all that matters to you is my past, now?"

"*Is* it your past?" Nia countered. "You've done this countless times with countless girls. Not even six months ago, you led on some other freshman, and when she wouldn't give in, you slept with her friend instead."

Six months ago... His eyes widened in shock.

"You don't know anything about what happened six months ago." The threatening tone probably didn't help their situation, but it was either that or lose his shit. The last thing he ever wanted to remember had been thrown like a knife toward his heart by someone he least expected it from. "If anyone's past is getting in the way here, it's yours." Her jaw dropped, and he walked past her to the door. "Next time you decide to do your homework on me, maybe ask instead of snooping around."

Sparing a glance at her one last time, he looked her in the eye. Instead of cursing or yelling an insult like he expected, she only cried. That hurt more than words ever could.

"I just wanted you to l—" A sniffle cut off the sentence.

She wanted him to leave.

But he couldn't move. Frozen, he mulled the situation over and over, but his brain refused to function. The synapses just weren't firing.

Fuck.

So then, it was over. She was the first girl he wanted to shower with cuddles and late-night conversations and to *stay.* Now this.

Silently, he turned and left.

The drive home was filled with static, like his mind got stuck on a broken channel. He couldn't even tell if his heart was still beating or not. Then, after the first step into his apartment, he noticed it. No traces of Nia. Not her laughter, or her no-nonsense comments, nor her listening ear.

Pushing aside a stack of notebooks, he sat down on the couch. Where he usually sat with her. Images of their short-lived time together crowded his mind. Nia at the park, hair shimmering in the sun. Nia deep in thought, absorbed in her studies. Nia rolling her eyes and giggling at his lame jokes. Nia returning his gaze, looking into his soul. Nia calling out his name...

Nia crying, alone, in her dorm.

He bent over and pushed a tear back into the corner of his eye. His fingers still smelled like her.

THIRTY-THREE

Nia

THE ALARM SIGNALED THE BEGINNING OF A NEW DAY, AND SHE struggled through routine movements. Get dressed, brush teeth, straighten hair, walk to class, take notes.

Don't think about Caspian.

The latter was considerably hard to do, not only because of her emotional state but also the collection of dark blotches unceremoniously lining one side of her neck. She vaguely wondered how such painful-looking bruises got there without her noticing. Well, she had noticed, but receiving them certainly didn't feel the same as how they looked.

Of course, she hadn't seen them until just before walking out. Fate must have pitied her because she checked the mirror just in time to snatch a scarf and sent praises to the sky that it was cold enough to justify the extra layer.

Memories of last night continued to suck warmth out of her spirit. The blue pillows she had once thought were cute and chic now reminded her of Caspian's eyes and the bed sheets— she'd have to buy new ones.

The hardest part was that sharing such an intimate experience with him had been good, euphoric even, but temporary. Worse, being alone felt emptier ever since he left. She hadn't been able to keep things slow, to keep it safe, and the more time she spent with him, the harder it would get.

She couldn't help but recall how one-sided her past relationship had been. How easily her ex had faked feelings, faked a sense of attraction, and said who knows what behind her back to his friends. She *had* to brace for the downside, the recoil before it took her by surprise. Maybe she hadn't been Caspian's easiest catch, but he still caught her in the end.

She accepted he was right, that the flaw lay in her past—in her very genes. None of her mother's relationships lasted longer than a few years, and her mom had used it as an excuse to never get married. Nothing could last forever. Nia always questioned that line of logic: why start something you don't want to finish? Then Caspian came and adjusted her perspective. Although she never tried to assume how long she and Caspian would last, she didn't expect it to end so soon.

She couldn't let the pitter-patter of her heart start up again. Ever. It was impossible not to get hurt. The pain simply outweighed the pleasure. Letting herself feel had been a fatal mistake—and now she felt numb.

For a while, she soothed her consciousness by placing the blame on him. On men in general. She told herself this heartache was Caspian's fault for being so tempting. And if only men took all relationships seriously, broken hearts wouldn't be so common.

Eventually she admitted she had been stupid enough to fall for him.

Caspian's number should have been deleted long ago. It was too late now. She had a feeling if she turned on her phone, his messages would be waiting. A pit in her stomach formed every time she thought about reading his words, whether they pleaded for forgiveness or hurled insults. Or worse, said nothing at all. All that mattered was she wouldn't be greeted with his usual "good morning" or playful emoji.

Rounding the corner to her section of the dorms, she stopped in front of her door. That was the last place she wanted to be right now. Besides the bitter memories of last night, she felt sick at the thought of being alone.

Looking further up the hallway, she eyed the common area where Ivory, Serena, and Avril were talking around a table piled high with textbooks. Their smiles and laughter brightened the bare modern furniture and beige walls. Nia wondered why she hadn't at least tried to study more with them earlier. She tugged the scarf to cover her neck and walked toward them.

"—so I was like, boy, bye!" Avril finished, then noticing Nia, turned to give her a welcoming smile. "Oh, hi, Nia."

Serena met Nia's eyes, and her smile wavered for a moment but quickly recovered. Something softened in her eyes, and she returned to being as chipper as usual. That was a relief.

Nia attempted a smile and a friendly wave. "Hey."

"Come join us," Ivory said, waving and clearing out a spot on the table.

Mumbling thanks, she pulled out the remaining empty chair and sat her backpack on the table. Their textbooks lay open to the chapter title and pens were scattered on the table. It was clear the girls hadn't been doing much studying, but she wasn't ahead on homework like normal, so she brought out her own textbook in hopes to get back on track.

"I was just retelling my horrible dating life," Avril informed with a dramatic sigh. "You didn't miss much, not if you want to hear about me puk—"

"Please not again!" Ivory and Serena exclaimed at the same time.

Nia laughed, for a moment forgetting her own troubles.

"Sounds bad enough without me having to hear the whole story."

Avril rolled her eyes. "Believe me, it is."

"How have you been?" Serena asked, directing her attention to Nia. Though innocent, her question felt strangely personal. The one time she had to ask, the answer wasn't so simple.

"Um, not bad. You know, school and stuff," she mumbled, toying with the ends of her scarf.

"I heard you've been hanging out with Caspian a lot lately." Avril wiggled her eyebrows. "Quite the looker he is."

Nia's face flushed and her hands clenched around the delicate fabric. Her reaction must have been obvious because concern colored Ivory's face. "Oh no, did something happen?"

"Kind of..." Nia looked down, not wanting to put her personal life out there. "It's not something anyone needs to worry about. I'm not sure we were even together, but we aren't anything anymore, so it's not important."

"I'm so sorry to hear that," Serena said, a sympathetic edge in her voice that didn't quite reach her eyes.

"Give me the word, and I will *break* him." Ivory sounded serious, like she had done this before. Nia wasn't sure if she should be scared or grateful but settled on the latter.

"Thanks, Ivory, but you don't need to. Besides, I doubt you'll be able to do much damage. No offense," Nia said, attempting a joke. Ivory was taller than her but much thinner. Compared to Caspian's brick wall of a body, she looked like a feather.

Ivory pouted and squared her shoulders. "You think I would risk brawling with my bare hands? Oh no, can't scar these beauties." She held up her hands, wiggled her fingers, then made a swinging motion. "Give me a crowbar, however..."

"Woah, hold on, I don't need anyone to end up in jail for assault." Nia opened her eyes wide in mock protest. "But at least I know not to mess around with you." Serena and Avril laughed at Ivory's antics, and Nia joined in. It felt good to be laughing today, something she didn't think would happen for a while.

"I really don't want to rain on your parade, but that's Caspian for you. The local heartbreaker," Avril said once she caught her breath.

"What do you mean?" Nia asked. Avril was a sophomore like Caspian. She had never thought about it before, but maybe Avril had known Caspian from before.

"He's always leading girls on. I've heard from a few of his previous interests that once they turned him down for sex, he left them for someone else just like that. Typical playboy, only in it for one thing." Avril shook her head and gave a sympathetic half-smile. "Don't feel like you're the only one. I'm sure he brags about exploiting a new girl almost every weekend."

A pit settled in Nia's stomach. Would he go around bragging about her, too? She knew she wasn't the only one, but still...she had turned down Caspian every day they spent together. It had even become like an inside joke, and he never seemed bothered by it. Then again, maybe he just got better at waiting.

"Glad I don't have to deal with him," Serena said with a wave of her hand. "I'm not ready for the dating game yet."

Avril turned her attention to Serena and rolled her eyes. "Maybe you're not ready for the dating game, but playing truth or dare is right up your alley if I remember correctly." They both burst out in a fit of laughter.

"What happens at Beta Rho stays at Beta Rho," Serena said between giggles.

"You're still going over there?" Ivory asked them.

"Yeah," Avril answered. "They're fun. You should join us sometime, Nia."

"Oh, parties aren't my scene," she quickly declined.

"Come on, the guys there would love you," Serena said. "I'm sure you can find a replacement for Caspian."

"He doesn't need to be replaced," Nia interjected. Not only had this conversation become uncomfortable, she was starting to feel targeted.

"Don't worry, not all guys are looking for sex. You can just come to unwind, ya know?" Avril said.

"It's not like Caspian only wanted sex." The words flew out of her mouth before she knew what had happened.

Whether true or not, she didn't want to be put in the same category as his other flings. And she didn't want the others talking about Caspian like he was the worst guy on the planet. She'd known plenty of men who were far worse, and she had gone along with his game in the first place.

"Nia, we didn't mean to insult you," Ivory said gently.

Avril and Serena looked away, their mouths clamped shut. Nia's stomach dropped further. Just a moment ago, she had been enjoying their company and had to ruin it with her sorry excuse of a life. "My bad. I guess the whole thing is still fresh."

"Well, in any case, you're always welcome to join us on the weekends," Avril said, all awkwardness forgotten.

"When we don't have to pretend to be studying," Serena added.

Ivory sighed. "Speaking of, we should get to work. My assignment is due by midnight."

Nia smiled, happy her comment didn't cause more issues. She cracked open her textbook, for once looking forward to the monotony of homework.

"Nia."

She froze mid-page and felt the others do the same.

It was Caspian.

THIRTY-FOUR

Caspian

THE BLESSING OF AN ENTIRELY SLEEPLESS NIGHT WAS HE DIDN'T give a rat's ass what others thought of him the next morning. Drained from hours of punching out raw emotion in the gym and equipped with dark circles under his eyes, he left on a mission.

He would find Nia. Track her down and make things better. A single evening turned sour wasn't a good enough excuse to ruin what they had. One misunderstanding didn't need to lead to questioning everything else.

The past year, he'd spent his energy finding women he could easily let go of, people who he didn't care to keep. Now confronted with the possibility of loss, he came face-to-face with his best-kept secret, guarded even from himself. *He* was the one scared of getting hurt.

But after his night of self-reflection, he concluded that he never wanted Nia to feel how he did now—abandoned. He never wanted her to feel unappreciated, taken for granted, or alone.

He would do whatever he needed to make her see she

meant something to him. She wasn't on a list and she wasn't just another girl. She was *his* girl.

Or, he wanted her to be.

This time, he'd be prepared, armored against her harsh words and emotional outbursts, and he'd hold his ground. In other words, he was going to man up.

What he'd been too dense to see in the moment was how vulnerable she felt, and to compensate, she became defensive. From day one, she told him about her insecurities, but addressing them once didn't make it magically disappear. He'd also left out details from his past and waltzed around like he didn't have any issues. Then when they came out, it blinded them both.

He waited until her classes finished for the day and drove to the dorms. Not sparing any more time to think of what state he'd find her in, he strode in, and as he came to her door, her voice drifted from down the hall. The sight of her felt like a punch to the gut. There she was, smiling around a table with the other girls. Like any ordinary day.

Except, Nia looked better than any ordinary day.

His heart constricted, and the plan he'd made crumbled into pieces. Clearly, he needed her more than she needed him. Would she be happier without him? His chest squeezed in adamant protest, and his legs carried him toward her voice, toward her shining, pale blue eyes and impeccable face. His sleep-deprived brain could only muster up one word—one word that had passed from his lips endlessly in the past 24 hours.

"Nia."

He hated how he sounded, but he'd gone past the point of caring. This was too important to let pride get in the way.

All four girls froze. Nia was the last to look up. His gaze fixed on her, registering the flash of pain that flickered across her features before defiance rose to the surface.

"Nia, I need to talk to you," he tried again.

The sharp scrape of chair legs against linoleum filled the deafening silence as she stood in a rush then stared back at him.

"Give me a moment, okay?" She directed her question at the other girls, but her eyes didn't leave his. Ivory whispered something, and Nia nodded, a fragile smile tipping up the corners of her mouth before being replaced by a firm line.

She walked up to him, then veered past without another word. He followed into her dorm, the joyful and carefree attitude he usually wore transformed into something he usually avoided at all costs.

The door closed with a muted click, and he opened his mouth. "Listen, I know—"

She stopped him by holding up a hand. "You don't have to explain." Crossing her arms, she chewed her lip, eyes cast down as she continued. "I let things go too far last night, and I should have known better."

Regret coursed through him like a thick drug. They chose to be intimate together, but now she blamed herself for what he could've corrected. Up close, he saw her eyelids were swollen and puffy, and from the looks of it, more waterworks were on the way.

Brushing her scarf aside, he gently skimmed the darkened surface of her skin with the pad of his thumb. "I gave you these to make you happy, not so you'd feel ashamed."

She kept chewing her lip, either not willing—or not able—to speak.

"The past can stay in the past," he continued, keeping his tone soft and neutral. "What matters is the present and that I want you in it."

She raked her eyes up to his, voice hoarse but firm as she asked, "What about the future?"

The future.

That thing that had been his Achilles heel ever since he learned it was out of his control, no matter how hard he tried or how often he wished it was. Last night had only been further proof.

For a moment, he stared at her, searching every crevice of his brain, every dark corner of his heart for the right words. "Believe me when I say you mean more to me than anyone—I care more about you than I care about myself." He sucked in a sharp breath. "We just need to keep going and figure it out as we go."

A whimper died on her pursed lips, and she shook her head. "I can't do that."

She wiped a tear away, and he cupped her cheek.

"Nia." That was the only word he had left—all he had left. And he was losing her.

"I've seen what that leads to," she continued, composing herself as she clutched the golden heart pendant around her neck. "One day, things fall apart, and there's nothing else you can do because you weren't looking for it."

Her icy gaze pierced into his soul, and for a moment, he saw below the surface. The entirety of a looming glacier she hid from everyone else. He felt every cold, jagged edge she'd been forced to climb over before she should have even been exposed to it.

"What's the difference if you leave now or if you leave later?" she asked in a whisper.

His air supply cut off. What was breathing when all he could think of was her pain? He hadn't foreseen the consequences of last night, so how was he supposed to prevent the things that would come up down the road? He hadn't even protected her from himself.

At the end of the day, all he could offer were empty promises for a life he'd always believed was out of his reach.

The promise of till death do us part hadn't worked for his parents—why would it, or anything less, work for him?

"Don't ask me to leave again," he whispered. "Just don't..."

"Again?" she asked, confusion contorting her face. "I never asked you to leave."

"Yesterday, you said that's what you wanted—"

"No." She shook her head. "I was saying I wanted you to *love* me."

His eyes widened.

"Then I realized," she continued with a sad smile. "You probably don't even know what that word means—you said it yourself."

The anvil fell.

The word he needed was right there, forming in his brain, but it stuck to the roof of his mouth, coated his tongue like syrup too thick to swallow. She was right.

He had no idea of love, no experience. He had no right to use that word.

An unrepentant playboy couldn't put on shining armor one day and call himself a prince the next. He wasn't meant to rescue the princess—he was no cure for her curse. Why had he ever thought someone like him could be enough for someone like her?

Straightening the scarf, Nia squared her jaw and chased away all traces of sorrow. "It's okay. You don't have to try anymore, Caspian."

The look she gave him was absolute. Awkwardly, she walked around him to open the door and went back to the common room.

He lost. Everything.

Unable to speak, he shuffled out of her dorm, back outside, and into his car.

He pulled out his phone in hopes something changed in

the last five minutes. Maybe this was Nia's way of getting back at him. Maybe there'd be a text saying it was all a joke.

Nothing.

He opened his messages and scrolled until his thumb stopped on a conversation. The one person who wouldn't throw shit in his face. Well, no more than he deserved, anyway. A part of him wondered if this was karma, if this experience was something he was required to go through for all the times he disregarded what others thought was important.

> You free tonight? I might need a beer.

> Or two.

PUKE HAIR

> I think I have a few in the fridge.

THIRTY-FIVE

Caspian

ADRIAN PUSHED OFF THE COUCH, BEER IN ONE HAND AND A PACK of cigarettes in the other. "Need a smoke break, wanna head out to the porch before we go another round?"

"If there's a breeze," Caspian replied. "You know I hate the smell of those things." He paused the video game and got up anyway. The only light in Adrian's apartment came from a blue glow from the television, but since the layout reflected his own, he knew his way around. Stopping at the fridge, he pulled out another beer and popped off the lid, metal clanking as it joined a pile of others on the table.

The alcohol hardly held its taste, but the tension inside him eased a little with every bottle. He didn't know if tomorrow was a weekday or not. It didn't matter. He'd gotten so far ahead from studying with Nia that he didn't need to go to class. A hangover was the least of his concerns.

Drinking like this normally didn't appeal to him, but he did indulge from time to time. Used to drink a lot more than he should've at all the parties. Those times felt different, like a prelude to a crash rather than trying to pick up the pieces from one.

By the time he made his way out into the cold night air, Adrian had already lit up a cigarette and positioned himself downwind on the porch. The tiny space could hardly fit both of them, built for the mandatory fire escape laws rather than actual use. The laid-back atmosphere reminded him of the first time he drank on his sixteenth birthday. His dad had given him the whole safe-drinking speech, followed by a lesson on which beer brands weren't half bad for a cheap price.

He'd never noticed if his parents drank much outside of the occasional glass of wine, but after the divorce, beer cans started to fill the recycle bin. Though it hadn't seemed like much, since the entire house steadily got messier every year. That'd been just one thing on the list of changes.

Ever since then, he and his dad drank together every once in a while, mostly on holidays when his mom was off living her new snazzy life with her rich CEO husband. Celebrations weren't the same without her.

Without warning, images of him and Nia conjured in his thoughts. Them opening Christmas presents, blowing out birthday candles, kissing under a grand display of fireworks. He took another swig of the tasteless beer.

"Gonna say what's on your mind, or do I have to play twenty-one questions?" Adrian asked through a puff of smoke.

"Ask away." Some conversations were too hard to start.

Adrian scoffed and looked over the railing to the street below. Caspian followed his gaze. There wasn't much going on tonight, just a few people walking on the sidewalk as the streetlamps poured sickly yellow light into the darkness.

"What'd you do?" Adrian asked.

He should have known better than to play this game with Adrian—he always got to the heart of the matter. "I fucked up."

"Give me another reason why you're on my porch drinking yourself into oblivion." Adrian sighed and took another drag on his cigarette, the end glowing orange before dimming again. "What happened to your girl?"

"She's gone."

Adrian pursed his lips and let out a steady cloud of smoke from his nose. He took his time crushing the end of his cigarette into a metal sardine can, then turned to look Caspian square in the eye. "What. Happened."

Caspian set his beer down and swallowed the lump in his throat. This was the reason he came here in the first place. Hours of drinking and smashing buttons didn't change that. "I pushed her too far. She got scared, thinks I just wanted to fuck." He rubbed his temple, frustration and fatigue splitting open his head. "Worst part is, I can't prove her wrong."

"Mhm," Adrian hummed. "Sounds like you fucked up."

"Thanks for the clarification."

"Think you can get her back?"

He sighed and gave the beer bottle a longing glance. "Unlikely."

Adrian paused, a grim look weighing down his angled features. "Tough luck." After a stretch of silence, he continued. "All I can say is don't mope around forever. And—" He shot a pointed stare at Caspian. "Learn for the next time."

"The hell is that supposed to mean?" Caspian scoffed. As far as advice went, that was pretty cut and dry.

"If you love someone, don't beat around the bush," Adrian said flatly. Caspian's chest tightened. "There's more to communicating your feelings than being a good lay."

Caspian turned to face the street, preferring to stare into the night air rather than contemplate Adrian's words. Tiny specks of dust floated in and out of his vision like microscopic aliens.

"Oh, my bad, are you allergic to the "L" word?" Adrian joked, reopening the barely sealed wound. "Listen, I know deep down you're a decent enough guy, or else I wouldn't be entertaining you right now. You picked a woman who doesn't fool around and saw through your crap. It's no wonder you fell in love."

"Is that so?" Caspian mused, picking up his beer again, but not lifting it to his lips. The liquid swirled as he turned the bottle.

"That girl tolerated you even though she wanted nothing to do with your lifestyle. She cared about you. No matter what you think, you cared about her, too," Adrian said. "I could hear you two laughing from across the hall, and I know you avoid letting girls stay in your apartment."

"Shit," Caspian cursed. Pain seeped through the wall of alcohol poisoning his veins. Those happy memories reduced to ammunition, firing from the subconscious straight into his heart.

"Did you ever make it clear what exactly you wanted from her?" Adrian asked.

Caspian furrowed his brow. "I don't want anything from her, that's the point. I want *her*."

"For how long?"

The question threw him off guard. "That's never been a part of my thought process. All I know is that I want her here." He paused and remembered to breathe, relieving some of the pressure in his chest. "Even if she's mad at me, her standing right here would make life a million times better."

Adrian reached for his beer. "You got some sorting out to do."

A thought pricked Caspian's brain like a splinter. "What if I *had* confessed everything sooner, went all mushy, and she still had this trust issue business? What if she asked for space after all that? I wouldn't be able to pick myself up off the damn floor." He downed the rest of the beer, and this time it left a bitter taste in his mouth. "There are reasons I don't go throwing my heart out to people."

"I know," Adrian replied. "Even so, a player isn't boyfriend material, no matter what people think or say. When you decide to change your modus operandi, expect backlash. You'll always have to work harder when you try to improve."

The night air stood still around the pair as Adrian's words sunk in, and he couldn't deny their truth. He'd barely mentioned his own past, never even brought up what happened between him and Jewelle six months ago. On the other hand, Nia had been completely vulnerable with him.

A heavy sigh pierced the silence, and with a raised eyebrow, Adrian employed one of his favorite sayings. "Love can be a fucked-up game, and if you play fucked up games..."

"...you get fucked up prizes," Caspian finished.

Adrian nodded and gazed off into the distance, lost in his own world of who knows what. "I hear love is worth it, though."

"Think you'll ever give it a go?" he asked.

At first, Adrian didn't respond; didn't even move a muscle. Caspian wondered if he'd officially had too much to drink.

"If I ever get to play at love, it will be love that finds me, not the other way around." Adrian pushed off the railing. "Ready to play another round?"

"Yeah," he replied. "You're not going to get another win tonight, puke hair. I'm ten times better drunk than sober."

Adrian laughed and shook his head. "Hate to break it to ya, but you've been drunk the whole night, dog breath."

THIRTY-SIX

Nia

NESTLING DEEPER INTO IVORY'S BEAN BAG, SHE PEERED INTO HER bag of popcorn. About halfway through the movie, she'd forgotten all about the snack's existence, so plenty of buttery goodness was left over. "That was really good," she said as the credits rolled. "We should watch more spy movies."

"Yes!" Ivory squealed from on the bed. "There are two more movies in this series, and after those, I know you'll like my other favorites..."

"Sounds fun," she replied before Ivory could add any more movies to the already long list. "I thought spy movies were all action, but there were some cute romance scenes in there, too."

Ivory giggled and clutched her pillow tighter. "I *know*. I swear I would marry that man if I could."

"Says the girl who's afraid to ride a motorcycle." Nia rolled her eyes, though Ivory probably didn't notice.

"Hey, I've been meaning to ask..." Ivory sat up, crinkling the purple bedspread, and fixed her eyes on Nia. "How are you doing with the whole Caspian thing? It's been a few weeks now."

She tried sinking into the bean bag completely, but it didn't work. "We haven't talked since..." Her voice faded, and her attempt at a neutral smile failed. Instead, she looked away, hiding what she could of her face. "I don't know if what I'm feeling is real." She took a deep breath. "I changed with him, and I needed a break to figure it all out."

Emotion welled up in her chest, and she stuffed a handful of popcorn in her mouth. She had been wrong to think life would feel the same as it had before. It would never be the same again.

"Changed in what way?" Ivory asked.

She swallowed, the placebo of the salty snack taking effect. Her stomach growled in approval—or maybe in protest.

With Caspian, she hadn't doubted herself or her actions, but as soon as he left, her trust issues hit harder than ever before. In such a short time, she had become addicted to him—his touch, his words, his presence—and she hated how he could've capitalized on it.

The same thought plagued her every night. Would that moment have been different if she hadn't let herself catch feelings? If she accepted his attention as he first presented it—limited to sexual attraction and nothing more?

She didn't have any answers, so instead asked the other question rattling around in her head, "Do you think sex really means anything? Or is it only a chemical reaction?"

Ivory leaned back and sighed. "Depends, I guess. Sex can be many things. Physical, emotional, spiritual...good and bad, in-between. The problem is judging what it means to the people involved. At the very least, I doubt it equates to love."

Nia's frown deepened. She knew sex didn't equate to love. But whenever she thought of Caspian being with other girls in that way, it made her sick, unrightfully so. They hadn't even been official.

A soft knock came from outside the door.

"Come in," Ivory called.

A blonde head popped in, and after seeing the two of them, Serena slipped inside. "I'm *so* bored, but I have a test tomorrow, and if I don't get at least a B, I'm gonna fail the whole stupid course." She plopped down next to Ivory on the bed. "Which means I can't go out tonight. Which *sucks*."

"I feel you," Ivory sympathized, moving over to make space. "Good luck on your test, though."

"What are you up to?" Serena asked, directing the question at them both.

"Movie night, but it just ended," Nia replied. Things had been more or less patched up between them. Although, she guessed it had more to do with her falling out with Caspian than Serena changing her tune. Serena still made it a point to mention how Caspian didn't show up at parties, and Nia thought it odd how she noticed when it shouldn't matter. "Can I ask you a question?"

"Yeah." Serena shrugged, running her lime green toenails through the furry rug.

Nia hesitated and chewed her lip, unsure of how to word her question without giving too much away. "Do you think sex is important?"

Serena snorted. "In my opinion, only if the guy knows what he's doing."

Ivory rolled her eyes. Nia almost copied the action but got caught too deep in thought.

Serena continued, "That means with most of the guys here, no, sex isn't very important." She looked up, a curious gleam in her eyes. "Was Caspian any good?"

Nia choked on a fistful of popcorn.

"A bit soon, don't you think?" Ivory shook her head and gave a nervous laugh.

"What? It's been more than a week," Serena defended, not fazed in the least.

After her coughing fit died down, Nia managed to gasp out, "We—we didn't actually—"

"Oh." Serena sounded disappointed. "I was hoping to get the full scoop."

Both Nia and Ivory gave her an incredulous look.

"No matter. But if you're looking for some action, there's a big costume party on Friday," Serena announced.

"Oh yeah! I almost forgot." Ivory jumped up and bolted over to rummage through her wardrobe. "I got this super cute outfit from the thrift store. Just wait until you see it."

"You coming, Nia?" Serena asked.

"Oh, I um..." Her only other experience with these types of events had been at the club, and she was sure a costume party would get a lot more wild. Especially with the stories she'd heard about the frat parties, and those never sounded very fun in the end.

"It might be good for you to get out, be around some new people," Ivory suggested, voice muffled by a rack of hanging clothes. "This party only happens once a year."

A costume party didn't sound half-bad. If she was sensible, it might even be fun dressing up. Or at least Ivory would have fun in the role of costume designer.

"You could go to find out what's important for yourself," Serena added with a wink.

Nia's eyes widened. That was it—her issue hadn't been going too far with Caspian. It wasn't her fear of sex, but rather tossing her heart on the line. Of placing too much importance in something that might not mean anything.

She needed to try something different.

Sitting in the dorms had only stuffed her feelings down further, left them to grow mold like all her other issues. A lot of progress that made. If she wanted answers, she needed to take action.

"Okay, I'll go."

Serena and Ivory gave her a little cheer. "Yay!" Serena chimed. "I'll ask Avril if she can drive all three of us."

"Do you have a costume?" Ivory asked, turning with a ball of crumpled fabric in hand.

"I figured you could help me with that part?" Nia replied sheepishly.

No sooner had the words left her mouth than Ivory's arms flung around her neck. "Oh, yes! You are not going to regret this."

She hoped not.

"I have a request, though." Nia untangled herself from Ivory and looked between the other two girls. "For both of you."

"Hm?" Serena looked up from her phone, most likely messaging Avril.

"I might not have the best style sense for these things, so can you make me look...um, sexier?"

Serena gave her a radiant smile. "Oh, definitely."

Ivory's voice became muffled by clothes as she went back to digging through her wardrobe. "Have no fear, Nia dear, your fairy godmother is here!"

3

Strips of chiffon-dyed burgundy and deep violet billowed around long, pale legs. Ghostly smooth skin peeked through small gaps in coy flirtation, and a clasped cloak cascaded down from shoulders decorated in lace. Underneath a pointy-brimmed hat, Ivory's lips boasted a sinful plum and her olive eyes shone mischievously through a shadow of smoke and sparkles.

"Ahaha! Double, double, toil and trouble! 'Tis time to make my love potion bubble!" Ivory made a swirling motion with her hands and scrunched up her face.

"*Pffft.*" Nia couldn't keep her laughter in any longer.

Serena doubled over, trying not to mess up her winged makeup. "—please!" She gasped for breath. "I don't think you'll bewitch anyone looking like a madwoman."

An uncharacteristic pout broke Ivory's evil demeanor, and she transformed from a troublesome witch into a disheartened young maiden. "Maybe if I try in the dark, I'll look scarier."

"You're not supposed to be scary. You're supposed to be cute," Serena countered.

The point was well-backed by Serena's costume, a skimpy red dress paired with a short pointy tail and two miniature horns poking out of her golden hair. The dress flared out at her hips, not shy about revealing the origin of her temporary devil's tail.

"I think if you give up the chanting and potion brewing, you'll look just fine. There are good witches too, you know," Nia offered.

She also sported a dress that fell to her ankles in two cream-colored sheets, separated by slits that traveled up the side of each tanned thigh. A golden rope cinched her wait, similar pieces knotted around one arm and her temple. Long brown curls tumbled to her mid-back, red hair tucked neatly under a wig. Her makeup, compliments of Serena, looked flawless— deep brown eyeshadow accentuated golden flecks that gave her blue eyes a special pop.

Ivory huffed and gave up on the witch act, returning to her upbeat demeanor. "Can't argue with the goddess of love. I'm so proud. Your costume came out great, Nia."

"Thanks." Nia beamed. Ivory had the idea to dress her as Aphrodite, and it was absolutely brilliant. She'd never felt so beautiful, or so prepared to tackle the night ahead. If Caspian had only been a whim, a detour on her road to true self-awareness, then she'd prove it tonight.

Avril rounded the corner and walked into the dorm common room. Her costume matched Serena's in style, but instead of flashy red she wore pristine white topped off with a feathery halo. "Thanks for waiting guys, I'm all set." She dangled her keys for them all to see. "Shall we?"

They clambered outside, rushing to the safety of an enclosed car against the icy breeze. Nia shuddered to think of what would've happened if she tried walking in the two-inch torture chambers the others suggested instead of her modest sandals. Arriving first, the lights flashed as Avril unlocked the doors and Nia took shelter in the backseat.

Serena followed close behind and plopped in the passenger seat, skin covered with goosebumps. Ivory and Avril climbed in at the same time, and with a roar the engine started.

"Heat, heat, *heat*," Serena chanted as she fiddled with the controls. Soon heavy pop music filled the car and the road sped up beneath their feet.

She watched as streetlights and shuttered houses went by in a blur. The others sang along to a song she didn't know, but it had a good vibe and got her heart pumping. The last time she sat in the back seat of a car dressed to go out was the night Caspian took them to the club.

A sickly scoff left her lips, drowned out by the sound of mingled voices and a bumping bass line. Her thoughts were so different today than they were then. She hadn't been able to write anything with real emotion these past weeks. It'd all fallen flat. What she had first thought was writer's block turned out to be inspiration, and once Caspian left, the real creative shutdown set in.

As they got close to the frat house, she spotted a costumed couple walking along the sidewalk. Her gaze followed the pair until the car swung into a parking spot and cut them out of view. The street filled with groups of students clad in various stages of dress, all headed toward a large but otherwise ordinary-looking house.

Showtime.

"All right, girls, before we go in…" Avril turned in her seat to lock eyes with each of them. "I'll be sober in case you need me or a lift home."

"You're the best, Avril," Ivory said. Usually, she stayed sober at parties to drive, but this was her break.

Avril giggled. "Trust me, I drank more than enough at this party last year." Her face straightened. "Okay—let's go have fun!!"

"Can count on that," Serena giggled along and swung open her door.

A blast of cold air spiked Nia's nerves and gave her heart a jump. She stepped out onto the street and placed a hand over her chest. With each step toward the bustling house, her conviction grew. Tonight was the night she'd let go.

It might not be her element, but for once, she welcomed it. Change had been coming for a long time. She'd been to heartbreak point and back, so there was nothing to be afraid of anymore.

Tonight, she was untouchable.

THIRTY-SEVEN

Nia

THE PULSE IN HER VEINS RACED TO THE BEAT OF POP MUSIC. Small groups bounced as they danced or chatted, casting aside all worries along with their identities for a night.

Nia wove through the crowd, using the low lighting and anonymity of her costume to avoid sparking any immediate attention. Whispery traces of the exposed skin on her legs and arms warmed as it brushed others, the chill of the night soon replaced by a collective fervor. Wandering eyes left an invisible imprint on her back, and she glanced around, wondering whose gaze she'd attracted.

Instead of locating any onlookers, she spotted a large table of refreshments that beckoned at the side of the room. That should do. She'd left the others to poke around by herself and now needed something to relieve her pesky nerves. For this plan to work, she needed to loosen up.

Making her way over, she turned to accommodate a tall figure. "Excuse me," she muttered.

"Oh," a rumbling voice answered, blending with the music. The man turned to the side. "Here, that better?"

"Yeah, thanks." Her eyes traveled up...tipping her head to see his chest, now pressed closer to hers, and further to land on a chiseled face with several false gashes and a few fake stitches. Thick, dark eyebrows stared down above a friendly smile.

"Woah, you're a tiny one," he noted, bending closer to avoid shouting. "Nice costume." A hint of beer and something stronger tainted his breath. Her heart jumped in her throat. The space felt considerably more cramped than before, but she forced herself to calm down and roll with the punches.

"Glad you like it." She felt a blush heat her cheeks and was grateful the reaction probably went unnoticed— something Caspian would lock onto no matter how hard it was to see.

"If you need some company, we're about to head downstairs for a game of beer pong," he offered.

She weighed her options. "I don't know how to play."

"That's all right." He chuckled and tossed his arm around her shoulders. She flinched away, but he didn't notice. "I happen to know some great tricks, and if you team up with me, you're guaranteed a win."

"Found a new partner, have you, Dane?" A girl in the circle of friends smiled at Nia.

She smiled back and gave a nod to another man she assumed to be the girl's boyfriend. His arms settled around the girl's waist as he handed her a red plastic cup and added, "His promise of victory only holds true if you're not playing against me."

"Hey—" Dane chided.

Their interaction seemed nice enough, but even that weighed on Nia. Could she pretend to be a part of this group when she intended to never see them again?

"Maybe I can meet up with you later?" she asked, returning her gaze to Dane and concluding that, if anything, a drink of two of her own was a top priority.

"Sure, sweet cheeks," he replied and gave her elbow a squeeze.

Any further reply faltered on her lips. With a quick side-step, she slipped away. He'd met her a minute ago and was already using pet names? She expected flirting, but she hadn't been ready for *that*.

Not when it reminded her so much of someone else.

Ducking behind another group next to the refreshment table, she let out a sigh of relief when Dane and his friends were no longer in sight. Her attention returned to the current objective, and she surveyed the available goodies.

Among various treat options, small cups of colorful jello appeared to be a crowd favorite, with one tray already devoured and another dwindling in selection. She grabbed one and popped it in her mouth. A potent, very not-jello flavor hit her tongue. She swallowed quickly.

Craving something to soothe the bite of alcohol, she took a sugar cookie and, despite it not tasting quite the same as she remembered either, discovered jello shots weren't half bad when mixed with something sweet. Another shot got quickly consumed, followed by a cookie chaser. The back of her throat and center of her chest burned. If the effects were already kicking in, then that should do the trick. She grabbed a final cookie and forced herself away from the tempting goodies. The more she ate, the better they tasted.

She wandered around the room and let music flood her ears. Soon, she was swaying, enjoying how the fabric of her dress swished each time she rocked her hips. Her mind settled, watching others with half-lidded eyes as she waltzed along and surveyed how people did this 'party' thing.

On the dance floor, Serena and Avril danced with another girl with long shiny black hair dressed as a fallen angel. She looked familiar, but Nia couldn't place her. The three were all so stunning together. They moved expertly, laughing and singing and grinding in a cluster of bodies. Serena turned to kiss her partner between attempts at belting the lyrics. None of the three cared about who might be watching, or where wandering hands ended up.

The urge to look away slammed into her like a semi-truck. Pivoting faster than her balance was prepared to handle, she lurched forward and face-planted into someone's back.

"Woah, you okay?" The guy turned and steadied her.

"Yeah, I'm fine." She groaned and checked to make sure her nose wasn't bent or bleeding. How embarrassing...did she really expect to dance when she couldn't even walk straight?

"Are you sure?"

The floor tipped beneath her and she stumbled. Reaching out, she grabbed onto a pair of strong arms. But something about them wasn't right.

A concerned face returned her stare, eyebrows knit in concern. An argyle vest and bow tie hung unceremoniously over his white t-shirt, face clean of the showy make-up others had painted on. How fortunate. He was both helpful and attractive.

"What are you supposed to be?" she asked, voice raised above the roar of the party.

He smiled and shook his head as if she told a joke. His hands slid down to her elbows, holding on just enough to make sure she stayed on her feet. His touch felt nice, much better than the jostling contact she'd gotten earlier. She didn't mind how he stepped even closer to speak at a normal volume. "I'm a nerd—or I'm dressed as one."

"Oh, okay." She stared at him, unsure of how to continue. She'd made a fool of herself twice and expected him to turn away by now. A girl came up from behind and tapped him on the shoulder. He looked over as she whispered in his ear. At once, Nia's eyes widened and she took a step back. "I—I didn't know you were here with someone."

He laughed and shuffled closer, eliminating what distance remained between them. "I'm not, she's just a friend." Turning to the girl, he said a few words, to which she winked in reply, then disappeared. "And you?" he asked, returning to Nia. "Are you with anyone?"

"No! Not at all." Her eyes tried to read his face, but for what, she wasn't sure. It was hard to make out his features since everything else was spinning.

"Do you dance?" The music spiked, and she had to focus on his lips to understand. They looked nothing like...she snapped her mind back to the present. *He* was in the past.

Still, maybe this could be done without the kissing part.

She nodded and stretched up on her toes to speak into his ear, bracing her hands on his chest. Now wasn't the time to think about what he looked like. Or who he didn't look like. "I dance, though I'm not very good."

His hands smoothed over her hips as he whispered into her neck. "From what I saw by the snack table, you're more than good."

Their bodies melded together, and he began to guide her steps. She turned her head away and rested it on his shoulder, letting her eyes close. His hips rocked into hers with the music, and magically, she could follow his lead. Her skin blazed, breath caught all in a lump. His hands moved lower and pulled her into him, compelling their movements. A groan vibrated against her neck, but instead of the exhilaration she'd grown accustomed to, it rattled around her.

He was foreign. A wild card that could turn in an instant. Her mind protested, and her muscles tensed.

"Mm, you feel so good," he hummed, lips skimming from her neck to her jaw.

She didn't want this. Not him. Not now. Not ever.

Abruptly, she jerked away, relieved at not feeling his face near hers. But he pulled her back, hot breath fanning her face as he chuckled. "I see we still have to work on your balance."

"Hey, it's about time!" another voice called next to her. She jumped. "I've been looking all over for you." A tug in the opposite direction came from her shoulder.

"Come on, I'll get you away from his guy," the newcomer whispered in her ear.

Wishing only to be free from them both, she stepped back. "Leave me alone."

She turned and sped around a corner, not caring who she bumped into along the way. Once in a less populated and less chaotic hallway, she leaned against the wall for support. Any ideas she had about tonight had been wrong. Her head throbbed as all five of her senses faded in and out.

"Hey," the second voice called again. She looked up to see a green man with an orange headband. "You looked panicked back there." He leaned against the wall beside her.

"Yeah, but I'm okay," she said. "No offense, but I really don't want to talk." The only interaction she wanted at the moment was with someone she knew. If she could find Ivory, maybe there would be some way to salvage the night or simply go home.

"Come on, you're too pretty to be having a bad time," he offered.

You're too pretty.

Her whole body went rigid, alarms sounding loud and clear through the fog in her brain. That's what they said to her back then, too. When they cornered her and tried to strip off her clothes. Bile rose in her gut.

"Get out of my face," she snarled and stepped away. He grabbed her wrist before she could escape. She yanked away in protest, but his grip was stronger than anything she'd felt before.

"Let go of me!" she yelled. His eyes flashed, watching

something behind her. She was one second from kicking him between the legs when he let go and vanished. At the same time, a loud group of guests stumbled into the hallway, singing a muddled version of the song blasting through the house.

Nia backed out of the hallway in search of Ivory. She'd had enough.

THIRTY-EIGHT

Caspian

RECLINED AGAINST THE ROUGH, UNFINISHED BASEMENT WALL AND surrounded by a murmur of drunken conversations, he watched as two tipsy people attempted to play beer pong. It'd been entertaining for a while, but soon became apparent the girl had more talent than her partner, who in turn kept *accidentally* bumping the table to make her miss.

If losing injured the guy's confidence so much—and to a beautiful woman at that—he should've practiced more. Or, preferably, not disabled himself by drinking to the point he couldn't stand straight.

The half-finished beer in Caspian's hand swished as he turned his attention elsewhere. He didn't come to get drunk or to socialize. The only reason he'd been convinced to go out was to get his mind off Nia. To admit it was really over and move on.

If only he didn't look for her in every girl he laid eyes on.

At least the costumes helped, and lots of attractive options had generously showed off their assets, but he couldn't quite let go. He'd already turned down several offers, storing their contacts in his phone for later. Later—as in a time when less drugs were being passed around and the girl might recognize him in the morning.

Then again, perhaps he needed a little inebriation. If he took the plunge and let his body do the talking, some decently attractive kitty-cat would be easy to score. Maybe he could forget, effectively drown his sorrows in someone else. Someone who didn't care about him just as much as he didn't care about them.

But even that felt like a disgrace to Nia. Mindless sex was easy, but it no longer appealed to him. Sure, she'd said it wasn't his fault, but he couldn't put all the blame on Nia either.

The wrong kind of men had torn apart her life and left her with the need to feel safe—he had never been the safe option and probably never could be for anyone else. Before Nia, he simply hadn't been the guy she deserved, and because of that he hadn't wanted to disclose parts of his past. But now it was too late. They didn't need any more drama, and he wasn't going to hold on to the hope for a relationship she didn't want.

He took another sip of beer in hopes to dull the ache of over-thinking. Between working on schoolwork and obsessing over his latest masterpiece, he'd barely left his apartment. Not even Adrian had seen him for a whole week.

"That one has a good ass." Beer in hand, Adrian motioned to a brunette across the room. The woman in question teetered in red stilettos with some friends, her bodysuit more like a stripper's outfit than a fireman's costume. "And she isn't looking for any type of commitment."

"Should I even ask?" He knew Adrian had facts to back up his words but didn't want to sit through the lengthy details.

"Tattoos and piercings." Adrian glanced over, expecting him to catch on. When he didn't, Adrian expanded. "Everyone in her friend group has at least one, but not her. The only jewelry she has is a charm bracelet. They share casual touches, which means they're close, but she doesn't carry anything to symbolize that bond except the bracelet, and that can be taken off. Clearly, she won't commit to something permanent unless she knows there'll be no regrets later."

"But she'll still sleep with a stranger," Caspian wondered aloud.

Adrian gulped a long swig of beer. "In the end it's her choice, but all it takes is someone who knows how to play their cards right."

Caspian hummed in acknowledgement. "I'll give you that, but the brown hair isn't doing it for me."

His eyes roamed the room for the umpteenth time. To his dismay, there remained a severe shortage of Nia-clones. Zero, to be exact.

A curvy masked maiden looked up in time to catch his eye. Lingering on him for a few extra seconds, she gave a cute smile and glanced away, then snuck a second glance at Adrian. She tucked a strand of hair behind her ear and turned to the side, biting her lip.

"Another at 3 o'clock," Caspian muttered as he took a swing of beer.

"Sure you don't want that one?" Adrian looked bored, his go-to emotion at parties of any kind. "If you tilt your head at a 45-degree angle and squint just so—"

"She's too tall," he interjected.

Adrian gave a disappointed grunt, then set his beer down as the maiden walked by, pretending to throw away a scrap of plastic much smaller than half the trash littering the floor.

"You know," Adrian spoke above the music, turning to face her as she passed the second time. "I could enjoy the evening a lot more if you didn't keep staring at me."

She turned on a dime, mouth open in surprise. "I wasn't—"

"If you want my attention, all you have to do is ask." Adrian brought the beer bottle to his lips, smirking as his target searched for a reply.

"What are you—excuse me?" She looked down, any courage she'd built up now obliterated. Sucking in a breath, she braved, "Would you want to, um, get a drink with me?"

"Naw, I already have one." Adrian raised his glass and took another sip of beer. "But I'll take your number instead."

"Oh," came her breathy reply. "Sure."

That's how Adrian worked. He hadn't even put in the effort to wear a costume tonight, although Caspian was sure his newest admirer didn't connect his leather jacket with Adrian's love of bikes. She left with a small smile on her face and a lightness in her step.

"Trouble, incoming," Adrian muttered as soon as his newfound maiden returned to her friends. Caspian looked to his right and saw exactly what Adrian said...trouble.

Tall, thin, and seductive in a short black dress, Jewelle weaved through the crowd of bodies with a coy smile. He snorted at the irony of the two torn and sooty wings hanging from her otherwise exposed back. She wasn't any fallen angel; she was Lucifer incarnate.

His muscles tensed as she approached.

"I see you two are as popular as ever." The woman raised an eyebrow to Adrian, then turned to face Caspian. "And what are you supposed to be, sex on a stick?" Her fingers brushed provocatively down the trident leaning on the wall at his side, raking her eyes over his bare chest as if reliving a fond memory.

"Poseidon," he spat, swiping his trident from her grimy hands. "But to you, I'm Not Interested."

Figures she'd turn up at the first big party he decided to attend. Jewelle had probably been waiting for a chance to sink her claws in his back a second time.

"Aw, that's too bad." She twirled a strand of long, shiny

black hair around her finger. "But at least you remember me this time."

If he weren't trying to be a reformed man, he'd have punched her for that comment—regardless of the fact she was a girl. Adrian shifted beside him, and Caspian wasn't so confident his friend would hold back. Six months ago, Adrian warned him to be careful around Jewelle, but he hadn't thought much of it. That was, until he found himself phasing in and out after a handful of beers. He'd never been a champion drinker, but he hadn't had nearly enough to make him blackout, either.

The next morning, he woke up to the worst hangover of his life, accompanied by a slew of angry texts from the women he'd been chasing—Jewelle's best friend—with no recollection of the night before; but there were enough pictures on the internet to give him a good idea.

The entire school had seen incriminating photos of him and Jewelle naked in a bed, posted along with a rant written by her friend that exposed him for being a useless fuckboy as she cried over a broken heart. Needless to say, he didn't speak to either of them after that. The rumors had been loud enough.

"I remember quite well how much I'd love for you to *fuck off*," he growled. "Nothing's changed. I didn't want you then, and I sure as hell don't want anything to do with you now."

"Oh, don't make me cry," Jewelle sighed. "I only came to see if you could use someone who knows what you like, since you haven't been making your rounds lately."

He scoffed and shouldered past her. What a waste of time— nothing she tried would ever have an effect, despite her pathetic attempts to be relevant.

"Get lost, before I decide you need a shove in the right direction," Adrian warned, voice low and firm. Once she was well behind them, he turned to Caspian. "Gonna grab another drink from the kitchen, want one?"

"No," he replied with a bitter taste in his mouth. "I'm about to find a different type of distraction. He settled against a new wall, searching for someone who could take his mind off both the best and worst women he'd crossed paths with. Suddenly he had a lot to forget, and that's exactly what he was going to do.

THIRTY-NINE

Nia

"OH HEY," IVORY CALLED, DRAWING OUT THE SYLLABLES AS NIA came up beside her. Witch hat skewed to the side, Ivory was all smiles and flushed cheeks, hair frizzed out in true witch fashion. "Whatchu been up to?"

"Nothin impourtant," Nia replied, voice loud and more slurred than she anticipated.

Ivory frowned. "Awww that makes me saaad. How can I cheer you up?"

"Already better." She cracked a smile, feeling lighter and overjoyed to see a friendly face. She let herself sway along with the music. "And I think I'm getting a hang of navergating when the room does song—somersaults."

"Oh dear, you sound like you need a glass of water." Ivory grabbed her hand and guided her through the mass of twisting bodies and scattered cups. "I know just the thing. Or—" She giggled. "—maybe it's more for me than you."

Appreciative of her enthusiasm, Nia happily trailed along. Bright light washed out from an open room and chased away the shadows veiling the rest of the house. Just before they passed through the doorway, Ivory let out a startled squeal, and then her face smashed into Ivory's back. Nia groaned as Ivory abruptly pushed them both in a corner.

"Oh my gosh, I didn't mean to shove you," Ivory apologized in a not-so-hushed whisper, fumbling with the brim of her pointed hat as it combated with the right angle of the wall. "I wasn't expecting...he hasn't been..." She finally got her hat situated and stared at Nia with wide eyes, tongue-tied.

"What? Who?" Nia probed. Ivory couldn't be this agitated over Caspian.

"The guy..."

Nia grabbed her shoulders and looked Ivory square in the eyes. "Who?"

"From before." Ivory's green eyes begged her to connect unseen dots.

Nia furrowed her eyebrows and tried to decode the message. What was she talking about? They hadn't been to any other parties together...

Then, a conversation from weeks ago came back; in the cafeteria, Ivory had told her about a certain someone who caught her eye. That was the only guy Ivory ever brought up, the one who she still must have a thing for.

"*The* guy?" she asked.

Ivory nodded. "*The* guy."

Who could be so scary even Ivory was afraid to be in the same room with them? She clearly hadn't spoken to him yet. "Are you scared of him?" she asked. "Or just nervous?"

"Maybe both?" Ivory giggled. "I'm scared I'll sound like an idiot." She glanced over Nia's shoulder. "Has he left yet?"

Nia sighed and pursed her lips. Chances were she'd feel the same way, but Ivory was the one who pushed her to act on her feelings in the first place. Shouldn't she encourage her to say something? At least hello?

The first good idea of the night crossed her mind. Ivory might hate her later, but she'd take the blame if anything went wrong. If it went right, however, then she'd be the only one to look foolish, and Ivory would get her introduction.

Courage surged from a hidden storehouse, and she grabbed Ivory's arm, dragging them into the kitchen before Ivory could get away.

"Come on," Nia insisted as panic played in slow motion across her friend's face.

They barged in at the same time a couple walked out, leaving them alone with the mystery man who was currently reaching into the refrigerator. Nia's eyes latched onto his back, where long auburn hair fell past his shoulders. The pale pink ends sparked her recognition. Ivory began to shrink back as Adrian glanced up, golden eyes landing on Nia.

"It's *you*?" Nia asked, impervious to the lack of context.

Adrian's face twisted in confusion. "...Me?"

Ivory and Adrian glanced between each other, then at her, trying to piece together different sides of the same puzzle.

"You're the guy from the hair salon," she clarified.

Adrian straightened and shut the refrigerator, frosty beer in hand. "Ah, yes. Can I help you?"

"My friend Ivory wants to dye her hair," she blurted, slipping over the words. Riffling through everything she knew about Ivory, she added, "Purple. She wants purple hair."

Nia cleared her throat, proud of the impromptu performance. Ivory, on the other hand, looked like she was going through several stages of shock, much less of a maleficent witch and more of a cute embarrassed one. "I...ah..."

"Do you need it done right now?" Adrian asked, eyebrows raised in sarcastic inquiry.

"N-no!" Ivory stammered. "I came for a refill, that's all." She took two quick steps to the counter, where several large juice coolers sat next to a stack of red cups. Pouring a cupful of clear liquid, she explained. "I've been talking about my hair for weeks you see, so when Nia saw you, she had to say something."

"I saw an opera—opportunity and took it." Nia smiled and took the cup Ivory handed her, then watched as she filled two more with a bright red drink.

"If it's that important, I'd be glad to do it for you. We can dye it in my apartment, and I'll waive the salon fee, providing you buy the dye." Adrian made himself at home and leaned against the counter, popping off the beer cap with one of the thick, gold rings around his fingers.

Ivory nodded, having again lost the ability to speak as she handed Nia a second cup. Deciding this drink looked a lot better than water, Nia took a sip. Hints of lime and strawberry smoothed over a sharper flavor as it coated her tongue. She quickly downed half the cup and her chest warmed. Ivory knew her stuff. If only there were more cookies to go along with it.

Adrian shifted his attention to Nia and tipped the beer bottle against his lips, Adam's apple bobbing as he swallowed. "I don't remember you, must've been a while ago."

"Oh, yeah. Plus, this is a wig." She pointed to her head, lest he think the wig she spoke of was somewhere else.

"Ah, now I recall." Adrian's lips twitched. "You're the redhead."

"Yep." She went to refill her cup, needing as much of this as she could get before getting a ride home.

"Do you need a touch-up?" Adrian offered. "I'd be happy to give you the same deal."

Watching the liquid fill her cup, she didn't bother looking up as she answered. Time to put in motion the second part of her plan. "Oh no, I'm good." She struggled with the lever as some precious liquid splashed over the edge. "Take care of Ivory, okay?" Turning with a final wink at her friend, whose face looked much less pale than before, she added, "I'm gonna find Avril. You get Adrian's contact info, and I'll catch ya later."

She half-walked half-skipped out of the room without waiting for a response. A grin stretched over her face, mood greatly improved. Now she could go home feeling accomplished. All she had left to do was find Avril.

Side-stepping other wobbly three-legged guests, she wandered around in an attempt to find the last place she saw them dancing. The red drink turned sweeter with every sip, and she licked her lips before tipping the cup back, only to find it empty. She frowned at the plastic bottom, wanting more but unwilling to go back into the kitchen and disrupt Ivory.

Avril and Serena were nowhere to be seen. Her eyes landed on a staircase. Oh, they were probably downstairs. She faintly remembered someone mentioning drinking games down there.

As she approached, the steps loomed steeper than normal. To be safe, she grabbed the railing with both hands and descended, giggling at the thought of how Ivory and Adrian might be getting along.

In the basement, music boomed louder and vibrated her to the bone. She swept her gaze over the crowded space for Avril but didn't get very far before locking on to a head of black hair. As untamed as ever. Eyes just as piercing but focused on someone else.

Carelessly put together and achingly familiar, the person forever burned in her memory stood a few paces away. Her heart squeezed, then stopped altogether. Caspian's lips parted in a light chuckle that drowned out everything around her. Even her pulse became swallowed by the deafening bass and scene before her eyes.

Caspian wasn't *really* laughing, not the way he used to. The girl clinging to his side echoed his laugh, but his eyes were so focused on her chest Nia wondered if he even noticed his companion's expression.

She took an involuntary step toward them, the hairs on her skin bristling.

If he was going to mess around anyway, why not play into his hands? He wouldn't recognize her, not with the costume and dim lighting. Then she'd get to experience him when he wasn't pretending to be a model boyfriend. What he'd been like before—no, who he really was.

The burn building in her chest exploded into a white-hot fire, spiraling out of control. Right now she didn't need to be Nia, she was Aphrodite, the goddess of love, and she knew *exactly* what—or who—she wanted.

FORTY

Caspian

HE TIPPED HIS HEAD DOWN, FOCUSING ON ANYTHING BUT THE petite blonde's face. She looked nothing like Nia.

Not that the rest of her could measure up to the woman he wanted, either. Those hips didn't flare out the same way, and when he brushed over the point of a nipple eagerly poking through her halter top, the sigh sounded all wrong. The beauty mark next to her belly button wasn't there like it should be, and her thighs lacked substance—but at least she was short and feminine. His beer did its best to fill in the mismatched details.

Someone else's hand slid up his arm, and then a sultry whisper floated to his ear. "You'll find I can be *much* more entertaining."

His grip loosened on the blonde in surprise, and he turned toward the source of the voice.

The reaction to seeing her was almost instantaneous.

Heat flooded his veins, eyes drinking in the alluring mirage. A goddess stood before him, one hand on her pushed-out hip while the other continued to smooth up his bicep. A trail of sparks followed her touch.

He blinked once, then twice, eyes gliding up and down the

long dark locks that outlined her petite silhouette. The alcohol must really be doing its job, because although her eyes were much too smoky and dark, the goddess's face and build matched Nia exactly.

What fortune.

Disregarding his old distraction in favor of this new one, he took her hand and slid it up to the flat of his shoulder, flexing his muscles. "Really now?"

She gave him the sexiest smirk he'd ever seen and wordlessly flipped her body, pressing all her curves into him. He couldn't care less about the blonde, consumed by the goddess's hand slithering up to his neck, her skin hot and smooth.

Then her hips rolled.

He groaned and reached down to capture her in his arms and swayed along. She even smelled like vanilla, like Nia...

He was losing his mind. But he didn't care. Delusion or not, he was going to enjoy himself. Consciousness receded as his body took the reins, nose skimming along her neck and his fingers seeking out her thigh between the gap of her costume. When his fingertips brushed over bare skin at last, they both shivered, then pressed more fervently into each other. Her head tilted against his chest, long hair tumbling over tan shoulders as her lips parted.

"Entertaining indeed," he hummed into her ear, voice husky and laced with renewed desire.

She sighed.

Fuck. He wouldn't—couldn't forget that sound. Not ever.

"Nia..." he whispered hesitantly, breathlessly. She didn't go to parties. This couldn't be her.

The woman in front of him continued to dance, either too drunk or too deaf to hear. The moment of doubt didn't last long —his body had other, much more pressing plans. Roaming his hands over her thighs and under the thin fabric of the dress, he squeezed her generous hips. The silky skin molded to his fingers just right.

"Come," she whispered, pulling him along before he could question her again.

Believe me, I'm about to. He obliged and let her lead him upstairs while his pants tightened. At the top, he was ushered into a hallway and pushed ruthlessly against the wall. The music swelled around them as she attacked his lips, leaning in and taking what she wanted. He let her tease him with her talented tongue, growling as she drew his bottom lip between her teeth.

The kiss was hot and demanding, but this passion felt out of place for a random hookup at a costume party. Through the fog of denial, he recognized an emotion deeper than lust. A sentiment rooted to his being, almost sacred.

He froze. No, this *was* familiar. As much as he wanted Nia, he couldn't replicate her, not like this. Yet it had to be her. Her lips, her curves, her raw desire.

What was she doing? And why?

His brain reeled to catch up, but to no avail. The search for answers battled with basic impulse, and his body favored impulse.

Nia stole each breath from his lips, canceled out every rational thought as she plundered his mouth and skimmed her hands over his body. Her touch was light yet inebriating, her lack of communication infuriating.

In a swift motion, he turned them and pinned her against the wall. She rolled with the motion, hooking a leg around his waist, and for a moment he faltered, lost again in her taste. In the feel of her being near to him again. Knowing who she was made it that much harder to pull away.

Then he tasted the alcohol on her lips and remembered she didn't like to drink, at least not the bitter stuff that diluted her tonight. He reached behind her neck and hooked one finger under the seam of the wig, pulling out a strand of ruby-red hair.

"Wh—don't," Nia murmured, sloppy in her reaction. She raised a hand to redirect his attention, but he gripped her chin instead and forced her to look at him. God, that face. Seeing her, *feeling* her was the best kind of punishment.

"Nia." No trace of doubt lingered in his voice.

Her eyes widened into large, dark-as-midnight orbs. Only a sliver of her pale blue irises remained. She squirmed in his grip and reached out to pull him closer, to draw him under again.

"Nia," he repeated as if scolding a child.

Another drunk couple stumbled into the hallway, doing much the same as he had earlier, but one look at his expression and they retreated.

Nia must've also sensed his shift in mood because she dropped her hands, eyes focusing in between his lips and eyes. "Please, no. Pretend it's not me, just for tonight." Her hands brushed over his nipples and went up to his jaw, touching what her mouth could not.

He steeled himself against the temptation. "Why the hell would I do that?"

"I'm just someone random tonight. Someone..." She struggled with the next words, closing her eyes, and releasing a shaky breath. "Someone you want to sleep with, nothing more."

A grating sound filled his head, and he realized it was his teeth grinding against each other. She wanted him to treat her like some trick? Like a party favor?

"No."

"Caspian," she pleaded. Her hand snuck between them to grab the bulge between his legs.

Dammit. His body was painfully on board with her plan, but he wouldn't let it take control.

"I won't let you use me to play out a page in one of your

fantasies." He caught her wrists and anchored them to the wall. "If you want me, then I'll be the one to fulfill *all* of your fantasies. On *every* page. *Every* night. And if you don't start behaving yourself, I will put you in your place."

He could play along, but it would be by his rules.

His voice lowered to a dangerous level, hissing in her ear. "Keep going and I'll make sure the only word you remember is my name, and the whole block will hear you scream it."

She was delusional if she thought he wouldn't want her as more than a stranger at a party. He wanted much, much more. But this wasn't the time or the place.

Her breath came out in a gasp as she stared at him openmouthed. "You'd still want me?"

Hell, he'd want her any way he could take her, but he needed answers before giving any of his own. "Why did you come here like this?"

She came dressed to impress, that was for sure, but frat boys didn't care for clear consent, much less how conscious a girl was. He didn't trust them on a regular day, and especially not after drinking and smoking themselves into oblivion at the biggest party of the semester.

"I—I thought..." Her lip trembled, dark and swollen from their kiss as water welled in her eyes.

His patience broke. "Do you know what some of these guys would do to you? Walking around drunk?"

"I know," she whispered, eyes falling.

The answer only served to irritate him, but he tempered his voice. "Why, Nia?"

"Because..." She hiccupped as more tears welled in her eyes. A thousand needles shot through his heart. "I needed to figure out why I felt so much with you. Romance wasn't a part of my life plan, and I had no idea what to do. When you came, I'd never—" She hiccupped again.

He wiped the tears away with his knuckles. Seeing her

261

break like this was enough to break him, too. Her small frame fit between his wide shoulders, and he did his best to shield her from curious eyes.

"I was scared of getting hurt. Scared of giving in, but I ended up hurting us both. All I've known is to run away. Run from pain and from happiness, but the emptiness you filled—" She closed her eyes and shook like a leaf. "I want to get better, to fight for the good like I should have all those years ago. I should have—"

She started sobbing, and he cradled her in his arms. Her tears ran in a hot torrent down his bare chest and quickly put out any lingering flames of anger. All he felt was her pain as his own.

Nia sucked in an unsteady breath. "I couldn't—I didn't fight for her—my mother, and we both suffered. Then I didn't fight for you, and now..."

He pulled her closer, held her tight enough to keep her in one piece. What happened to her as a child wasn't her fault. Despite this breakthrough, he made a mental note to tell her in the morning to go easy on the drinks. Yet he knew every word she said was genuine. That would have to be addressed at some point, but preferably when they were alone and both sober.

As she quieted, he whispered, "I'm going to take you home now, okay?"

She shook her head. "Don't, I'd rather be here than alone."

He stroked her back. "Okay. I'll take you back with me, but we'll have to walk."

He hadn't planned on bringing anyone home with him and left his car at home so he could have a few more drinks than usual. Earlier, he hadn't even been sure if he'd be going back.

"Okay," she whispered with a nod.

He put his arm around her waist and walked down the hallway, opening the few doors on the way and eventually finding a bathroom. The walk would only be about ten minutes, but he worried about Nia not having a jacket. Snatching a towel, he wrapped it around her.

Once they got outside and away from the party, he paused to send both Adrian and Ivory a text. A retching sound interrupted his typing as Nia doubled over. He grabbed the wig and pulled it out of the way as she heaved up the remnants of her good time.

They were going to have a long walk back.

FORTY-ONE

Caspian

NIA HAD REFUSED TO LET HIM OUT OF HER SIGHT, SO HE PULLED
the blanket around her shoulders as she drooled on the pillow
next to his leg. Considering she might not remember much in
the morning, he thought it a bad idea to sleep in the same bed
and wasn't about to risk his sheets getting covered in vomit. The
couch was the safest option.

Once her eyes slid closed and her breathing evened out,
he'd planned to retire to the bedroom. But he didn't.

Just a little more, he told himself as he gazed at her peaceful
face. Tonight, he saw a new side to Nia, one he knew existed but
rarely got to see. Whenever she talked about her past before,
her words had been hollow and withdrawn. This time she
didn't disassociate.

The struggle of coming from a broken home and burden of
carrying a generational curse felt all too relatable. Caspian
stroked his fingers through her soft hair as he thought about
his own voids, how he'd filled them the exact same way Nia
tried to tonight, just with more expertise.

It never worked, and he knew that. Somewhere deep inside
he recognized satisfying lust wouldn't fill the hole dug by

feeling unloved. Abandoning others wouldn't ease the pain of being abandoned.

He, too, had been willing to pass up on a real relationship in exchange for easy rewards. Before Nia, he never wanted anyone permanently, but he only recognized his need for her when she was gone.

Her courage to try and live better despite the examples in her life made him want to cherish her, to get down on his knees and worship her. She taught him how to enjoy being around someone else, to share good times as well as bad. She expected so much of him and tonight, he realized he needed that.

As he pulled her close, her soft body fit perfectly with his hardness—inside and out. Forced to confront his choices, he pondered the difference between love and lust. Not only in meaning but significance. Nia deserved to feel irresistible, to be championed as the sexy woman she was—and she deserved unconditional love.

She deserved his soul.

He hadn't even considered if he had one until she came into his life. Maybe that's what a soul was—something you don't actually use for yourself but give to the people you love. He vowed to try his best. To give her his soul. To give her everything.

Swimming in too many thoughts and feelings, he slipped into a light sleep.

Several hours later, Nia's voice cut through the darkness. His neck cracked as he looked over, stiff and knotted from leaning on the couch. She seemed to still be asleep but looked distraught as her eyes moved under closed lids. Another whimper came from her lips.

A nightmare?

He gently stroked her hair, watching with a furrowed brow. She tensed at his touch, then relaxed. Leaving her like this wasn't an option. He looked around for something to use as his own pillow and bent down to grab a sweatshirt off the floor.

Nia cried out, voice hushed but urgent. "Don't leave."

"Shhh," he soothed, returning his hand to her head.

"Caspian," she breathed.

He would never leave.

Stroking her cheek with his thumb, he waited until she calmed down.

"I love you," he whispered. Then let his eyes close once more.

3

Light stung the back of his eyelids. He raised an arm to block the sun that had brought him back to consciousness much too early. His body ached. Everywhere.

Turning his head, he noticed he wasn't in his bed. Or in a bed at all.

That explained the aches, but what explained the sleeping arrangement? Eyes still shut, memories of last night resurfaced.

Nia.

He looked over to find her curled up next to him, sound asleep. Her hand had stretched out to touch his leg, and his fingers were nestled in a halo of red velvet. Crumpled from sleep, her hair swirled around the pillow and poked out in all directions. The sight made him grin despite his fatigue.

Tracing a strand back to her scalp, he noticed a hint of blonde emerging. Her shade of red was too bright to be natural —he'd always known that, but discovering this felt intimate, personal. Tiny nuances like her true hair color were priceless; he wanted to know every detail about her, down to the base of a strand of hair.

He sat forward, muscles protesting as he lifted his hand and stroked Nia's skin one last time before rising to his feet. Better to get a few more hours of rest and at least one solid door between them before she woke up.

If he got lucky, she might leave before chewing his head off.

He didn't assume after last night, everything would instantly fix itself. She was going to wake up to one hell of a headache, and worse, he would have to be the messenger of why.

No sooner had he clicked his bedroom door closed and lay down, than rustling came from the other side. So he did what anyone else would do in his position—pretended to be asleep. More rustling and a grumble signaled Nia had woken up.

"Shit!" she cursed.

Yeah, and not in a good mood either. He braced himself. A door slammed. He stilled.

"Caspian!"

He contemplated how much longer he could pretend not to be awake, and if snoring would either help or hurt his cause.

"Are you there?"

Groaning, he went to assess the damage. But upon entering the living room, instead of Nia, he found the blanket abandoned on the couch and the bathroom light on underneath the closed door.

He knocked. "Nia, you okay?"

"No, I won the lottery—of course I'm not okay."

She was even less of a morning person than he was.

"I swear we didn't do anything," he assured. "Although you were very convincing and if..."

"Caspian, please not now." She sounded genuinely upset.

"What's wrong?" He wished he could see her face, look her in the eyes. Was she still sick? Not knowing what was the matter ate at him.

She groaned.

"Are you sick? I can help, let me in." He tried the knob, but it was locked.

"No! Don't come in, just...." A massive sigh came from behind the door.

"I don't care how bad you look, okay?" He rested his forehead against the door, frustrated at the barrier. "Tell me what's going on."

Her voice lowered and the irritation disappeared. "Do you have a tampon?"

A...*what?*

He stared stupidly at the door for a few seconds. "We were about to have *sex* last night and you were on your *period*? Shouldn't you have mentioned that?"

"I wasn't! I swear I didn't know, okay? I woke up and the cramps came in, along with this massive headache and when I checked there was..."

"Aren't women supposed to have a calendar for that? An app or something?"

"Well my body isn't exactly a well-oiled machine, you know," she shot back. "I've been late since...well, I haven't had one since we separated."

To him, missing a period only meant one thing. "Fingering did *not* get you pregnant."

"It was *stress*, you idiot," she hissed. "That affects things too."

He turned and rested his back against the door, breathing through his nose. This was a lot to digest, and he had not been prepared to wake up to a discourse on female menstruation irregularities. She'd been so stressed that her body...malfunctioned?

Sighing, he figured this was a problem that needed to be dealt with, and sooner rather than later. "As you might have guessed, I don't keep a secret stash of feminine hygiene products. Give me the key to your dorm, and I'll grab whatever you need."

"You might as well take me ba—" a groan cut off her sentence.

"Cramps?" he asked softly.

"Look who's catching on."

"You're staying here, and I'm taking care of you."

Silence. He knew she didn't want to accept it, but he wasn't taking no for an answer. They had a lot to work out, and he didn't want to leave her feeling miserable. Again.

A key card slipped under the door. "Under my bed, in a blue bin."

He took the card and shoved it in his jeans, then shrugged on a hoodie. Returning to the bedroom, he pulled out a new pair of boxers and grabbed a roll of paper towel from the kitchen.

"Here." He placed the supplies by the bathroom. "You don't have to stay locked in there while I'm gone."

She mumbled a thank you. This would be a sharper learning curve than anticipated, but he hardly viewed it as a setback.

It was their second chance.

FORTY-TWO

Nia

COULD THIS DAY GET ANY WORSE? SHE CRADLED HER THROBBING head, staring at the goosebumps on her bare legs as silence settled over the apartment.

She didn't want to consider what happened last night. Only twenty minutes into the morning, and she was already physically and mentally exhausted. Her organs must be conspiring against her.

On top of the cramps, a pounding headache, and the black hole that was her stomach, she had no clue what to say after her breakdown. Although she remembered walking back to Caspian's apartment, the details were foggy, and she didn't remember falling asleep on his couch at all.

Taking a few steady breaths to distract from the sharp ache in her abdomen, she cracked open the bathroom door and snatched what he'd left. A smile curved her lips. Even if he hadn't experienced what she was going through, he was doing a good job.

He'd always done a good job.

Last night dispelled any doubt his feelings weren't genuine, and the same for hers. At the party Caspian had all right to disregard her, or to use her for his own sake, but he still chose to take her in. A last act of kindness before the inevitable.

He wouldn't want her back, not now.

Dejected, she crafted a make-shift pad and pulled on the boxers. They fit snug around her hips. It might not be the sexiest, but they sure were comfortable.

Rummaging around a little more, she found a spare toothbrush and did her best to clean up. The mint toothpaste felt wonderfully refreshing, but she had to push out why he had an extra toothbrush in the first place.

Unfortunately, the Caspian Suite didn't come with every amenity. Namely, the all-important hairbrush. She did what she could with knotted and wind-blown hair, then decided to reevaluate the couch. To her relief, stains had only gotten on her clothes. The underwear and dress she'd worn to the party were goners, but at least none of Caspian's things were ruined. Not that his apartment was very tidy. Even more clutter than she remembered covered the floor and almost every other flat surface.

Searching for something but not knowing exactly what, she inhaled Caspian's scent. Her heart swelled. The happiness she'd felt with him came back full force. The pain in her body subsided at the comfort of being back, both body and mind recognizing it as a safe place.

His voice this morning calmed her more than she liked to admit, and he was about the only thing that stood between her and another mental breakdown.

She wandered into his bedroom and pulled on a pair of his sweatpants, then dug in his dresser for what she hoped would be a clean shirt. Encased in sentiments of Caspian, she turned to the kitchen.

The trash had begun to overflow with paper plates, and bottles were scattered over the counter. She'd seen worse. After a particularly intense fight or breakup, her mom didn't clean for weeks, but mending hearts was more important than keeping a clean house.

Still, one thing remained clear—if she was going to stay here for any amount of time, it needed to be tidied. Her stomach growled, and she feebly wondered what food he had on hand and if it would be edible or not.

Finding trash bags under his sink, she collected the bottles, replaced the bag in the trash can, and went to work on the living room. Clothes went in one bag, papers and old assignments in another. The one area she left untouched was his desk, not wanting to disturb any of his drawings. Before much time passed, the jingle of keys came from outside, and the door swung open.

"Honey, I'm ho—" Caspian's jaw dropped as he closed the door behind him, eyes trained on her. Then, his eyes crinkled with a smile. "You can keep that shirt. In fact, take my whole closet." He strode toward her, the strap of her backpack hanging over his shoulder.

"You look amazing," he murmured and pulled her into an embrace, placing a kiss on the top of her head.

If she looked 'amazing,' he must be one of the seven world wonders.

"I haven't even brushed my hair yet," she mumbled. "I'm sure I look terrible."

He smoothed down her hair, and she fought a blush as he tilted her head. Studying his face, she absorbed everything from his impressive jawline and sharp nose to intense blue eyes that searched her own. How did he look so...happy? She ruined his night and now crashed whatever plans he had for the day.

"I'll take it," he said. "All of it. Blonde hair, self-deprecating comments, and all."

A rush of self-consciousness flooded through her, then Caspian brushed his lips against hers. Her heart all but burst. She couldn't even call it a kiss, more like the ghost of one, but it unraveled her. Considering recent events, she didn't think he'd still have any interest in her, yet this kiss said something else.

"Why are you cleaning?" he muttered, pulling her to the couch. "Shouldn't you be curled up with a good chick flick?" A smile touched the corners of her lips. He knew her too well.

"Actually, Ivory turned me on to spy films. I'm not a one-genre girl anymore." Speaking of Ivory, she made a mental note to check her phone.

He chuckled at her statement. The rumble from his chest warmed her much better than the shots had last night. "Good to know." Caspian shrugged the backpack off his shoulders. "But I can't let Ivory have all the fun now, can I? Maybe I'll turn you onto horror next."

"Oh no, that's a hard limit." She narrowed her eyes, having a hopeful hunch as to why he wanted to watch horror movies with her. Plus, she had enough nightmares as is.

He shook his head, digging through the backpack. "Here's your supplies." He handed over the bin containing her tampons. "I brought some clean clothes—which you don't need cause you're keeping mine on—your laptop, and whatever else was already in the backpack."

She stared at the bag, then at him, then at the bin in her hand. This was too much kindness. When he said he would take care of her, she hadn't imagined he'd be this thorough. Literally, everything she'd wanted he'd brought, when all she had asked for was a single tampon.

"Oh, and some food from your fridge," he added. "You need to be drinking water. After way too much alcohol—" He stopped, then sighed.

"Sorry," she mumbled. "About last night. And today. And..." *For not addressing my problems...* but the sentence died on her tongue.

Wordlessly, he stood and walked to the kitchen. The removal of his presence stung as much as a ripped-off band-aid.

She took the tampons and retreated to the bathroom, very aware of the literal and metaphorical distance between them.

Maybe a part of Caspian still cared about her, but that couldn't make up for the past they shared. He wouldn't want a repeat of their argument or of last night.

"You okay in there?" he called from outside.

"Yeah," her voice cracked. "I'm fine." She berated herself for her miserable attempts at being a girlfriend and a hook-up. Apparently, neither were meant for her.

His clothes blanketed her skin, soft and comfy. Would they be the only reminders she had of him after today? The only guaranteed keepsake from this twisted amusement ride they got on?

She stepped out and walked over to the kitchen, where Caspian had pulled out milk and butter from the fridge. "Do you like mac n' cheese? About the only thing I have on hand."

For reasons she didn't have the mental capacity to process, she giggled. He had managed to surpass the pessimistic turmoil and cramps in her abdomen. "Yes, but I have to say, my mom's recipe is better than the boxed version."

He pulled her close, arms wrapped tightly around her back. She exhaled into his shoulder and returned his touch. Her breath caught, the trademark mint and cologne filling her nose, sturdy heartbeats drumming an eternal pattern into her soul.

"Then you'll have to make it for me someday," he whispered. His voice sounded like home—felt like home—right down to his deep inhale.

She wanted to say how she'd missed him. How, in the past few hours, she realized just how painful being apart had been. If there were a chance, even one in a million, to keep what they had, she'd take it.

"I'm sorry," she whispered again into his chest. Her limbs froze, they wouldn't detach from him even if she wanted them to. There was so much more to say, but the things she needed to know were too hard to ask. Rejection would feel like hell if it came with him being so close.

"I'm sorry, too. I promise I'll say everything I need to, but first, you need to eat, okay?"

She nuzzled deeper into his jacket. "Okay."

FORTY-THREE

Caspian

HE SETTLED INTO THE COUCH, ONE ARM AROUND NIA'S shoulders and a hand on her knee as she drank a third cup of water for the day. His favorite movie had just gotten to the big exposé, but he wasn't watching.

He'd rather count Nia's breaths. Take in every movement and relish her very existence next to him.

Somehow, he needed to make things right between them. This whole time, he thought he'd be the one to catch her, maybe even bring her out of her shell, but it was him who got caught.

He had no idea how to express that.

A lack of finesse was part of why they broke apart in the first place, and he had no practice communicating emotions that felt like apocalyptic hurricanes in his heart.

The credits began to roll, and Nia snuggled her head into his chest. Although her breaths were soft and steady, he knew she wasn't asleep. Soft light filtered through the drawn curtains, almost as a sign not to leave their issues in the dark. The entire morning, unspoken words had hung over them like storm clouds, preventing any real relaxation.

277

"Hey," he started, rubbing her knee. "I made a promise, so I'm going to keep it. You just have to listen, okay?"

She nodded, curling into him.

This felt like being trapped in a dream where no matter how fast he ran, the ground under his feet wouldn't move. Even though he was treading water, he still sank. "If it were as simple as explaining my past, I would have, but that's not what you wanted or what you needed."

His heart plunged at the memory. Having her in his arms now was surreal, enough to make the next words spill out despite how vulnerable they made him.

"I may have messed around with a lot of people, but there's only been one you, Nia." He stroked her back, the soft cotton of his shirt and her familiar form directing his thoughts. "From now on, I only want you. Hell, I can't think of anyone else. I know I'm not the best but—"

"No," she whispered, shaking her head. "Last night I realized *I* caused my doubts. It wasn't right to pin them all on you." Her hand wrapped around his—small, delicate fingers interlaced with thick worn ones. She ignited hope, a hope he desperately didn't want to end up destroyed by again. "If you want me, I want to stay. No more running away, I promise."

He exhaled, not realizing he'd been holding a breath. "Then stay." Truth was, ever since recognizing her last night, he hadn't wanted her to leave his sight. "You're not just some girl, Nia." He tightened his grip on her hand. "I want you to be *my* girl. I want—"

His throat closed up, and her hand returned his fervent grip with abnormal strength. "You want me...like that?"

"I do."

"Tell me you really mean it." Disbelief wove into her voice. "Tell me we'll work things out, and when we fight, tell me we'll get through it. Tell me if I stay...you'll stay, too. Not just now or for the time being. I want to do this right. That's all I need to hear." She turned into him and hid her face.

His heart beat stronger, crashing against his ribcage in an effort to get through to her. "I won't leave. I never wanted to." He cleared his throat. "I won't take you for granted. Ever."

Nudging her to sit up, he brought their clasped hands to her face and tipped up her chin. His eyes pleaded for understanding. "But I need to hear it from you, too. Stay with me. You have to want it, to want me."

Her eyes wavered, filled with melted ice, then spilled over. "I'm sorry, I..." She wiped away her tears with her spare hand. "I want to be with you. I shouldn't have ended things the way I did, shouldn't have kept my doubts bottled up."

Despite the calm in her voice, tears continued to roll down. She tried to catch them as they fell, to smile through the onslaught of emotion, but her eyes were bloodshot, and uneven red blotches rose on her skin.

"I meant what I said." He tucked her hair behind her ear. A pit sunk in his gut, and he wished he could've been there for her before.

"I'm happy, I swear." She tried to laugh, but it caught and turned into a sob.

He gathered her in his arms and pulled her sideways into his lap, her back against his arms and legs bent over his thigh. "I know, but it's okay to be sad at the same time."

All her pain was coming out at once, and that was all right. He would be a shield and a sword, whatever she needed. As long as she was here, they would both be okay.

With shaking hands, she sniffled and smeared tears and leftover makeup across her cheeks. "This is so bad, I'm s-sorry."

"Don't apologize," he whispered and brought her head to his shoulder. He needed this as much as she did. The show of affection only seemed to make her condition worse as she gasped for air.

"I really c-can't control it. I..." She lifted her head to wipe her nose.

"Use my shirt, it's yours."

"No, this is gross. Let me get—"

"—don't get up." He enclosed her in his arms. "I need you here." Body fluids were the least of his concerns. He wasn't ready to be apart from her yet, not even by an inch, and especially not when she was having a hard time.

She trembled and sunk into him. Twisting his shirt in fists, she tried to speak through the sobs. "It's so irrational. I don't know why..." He held her head, doing his best to give her comfort, bring her some sort of peace. "I've never depended on validation." She managed to suck in a larger breath. "But sometimes, I can't shake the feeling that I deserve to be alone. Sometimes, I want to feel loved, and a part of me, for whatever fucked up reason, always remembers that my own father didn't—"

Her voice cracked, and he knew how the sentence ended.

Words at this moment wouldn't be powerful enough. He needed to override the voice in her head and smashed his lips to hers.

She gasped for breath as he went back for more, her salty tears a delicacy more exquisite than fine champagne. Her puffy skin, soft and heated, was more addictive than the strongest drug.

Her sorrow became his, her demons forced to reside in them both. They would have to battle him to get to her.

He cupped her face and held her like a crown, a symbol of power and dignity, of strength and accomplishment. The intricate feelings of her soul were encased in gold—no matter how dark or deep they ran, they shined. Because they were hers, and she was his.

Her chest rose, and she shuddered, regaining control over her lungs and returning the kiss. She clung to him, pressed her swollen lips to his, then wrapped her arms around his neck. He let her steer him, parting his lips and reveling in her sweet assault.

His hands dropped, one circling her back and the other sliding over her waist. She took her time to explore his mouth, nibbling at his lip and sweeping her tongue over his. Eventually, she grew greedy and bit down, pulling at his hair.

"*Ah*," he hissed and pulled back. Thankfully, the skin was unbroken, but his lip still stung.

"Sorry," she mumbled.

"Don't be," he said and planted a chaste kiss on her now-tempered lips. Her skin soothed the pain, a salve he yearned for above anything else. At last, their hearts had begun the process of healing.

FORTY-FOUR

Caspian

"DO YOU FEEL BETTER?" HE PEPPERED KISSES ON HER CHEEKS, UP the bridge of her nose and over her puffy eyelids, across her eyebrows, then up her hairline and back down again.

"Mhm." She let out an exhausted sigh. "Thank you. I haven't felt this light in a long time...maybe ever. I owe you."

"You owe me nothing." Reluctantly, he drew back and observed her calm expression. "This is what being together means."

A smile turned up the corners of her lips, finally a flicker of humor in her eyes. "I hope that doesn't mean I'm going to be a blubbering mess every day."

He chuckled. If she did, he'd find a way to patch her up. Every time.

"Your eyes are so clear now," he murmured. The texture in her irises stood out like a maze of small streams cascading into the depths of her soul. At last, he remembered to take a breath and glanced down. "Your lips are so soft, so dark..."

He was amazed that such a tiny mouth could overwhelm him so entirely. As if hearing his thoughts, she leaned in for another kiss, simple and sugar-coated. Her smile widened over his, and she pulled back to look at him.

"Nia," he addressed her with as much sincerity as he could muster. "I can handle your pains. Never be afraid to share with me."

"Okay," she whispered, biting back a grin. "They never last long with you, anyway. I'm too happy for my own good. That used to scare me, but now I know it's because what we have is real."

He smirked, pride glowing. Without warning, he rolled her hips and pinned her beneath him. She squealed and laughed, breath fanning his neck.

If this wasn't heaven, he didn't need to visit the pearly gates. He'd take her angelic laughter and wholesome presence any day.

"Tell me one more time," he demanded as she squirmed, dwarfed by his larger frame. "Tell me how I make you feel."

She struggled to catch her breath, giggles dying out. Challenge flashed in her eyes. "You heard me."

A wicked smile curved up his lips. "You're not in a position to sass, baby girl."

He lowered himself to let her feel more of his weight. In turn, her heat radiated beneath him, every curve of that soft, delicious body coming in contact with his. Propped up on both elbows, he trailed his fingers along her neck, lightly tracing her collarbone and dipping down to the hem of her—*his* shirt.

"Stay with me?" His whisper was barely audible, but they were so close it didn't matter.

"I am, I will." She looked up at him and pressed her hands over his chest. His heart rate spiked under her fingertips. "I already said I would."

"I mean, tonight." He lowered his head the few inches that separated their lips and drank her in. "Don't go back to your dorm. I want to sleep next to you."

Again.

But this time, she wouldn't be drunk, and he wouldn't wonder where they stood. His neck still felt sore from last night's awful sleeping position, and letting Nia out of his arms wasn't going to happen. He needed his bed and his girl in it.

"But we can't, you know, 'cause I'm..." She blushed and twisted his shirt.

"What, can't handle a little teasing?" He kissed the corners of her mouth, fully addicted to the taste of her skin and the sound of her shallow breaths. His lips followed her jawline to her neck while his hand slid along her side to hold her still. "We can order food, or I can take you out somewhere nice. Whatever you want."

She groaned, running her hands up to the muscles in his shoulders and arching her back. "I'd rather stay in."

"Then we stay right here." He licked the spot where her pulse called out to him, pressed into her with his lips as his entire body responded to hers.

"Maybe not r-right here," she stammered.

"Right here," he emphasized and ground his hips into hers. This was how being with her felt. Even when they had crying and misunderstandings, even a couch on an average afternoon wearing baggy clothes and smeared makeup, every cell in his body craved it.

"Nia, I'm going to give you everything." He kissed her chest, right above her pounding heart. "I've never made that promise to anyone."

His hand wandered under her shirt to pull down the cup of her bra, and her fingers dug through his shirt into his shoulder. "*Cas—*" She gasped.

He needed more. Needed everything.

"And I'll never make that promise to anyone else," he hummed, nuzzling his way down her neckline and brushing his nose against a pebbled nipple.

She sucked in another sharp breath. "I-I'm a little sensitive right now."

"Oh?" The subtle waver in her voice, the way her scent and warmth washed over him, almost pushed him over the edge. "I'll be careful then."

He covered her taut nipple with his mouth, rolling a flat tongue against her soft skin. With a moan, her hips bucked into his, coaxing out a groan of his own.

"So you are," he confirmed, voice thick and husky, arms trembling as he rolled his body to match her movement. Memories from last night jumped into his brain. Seeing her in that dress, feeling her hips push into him...

"Tell me you're mine," he growled. A tiny gasp left her, the one she couldn't hold back whenever he said something she liked.

"Tell me you're mine to taste, mine to treasure, mine to keep." He grabbed her hips and sunk his fingers into her thighs, fitting his hard erection perfectly between her plush legs. Their bodies clashed, slow and hard, mingling with pent-up frustration. The pain and desire they entrusted to each other transformed into hunger and bliss, a connection that surged with every touch.

She threw her head back, barely able to catch enough breath to answer. "I'm...I'm yours."

Her fingers wove into his hair, holding him gently as he branded hot kisses over to her other breast. He rocked into her soft body, absorbing each moan and quiver as it took him apart. Another low groan rumbled out from his chest, and he buried his face in her neck.

"Mean it," he panted, letting the last ounce of control evaporate.

She held the back of his head, stretching her body against his as she poured her soul into him. "Caspian," she emphasized. "I'm yours. Forever."

The fervent whisper shook his soul. As he let go of all the fears and misery that held him back, Nia's delicate vanilla and lavish arousal consumed him. Whatever life he searched for before her, whatever dreams and goals he stumbled toward, now became anchored to her.

"Come apart for me," she breathed. "Please."

Damn. That was all it took; her wish was his command.

Muscles seizing, he jerked and came undone inside and out. His arms clamped around her back, clinging onto her as his chest heaved. For a moment, his world went dark and silent. Complete.

"Are you crying?" she whispered after a while, breaking through his willful abandon as her fingers massaged the nape of his neck.

He blinked as wetness leaked out from the corner of his eye. "Guess it's my turn." He let her delicately brush away the tear with her finger. "Didn't want you to feel like the only one who gets to cry."

He studied her face, flushed pink and exhausted. She smiled at him, eyes lidded, hardly able to stay open. Then he remembered they had only gotten a few hours of sleep and moreover, had an exceptionally emotional morning.

"Let me clean myself up, then we can put on another movie and take a nap together," he said.

Her eyes shut and a contented sigh escaped her parted lips. "That sounds nice. I should shower, too, if I'm staying the night." She stiffened, then peered up at him. "Did you hear... did I do anything weird last night?"

He mirrored her furrowed brows, wondering why that mattered. "No..."

The nightmare.

She'd barely spoken, though. Nothing was wrong with having bad dreams, and she had them often, all the more reason for him to be by her side.

"Don't worry baby girl." He swooped down for one more kiss. "The only bed bug that will bite you is me, and if any others try, I'll kick their ass."

She managed a weak giggle, her eyes slipping closed again. "Don't bite me. I'm not responsible for punching you in my sleep."

He chucked and sat up. "I'll keep that in mind."

Reaching for a blanket, he laid it over her before stepping into the shower. Chances were that nap was happening sooner than she anticipated.

FORTY-FIVE

Nia

SHE ROLLED OVER AND PULLED THE SOFT COMFORTER UP TO HER chin. Upon discovering more space than usual, she continued the roll and stretched out her legs, tension leaving her muscles until she bumped into another warm body. For a split second, she stilled.

Caspian.

His name, even as an unspoken thought, wrapped around her like a soothing blanket. She melted back into the mattress.

Sharing a bed had been less eventful than she'd anticipated, but that had been for the best. After waking up from the impromptu nap, she found the room dark and a gaping hole in her stomach. Caspian ordered food while she took a heavenly shower, then they spent the rest of the night watching movies and playing video games. She actually won a few rounds without him going easy on her and wondered if it was due to her increase in skill or his lack of it.

Either way, she had ended up so exhausted—mentally and physically—that Caspian had to carry her to the bedroom. He cocooned her in warmth, and she soon passed out.

During the night he must've let go, or she fought him off, because now he sprawled almost as spread-eagle as she was. Their feet tangled in a pile at the bottom of the bed, and his leg fur tickled her under the sheets.

He shifted, twisting the comforter toward him. She cracked open her eyes to see if he was awake, but he only rolled on his side and pulled her closer. A heavy, muscled arm snaked around her waist as his leg trapped her against him.

The position would've been pleasant if not for his suffocating body heat. That, and the fact he only wore briefs. Hot-as-the-Sahara skin melded to hers, and she felt just *how* toned his abdomen was. The dead weight of his body left her with no ability to escape and no wiggle room.

She huffed and glared at his peaceful face but couldn't stay mad. For once, his eyes were shuttered, and thick eyelashes fanned his cheekbones. He looked young, almost boyish and innocent.

Being with him felt better now than before, more solid than the shifting tides of their first week. Not only did she know where his head was, but she finally let go of her reservations about falling in love.

Well, mostly. As much as she wanted to believe in 'and they lived happily ever after,' she knew one sentence could never sum up the rest of her life. A handful of words hardly described one day, much less years or decades.

Besides, she wanted the rest of her life to be written on pages upon pages, filled with beautiful discoveries and well-deserved accomplishments. The road ahead of them may not be paved with gold, but it led to riches nonetheless.

Hearing him laugh and joke came second only to listening to him confess his love—not in so many words. In fact, his heartfelt attempts to express emotion were better than simply saying, 'I love you.' She was sure that would come someday, but this weekend, they took a large enough step. They both came a long way from flirtatious texts and teasing exchanges.

Realizing her eyes had slipped closed again, and Caspian's body heat was about to put her in a coma, she squeezed both arms out from between them and pried herself away.

With a grunt, he peeled open one eye, staring at her through an ocean abyss all his own. The blue of his eyes looked much softer in the morning light as if the sun shone through the other side. Caught in his stare, she didn't have time to block his arm before he captured her again.

"Ugh," she whined. "You're suffocating."

He grunted again, apparently incapable of speech. His body lifted, and she almost sighed in relief, but then he pulled her under him and caged her between his arms.

"Caspian! *No.*" She laughed and shoved at his chest with feeble hands, writhing under his rock-solid body.

"Shh, let me enjoy waking up next to my girlfriend," he croaked, voice gritty and deep, like a stroke of thunder.

He nuzzled his way past her hair to her neck and pressed his lips to the hinge of her jaw. Her arms breached the surface, and fresh air cooled her skin. The relief was short-lived however, as Caspian quickly claimed the space her arms had occupied.

She groaned and felt him smile against her skin. "Good morning, baby girl."

"Morning, overheated toaster."

"*Sexy* overhead toaster," he corrected.

She responded with a strangled sound halfway between a laugh and a whine. He seemed intrigued at that, trailing his lips down to her throat. "I could listen to the sounds you make all day."

If possible, her body flushed with more heat. The sounds he coaxed from her lips often entailed other things, of which her body seemed very excited about, but she wasn't ready to handle that at the moment.

"I'm serious. Get up," she said.

He exhaled and lifted, hips hovering a hair's breadth away. Her chest expanded at last, and sweet air filled her lungs. She gazed up at him, a lazy smile on his lips that crinkled the corners of his eyes. Knowing Caspian was happy to wake up next to her made her feel warm in another way, in a place she didn't know was cold before.

They stared at each other, oblivious that neither said a word or made a move. For perhaps the first time in her life, she didn't feel vulnerable, her heart content to share a space with someone else entirely.

At last, he rolled off and sat up on the bed. "What's happening to me," he muttered, shaking his head then looking over at her. "What are your plans today?"

As much as she didn't want to, she had classes tomorrow and tests coming up this week. "I really don't want to leave, but I should spend some time studying."

One look at him told her he wasn't pleased but didn't expect anything less.

"Maybe I can stay until dinner, and you can take me back after that?" she offered.

"Sure." He stretched his arms above his head and displayed a mouthwatering collection of muscles. She blushed and got up, retreating to the bathroom to collect herself.

Once there, she brushed her teeth and realized that, again, one essential tool was missing—a hairbrush. Not even Ivory had seen her without straightened hair, much less hair left untouched for two days. She couldn't go to the dorms like this.

"Um, Caspian?" she called.

"Is something wrong?" Footsteps approached the door.

"No, well—kind of. I need a hairbrush." She opened the door to him, staring down at her. It took great effort to keep her eyes on his face, but she managed to keep her composure instead of inspecting every dip and furrow of his exposed chest. How could he be so casually sexy all the damn time?

"Need one or want one?" His eyebrows quirked up.

She pouted and glared back. Of course, he wouldn't understand; bed hair was his normal. "Both, you can't tell me you don't use at least a comb."

"You'd be surprised," he sighed. "Give me a minute, then I'll find a comb for you."

"Okay, thanks." She walked past him, breath faltering as their bodies brushed together. His skin still felt so hot.

She turned and wandered into the kitchen, focusing on food instead of what she craved most. The only thing suitable for breakfast was cereal and the extra sweet kind at that. Leftovers for breakfast and dinner didn't sound so great, but it looked like her only option.

Then she remembered the food Caspian brought from her dorm and, upon inspecting the contents of the fridge, happily pulled out a yogurt.

A shiver ran down her spine. She looked up to see him leaning on the counter a few feet away. Still very shirtless. Watching her with a look that sent tingles all over her body.

"What?" she demanded, setting the yogurt cup down.

He smirked.

She shifted to press her thighs together, aroused but unwilling to cave so easily. Some things would never change. She stood her ground and stared back, even as it made her all the more weak in the knees.

But she couldn't keep her eyes from wandering. The male figure had been a mystery she never sought to unravel, and now she had ample reason and means. He'd been shirtless around her plenty of times, but now his aura was different. He presented himself reverently, not to impress or intimidate, but akin to an offering. He wanted her to look.

He was hers, in all his glory.

Her man.

She refused to ease up, ignoring the heat crawling through her veins as she examined him to the fullest extent. His shoulders seemed broader, pectorals stronger, nipples harder. Her body remembered being pressed against him all night, the contour of his hard lines and smoothness of his skin. Deep desire pooled and settled in her womb.

Neither of them made a move.

Determined to fluster him as much as did her, she dropped her gaze lower. Hugging the outline of his six-pack, an Adonis belt carved out an arrow that pointed to his unmistakable bulge. One that had been nestled snug against her all night and fueled her imagination more than she'd admit.

She bit her lip. His cock jumped, stretching his briefs and growing larger. Her eyes flicked up, assessing if her plan worked.

From the gleam in his eyes, it hadn't.

However, his smirk faded into a clenched jaw. Silence cloaked her as she clamped her mouth shut, stuck in this strange contest but feeling as though she'd already lost.

Caspian took a slow, steady breath, his chest expanding and triggering a snap of tension across her faltering heart. "I know I'm a work of art, but this isn't a museum," he started, bearing down on her with intense eyes. "You can do more than just look."

Her mouth went dry, all the moisture in her body flooding between her legs. Cautiously, she stepped closer and brought a hand to the center of his chest. The tips of her fingers landed on scorching skin and traced the valley over his heart.

She swallowed and looked up into darkening eyes, voice barely a whisper. "Do you feel anything when I touch you?"

His heartbeat pounded, carving its print on her fingers. "I feel everything when you touch me."

Emboldened, she watched his face as she drifted lower and eased over the gentle slope of each smooth abdominal muscle, dipping into his navel. His breaths were heavy with restraint, holding back so she could take her time. When she continued the descent, he hummed and pulled his lip between his teeth. Her smile twitched upwards, basking in the gratification of his reaction. Hesitation stopped her at the waistline of his briefs, and she locked eyes with him, asking for permission she knew she already had.

"Everything," he whispered, then took her hand and guided it over the fabric. Their fingers wrapped around his length, and her jaw slacked. The muscles had been hard, but this...this was on another scale. He pressed her palm to him, and she gave what she hoped was a gentle squeeze.

A sigh left his lips, one that wavered as it petered out. At the same time, his eyes closed. He tipped his head back and parted his lips. What was this newfound power she discovered? She liked it. A lot.

Moving her hand down, she caressed his tip, the softer blunt intriguing. Would that really fit? A low groan crawled from his throat as she pressed her thumb over the top.

"Baby, I want to feel your skin," he rasped.

She gulped.

"You feel so good." He caressed her jaw, eyes filled with a need he never expressed before.

"Here." He showed her the opening in his briefs.

Peeling back the fabric, she wiggled her fingers underneath and found his arousal straining to be released. It bounced up to his stomach, hard and proud. She curled her hand around as much as it would go. His skin was tender, radiating the same heat she felt all over.

Caspian guided her head up, meeting her lips with his, and started to pump his hips. Her hand slid up and down as he groaned into her mouth. She kissed him back, intoxicated by his pleasure and feeling her own build.

A series of sharp knocks split them apart. She all but jumped out of her skin and spun her head toward the front door.

"Fuck," Caspian hissed.

FORTY-SIX

Caspian

Whoever stood on the other side of that door was about to get their head chewed off. Not even someone dying would be a good enough excuse to interrupt *that*.

He shoved his dick into his briefs and looked down at Nia, her brows knit in silent inquiry.

"No idea," he grumbled, stomping off to his room to put on more clothes. Exactly the opposite of what he wanted.

"Caspian, open up," an impatient feminine voice called from outside.

His frown deepened, skin pricking with a thousand needles. The hell was *she* doing here?

Nia popped her head in the room. "Should I wait in here?"

"No." He forced his gaze away from the little crumples their make-out session left her clothes and how it draped just so over her hips. Nothing appealed more than ignoring their unwelcome solicitor, but he knew she wouldn't go away. He glared in the general direction of his annoyance, and Nia shrunk away.

With a heavy sigh, he dragged a hand over his face and

swooped her under his arm. She shouldn't have to get caught up in his mess, but it looked like they had no other choice. "You belong next to me. Come on."

"Ohhh no," she protested, pushing off him. "I'm not in any state to see visitors."

Two more impatient knocks rang from the door.

He kissed her on the forehead and squished her closer. "This is no visitor. Trust me, it won't matter how you look."

"Yes, it does!" Her wide eyes pleaded as if to deny even now she wasn't stunning in every way, that a few hairs out of place would change how she took the very breath from his lungs.

If a certain pest wasn't at his front door, he'd make a point to turn her into an even hotter mess for her objections—but fate had other plans.

"Listen." He took her chin and tenderly stroked her jaw. "I don't give a fuck what this particular person thinks of you, but believe me, I think you look fine and I want you with me."

Especially in his clothes, in his apartment, under his arm. There was no room for anyone else.

"*Sure.*" She rolled her eyes. "With your vice grip, I guess I'm stuck here, but I'm blaming my bad looks on you."

The corners of his mouth twitched. "If you must. Although," he added, steering them to the door, "I take that as a compliment."

She pursed her lips and huffed in disapproval, but her arm wrapped around his waist. *That's right. Mine.* His mood lifted a smidge.

Well aware of who stood on the other side of the door, he didn't bother looking through the peephole and swung it open mid-way, wide enough to show he was otherwise engaged.

Jewelle glared back, hard onyx eyes in stark contrast to her warm, sappy smile.

"As you can see, I'm busy," he snarled, not giving her a chance to speak. "Get off my doorstep."

Whatever havoc she wanted to stir up wasn't going to happen. Not today, not tomorrow, not ever again.

Through the corner of his eyes, he noticed Nia's shocked expression and rubbed his thumb against her waist. His words came out harsher than she usually heard from him, but not everyone deserved his hospitality.

Jewelle almost scowled. *Almost.* But then she tucked a strand of shining black hair behind her ear and managed a blush. "Oh, did I wake you up? My bad, I know how you get in the mornings."

Her eyes drifted down to Nia. "I should have known...when will you be done?"

"Jewelle," Caspian said through clenched teeth, "This is my girlfriend—we aren't going to be *done*. Ever."

Nia gripped the hem of his sweatpants tighter, and he felt a wave of anger roll off her toward Jewelle. Despite the situation, he found her possessiveness adorable and sexy. All the things he'd rather be doing right now...

"Ah, so that's what you're calling it," Jewelle cooed. "I came by because Serena was worried."

"Serena?" Nia spoke. "What's she worried about?"

Jewelle's smile split, sparkling white teeth showing through Cheshire lips. "She didn't say, not in so many words."

"Caspian and I are perfectly fine," Nia said and narrowed her eyes. "There's no need to worry."

He watched as his girl stood strong and squared her shoulders, reduced to admiration at Nia's definitive words. She truly was his.

"Oh, but you don't know him like I do," Jewelle countered.

"You don't know shit about me." He flexed his hand to keep it from balling into a fist. He couldn't be sure of what he would do at the moment. More drama was the last thing they needed, but the thought alone piqued his satisfaction.

"If you need anything, you have my number." Jewelle

flashed a presumptuous smirk, then turned on her heel and retreated down the hallway.

Nia crossed her arms. "Who the hell was that?"

Jewelle wasn't yet out of earshot, and he was sure she was listening intently, her mission accomplished.

"A bitch from the past." Caspian stepped back and shut the door, then walked into his bedroom. He snatched his phone off the dresser and shoved it in Nia's hands. "Name is Jewelle. Block her."

She took the phone but re-crossed her arms, feet planted firmly to prevent his escape. "That's not gonna cut it. I need answers. Who is she to you?"

"She's no one to me." He reached out, but Nia stepped back to evade him. Concern knit his brows. "You've never met her? She said she knows Serena. I thought—"

"I haven't, but seems like you have," Nia retorted. "Why does she think she can come here to check up on you? Or me, for that matter?" She bit her lip, and much too hard for his liking. It was going to draw blood, which bothered him more than Jewelle ever could.

"Nia, stop. You're going to hurt your lip."

"You're going to hurt *me*." Her voice rose as she turned her back to him.

He raked his fingers through his hair. Please, no. Not a repeat of last time.

At last, he sighed. "You want to know what happened six months ago?"

Feeling the sudden weight of gravity, he sat down on the edge of the bed. It felt too big, too empty without Nia. "Sit down, I'll tell you whatever you want to know."

Watching her back, he waited to see if she would run or stay. She turned and pinned him with a savage glare. "You slept with her."

His elbows went to his knees, tension strung through each limb. "What did you hear?"

She sighed and shifted on her feet, feather-like shadows from her eyelashes framing the worry in her eyes. Wordlessly she sat down, keeping at least a foot between them. "I recognized her from a blog. She was at the costume party dancing with Serena, but I only remembered where I saw her from just now."

"A blog?" He eyed her, knowing whatever Jewelle touched—in real life or on the internet—was not good news.

Nia fidgeted with his phone, tracing the lines of the case as their faces reflected in the screen. "Yeah, her friend wrote it or something. There were pictures of them...and you. That's how I found it. The stupid selfies you pass around like candy—"

"—like candy?" he scoffed.

"That's not the point." She rolled her eyes. "The girl who wrote the blog thought she was dating you, and then you slept with that Jewelle girl because she was willing. There were even photos of..." Her voice faltered, and she bit her lip again.

Oh. Those.

It was never easy to remember. From the pain that swirled in her eyes, he knew she thought the same thing would happen to her. That killed him even more. "That story isn't entirely true."

"Which part?" she asked. "You sleeping together, or why you did it?"

He closed his eyes and took a deep breath. Looking up, he fixed his eyes on her. "This isn't something I talk about. Got it?"

She nodded, hands stilling.

"Come here." When he stretched out his arm, she slid closer. He picked up her palm and idly inspected each slender finger, toying with her tiny knuckles.

Now that he had her, she deserved to know everything. He

wouldn't pretend to be the victim, never had, but he still didn't know how she'd interpret his words. Best to get the facts out of the way first.

"Last year I had no direction," he started. "It's true I slept with a lot of people, but I never promised anything—no relationships, no commitment—and I didn't sleep with one chick while leading another on. Jewelle's friend and I started messing around, nothing serious." He gave her a sideways glance. "She liked to play hard to get, and I didn't mind, but now I think it may have been something else. One night after she'd turned me down, Jewelle invited me to a party. I thought nothing of it at the time."

He brought Nia's hand to his lips and placed soft kisses on her joints. "I admit I might've ended up interested in Jewelle down the road, but not that night. Then..." Nausea swept over him, and he had to push bile back down his throat. "Then she slipped a roofie in my drink."

"What?" Nia breathed, eyes softening.

Her surprise didn't sit well with him. Two nights ago, she'd been drunk and practically alone—at a much larger party. The same thing could have easily happened to her, and if...

He swallowed and realigned his thoughts. One thing at a time.

"The next morning, I woke up groggy with hardly any memory of the night before. I had to find out what happened from everyone else, and their narrative all painted me as the bad guy. Jewelle said I took advantage of her because of her friend's rejection."

Nia leaned over and placed her head on his shoulder. "That's messed up. I can't believe they would take things that far."

"Defending myself was pointless," he said. "I was the guy who slept around, and they were innocent victims. But you don't need to worry. I'm fine, and life goes on." He stretched his arm behind her back, glad that she had believed him. "I only regret that it caused a rift between us."

"So there's nothing between you and Jewelle?"

He nudged her to look up, raising his eyebrows to get the point across. "No. That shit should've been buried a long time ago. I have no idea why Jewelle showed up again."

"It's Serena," Nia muttered. "I don't know why they are hanging out, but neither of them can get over you." She straightened; mouth set in a hard line. "You don't think they'll try something again?"

"They already did." He pulled his legs up on the bed and wrapped them around her, heart-melting at her smile as she nestled into his chest. "Jewelle tried to talk to me at the party, and then showed up today." He sighed. "It doesn't matter. They won't get anywhere, and I won't let anything happen to you."

"I won't let anything happen to *you*." Nia emphasized. "I should block her."

He chuckled. "That is why you're holding my phone. You can go through all the names if you want. I won't keep anything from you."

Turning the phone in her hands, Nia tapped the screen, then hesitated. "I know it's none of my business, but...how many girls did you get with since I left?"

"I didn't."

She tipped her head up, eyes full of curiosity. He stroked her face, lost in her for a brief moment. "I was trying—and failing horribly—to get you off my mind at the costume party, but you sort of crashed those plans."

An amused grin flashed on her face and spread to his. She shouldn't be so proud of her drunken self. But he did have to give her some credit.

Just a tiny bit.

303

"My little vixen."

She glowed with pride. "Well, I was the goddess of love, you didn't stand a chance."

"I still don't," he whispered, leaning down to kiss her, and pulling them both down onto the bed.

FORTY-SEVEN

Caspian

ABDOMEN GLISTENING WITH SWEAT, HE THREW A QUICK JAB AND followed through with a right hook. The punching bag jolted, and Nia grunted.

"You okay?" he rasped.

She hummed in confirmation, body dwarfed as she braced the bag from behind. He didn't often get a partner at the gym, but she was by far his favorite. Especially with the way her eyes roamed over his torso, licking over his abs and sizing up his pecs like they were her next meal. Which they could be, and if he got any say in the matter, they would be. Anywhere, anytime.

Her gaze flicked around his biceps as if they earned her admiration a little more with each demonstration of strength. His muscles burned deliciously under her approval, endorphins singing through his bloodstream.

"Your hits are so much more forceful than mine," she pouted, tucking back a few strands of ruby hair that had fallen out of her ponytail.

"I'm not demonstrating strength; I'm demonstrating technique. More power will come with time." Although she was right that he had the upper hand now, seeing the strength she already used had been enough to strike fear into his heart. He had no doubt she'd become a force worth reckoning with in no time. "Once your muscles become accustomed to the motion, you'll be able to do just as much damage."

"I doubt that," she muttered, face scrunched into a cute frown.

They switched places, and he secured the bag with his hip. "Let's not test the theory, okay? I'm already nervous about the next time I get on your bad side."

"Oh, don't be scared of little ol' me." she chuckled, but he didn't miss the gleam in her eye.

Eyebrows raised, he faked a grimace. "You're terrifying."

"Ha." Rolling her eyes, she replicated his stance and performed a one-two combo, turning her body into the punch. Her tits and ass jiggled as she moved, and he enjoyed the view as much as her improved skill.

"Good. Again," he instructed.

On the next combo, she focused too much on power and speed, short-changing her posture.

He tsked.

"I know," she huffed. Her next hit was on point, smacking the bag with a loud *thwack*. After ten combos, her consistency greatly improved, and the force behind her punches steadily increased. With that kind of fierce concentration, Nia learned much quicker than most, even faster than he had.

Finished, her arms dropped like dead weights. "I'm already feeling sore; tomorrow's gonna be hell," she groaned.

He stepped around the bag and cupped her jaw, giving her a chaste kiss. "Sore is a good thing. You did well."

"If that's supposed to have a double meaning, I'm about to practice my punches on you," she grumbled.

Her brain was a dirtier place than he gave her credit for.

And he loved it.

306

"Remember, for now, I can still take you. I'm not afraid to tackle you to the ground." He grinned as she shot him a glare, almost forgetting where they were. "Let's go back and shower, *then* we can talk about being sore." He dodged a punch aimed at his side and wrapped his arm around her waist, pulling her into a sweaty hug.

"Ew! Let go!" she exclaimed, turning her nose away.

He chuckled and released her. She didn't smell so good herself, but her body odor didn't bother him as much as he thought it would. Plus, seeing her slick with sweat turned him on more than he'd admit.

The constant state of arousal from being near her had become more bearable with practice and lots of patience. But he'd never quit fighting the battle to win her over, even after they got over their hurdles. After admitting the depth of his feelings, waiting had become a privilege instead of a chore. He didn't mind the simple kisses, their simple touches—because, in reality they weren't simple or small at all. His whole world was a tapestry of Nia, woven from a collection of those tiny moments. The rest would come in time, and no matter how long or short it took, he knew it'd be well worth it.

They gathered their things and walked to his car, a near-winter breeze licking their skin as they gulped down water. Nia updated him on her midterms and how ecstatic Ivory had been that they were back together, all the while clinging to his arm like a little koala.

He happily listened to her rambles, loving the passion in her eyes when she talked about whatever was on her mind. But his mood shifted when she mentioned Serena had been avoiding her for weeks, ever since the Halloween party. At least if they got into any kind of fight, he was certain Nia would win, but he'd do whatever he could to prevent that.

Once they got to the apartment, he let her shower first while he prepared the kitchen. They'd agreed to exchange boxing lessons for her cooking mac n' cheese, and he was looking forward to his end of the deal. If only all his Saturdays could be filled with boxing and good food—and, most importantly, Nia.

The water shut off, and a few minutes later the bathroom door creaked open. He turned just as she walked out, then his eyes widened. Tiny droplets sparkled as they slipped over the swell of her breasts, peeking out over a small towel that hardly hid the curve of her ass.

He swallowed, dragging his eyes back up as her steps halted. She knew better than to come out like this and not expect him to enjoy the view.

She hesitated as a blush colored her face, then curled her lips into a sweet smirk. "I know I'm a work of art."

Recognition flashed through his brain. Those were his words, and he knew all too well how that sentence had ended.

"I'd watch my next words if I were you," he warned, stalking closer. This day was getting better and better. The light aroma of vanilla encompassed the air, taunting him with the smooth taste he knew would be on every inch of her radiant skin.

"Oh?" she hummed, chewing her lip as he tested her resolve.

A hair's breadth of space separated them—but he stopped, daring her to make the first move. The normal doe eyes she wore transformed into something sinister, shining in a sinful way that made his pulse throb harder. Normally, she'd back down by now, but she met his gaze head-on.

"You know," she whispered. "I almost invited you into the shower with me."

His breath caught. He never knew her voice could sound so sultry, dripping with an invitation he was more than ready to accept. She had no idea what she just got herself into.

"It's never too late." He grinned wickedly as she stared at him. His little goddess remained unwilling to move but more than happy to tempt. "I think that dirty mind of yours needs a little extra cleaning."

He reached down and hooked his arms around her rear. She gasped as he hauled her over his shoulder and dragged her back into the shower. "What? No! Not in here," she protested.

He turned on the spigot, and hot water soaked right through his clothes, slicking off the salt on his skin.

"Now, what am I going to dry off with?" she pouted as he set her down, motioning to the towel that clung even tighter to her curves. The fabric slipped off further and exposed a hint of her dark pink areola. Shit. He couldn't take this any longer. He needed her.

Every. Fucking. Inch.

"My tongue," he answered and peeled the damn towel off, tossing it on the tile outside. She moaned as his lips latched onto hers and hungrily devoured them with a greedy kiss, then roamed to her jaw and down to her chest. He couldn't get enough.

Wrapping his hands around her wet body, he filled his palms with her heavenly skin and released a guttural growl. Her sighs and heavy breaths fed his desire, redirecting all his thoughts and energy to the woman who owned them.

High on arousal, she let him claim her—but not without enjoying him as well. She dropped her hands from his jaw to his chest, brushing over his nipples and skimming down his abdomen. Her touch was feather-light, yet it branded him, marking deeper than a red-hot iron and leaving scars he never wanted to heal.

His cock throbbed, straining toward her through his sweatpants. The fabric had become too heavy and much too tight, but he couldn't take his hands off her, and his lips were too busy for words. He kissed and licked up the tiny streams of water that ran over her skin, nibbling around her stiff nipples before taking them in his mouth. She tasted sweeter than syrup, softer than marshmallows, more enticing than his favorite meal.

Scratch that. She was his favorite meal.

"I've waited too damn long to taste you," he rasped, making his way up her shoulder as she tipped her head back to give him proper access.

Her response came as an incomprehensible sigh. She dragged her hands through his hair and pulled him again to her lips. Fuck, her little tongue was wrecking his mouth, down to his last ounce of self-control. Holding the back of her neck, he slid his tongue over hers and explored the neat row of her teeth.

At first, she fought to reclaim control, but he wouldn't give in. They collapsed on the shower wall, and he pressed her against the smooth, hard tile. Bracing a hand by her head, he savored the taste of her lips as he teased them between his teeth, then parted her legs with his knee. The gasp she made was cute, but there was nothing innocent about the way she rubbed her hot pussy over his thigh. He couldn't concentrate on anything else. Her heat rivaled that of the shower and soaked through his pants.

An invisible force drew his hand down, and his fingers grazed over her sex.

Oh, shit.

He was so fucked.

She quivered and spread her legs, allowing him to dip further between her folds. For a moment, he became utterly lost, coating his fingers with the luxurious warm silk and skating back up to her perked breasts.

"Please let me have you." His voice came out gritty, and dammit, it sounded just as needy as he felt. "All of you."

She whined, a sound that had his dick nearly tearing through his underwear. Taking notice, she pawed at the elastic of his sweats.

"The knot," he croaked. "Untie the knot."

He wanted to help, but she was being such a good girl and managed to get the job done herself. That left his hands free to tweak her nipples while his mouth went back to hers.

To his surprise, she yanked down his briefs as well, and he kicked off the last of their clothes, finally able to enjoy her completely, skin to skin.

Steam swirled around them as he drank in the sight of her —the smell, the feel of her sharpened nipples under his fingertips. About to drop to his knees, he came to an abrupt halt as a rush of pure pleasure stole the breath from his lungs.

Nia was more than eager to please, and her hands had wrapped around his manhood. She remembered the earlier lesson well, going straight to the sensitive spot on the underside of his head.

Before he could register what was happening, she slid to *her* knees. Clear crystal blue eyes peered up at him, her back arched so he could see the swell of her ass.

His lips parted, but nothing came out, and she beat him to the punch.

"Let me taste you first."

FORTY-EIGHT

Nia

THE THRUM OF BLOOD, HOT AND THICK IN HER VEINS, CARRIED heady arousal and a rush of endorphins through her entire body. But nothing compared to the way Caspian was looking at her, jaw unhinged, chest heaving like he'd just run a marathon.

Priceless.

Her nipples ached from his touch, lips swollen and tingling, clit pulsing as she felt arousal drip down her thighs. Every pore felt heavy with need, overcome with the impulse to tease and taste and *indulge*—to embody the sexy women she read and wrote about.

The same woman she'd pictured ten minutes ago as she carefully ran a razor over her legs and everywhere between, scrubbing her skin clean and summoning her best fantasies.

The woman Caspian had always championed her as.

"Like what you see?" she asked, intending to sound full of confidence, but instead, the words came out as an uneven whisper.

He inhaled sharply, cock surging in response. "Baby girl, I'm not even sure you're real right now, but if you stop, I think I might actually die."

313

The awe in his stormy eyes made her feel immortal. Desirable. Special.

He looked no less than a god himself. The spray of water landed squarely between broad shoulders, steady streams running over his chiseled chest and refined abdomen before evaporating into thick steam that filled her lungs.

Face mere millimeters from his glistening erection, her jaw ached at the concept of taking him in. He smelled of earthy musk and salt, but also of sweet skin and spicy masculinity. Their renewed dynamic unlocked many parts of her—and though before she would've felt weak for letting a man enrapture her this way, for making her want to get on her knees —now she felt empowered.

He supported her desire to learn to fight, helped her cope with emotions she'd banished for so many years, and welcomed her desire to please. Even though she had no prior experience, her tongue tingled with anticipation. Both hands were necessary to encircle his girth, and tentatively, she placed a kiss on his tip.

"*Shit*," he hissed, eyes trained on her. "Just like that, keep going."

She grinned, lips pressing into the bulb of his swollen, tight skin. Palming him more firmly, she moved her hands up and down like he'd shown her. Then, a little faster, to test how he liked it.

His hips jerked out, stomach quivering as a debased, caveman-like noise came from the back of his throat. Oh, he liked it.

She sped up, squeezed a little more, and kissed more courageously until he made that toe-curling sound again. The way his body responded captivated her, pulsing outward to fill her hand as if his life depended on it. Relaxing her lips, her tongue ventured out to lick up the dew that collected in his slit.

He tasted rich and slightly tangy, a savory blend that made her mouth water.

Groaning, he shifted to brace his back against the tiled wall and brought a hand to the top of her head, wiping away wet strands of hair on the side of her face. "Take whatever you want, baby girl. I'm all yours."

The words, accompanied by a look of pure bliss and a hint of agony, unlatched a hinge inside her. She ran her tongue up and down his length, delighting in the silken texture, the hard-as-diamond rod slick with water and saliva. His fingers tenderly brushed the corner of her jaw, his touch loving, appreciative.

She looked up, eyes ravenous for his sculpted body and memorized by the force that pulled her to him. Their eyes locked as she took him into her mouth, hardly able to keep her teeth from scraping skin as she swallowed as much as she could.

"Fuck," he moaned, head rolling back as his hand caressed her jaw.

His response pleased her as much as she seemed to please him, so she pulled away and swallowed him again, impossibly deeper, until she felt him tickle the back of her throat. His hand tensed, and he let out a heavy exhale. She could feel how he strained against the urge to move, thighs bunching and breaths ragged.

Instinctually, she wanted to keep going, to give more, but her body had other plans. She gagged and jerked away, sputtering.

"Mmm." Caspian's groans soothed her embarrassment as he searched her watery eyes. She gave a small grin, and his hand came back to stroke her face, thumb rubbing her lip. He didn't pressure her to continue but didn't seem bothered or turned off by her reaction.

Aware of her limit, she took him in again and let him glide along the flat of her tongue, drawing back enough to tease his slit before pushing in again. He felt incredible, strong and commanding, yet let her take complete control.

"It's so good...*damn*," he growled amidst another earthquake of groans. "You're such a good girl."

With *that*, her head bobbed all the more, coaxing out shudders and audible grunts from her willing victim. His hips flexed, thrusting with her movements and gradually increasing the speed. She anchored herself with one hand around his thick base and let the other explore, moving between his thighs and massaging his tender sack. His skin felt softer there, pliant and delicate.

"Don't stop," he rasped, hand guiding her head up and down. "I'm about to come. If you don't w—"

She wrapped her lips tighter around him, sucking as she moved back and forth. Caspian let out a string of curses and jerked into her mouth. She would have chuckled at his incapacity for speech if her mouth wasn't in the same predicament.

Instead, she moaned around his arousal, her own heart rate spiking. She tightened her grip on him as if trying to help contain the inevitable, but it only pushed him closer to the edge. His breath came out in short, punctured rasps as he clenched his jaw and literally collapsed.

Knees buckling, he fainted into the wall. Hot, creamy liquid filled her mouth. She swallowed, captivated at consuming a part of him and drawing out his shudders.

A single heartbeat of silence mingled with the sound of running water, then he cradled her jaw and pulled her up to his lips. She stood, red circles decorating her kneecaps and lips marked with his cum. His blue eyes shimmered, an ocean of reverence and rapture.

"You have no idea what you just did to me." His voice was all gravel and grit, the most threatening whisper she ever heard. He kissed her excruciatingly deep, turning her insides to mush before coming up for air. "But I'm about to show you *exactly* how proud I am."

Before she could blink, he braced her against the adjacent wall and sank down to her sex. His lips latched onto the skin at her hip and sent a shock of electricity straight to her core. She gasped at the sudden intensity—and he wasn't even *there* yet.

"Ah...*Caspian*," she warned. This was almost too much to take.

He sucked on her skin until she couldn't stay still, both pushing him away and pulling him closer, her nails marking little crescent moons into his shoulder blades. His teeth nipped and scraped across her belt line, veering down to nuzzle her trimmed bush.

"This is different from how I remember it," he murmured, flattening his tongue around her outer lips.

"Shaved," she gasped, fighting for air. "But please, ahh—" She squirmed as he sucked her into his mouth. "Careful, I accidentally cut myself."

He placed a kiss on the center of her silken fur. "Next time, let me do it."

The thought of him holding any kind of shaving tool between her bare legs terrified her, but she didn't have much time to dwell on the thought as his lips roamed to her other hip, repeating the torture from earlier. He focused on the dip right below her bone, unrelenting as his tongue flicked out and elicited a cry from her lips.

"*Too much*," she gasped as her leg kicked involuntarily.

He caught her thigh in his palm and with an expert twist, hooked it over his shoulder. She grabbed at the wall for support, searching for some kind of tether. However, her imbalance was more mental than physical. He held her steady with a hand on her waist, her heat positioned directly in front of his face. If she hadn't felt exposed and vulnerable before, she did now...but more than that, she was excited, strung up in palpable anticipation.

He admired her, watching with the intrigue of a cat before it pounced. Her muscles clenched as one long finger reached out and lazily circled her entrance.

She didn't know his plan, but it was working marvelously. He barely touched her, and she'd become a mess, absolute putty in his hands.

"So warm," he breathed, easing into her until his knuckle met her soft folds. Unlike a wand, he could flex and wiggle inside, and he did. She mewled at how he stretched her delicately, so deliciously, and her walls gripped him as if to hold him there forever.

"Fuck baby girl, so soft." He groaned. "And so fucking tight." Awe coated his voice as he swiped his thumb over her clit, pressing into her overzealous bundle of nerves. She could only sigh and grip his shoulder, unsure of what would come out if she tried to form coherent words.

He looked up with sapphire eyes, and she all but fainted. "Let's see how many licks it takes me to get to your center."

She hated to break it to him, but he was already there. His tongue met her clit, and she released a strangled moan, head thudding against the tile as her hips flexed outward to chase the pleasure. How did his mouth feel like molten lava, both burning and liquefying her insides?

"*One*," she panted. "It—ah, it only takes one."

He chuckled, the vibrations going directly to the place she felt them the most. "Oh, you'll take more than that. Here, let me show you."

His tongue flattened, rolling and circling, probing with greater concentration after each round. The arousal building within her became so great that she moaned again, her voice alien as it bounced off the shower walls. Just when she thought he would give her a break, another finger wiggled inside her.

"*Caspian!*" At this point, she didn't know if she was begging him to stop or to keep going. All the air got sucked out of her lungs as he curled his fingers in response, bringing his lips back to her clit. He sucked her into his mouth, swirling his tongue and constricting his lips.

Her muscles seized and convulsed around his fingers as he continued to massage her. She gushed against his lips, and he readily licked her up, leaving nothing to spare. She felt as if every cell in her body was focused on handling the pleasure he doled out, her senses primed only to take in what he gave. But it still wasn't enough—she was overflowing and yet craved more.

The sheer flood of sensation made her wobble and forced her to hold on to his head, which worsened—or bettered—her circumstance. His lips parted from her searing sex to nibble on the tender skin at the start of her thigh. The electricity he stirred up earlier came back to life, zapping her nearly useless legs. "Ah, Caspian, I..."

"*You* are addicting," he finished, before he went back to finishing *her*.

"Caspian...*please*." Reduced to a shallow whisper, she felt herself fade into a blind ecstasy. His fingers stroked her over and over, enticing her pulse to throb stronger against his merciless tongue. Without conscious effort, she rolled her hips into his mouth, nectar coating his chin. Her thighs trembled, held in place by his hand and the sheer willpower to reach the top of her high. She was so close, nearly there...

And he stopped.

Head snapping down, she conjured up the most irritated face she could, which probably looked more pathetic than anything else. His lips curled into a deadly smirk against her skin, his eyes darker than pure onyx. A third finger nestled into her, and a breathy groan exited her lips.

"Watch," he whispered. *Watch what I can do to you.*

She did.

Jaw-dropping, she felt him nudge her clit, saw his satisfaction as he sent sparks up and down her spine that curled her toes and jump-started her heart. She couldn't look away, couldn't even scream as he stroked again and again, his fingers stretching her innermost region while the tip of his tongue flicked against her clit like a whip. Her world reduced to a pinhole. The coil of tension snapped. She surrendered.

All was lost. Everything was gained.

Her fingers dug into his scalp as he held her to his tongue, humming contentment with a low growl as she unraveled in merciless, undulating waves of pleasure. At last, consciousness resurfaced, and she felt his fingers rocking inside, coaxing the last of her nectar out into his awaiting mouth.

Overwhelming satisfaction gripped her down to the root of her being. This time, she knew their intimacy meant something to him. She had seen it in his eyes, and he saw it in hers. Her climax had been as emotional as it was physical.

"Caspian," she whispered faintly, too weak to say more.

He stood and encircled her in his arms, holding her while her heart returned to a normal rhythm. "You're mine, Nia."

"Yes." Her arms remembered how to work, and she hugged him back. "That was amazing."

Something impertinently prodded her thighs. Caspian cleared his throat. "I think it's my turn to take a shower." He pulled away slightly. "A very cold one."

She looked down to see him hardening *again*.

"You're a monster." She couldn't go another round even if she wanted to.

He chuckled and pecked a kiss on her lips. "No, that's all you, baby girl. Now go put some clothes on before you see how much of a monster I really am."

She didn't know whether to roll her eyes or gasp, but a very over-stimulated part of her body couldn't help but believe him. So, instead, she shook her head and stepped out of the shower.

As her foot landed on the cool tile, a small sting bloomed across her rear.

"Hey, what was that for?" She turned and glared.

"Maybe next time you'll remember to invite me in *before* you get out of the shower."

FORTY-NINE

Nia

"Mm, sounds delicious," Caspian hummed, wrapping his arms around her waist as she dragged a spoon around the overflowing pan. "Smells good, too."

His breath tickled the shell of her ear, and she giggled. The fresh scent of his soap and the coolness of skin sent a wave of chills along her spine. She swayed her hips as his bare chest pressed into her back. "I hope you like it. This is pretty much the only thing I can cook from scratch."

"My mouth is already watering."

A smile pulled her checks up so far it hurt. Too many happy memories had filled this morning, so much that it was nearly impossible to contain them all.

"I see you couldn't manage to find a clean shirt?" she teased. Caspian's habitual state of undress wasn't really an issue, but she had to get him to wear a shirt *sometimes*. What if they invited friends over? Or if there was an emergency evacuation, and they had no choice but to stand out in the snow?

What if it just became too distracting for her poor self to handle?

She thoroughly enjoyed their fun earlier, and although her

current appetite extended beyond a bowl of mac n cheese, she wanted to savor every tiny step they took as a couple. His hugs and kisses were just as gratifying as steamy shower excursions.

"Nope, couldn't find one." He placed a barrage of delicate kisses on the back of her neck.

A wave of tingles followed his soft lips, and she renewed her efforts to ensure the noodles didn't burn. "Guess your wardrobe was hiding again."

"Mn." His mouth was too busy to spare a proper response, traveling down her spine and leaving a warm, ticklish trail.

"Okay, okay, enough," she gasped, spinning to push him off. He liked to press buttons she didn't even know she had.

His arms loosened around her waist, and he smiled down at her, damp hair falling over his eyes. "You're making me way too cheesy, you know that?"

She stifled a grin and turned back to the pot, ignoring the blush creeping up her face. At this rate, they wouldn't get anything done. "I'm trying to make these noodles cheesy, but you aren't letting me."

"I got you something," he said with a warm inflection.

"Oh?" It was her turn to be too occupied to respond, adding in some herbs and a pad of butter to the pot.

"Look." He stepped back and tugged on the waistband of the briefs she "borrowed" from him—with no intention of giving back. While Caspian couldn't find his clothes, she did.

She turned off the stove and spun around. This time, warmth fanned across her cheeks in full force at the sight of him, dark eyebrows and high cheekbones, wide shoulders, and rippling muscles.

He smirked. "Not there, lower."

She raised her eyebrows and swept her gaze down his body, landing on... *oh my*.

"You're kidding."

"I think it's a nice touch." His grin was audible as she read the words printed on his new pair of briefs, *Property of Nia*, with puckered lips imprinted over the proud, semi-hard bulge. "Came in the mail yesterday, but I have to say I'm glad I waited to show them to you, considering how today's gone."

The heat in her cheeks flared as it wound between her legs, and she went back to stirring the mac n cheese, although it was already finished. "I don't see how those are necessary."

He chuckled, reaching over her head to grab two bowls from the cupboard. "It's my way of saying as much as you're mine, I'm yours. No one else comes near this dick but you."

She laughed and rolled her eyes at his choice of words, but inside melted into a mess of goo, not unlike the one on the stove in front of her.

"That's a big responsibility, you know," he added.

"Oh, I'm aware of how *big* it is," she scoffed and took a bowl from him, spooning in a generous helping of the creamy goodness. She handed him the bowl, leaning in to grab a stealthy kiss. "I appreciate the gesture."

Their eyes connected, causing a stream of butterflies to flutter from her belly to her heart and then invade everywhere else.

"I appreciate the meal." He dazzled her with a smile and a wink. "Both meals, actually."

She grabbed the second empty bowl and pivoted to hide her face. Maybe someday she'd get used to his flirting, but not today.

After serving and grabbing utensils, they sat together on the couch. Caspian had never invested in a table or kitchen stools, but it didn't bother her.

They *mmm*'d in unison on the first bite, too busy eating to talk for the first few moments. She'd called her mom earlier in the week to get the recipe and followed it exactly, and to her pleasant surprise, it tasted the same as she remembered.

"Baby girl, you are amazing," he praised, already going back for seconds.

"Credit goes to my mom," she called over her shoulder, grateful she made the full recipe instead of halving it.

"Speaking of moms," he said, sitting down again. His thigh brushed hers, and she leaned a little closer. "I decided I should reach out to mine."

"Really?" He rarely talked to either of his parents, and last she heard his mom was on his blacklist, so she wondered what brought on the change. "That's good, I mean...I hope it goes well."

"I'll let you know. How's your mom?" he asked, changing the topic.

"Oh, she's sad I'm away at college but glad I'm doing well. In other words, a normal mom." She moved her spoon around the bowl, collecting spare noodles. "I haven't told her about us yet. I wanted to wait until we were...solid. Didn't want to jinx things since I'm not sure how she'll react to me being with someone."

"Mm," he hummed around a mouthful of noodles. "So, are we? Solid?" His tone remained casual, but the question carried all the weight in the world.

A small smile lingered on her lips, and a larger throb loomed in her heart. "Well, I don't want to be with anyone else. Ever." She looked up to meet his eyes, anchoring herself in their depths. "This may sound naïve since we met a couple months ago, but I only want you. I'm sure there'll be lots of bumps along the road, and I'm terrified of trusting someone with this much of me, and if we ever..."

She paused, not sure how to finish. "I need to see that we can keep working through our problems together this time. I've watched my mom run through too many relationships because they wanted two different things and couldn't work it out."

Caspian set his bowl down. She held her breath as he took her hand between his, encasing it between his palms. "I'm no good at using words like you are." He smiled down at their entwined fingers. "I'd rather just show you, but I know that's not always how it works."

She gave his hands a squeeze. Words didn't have to be eloquent to mean something. They just needed space to exist.

His gaze flipped up to hers. "I can please your body all day, but what I need to do—what I want to do—is please your mind. I can't guarantee I'll get a fancy job, or get a nice house, or take you on vacation every year. Pretty much what you see is what you get, but Nia..." He swallowed, dropping his voice. "I'm willing to give you everything I have. Will that be enough?"

Tears pricked the corners of her eyes. That's all she ever wanted, and he was asking if it was enough?

Heart at capacity, she smiled as their knees bumped, remembering all the times they spent together on this couch. The pain from being apart was still a not-so-distant memory, and she realized—just as much sorrow as she felt then, she experienced as joy now.

No argument, no obstacle, could be worth losing him. Losing this.

Them.

She took in every detail of his face, every line, and every shade that colored the man she loved. "Caspian, you care for me in a way no one else can. In a way I couldn't imagine wanting from anyone else. You're more than enough."

His lips parted, but instead of speaking, he leaned in and touched his lips to hers, a sweet cotton candy kiss that melted on her tongue. His hand floated up to cup her neck, and though the kiss didn't deepen, her lungs burned from lack of oxygen. She pressed into him, fusing not only their love but their hopes and dreams, fears and nightmares, giving him her everything as he did for her.

Noses brushing, she opened her eyes and felt the flutter as their eyelashes met. He leaned his forehead against hers and stared into her eyes. She could look into his eyes forever, watch as they spilled out his soul and gathered hers up.

"I love you," he sighed.

Those words, which at one point she was certain he couldn't truly mean, sounded as natural as breathing. Words he'd meant before but never explicitly said. A phrase that became a million times more meaningful the second it left *his* lips.

Humble in its wholeness, the moment overtook her and expanded—burst the seams of her stitched-up heart and reverberated in her ribs, between every heartbeat.

FIFTY

Nia

"That's...a lot."

"I know, it's huge."

"Like really *really* huge, the biggest—"

"—*sweetest* thing. I never expected him to say it," Nia gushed. She couldn't keep child-like glee out of her voice as she spoke to Ivory. With midterms and fall break approaching, they had been too busy to chat, but made time tonight to catch up in Ivory's dorm.

She'd been especially eager to know how things went with Adrian after she'd left them alone at the Halloween party, but Ivory promised to tell only after she got the scoop on Caspian.

Speaking out loud about all the time they spend together put the relationship into a larger frame, and repeating it solidified the reality of each detail. It took her breath away all over again. A few days had passed since Caspian's outright confession of love, but emotion still vibrated inside her like a high that wouldn't end.

"Did you say it back?" Ivory asked, eyes wide with curiosity, lips pressed into an excited smile.

Nia hugged a purple pillow closer to her chest, attempting

to fill the Caspian-shaped imprint in her chest. "Well...not exactly, but it's not because I don't feel the same way."

Ivory nodded, listening intently.

"I want to do something special," she continued. "Say I love him in my own way. So..." She bit her lip. "I wrote a letter." Heat crept into her face as the nerves started kicking in. The first few times around Caspian she'd been anxious, but not anymore—not unless she thought about giving him that letter.

"Aww you two are so cute!" Ivory's smile radiated on her whole face. "I'm so happy you were able to work things out."

Nia felt her blush deepen. Sure, from the outside she and Caspian were cute, but being a part of the story had her on edge with every plot twist. This latest chapter was the summit of a long journey, and after enduring the climb, she just wanted them to stay at a simple plateau.

"Okay, your turn," she mumbled. "I told you my sappy details. Is Adrian actually going to dye your hair?" She covered her mouth and giggled. "I really threw you under the bus that night. I'm sorry..." Her giggle turned into a grimace. "I was a little more impulsive than usual."

"Oh, um..." Ivory's mouth opened, then closed. "Don't worry about it. I was the awkward one, really. I don't think... well, Adrian isn't as keen on doing the relationship thing as Caspian."

Nia frowned. She wanted Ivory to be as happy as she was. "What do you mean?"

"He point-blank told me a relationship isn't gonna happen." Ivory took a deep breath. "Which is fine." She exhaled. "I'm fine."

"You can't believe that." What guy wouldn't want Ivory?

"Which part?" Ivory tried to smile, but it turned into a sad flop compared to her usual.

"Well..." Nia hummed. "Caspian wasn't quite looking for a relationship when we met, so there's still hope, and I can tell you're not fine. Someone doesn't remember a guy they saw months ago like you did, then run away the first chance they get to talk to him. You can't give up like that."

"Wow, way to call me out." Ivory shifted and slumped on her side, falling into a pile of fluff. "To his credit, he did say he'd do my hair despite...everything."

Nia raised her eyebrows.

"I'll think about it," Ivory said, narrowing her eyes in a *don't-push-it* look.

A loud laugh chimed in the hallway, followed by the click of a door opening and Serena's excited squeal. Both their eyes shot to the door, even though nothing could be seen past the slab of wood.

"What are you going to do about her and Jewelle?" Ivory asked, knowing the whole story—or Nia's side of it, at least. "Avril and those two have become inseparable, like the sisterhood of the traveling stilettos."

"You don't have to pick a side." Nia pursed her lips. "*I* have to. The things Jewelle has done..." she trailed off, knowing there wouldn't be a time she didn't feel rage toward that girl.

At first, she had questioned the integrity of Caspian's story, but she also knew what it felt like to be on the receiving end of an abuser. He didn't have to overplay being a victim for her to tell he'd been affected. Even when discussing his family issues, he didn't tense the same way when talking about Jewelle. Plus, he handed over his phone without hesitation, and she wasn't one to go through his messages, but took comfort knowing she had full access. He trusted her completely.

She scowled. "I swear the only reason I haven't said anything yet is I get so worked up over it all. Besides, I really don't think some people are worth the drama."

"I still can't believe Serena hasn't mentioned it at all..." Ivory bent her elbow and propped her head up with a hand. "I don't think she knows what Jewelle said or did."

"Doesn't know, or doesn't care." Nia spat the words like poison.

In direct contact with her venom, Ivory's eyes softened. "You know, Jewelle and Avril were close last year. I'm not vouching for Serena, but she's not involved."

"You think Avril was in on it?" Nia asked.

Ivory shrugged.

"Well, it doesn't matter as long as they mind their business." Nia knotted her fingers. "Something tells me they won't." History had a bad habit of repeating itself, and so far, the cycle had too fast of a turnaround for her liking.

"We should just ask them," Ivory said. "There's no use speculating—"

"Ask what?" she interrupted. "All I have to say is Caspian is taken, and they need to back off. Pretty sure I've made that clear."

Ivory giggled. "I bet if Caspian could see you right now, he'd be proud."

She huffed and rolled her eyes but let go of some of the tension. "You're right." Her tone lightened, and she set the pillow aside and slid off the bed. "I don't want this hanging over me. If Serena's here, I'm going to go talk to her."

"I'll go with you." Ivory stood up.

"You don't have to. I'll be okay." Nia turned and gave a smile. "It's my battle."

Ivory pouted. "I can be moral support."

"If you insist." Nia shrugged, but as she walked to the door, she had to force down the lump gathering in her throat.

This wasn't for her sake alone; it was for Caspian and anyone else Jewelle schemed against. She had to be called out. If Serena really didn't know anything, she could become prey, too.

Sure enough, as they stepped into the hallway and turned

to the common room, Serena sat conversing with Avril and Jewelle.

Her shoulders tensed. Jewelle hadn't come to the dorms before—normally, they hung out at the frat house.

"Oh," Ivory breathed beside her.

Nia steeled her eyes and kept walking. As soon as the trio noticed her approach, Jewelle smirked.

Serena, however, looked less than pleased. Her lips struggled to tug upwards in a polite smile. "Oh hey."

Avril waved, eyes darting between the tense energies filling the common room. Either she knew everything and decided to play dumb or sat in apprehension of their conversation.

"Did you send Jewelle to check up on me after the costume party?" Nia asked outright, a few feet from where Serena sat. The sooner she got this over with, the better.

Serena's eyes widened, and she shifted. "No, why would I?" Turning to Jewelle, she cocked her head and looked back at Nia. "I wasn't aware you even knew each other."

Nia shifted her gaze to Jewelle, who appeared completely unbothered. Her hands rested on the table as she observed everyone else, like this was some kind of soap opera, and she got to play director. Her calm demeanor was accentuated by smooth skin, no trace of worry or wrinkle. Confident in her complete control.

"She didn't *send* me." Jewelle's voice came out cool, gliding off her tongue like melted ice. "We all saw the way you were that night, practically opening up your legs on the dance floor. I know Caspian can break little hearts like yours, so when you didn't come back, I went to see if you were still in one piece."

Nia's scowl hardened. She didn't care if Serena had been involved with Jewelle's plot or not. As long as they continued to be friends, they wouldn't be hers.

"Why in the world would you say that?" Ivory cut in, her face drawn in concern and shock.

"It's true," Serena chimed in. "Caspian's broken you down enough. It was stupid to throw yourself at him like that, and you're delusional if you think he's any good."

"All of you? That's all you think?" She glared at the three girls, who exchanged sideways glances. That was a load of bullshit, coming from the girls who swooned over him the most. This was an outright attack, and Ivory's presence was the only thing left to calm her down.

"He's not the only one with a dick, sweetie." Avril coated the insult with a layer of sweet corn syrup.

"You would know," Nia sneered. Maybe she wasn't as brazen as them, but more than ever, she was confident they were the delusional ones. They weren't concerned for her in the slightest, and they couldn't care less how many girls Caspian slept with.

"At least we don't confuse one-night stands with boyfriend material." Serena's lips curved up in a smirk, empowered by her two comrades. "If you're going to be a slut, at least know when you're doing it."

Nia's jaw dropped, and she promptly reset it. She anticipated a battle of words, but she hadn't worn Kevlar around her heart. This bullet had been too fast to stop; it zinged right where it hurt the most.

The whole time, that's how the others viewed her? The one party she went to, the one time they *convinced* her to attend, that's all they saw?

"That went way too far." Ivory stepped up, blocking Jewelle from Nia's view.

"Let me handle this." Nia moved around Ivory, squaring her jaw and setting her shoulders. Her hands shook, heart pounding with anger and anxiety, but she needed to defend herself no matter how weak she felt. "The only reason you're attacking me is because Caspian *hasn't* broken any hearts lately. If he were still sleeping around, then you'd care more about getting in his pants than hurling insults at my face, wouldn't you? Not that you're opposed to *rape*."

Everyone in the room gasped and Jewelle stood up, peering down her nose at Nia. "Don't accuse me of things you can't prove. It's only a matter of time. You won't be able to keep him tethered to you for long, and I know where to find him."

The rush of air.

A slight sting. Tingling in her palm.

She felt the sensation of her slap before registering the action. A red print spread across Jewelle's cheek as Serena jumped up from her seat. "You bitch!"

"Leave," Avril demanded, standing up as well. "Jewelle is clearly the victim here."

"Show up at his doorstep one more time, I dare you," Nia hissed, then gave them all one last glare before storming out of the room.

FIFTY-ONE

Caspian

ANSWERING THE PHONE, HE CRADLED IT BETWEEN HIS NECK AND shoulder before picking back up his paintbrush. "Hey, baby girl."

"Caspian... "

Eyebrows furrowed, his tone changed the instant she took in an unsteady breath. "What's wrong? Did something happen?"

"I saw Jewelle."

He jumped up from the desk, paintbrush clattering onto the palette. "Shit, what did she do?"

He could tell Nia wasn't crying or distraught, but he didn't like it. Should he have stayed with her at the dorms? Calculating the potential severity of their encounter, he braced for the worst.

"Nothing, but I...I kind of slapped her."

He froze by the kitchen counter, hand clasped over his keys. "...Did she hit you?"

"No. She—we were talking about you, and it just happened. It's all over, though. I left."

He sighed in relief. Still, that didn't sound like a friendly conversation. "I'm coming over. Do you need anything?"

"No. Thank you." Her voice calmed, and his heart slowed to a regular pace. "I just want to see you. Can I stay the night?"

"You never need to ask, baby girl. I'll be there soon to pick you up, okay?" He'd already stepped out the door.

"Okay. Caspian I..."

Was there something else? He hated not being next to her.

"I'll see you soon," she finished, then hung up.

Ten minutes later, he stood in front of her dorm and knocked on the door. The hallway was noticeably empty. Even though he'd thought up a few choice words, Jewelle was smart enough to be nowhere in sight.

Ivory opened with worry in her eyes. "Hey, Caspian." She tried to put on a smile but had obviously been shaken up. "Looks like I can leave her to you now."

"Thanks." He wanted to ask if she needed anything, but he'd already honed in on Nia. Back turned, she occupied herself by grabbing things off her desk and shoving them in a bag. Ivory nodded and stepped out into the hallway.

Silently, he enveloped Nia in his arms, and she relaxed as he rocked her side to side. After a while, she turned around, a small smile back on her perfect face. Relief flooded him that the situation hadn't escalated further. Automatically, his hand went to cup her cheek.

She leaned into the touch. "You don't have to worry. Nothing serious happened," she reaffirmed. "But I couldn't let Jewelle think she can get away with whatever she wants."

He raised an eyebrow. "Sure you're good?"

"Yeah." She rested her head against his chest. "No one has the power to hurt me. Not Jewelle or Serena...only you."

His arms tightened, forming a barrier he hoped would keep her out of harm's way...from the hands of anyone. If he could absorb and mesh their spirits together, he would. "I'll never hurt you." He kissed the top of her head, taking in a deep breath. "Not on purpose. But if I do, promise to tell me so we can work it out?"

"Yeah." She pulled away to look into his eyes, hers soft with a kind of trust he knew firsthand wasn't easy to earn. "I don't expect life to be perfect. Frankly, I couldn't care less about things like this as long as we have each other."

Catching the nape of her neck in his palm, he bent and pressed a kiss to her lips. It was meant to be simple and sincere, but he couldn't pull away. She kissed him back, lips curved in a smile before loosening as she deepened the kiss. His other hand drifted to her waist, clinging to her as his world began to spin. This kiss became slow and excruciating, more intimate than anything he'd felt before—and he had felt a lot of things. Every part of him yearned for her, drenched in the desire to strip her down, feel her skin and savor her love.

That was the only way he knew to express whatever emotion had taken over.

She had taken over. This need for her was more than a drug. She was his life—the color between the sketches of his being, the blood in his veins, the purpose to his existence.

When she pulled away and sucked in a shaky breath, he groaned. He'd never felt so desperate.

"We should head back to your place," she whispered.

"Mn," he agreed, though he didn't particularly feel like going anywhere. "Is Jewelle going to be an ongoing problem?"

Nia stepped back, leaving him too hot and missing her warmth at the same time. "Erm, I don't think she'll be eager to see me again, and I'm not too keen on talking to her either." She let out a half-chuckle. "For the record, I *was* the one who started things tonight, but I'm done wasting time."

"Me too." The truest revenge would be to give Jewelle as little attention as possible, and from the sound of it, she'd realized her mind games didn't work on them. That only meant she'd grow bored and shift to another poor soul, but karma would catch up to her someday.

He suppressed a sigh as Nia tried to haul an overstuffed backpack on her shoulders. The zipper could barely hold itself together.

"I got that." He took it in one hand and swung it over his shoulder with ease but noticed it weighed a good three times more than usual. "You sure you're only staying for a night? This feels more like you're running away from home." Not that he was complaining.

"Ha—afraid you won't get rid of me?" she teased, picking up *another* small bag.

"Sounds like more of a blessing than a curse."

She turned and narrowed her eyes. "What does that mean?"

He hadn't put much thought into the words. All that mattered was when she was near, he was happy. On the nights she wasn't with him, he couldn't get her out of his mind, and despite not wanting to bother her all the time, he constantly debated on whether or not to call or text.

"I'd like it if you stayed with me," he answered.

She swallowed. "Like, live together?"

"Why not?" He shrugged, liking the idea more and more. They already spent the weekends at his place. Of course, there was getting her to classes on time, but he'd manage.

"I...I don't know." She turned and headed to the door, stepping out into the hallway. "There's a lot more to living together than enjoying each other's company."

"Yeah." He followed and closed the door behind them, remembering his first visit. In particular, seeing Nia dressed in pajamas, sexy and cute and oblivious to her effect on him. "So, if we lived together would you wear my shirt at night, or your pajamas? I'm not sure which I'd like more, to be honest."

She snorted and rolled her eyes. "That's what you're thinking about?"

"Which is it?" he insisted, walking beside her out to his car.

"If you must know…" She paused and he glanced over to see her bite her lip. Their eyes met for a millisecond before she looked ahead again. "Neither."

"I like where this is going." His palm felt restless and empty, and he reached out for hand. "Since there's no other option, I'm going to let my imagination answer for you."

"Then we both know what that answer is." She chuckled and shook her head. He bit back a grin, loving how open she'd become, even flirting as much as him. Okay maybe not *as much*, but he was hard to out-do.

The cold night air greeted them outside, a promise of overnight frost. He enjoyed how Nia cuddled closer to him and took his hand in both of hers. Reaching the car, he loaded her "vacation" bags in the backseat and turned on the heat.

"You wouldn't mind?" she suddenly asked once they were on the road. "Me being in your personal space?"

"Not at all." He looked over to study her face for a moment, seeing her deep in thought. "I do admit my bachelor pad needs some work." He'd have to get better at cleaning once in a while, and if she brought those blue curtains, the living room would look a hell of a lot better. But she could do whatever she wanted as long it meant she was there.

She laughed. "I can manage. I have so far." Her voice softened. "What about all my stuff? Getting to classes? Laundry and food? Shower schedules? There are so many things we'd have to think about."

"Relax," he murmured, habitually reaching for her hand. His finger pads played with the little crescents of her nails. "I'll give you all the space you want and take you anywhere you need. Even if I have to get takeout every day, we'll figure it out. If that's what you want."

She tightened her grip. "We could try."

"As far as showering, I didn't mind our last experience.

Would be up for that again." He gave her hand a playful squeeze.

She turned to the window and hid her expression. "I bet you would."

Was she embarrassed?

"I *definitely* would," he assured. "Anytime. Say the word and I'm all yours, for however long you want me."

"What if I ask for more than you anticipate?" she teased under her breath.

Wait.

Another quick glance revealed the blush creeping up her face, the one that always gave her away. *Oh, Nia.* She really shouldn't play games he was destined to win.

Instead of replying, he brought their clasped hands to his lips and playfully bit the pad of flesh below her thumb.

"Caspian!" She gasped and turned to look at him. "What are you doing?"

He smirked. "Don't say things you know will turn me on. I'll pull the car over a block away from home just to spread those gorgeous legs and feast on my favorite snack."

Her shocked expression was just what he'd hoped for. What he didn't expect was the comeback.

"Do it."

So, he did.

FIFTY-TWO

Nia

THE SNIP OF COLD AIR DIDN'T BOTHER HER IN THE LEAST AS THEY walked into Caspian's apartment building—their little pit stop proved quite effective at circulating her blood. He chuckled to himself and unlocked the door, then stood aside to let her step in first. "Didn't know slapping people would be your aphrodisiac."

"It's not!" she protested. Finding the light switch by memory, she flicked it on and set her smaller toiletries bag on the counter.

When it came to Caspian, she simply couldn't hold back. Turns out that went for defending him as well as succumbing to his ever-potent charm. "That slap was a one-time thing, and it had nothing to do with our...activities."

"I'm not complaining," he said, carrying her backpack into the bedroom. "Maybe I should've let you two go at it sooner."

She grunted her disapproval and followed behind him. Being here comforted her, but a blush spread over her face at the sight of his bed. Not because of what they did five minutes ago, which was very blush-worthy, but because of what she finally wanted...someday soon.

343

"Something on your mind?"

He just *had* to notice.

"Sort of." She pursed her lips and started unpacking miscellaneous things to avoid his intense gaze.

"Jewelle?" he asked softly.

She shook her head, then stepped toward him and sighed as he wrapped his arms around her. The past few hours had felt more like a whole month, and she melted into his touch. More than ever, she craved his proximity, to listen to his heartbeats and steady breaths for as long as she wanted, and lose herself in a heaven he provided solely for her. Today had been draining, not only from the confrontation but from wanting to return his words.

I love you.

She should've just said it by now. She'd tried but didn't want the declaration to be spur-of-the-moment or mixed with less than savory memories. Even though she couldn't get them out of her head, the words for all of the things she wanted to express only flowed right when she wrote them down. And now she had to toss living together into the mix.

"I like the thought of living together," she said against his chest.

His arms tightened. "I like it, too," he whispered. Running his hand along her jaw, he tipped her head up for a kiss.

She returned the favor and brought her hands to his chest, resting against his firm muscle. Before they got too far, she confessed, "I like the thought of...more."

He pulled away to look her in the eyes. "More as in..."

She blushed but couldn't finish her implication. Heat from his skin radiated into her palm, past the thin fabric of his shirt, and combined with her own to swirl into her chest. He pecked a kiss on the corner of her mouth and evaluated her expression. Her blush deepened.

Tentatively, he lowered his head to her collarbone and traced a small circle with his tongue. She moaned.

"More of what you got in the car?' he whispered.

Yes, that too, but...

"More."

Bending, he took her nipple in his mouth and bit playfully through her bra. "More." He groaned. "You mean that?"

For someone who never thought they'd say those words, mean what they meant, she was oddly at peace. The idea of going all the way with Caspian didn't scare or thrill her but felt complete. Sex wasn't something she wanted simply to please either of them, or to experience something new, but to share a part of her no one else would have.

The way he held her, kissed her, stayed with her even when they weren't flirting or happy...that was as intimate as it got. Not only did it feel right, but it was almost perfect. Perfect in a way where she knew flaws didn't matter. In how at the end of each and every day, she'd have someone who genuinely cared for her as much as she cared about him.

She looked into his sapphire eyes and smiled. "Yes. I want everything with you."

He stared back, frozen in time, then broke into a smile and switched to biting her other nipple. "If more is what you want, more is what you'll get." He kissed up her neck, lingering on her jaw and brushing the side of his thumb over her cheek, excitement lighting up his face. "Tell me a flavor, and I'll deliver. Rose petals and French vanilla? It's a classy choice..."

"Isn't that too cliché?" she teased, meaning it to come out as a tease, but her voice was airy and breathless. She had to admit it sounded good regardless. Still, he could do better.

"Ah, not with me." He tsked. "Let's see what else... A four-course meal featuring you as dessert?" He bit his lip as if he hadn't just gotten more than a generous serving. "Chocolate-dipped strawberries and extra whipped cream on the side? I can picture it now."

Her breath hitched as his other hand smoothed down her waist, sneaking under her shirt. She closed her eyes and felt his lips sucking her neck. "I'd be too drunk on you to need wine."

One hand stroked her pulse while the other teased the edges of her underwear, and though he satiated her need minutes before, she came alive all over again.

"Silk napkins should be enough to take care of these." He trailed his hand down and grabbed both her wrists, holding them hostage against his chest. "Then I can take a cube of ice and run it along all your tantalizing curves." He licked a line down her throat, and she moaned breathlessly. With a step, he turned them and pressed her into the wall, pulling her into him as he rocked his hips.

"Mm." She tried to speak, but it came out garbled. "All the above?"

"And all the below," he whispered, slipping two fingers inside her.

ᘓ

She decided to stay more than one night.

Finally, Friday morning arrived, and though classes hadn't started, they couldn't be over fast enough. The past few days, she'd successfully drafted her letter despite the looming threat of exams and convinced Caspian not to make any plans over the weekend—no gym, no parties, and lots of studying. And...more.

She was excited, nervous and giddy to hand over her well-crafted confession. And to show him the gift she bought along with it, especially when certain activities were bound to follow. While that would cut into her study time, she reasoned it would be better to unwind before tackling tests, and going down on Caspian might replenish her energy for cracking down on textbooks.

Running the last strands of hair through the straightener, she glanced at the clock. "We need to leave in five minutes!"

"Can't skip even on a Friday?" Caspian grumbled from behind.

"No. Even if I didn't need a participation grade, I can't afford to—" Hot lips at the back of her neck interrupted her brain waves.

"I know," he murmured, sweeping her still-warm hair to the side. "If you weren't so dedicated, I'd have kept you up the whole night." With his hands massaging her shoulders, that seemed much more appealing than sitting in a lecture room. Unless they were alone in said lecture room, with the lights off and—

"Wait...Caspian," she panted, protesting before her thoughts could get away from her. "I have—*ahhh*..."

His teeth found her earlobe while his hands roamed over the shirt she'd smoothed over. "About time I gave you a course in sex-education, don't you think?"

"I'd need a full demonstration," she whispered, trying to find the will to pry his hands off of her. Maybe after they glided under her bra...why did she even bother putting on clothes?

He smirked against her skin as his nose skimmed her hairline. "They say the best way to learn is immersive interaction."

"We need to go," she whined, not convincing even to her own ears, and bit back a sigh before twisting away from him. Not fast enough, he pulled her in for a kiss. The repressed sigh vibrated into his hot mouth and her knees wobbled as he held nothing back, lazily kissing her like she was his dose of morning caffeine.

Leaving her breathless, he pulled away and handed over

her backpack. She hadn't noticed he packed it. "Five minutes." He winked. "Time to leave right?"

She didn't know whether to scowl or laugh, so she ended up producing a weird combination of the two. "You—"

That gleam in his eye irked her, and she fisted his shirt and pulled him back, reattaching their lips. Her other hand reached out and palmed her ass.

"You are not convincing me to let you leave," he growled.

She smirked. "The classroom awaits."

CASPIAN, MY BELOVED.

I love you.

I love you so much that I can feel it pounding in my chest, coursing through my veins. You've been grafted into my bones and seep into my soul more and more each day. The feelings that flow through me as I write this, the ones that accompany the mere thought of saying those words to you, are almost inexplicable. The gratitude I have for your devotion reaches farther than the most distant star, and my pride in calling you mine is worth every pebble on the road we'll travel.

I've never felt more whole, more confident, or more myself than with you. You never expect more than what I can offer and are so content with what I can give. I have found a treasure in a vast sea of rubble, yet you act as if I'm the jewel. I love all parts of you, even those I may not understand or see at first glance. I want to be as strong for you as you've been for me. I want to support you and celebrate all that you do.

I enrolled here with an undecided future and a past I wanted to run away from. A hole will forever remain in my heart from the things I've seen and experienced, but you've filled that chasm with gold. Our connection is the cement that holds me together, and I am stronger alone because I stand with you. I hope it's the same for you. I've decided to declare a major and chose my path in life, and that path includes you. I hope a degree in marketing will help me share your art with the world, and let you reach your highest potential. Together we can reach for all the things we hope and dream for.

Forever your best friend, lover, and everything in between,

Nia

FIFTY-THREE

Caspian

His fingers gingerly ran up and down the edge of the paper, caressing each line. He should've expected incredible things from her by now, but this broke his heart all over again —in the best way.

The first time he saw Nia, he wasn't half the man he was now, and he knew a year from now he'd be twice the man he was today. Their time together had filled the cracks and missing pieces in his soul, reforged him into something worthy of her love.

He looked up, too astonished to care about the pool of moisture in his eyes. Nia sat beside him on the couch and fiddled with her fingers as soft daylight cast a golden glow on her skin, hair bright like the fire building in his chest.

Sensing his gaze, she looked up and gave a small smile.

His heart shattered.

Even if he had any words—which he didn't—he certainly lacked the breath to say them with.

Instead, he rose and walked over to his desk. Setting down the letter, lovingly pressed into perfect thirds, he pulled out a piece of cardstock hidden in a secret folder. He glanced over the masterpiece one last time and walked back, holding the paper to his chest.

"Thank you," he whispered. She waited as he struggled to find words, servants she could effortlessly summon but who continuously evaded him. "As a rule, I don't sketch people I know. I may use a similar body structure or expressions, but I don't bring the characters from real life into my creative one." He paused, lowering the paper just enough for him to absorb it again.

"Then there's you," he whispered reverently. He looked up and handed her the artwork. Her lips parted as she took it, eyes wandering around the page.

"I started the outline of you when we split apart because I couldn't focus otherwise. After we got back together, you didn't look right alone, so I put myself in too. Figured I'd paint it and finish up since..." He took in a breath. "Well, because it suits you. Not saying you're a damsel in distress or childish—"

"I love it," Nia whispered. Her sweet smile widened as she studied the painting.

Clad in a vibrant golden dress complete with puffed sleeves and a cinched waist, a girl with red hair danced with her prince —Prince Caspian. He wore a royal blue tailcoat with gold trim over a white frilled shirt and black trousers, hair uncombed as usual, and eyes a piercing blue while his lips curved into a notorious smirk. Princess Nia's eyes shimmered, hair tied up with a gold ribbon, and feet paired with glass slippers. The painting was a mash-up of traditional fairy tales, the pair frozen in a classic, tilted spin.

"I had no idea you'd write me a letter," he said as she continued to take it all in, "and I only finished this yesterday. The timing couldn't have been better."

She lifted her eyes, face alight with happiness. "I don't know what to say. I...thank you." She looked down at the painting again. "We should frame it."

"If you want." He reached for the paper and set it on his desk. They could look at it later when he didn't need to have her in his arms to function. "We'll put it next to your letter."

"Oh, I don't think we need to frame that."

He chuckled and pulled her into his lap. She settled into her favorite position, legs wrapped around his waist as he slid his hands over her hips.

"I love you, Caspian. I love you so much," she sighed. Her heart thudded against his chest as she nestled into the crook of his neck.

"I love you too." He hugged her back, taking the time to trace each vertebra up her spine until he reached the nape of her neck, then guided her to his lips. Placing a kiss on her cupid's bow, he pressed delicate fairy kisses from one corner of her mouth to the other. Her lips parted, and he swept his tongue over them, loving her familiar taste and how he always craved more.

She pulled him closer, hands wandering into his hair. His heart skipped a beat as he deepened the kiss, experiencing it like their first. Tasting her smile and swallowing her sighs like they were his last meal.

The universe must have a rule against being this happy because enjoying life this much made him feel like a criminal. If so, the only crime he could commit was stealing his heart back from the woman on his lap. But he didn't want it—that was hers to keep. Forever.

"You are my fairytale," he whispered.

She pulled back and laughed. "That's my line."

"No, really." His smile wrinkled the corners of his eyes, and he traced her lips with his thumb, plump and red from their kiss. "My happily ever after isn't about rescuing you or living in a big castle, it's learning to trust, to feel every emotion with you even when it's uncomfortable. I want to learn to love you —more intimately than anyone else—in every way. And I want to do that over and over every single day, for the rest of our lives."

A tear rolled down her cheek and caught in her smile, which he kissed away. "I would marry you right now, Nia." Her eyes widened and she stared back at him. "I promise to make it as special as you've made this for me," he murmured. "You really outdid yourself."

"But all I did was write," she whispered. "That's not like— like *proposing*."

"The sentiment is the same," he said, wrapping his hands around her waist.

"But you haven't gotten to the best part yet," she said, mouth open in bewilderment.

What could be better than having someone genuinely return his love? "There's more?"

She blushed. "Remember...the gift you gave me?" Her hands found the waistband of his boxers and tugged. "I got you one, too."

He sucked in a breath. So there was something better.

"Are you wearing this gift?" he whispered, hands skimming down to the edge of her pants. She bit her lip and nodded.

His fingers dipped below her clothes and his breath caught. Lace.

Fucking lace.

"This is why you asked about my favorite color?"

She nodded again. His eyes searched hers, wondering how she managed to surprise him at every turn. At this rate he'd never be able to return all the favors she'd given him.

He smirked. "It's a good thing this is exactly what I thought of when you asked."

Her forehead scrunched into soft creases, and she gave him an incredulous look. "Really? How?"

"I should have known you were waiting for something," he murmured. Her energy had been off the past few days. He could always feel when she wanted more but held back. The question was why. Now he knew—she'd wanted to gift wrap herself for him.

Her efforts would not go unrewarded.

This afternoon she'd had her turn bursting his heart into a thousand fragments, and now the evening would be his chance. He'd make sure to reinforce her every heartbeat, the heart that played a melody just for him.

"What do you—*woah*." She hooked her arms around his neck in a hurry as he gripped her thighs and stood, carrying her to the bedroom. "What are you doing?"

He hummed and gave her butt a playful squeeze. "Unwrapping my present."

FIFTY-FOUR

Nia

LIFTED IN STRONG ARMS, SHE GIGGLED AND GLADLY LET CASPIAN carry her wherever he wanted. In this case, that happened to be the bedroom.

She expected to be set down upon arrival, but he kept her pressed tightly to him, her plush body melded to his firm core. So, she clung on, closing her eyes and inhaling deep breaths of his cologne. By now, her whole system reacted to his touch, loosening and clenching in all the right places.

He supported her with one arm while typing on his phone, and soothing chords along with a complimentary voice filled the room. The music drew out emotion she'd so meticulously packaged in her letter, a seemingly endless stream of deep joy.

"You're my everything," Caspian rumbled into her neck, his breath leaving hot tingles over her skin.

Her lips brushed against his pulse as she smiled, and she held onto him tighter. Instead of responding with words, she kissed him, nibbling on his neck like he so often did to her. She loved his taste, his feel that had become so familiar and absorbed everything about him. Everything about *them*.

Her world went on tilt as she dipped into the crisp, cool

sheets. Caspian's lips caught hers before her eyelids could flutter open, and he dove into her mouth. This kiss was different from the ones before, hungry and dominant as if he had been starving his whole life and she was his first meal. In his arms she felt small, no more than a single rose petal in the palm of his hand.

"Shall I take a look at my gift?" he murmured, barely breaking the kiss as his fingertips traced along her stomach and inched up her shirt. She barely managed to open her eyes to see his enraptured expression, could hardly breathe as his head dipped to her waist. Her heart raced as his tongue flicked into her navel, teeth nipping at her sensitive skin.

She tried to stay still, to let him feast as much as he wanted —but his mouth alone made a mess of her insides, wrecked her pulse and convinced it to beat to his tempo. Air swirled over her abdomen, and she shivered in delight. The rest of her shirt was lifted above her head, but instead of pulling it off, Caspian let it encase her arms and effectively pin them up. Her midsection lie fully outstretched, covered in lace and love bites.

"Wow," he breathed in approval, pulling back to admire her bra, fingers tracing her chest and plucking at her nipples through the lingerie until they were stiff peaks. His eyes blew out into dark orbs, lips parting in awe. "I like this gift. White is outstanding on you."

Then his mouth crashed into hers, the small taste having only made him more insatiable. She arched her back and pulled him in with her legs, needing to feel his arousal, impatient to give them both the pleasure they'd waited so long for. Scorching her skin, he licked down her neck, then paused to suck on her sweet spot before continuing to the line of her bra.

"Truly divine," he whispered into her skin, "but you are much more beautiful—and taste much sweeter—than lace."

With one hand, he unhooked the bra and pushed it off to the side.

"Caspian," she moaned, impatient when he didn't readily move to touch her. This unwrapping business was starting to feel more like torture. But he probably enjoyed that aspect the most.

"Baby girl, I may have to do one more drawing of you." He tweaked her nipple with his thumb and finger, then smoothed down and pressed his hand to her navel. "That one will be for my eyes only."

He could do whatever he wanted later if he would only—

"*Ohh*," she sighed as his mouth closed around her peak, tongue circling the aching bud. His hand massaged her other breast, and her head rolled back in relief. Pleasure gathered between her legs, intensifying as Caspian unbuttoned her jeans and traced the lace leading to where she needed him most.

"Fuck, I can't wait anymore," he hissed, pulling his hand out of her pants and ripping off his shirt. She untangled herself from her clothes as Caspian curled his hands around the back of her jeans and pulled them down. His biceps bunched with the motion, abs straining as he took in a sharp breath. "Oh *shit*."

He froze, her jeans hanging midway down her thighs. Decorating her gold skin, a white lace thong and stockings attached to a garter belt outfitted her figure to perfection. His eyes followed the elastic to her panties, lingering and causing the pool in her core to grow by the second. As if unable to believe his eyes, he brought a hand to her heat and stroked her through the lace. She quivered, held at the mercy of a single fingertip, massaging circles over her clit.

"Mmm," he growled, rough and merciless in a way that sent a shiver down her spine. "So ready." He withdrew his finger and pulled her pants off the rest of the way. Gripping one of her feet in his palm, he kissed the top of her foot, her ankle, biting through the lace as he hooked her leg over his shoulder and closed in on the apex between her thighs. He placed a single kiss over her nether pulse before crawling on top, connecting their bare chests and indulging in another soul-incinerating kiss.

"Please," she sighed, cupping his cheek with her hand. "Let me feel you."

His erection jumped at the request, nestled into her hip and emphasizing his next words. "As you wish, baby girl. You deserve it."

Sweeping his tongue over hers one last time, he stood and tugged off his pants and boxers in record time, then fished out a condom from the dresser—she wasn't the only gift that would be wrapped tonight. She scooted to the center of the mattress, waiting to find out just how *he* would feel. Her body was entirely on board, wet and tight and needy, but the back of her mind fought with the uncertainty of the unknown. They more than satisfied each other, but would doing this make all that better or worse? What if she somehow disappointed him or couldn't...enjoy him the same way he did her?

She focused instead on the bubble of tension building between her legs, about to burst already. The only thing left for her to do was trust him, and she did.

His fingers wrapped around her waist, thumbs rubbing into the small valley below her hip beneath the lingerie. "I'm afraid this will have to come off," he muttered, voice almost sorrowful but fringed with anticipation.

He unhooked the garter belt and slipped it down, so the stockings were the only clothing that remained. Then ever so slowly, his finger worked into her, closely followed by a second. The level of fullness she'd become acquainted with fed her lust, and she rocked her hips forward.

He bit his lip and she moaned, their eyes both flicking up to connect.

"Is this mine?" he asked, fingers hooked deep in her pussy.

She nodded, warmth spreading to her extremities. He loved her, claimed her. No other woman had ever been *his.* "Yes," she hummed, arching her back as he curled and prodded her depths in the most delicious way.

"Good girl." He leaned over and reclaimed her lips, now sweet and tender. "Tell me you love me," he rasped, unrelenting as she trembled beneath him, on the brink of orgasm.

"I love you," she said as her body responded in kind. "Caspian..."

"Wrap your legs around me, hold on."

She did. His fingers receded, transitioning to her clit as she felt him at her entrance. How was he so much bigger than she'd thought?

"This is yours. *Feel* me."

She did. Her lungs protested, but she couldn't breathe. Couldn't move.

"Feel how well you take me." Warm lips coaxed out a gasp from her mouth and she held on tighter as he gently pressed a little more, marking her a little deeper. "Feel how you surround me in every thought, every breath, every *inch*..." His fingers glided up her side as he sunk in gradually—endlessly.

The ache between her legs made her squirm and claw into his skin. She knew it; he *was* too much. This was certainly not worth all the hype. Maybe she'd been right to think she'd never—

"I love you, Nia."

Her heart pulsed. His voice resonated the same way it had the very first time but now magnified a hundredfold. Since that day, he'd caused countless ripples in her life and become her biggest treasure. Caspian changed her life, taught her to not run away from dreams or nightmares, and she realized she didn't mind if he changed her body as well. Looking into his blue eyes, the color in everything else paled in comparison.

"I love you too," she whispered, voice as uneven as his. Both his arms encircled her. Bodies flush, she felt every bump and dip of his hot skin, their sexes combining in a miracle utterly unfit for words. Her hands explored his back as she tried to relax and couldn't help but notice how tense he'd become, his breaths heavy and labored as he held himself still. "I'm okay. Adjusting, but..." She relaxed further and smiled, overwhelmed. "I want to feel everything. All of you."

"Damn," he groaned and kissed her lips, then her nose and her eyes in a whirlwind of fluttering, wispy caresses. "I'm gonna marry you. And I'm going fuck you just like this every day for the rest of our lives." Bending her leg to his shoulder, he shifted and sunk deeper.

She gasped and hid her face in his neck. How much more did this boy have? She gulped in air as her body gave in, encasing him just like he said it would. Maybe it'd be better not to ask, but she had to know. "...is that all?"

He chuckled. "Not if you can still form words, it isn't."

Then he latched onto her neck, licking and sucking her skin, holding her as close as they could possibly get. Reacting to his kiss, she arched her hips and triggered another dull ache... and euphoria. Her walls clenched around him, swollen and slick with a newfound need, making her moan at the same time he bit down on her sweet spot.

Her body surged on a cellular level, experiencing more sensations than she could count. *What... how...* She raised her hips tentatively to test the waters. The ache became familiar, accompanied by a feeling much deeper and more desirable. Her entire body gripped onto him, clinging as if he kept her very soul.

"Nia..." His rasp sounded exactly how she felt. "You feel so damn good, *fuck*." He slid out, only to return with a touch of extra force. She braced for impact, but the pain only dulled as pleasure crept in.

"*That*," she gasped. "Do that again."

Not only did he do it again, he did it *better*. Her hands gripped his shoulders, wide and predatory in their strength, as he held himself above her. His girth became an honored guest as he made himself very much at home. One thing was certain, a vibrator would never feel the same again. Nothing could feel as good as him.

"*Ah*," she whispered. "Caspian."

"That's it, baby girl, say my name every time it's too much. I want to hear what I do to you." He shifted again, leveraging himself to stretch her with more precision.

"*Caspian!*" she gasped as her first ceiling shattered and pleasure skyrocketed.

His movements escalated with her ecstasy, a magnificent crescendo he masterfully orchestrated. Their breaths intermingled, bodies syncing as sweat beaded on their foreheads. She whined as his hand teased her breasts, flicking and stretching. A different kind of heat overcame her, all-consuming and blinding. Her hands twisted into the sheets to prevent her from falling apart. Never before had she needed release like this, but at the same time felt terrified it would rip her wide open.

"Please, Caspian..." She didn't know what to ask for, but he had to have the answer.

"My love," he answered, then huffed and raised both her legs. Hooking them around his shoulders, he grabbed her hips and thrust in hard.

Ohhh...

She hung on the verge of crying and screaming and everything in between. Unable to keep up, her whole body vibrated around him, opening to let him slip in and holding him there with all her strength. With swift, deep, electrifying jolts, he drove her to the brink. His name became a whisper of a plea as she burst apart beneath him. Her soul incinerated to fairy dust, full and complete and alive.

"*Ah, Nia.*" He bent down and devoured her lips while pushing in unabated, drawing out her orgasm while chasing his own. His passion overwhelmed her, and as his muscles contracted, she kissed him back, wanting to share every moment despite fraying at the edges. Several shallow breaths and a final thrust later, he collapsed with her in his arms.

Ꮳ

The room fell silent, yet it was anything but hollow. Emotion encased them so completely that words were unnecessary, dull in comparison with their profound heartbeats.

Satiated and surrounded by each other, the pair drifted lazily back down to earth. Caspian rolled to the side, and she nestled in his arms, enjoying his warmth. Her fingers idly skimmed his chest, over his jaw, and around his ear.

He grinned and tightened his arm at her waist. "Can't wait to do that again."

"Me too," she murmured. As she stared into the peaceful ocean of his eyes, a question rose to the surface. "At what moment did you first start to love me?"

"Mm," he hummed, brushing strands of hair over her shoulder. His fingers sent warm tendrils of delight dancing across her skin, the faint contact powerful even after the intensity of only a few moments prior. "I think a part of me knew the second I saw you, although I didn't recognize the feeling. I wanted to give you something special. At the least, I knew I wanted to spend more than one night with you."

"Wow, promoted to a *more-than-one-night* girl, how lucky was I?" She rolled her eyes, breaking out in a smile. Though a part of her loved that she'd been different from the very beginning. "When did that change from *more-than-one-night* to *for-the-rest-of-your-life*?"

His fingers ascended from her shoulder to her lips, tracing them as if he were sketching. "It just happened. Every day I spent with you, I wanted another and another, and that's still true. If I didn't get to see you, I wanted to talk to you, and when we couldn't talk, I wanted to draw you." He leaned over and pressed his lips to hers. "I never want to stop kissing you. Your smile tastes like pure joy."

She smiled.

He kissed her. Then kissed her again. She laughed.

"When did you start to fall in love?" he asked. "Other than noticing how sexy I am at first glance."

"Oh, that irresistible charm of yours." She couldn't help but giggle, and he placed another kiss on her happy lips. "I think I sensed it too, in the beginning, but I knew for sure on our first date."

His eyebrows shot up. "When we talked in the car?"

"Yeah, and..." She bit her lip. "Before that. You did something that was sort of a sign to me, but I didn't say anything because I didn't want to jinx it."

"Do tell more." He leaned back into the pillows, and she settled against his chest.

"Remember when you picked out this necklace?" Her hand went to the small heart charm around her neck.

"Mn." He nodded.

"This was a gift my dad gave my mom." She looked down, nostalgia rising from a memory that wasn't hers. "My biological father. The one part of him I haven't left behind."

Her fist closed around the charm, and Caspian clasped his hand over hers. That small motion alone brightened her world in places she thought would never see light, put wings on her back, and wrote a poem with her spirit. Reminiscing on their first date, the contrast was night and day.

"I felt like being with you could only go one of two ways," she continued, meeting his eyes. "Either we'd end up more broken or healed. For some reason, the first was easier for me to accept. I couldn't believe someone would actually love me, yet being with you made me feel so loved," she sighed, "but *feeling loved*, and *loving someone* are entirely different things."

"I love you," he whispered, pulling her to his chest.

"I know." She wrapped an arm around his waist. "I can finally let myself believe that."

"I'll always love you," he murmured.

She kissed his chest, right above his heart. "I'll always love you, too, and I want to be the one person you can trust and believe in."

He sighed deeply and tipped up her chin. "You are, more than you know."

She leaned in to kiss him, tasting his smile and his joy—which felt an awful lot like her own. Her absolute favorite flavor.

"Mm," she hummed, straddling him and testing out what it would be like on top. He truly was her perfect counterpart, and as she thought, he was well-equipped for what she had in mind. "This is what I call a night worth writing about."

He hummed his agreement, hips tipping up to meet hers.

Yes, the first of many.

EPILOGUE

Nia

GLITTERING BENEATH DELICATELY FILTERED MOONLIGHT, DEEP BLUE eyes shone clear and unwavering. Within the palm of his hand lie the symbol of her heart's truest desire, a sparkling white stone set in a golden band.

"Nia Fowler," Caspian began.

Tears slipped from the corners of her eyes as she met his familiar gaze, chest bursting with heat despite the blanket of fresh snow covering the ground.

"This is the place we first shared, where I promised to commit to you, where I promised to be more, for your sake and for mine."

She remembered the day well, their first official date. At that time, neither of them really thought there would be a second. Yet somehow, they'd ended up here again.

"I told you I wanted to remember that evening," he continued, "but now I don't just want to remember one special night with you, Nia. I don't want to remember ten nights or a hundred, even a thousand wouldn't be enough—I want to remember everything for the rest of our lives."

He paused and wrapped her hands in his. "Will you be my wife?"

. . .

Fresh emotion from that moment resurfaced as Nia twisted the engagement band on her finger, a smile growing at the memory. It was the plot twist she couldn't have written better herself.

Caspian's intentions had been clear for a while, but she hadn't expected him to propose so soon—on the last day of Thanksgiving break, under a sky full of stars. She hadn't even seen it coming when he said he wanted to take her someplace special, nor when her mom had hugged her extra tight after their dinner, and she certainly missed when Caspian's mother gave him the diamond ring at their Thanksgiving banquet.

Just like the stars and her highest hopes for the future, the ring shimmered and winked as she turned it in the light. If only she could live in that one moment forever.

But now, instead of looking at the love of her life, she faced a jumble of notes and far too many highlighted lines in far too many textbooks. The entire day had been nothing but study, study, study for hours on end, and she still didn't feel confident enough about finals.

College was *not* fun.

Her calculus class, in particular, hung in the balance, and the more she looked at the symbols, the less sense they made. Flopping both arms across the desk, she laid her head over the array of notebooks and groaned.

"What's wrong, baby girl?" Caspian hummed, coming over to rub her shoulders from behind. His warm fingers pressed firm circles over her aching muscles with a precision only he could master. "Studying worn you out?"

She gave an exasperated huff of confirmation.

He bent down and placed a teasing kiss in the crook of her neck, adding in a low whisper, "Hopefully, you're not worn out too much, so I can have my fair share of you later."

"Caspian," she scolded, glaring over her shoulder. Curse

him for knowing all her weak spots. Scratch that. He was her weak spot.

"What?" he chuckled.

She rolled her eyes. "You never change, do you?"

"Am I supposed to?"

"No, but..." A loud pop sounded as she cracked her neck. "I just can't figure out how you're not stressed about finals. Every single one of my brain cells are fried."

Caspian hummed, eagerly tasting more of her skin as his lips dipped to the collar of her shirt. "What about your other cells? Can I fry those as well?"

If only he wasn't doing that already. She turned, torn between caving in and staying diligent. "Right now, I *need* to focus. This is important, and if I don't make the grade check for scholarships, then..."

"You'll do fine." He pulled away, leaving tingles in his absence. "I even bet you'll do better than me."

"Easy for you to say."

He sighed. "Listen, I'll leave you alone for now, but give me the afternoon tomorrow. I promise I'll make it worth your time."

She had no doubt he'd make good on that promise but cast a doubtful glance at her workload. Last time she got distracted, the plan had backfired, and instead of renewing her energy, it made studying even more of a chore. "What day is tomorrow again?"

"Sunday, baby girl."

That meant her test was the next day, Monday morning. Her last chance to prepare.

"Only a few hours," he persisted. Sea-blue eyes melted her from the inside out.

She relented. "All right, okay." The smile from earlier returned. "But I absolutely have to finish going over every chapter."

Shaking his head, Caspian retreated to the couch. "I'll let you get back to work then, but don't think my patience won't run out—and when it does, you don't want to find out what happens."

Nia squirmed, *almost* tempted to see if he'd make good on that threat. But that could wait until tomorrow.

∞

Time was an aggravating thing. The whole night had passed in the blink of an eye, but this morning, when Caspian left to go to the store, minutes stretched into hours.

She double-checked the solution she wrote with the correct one and, in relief at their match, shut the textbook with a snap. She was drained. Grinding numbers had given her what she wanted—ample practice and assurance, but now an evening with her fiancé was more than needed.

Still, anxiety wedged into her thoughts. There would be no chance to make up for mistakes, and she hated not being able to predict the outcome. Caspian did much better with uncertainty. He'd take it in stride and wasn't afraid to try again and again. Guess he learned a thing or two from his playboy history of shameless flirting.

She tucked away the study materials and moved them out of sight, peeking out the window over the apartment's small balcony. The sight of drifting snow and icicles had her reaching for a fuzzy blanket.

Fluffy white globs floated past in a lazy course, some as big as her thumbnail and others too small to notice. Sunlight shone down through patchy clouds, alluding to warmth she knew was nowhere to be found. Frigid air clung to the glass pane, and when she touched it with the tip of a finger, fog encircled the small print.

It would have been better for Caspian to stay indoors today.

Whatever he had planned, her heart warmed with gratitude and willed him to return faster. She hoped he hadn't gone too far out of his way.

Drawing little hearts as her breath fogged up the glass, she stood and watched for his familiar car to pull into the parking lot. When it did, a thrill rocked her up onto tippy toes.

She'd never get tired of knowing he came home to her and visa-versa. Unlike the house she was raised in, this place felt like a true home, and she wouldn't give it up for the world.

Losing sight of his car while he parked, she turned and started toward the door, then changed course for the kitchen. He'd be cold, and she knew the perfect remedy. Now that she thought about it, she could use a little winter treat herself.

Soon, a small saucepan of milk boiled on the stove, and two mugs were set out on the counter. As she picked out two different flavors of hot chocolate mix, the door clicked open. A rustle filled the lonely space, and her eyes widened as Caspian maneuvered through the entrance, pushing his way though with more plastic bags than should be carried at once.

"What's all this?" she questioned, hurrying over to close the door.

Before an answer came, the bags landed on the floor with a thump, and he whisked her into a tight hug. "If you aren't done with that textbook by now, I'm going to burn it."

She giggled at the edge in his voice and leaned back into the embrace, all remnants of chilly air vanishing between them. "I did finish, but even if I hadn't—no burning allowed. It's only a rental."

"I'll burn anything that gets between us tonight." He took a deep inhale, and she felt his gaze lift to the kitchen. "You making something?"

Untangling herself, she went to mix the ingredients. "It's just hot chocolate. Looking outside made me cold."

Caspian walked past the bags and gratefully took a mug. "I can verify, it's chilly outside."

She took a sip of the steaming liquid. "Don't think your distraction worked—why on earth did you get so much? And what is it?"

A sly grin crept onto his face, accompanied by a boyish eyebrow raise. "Curious, are we?"

Too impatient to pry out a response, she walked over and picked up a bag. Metallic gold and silver garland fluffed out the top, hiding beneath an array of other colorful decorations. A quick glance confirmed the rest of the bags held similar festive items.

"Christmas decorations," he said.

One bag stood out, only partially able to conceal a large rectangular box with a mid-size tree pictured on the side. Her heart expanded. In all the worry about finals, she hadn't noticed the rest of the world beginning to celebrate the holidays.

Speechless, she continued to unveil various strings of lights, painted ornaments, and even a pine wreath. It made her feel like a child all over again, except without the burden of making up for the gaps in a broken home. "Christmas..." she whispered, "I completely forgot."

3

An hour and a half later, the apartment glowed with holiday fervor. Nia hummed along with nostalgic music and used the last remnants of her energy to piece together a festive tree. It was a mere foot shorter than her, but compared to Caspian, it looked more like a toy.

The tree sparkled with color, akin to the walls that were strewn with an unsymmetrical mix of garland and string lights. Two matching stockings hung beside the desk, replacing the former gloom of her all-nighter with lighthearted merriment. She stepped back and admired their handiwork.

"Last piece, it's for you to hang," Caspian said, standing by the doorway to their bedroom.

She turned and eyed a small bundle of faux green leaves in his hand, then giggled. When did he become the cheesier one? "Mistletoe?"

"Whatever you want to call it, all I know is I get a free kiss every time you walk underneath."

She grinned and took the plant. "Aren't we supposed to be standing beneath it at the same time?"

"Trust me, I'll be there every time you pass through this door." His cocky smirk sent a flutter of butterfly wings through her stomach, and a blush touched her cheeks.

"All that effort for a kiss? Wha—oh!" She squealed as he bent and grabbed her waist, lifting so she could reach the ceiling.

"Worth it," he said and pressed a delicate kiss to her navel.

Her eyes narrowed as she clung to his shoulders for support. Was he flexing on purpose? If so, it had the intended effect, and those same butterflies burst into embers of desire. She refocused her attention away from his heated contact and onto hanging the mistletoe, sticking the temporary hanger near her best guess of center. "There."

Without warning, his grip loosened and sent her plummeting down. She gasped, clenching her legs around his waist for dear life. He smirked.

"If you drop me..." she warned tersely, latching onto his chest like a lifeline.

The bite in her tone did nothing to deter the mischievous glint in his eye. If anything, it gave him incentive. "Now, what comes next?"

Her pulse began to race, and she wasn't sure if it was from the fall or what she fell onto. Despite that, she clung to the little composure she could maintain. Giving him what he wanted would only encourage this behavior more. But...

He was the one person who could—and would—get away with pushing her buttons. In fact, it softened her heart when she remembered just how deeply she trusted him. He hadn't come this far without earning it.

Warm breath fanned across her moistened lips, sweetened from the hot chocolate. Indeed, it didn't feel like she was on the losing side at all when their mouths met. Her arms nestled behind his neck, hips fitting perfectly against his.

She didn't know who deepened the kiss but clung tighter as he warmed her from the inside out. Their tongues danced, familiar and well-practiced partners. *This* was what cold weather was for.

Holding her with a matched and unbridled passion, he tilted their hips just right, and the seam of her sweatpants hit the oh-so-sensitive pinnacle between her legs. The friction set off a series of fizzling nerve endings, and she fell further into the clutches of impulse as the world around them faded away.

He pulled back, trailing kisses across her jaw, her skin soaking up the affection as if it were the finest lotion, and channeled it to the place he alone could touch.

"Caspian," she half-whispered, half-sighed, too tired to fight off the overwhelming need. Her head fell to his shoulder, and inhaling his cologne, she tenderly sucked a patch of warm skin between her teeth.

"Nia, *fuck*," he cursed under his breath and let out a low, broken moan. "This was supposed to be for you. You can't do that when I'm trying to pace myself."

"Then don't." Her body curled into his, motivated by the positive response and chasing further gratification. She never ceased to find as much enjoyment in pleasing him as she did in her own pleasure. The combination was a miracle in and of itself.

He groaned and shifted one hand to support her back, smoothing the other up under her shirt along the sensitive skin on her side. The tip of his thumbnail pressed a light line into her ribcage and sent electric shocks straight to her center. "You're not the only one who can be a tease."

She squirmed, unable to contain the pleasure that crackled over her skin like a ball of static energy. "I can't," she gasped. "I can't hold on."

A few steps later, her back dipped into the soft mattress as Caspian laid her down. Apart from the coil of anticipation in her core, all her limbs melted in exhaustion. In fact, she was unaware of the fabric being slipped down her legs until he replaced it with wet, hungry lips kissing up her thighs. Quivering, her legs fell apart in compliance. She moaned with anticipation.

"You've been so good, working so hard," Caspian murmured against her sex. "Time to let me reward your efforts."

Even if she was in a position to protest—which she certainly wasn't—this was an offer she couldn't resist. Oxygen rushed into her lungs as a finger hooked around her panties and pulled to the side. Cold air caressed her wet folds, and she opened wider in encouragement.

Slowly, exasperatingly, he took his time collecting the arousal that dripped down and circled closer to her clit, teasing until her hips arched off the bed. She opened her eyes, and just as a pleading whine was about to leave her lips, two fingers speared her weeping core. Her moan filled the room.

An ever so slight tug to the corner of Caspian's lips revealed a smug, triumphant smile, and any ability she had left to form words vanished, replaced by the singular focus of not combusting on the spot.

"Always ready, aren't you, baby girl..." His voice was a husky whisper, coated with beautiful dark lust and glowing in admiration as his other hand pressed down on her navel. "Ready to take everything I have for you."

The response she intended to offer transformed into a whimper, his silken tongue licking up her juices and nudging her swollen, aching nub in broad strokes. Her body thrummed to life, her sigh spiking into a cry as he pinched her nipple and elongated it between slippery, hot fingers. Her current state of helplessness amplified tenfold, reducing her to a trembling mess beneath his expertise.

Her fingers found their way into his soft curls, smothering the grin off his face as she held it to her sex and used him as leverage to relieve the pressure. Unfortunately, Caspian wasn't about to let it end so soon, and his fingers thrust even deeper, using a slower, deliberate pace that kept her on edge. She craved more, writhing and insatiable with need, yet desperate to escape the wave of pleasure that loomed just ahead.

Fingers curling, he hit that magical spot he was all too acquainted with, and her toes curled, muscles clenching at his mercy.

"Ah..." she begged, nearly tipping over the brink. She was past ready to topple into oblivion, losing touch with reality.

More than happy to please, his other hand pulled back the hood of her clit, and he feasted on his personal all-you-can-eat buffet. He sucked her between his teeth and rolled his tongue over her bundle of nerves.

She screamed. Thighs snapping shut, she tried unsuccessfully to get away as he gripped her thighs and didn't let up. It was too much and just enough at the same time. Her jaw dropped, back arching against him. A rumble came from between her legs—Caspian groaning deep and low as she fell apart, lapping up every last drop she gave.

Utterly spent, she couldn't even lift an eyelid. And she didn't need to, suddenly feeling even fuller than before. Raising her legs to his shoulders, Caspian slid his glorious length inside, all the way to the hilt. Her body gripped him with no intent of letting go. She bit her lip and let her eyes trace over the contoured muscles in his chest, down his abdomen, and to the flex of his thighs as he impaled her.

"I think you're the sexiest piece of art I've ever seen," she whispered.

A wicked smirk crossed his lips, and he pulled out only to plunge in deeper. "Then you must never have looked in a mirror," he panted as she split in two.

The ridge of his head slid along her walls, a tight fit that hit erogenous zones she didn't even know she had. Since starting birth control a few weeks ago, they'd gotten an even better taste of each other and could never go back. He insisted she didn't need to be the one to take on sole responsibility of using protection, but she grew to dislike condoms as much as he did and, in the end, got her way.

Not that he was complaining.

"Hell," he breathed, tipping his head back. "You feel so damn good."

Those words alone made her feel ten times better. And she couldn't agree more.

At first, he went at a steady pace, massaging her walls and gradually building back up to where they left off. The gentle rocking motion expelled the tiniest knots of leftover tension, her body surrendering completely to bliss.

Soon, beads of sweat dampened their skin, and a deeper yearning grew with every stroke. Her fists gripped the sheets, chest heaving with heavy pants. Heavenly soft lips brushed over the swell of her breasts as he lifted her up and tugged off their remaining clothes.

Melding together in a kiss, she basked in being skin-to-skin, heart-to-heart. He never ceased to fill her to the core, between her legs and knitting together every beat of her heart. Even more amazing was how she seemed to do the same for him.

His tongue swept over her lips, which parted as readily as her legs had, and tasted the product of their love. Their breaths intermingled, moans lost in a place where time didn't exist. Satisfied and drunken, their hands wandered as Caspian lifted them further onto the bed. He nipped at her lips, moving to suckle her earlobe, and breathlessly whispered, "Turn over."

In one fluid motion, he placed himself behind her hips and plunged in all at once, ramming her G-spot. She cried out and pushed back, collapsing on the bed as his hand traveled to her hips to keep her upright. His other hand acted as a brace as their speed and pressure built to an all-time high. He strummed her again and again, scattering kisses over every surface of her body within reach. Tunnel vision took over, and she crumbled, tightening as another string of elation prepared to snap.

"Baby girl," he panted. She hummed, answering the familiar words. "You never cease to amaze me."

As if to punctuate the statement, he pushed in deep and held the position. Stars burst in her head, caught in a tug-of-war between restraint and relief.

Then, pulling out, he penetrated her to the fullest extent as he spoke each following word. "You're beautiful, smart, sexy as hell, and..." He kissed up her spine, lingering at the back of her neck.

"Mine."

Diving in, he stretched her to the limit, stole the very breath from her lungs. An implosion of chaos consumed every cell. Nearly blacking out, she felt as he sowed seeds of pleasure and pushed into his climax. Riding out their peak, she could do nothing more but collapse in a pile of limbs.

After cleaning them up, Caspian crawled into bed and tucked the blanket over their melded bodies, encasing her with delicious warmth.

"Rest well," he whispered, drawing her as close as possible. "You're going to do great tomorrow."

Through the peaceful nothingness that filled her satiated being, all she could sense was his touch, his scent, his breath.

Only him. Forever him.

THANK YOU FOR READING

Don't forget to leave a review, share with a friend, and stick around for more heart—and panty—melting romance!

Sign up for Siberia's email list to get a free bonus chapter in Caspian's perspective: Bet.

"I'm a fucking mad man for you, Nia. I'm wild with the need for you. Whether you're trying to seduce me or not, I'll stake my claim on you every time. You can bet on that."

CURIOUS TO WHAT HAPPENED BETWEEN IVORY AND ADRIAN AT THE PARTY?

Find out in Ivory's Ruin, the next book in Lovesick...

Can a bad boy set on revenge find a path to redemption?

Everything about the man cloaked in shadow tells her to stay away—his black as night leather jacket, the bitter smell of cigarettes, a warning in his gold eyes. But Ivory can't ignore her intuition that something dark is weighing Adrian down. Meddling between rival biker gangs will put both of them in danger, even though being apart proves to be just as impossible. Ivory deserves a dominant worthy of her submission and Adrian knows exactly what she needs. In the end, this can only lead to ruin...or love, if they're strong enough.

ACKNOWLEDGMENTS

What does it take to write a book? I used to think the secret combination looked something like crazy impossible inherent talent, an excessive amount of time with nothing better to do, and questionable nightly rituals. And while some of that may be true, typing "the end" came down to the very same thing that kept Nia and Caspian together: not giving up. I owe an immeasurable amount of gratitude to the people who have supported me along the way, who kept me going when it would have been much easier to quit.

Thank you first and foremost to my husband, who is my inspiration, my motivation, my biggest fan, the love of my life, and my best friend. You are my everything.

Thank you to everyone who has read, critiqued, and reviewed this book, especially to those who took the time to mentor me while on this writing journey. Many of you believed in me more than I believed in myself, and to those who told me to scrap the whole book and do something else—look at it now.

Thank you to my editors, for answering all my questions and helping this book become it's best version. I'm so glad I found you, and look forward to many more projects together.

Thank you to all the other creatives who have inspired me and brought light to the world in dark times. I've always loved stories—in books, movies, songs, and art—and I wouldn't be who I am today without them.

Thank you to my characters, for incessantly demanding your story be told and being patient while I learned to tell it the right way.

And last but not least, I give thanks to God, who has blessed me so profoundly with all of these things.

On to the next page,

Siberia

ABOUT THE AUTHOR

Siberia writes sinful romance for the soul, featuring characters who are as unapologetically smutty as they are sentimental. She's a true romantic and can often be found trying new foods, making blanket forts, and taking long walks on the beach with her husband.

Join her email list to keep up with new updates, giveaways, ARC opportunities, and more!

Author website: beacons.ai/siberia
Reader Group: facebook.com/groups/sweetsinners
Instagram: @siberiathewriter

9 781963 206012